Myrrorball

Myrrorball
a fantascience novel

Major Roxbrough
and

Nik Gehenna

Major Roxbrough & Nik Gehenna

Copyright © 2020 by Mjr Roxbrough & Nik Gehenna

All rights reserved. No part of this book may be reproduced or transmitted in any form or by any means, electronic or mechanical, including photocopying, recording, or by any information storage and retrieval system, without permission in writing from the copyright owner.
This is not a work of fiction. Names, characters and incidents are used fictionally to protect the innocent and hide the guilty. Any resemblance to any actual persons, living or dead, is therefore entirely coincidental. Though events and locales are all correct.
Any people depicted in stock imagery provided by Getty Images are models, and such images are being used for illustrative purposes only.
Certain stock imagery ©Roxshot

Dedicated to
John,
thanks
for your continued patronage and support

Myrrorball

Other books by the same authors:-

Major Roxbrough.
Glimpserama
Remember Next Week
Axevictim
Axevictims
Axevictime
Invasion of the Zernoplat
Consolidation of the Zernoplat
Resolution of the Zernoplat
Murder Museum
Mirror of Mirrors
Mirrortome
Myrrorball
Mirrorganic
Xanthicology
From the Grave to the Cradle
Smoke and Mirrors
Banustib
Banisstwo
Second Life Syndrome

Nik Gehenna.
Mirror of Illusion
The Orrery of Power
Choose Your Mask
Mrs Meggins From the Pie Shop
Megwinda Meggins Goes East
Mirror of Delusion
Myrrorball
Dead Broads Don't Squeal
The Novel Not Yet Written
The Suicide Exposition

Major Roxbrough & Nik Gehenna

Myrrorball

plate 1

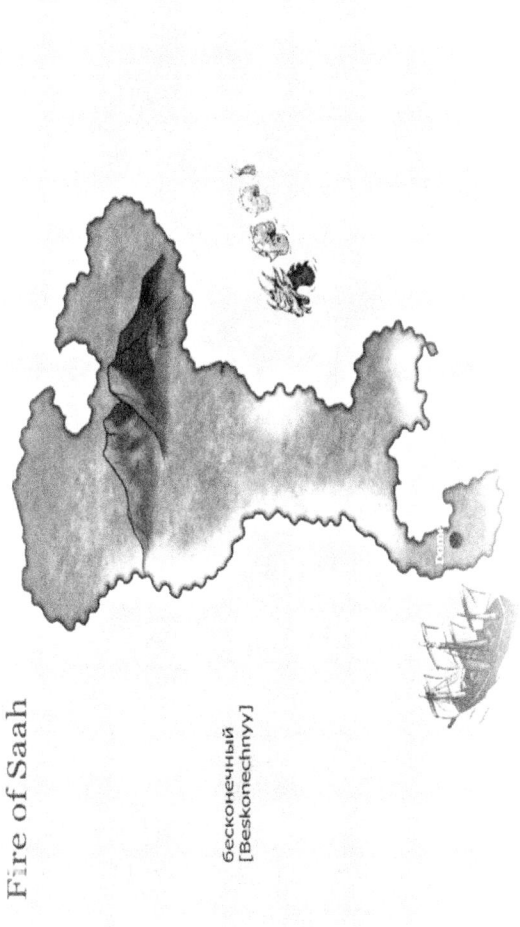

Fire of Saah

бесконечный
[Beskonechnyy]

Major Roxbrough & Nik Gehenna

plate 2

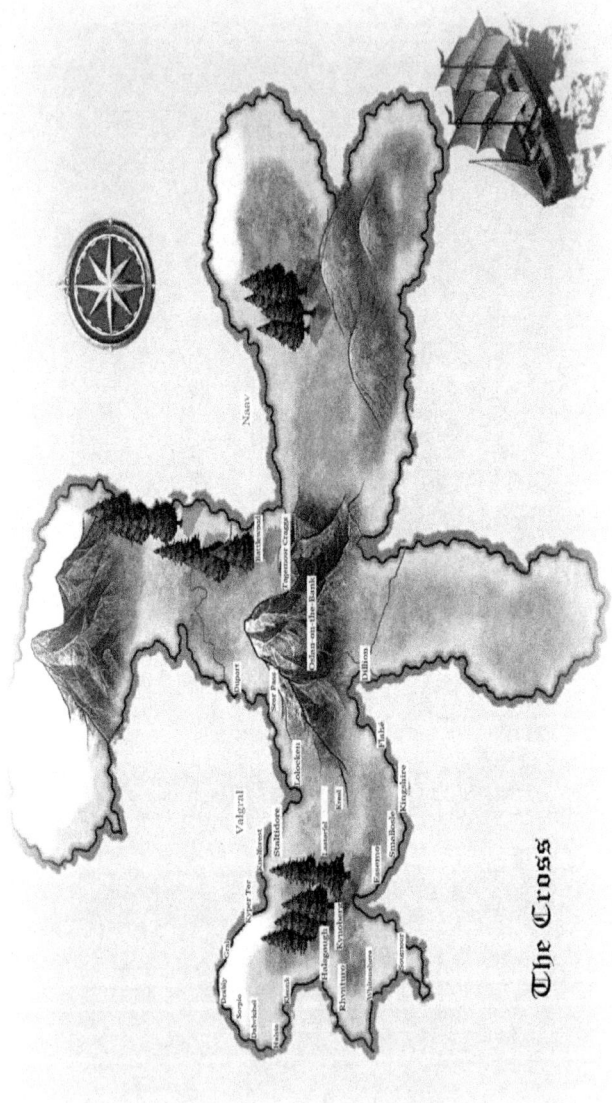

Myrrorball

plate 3

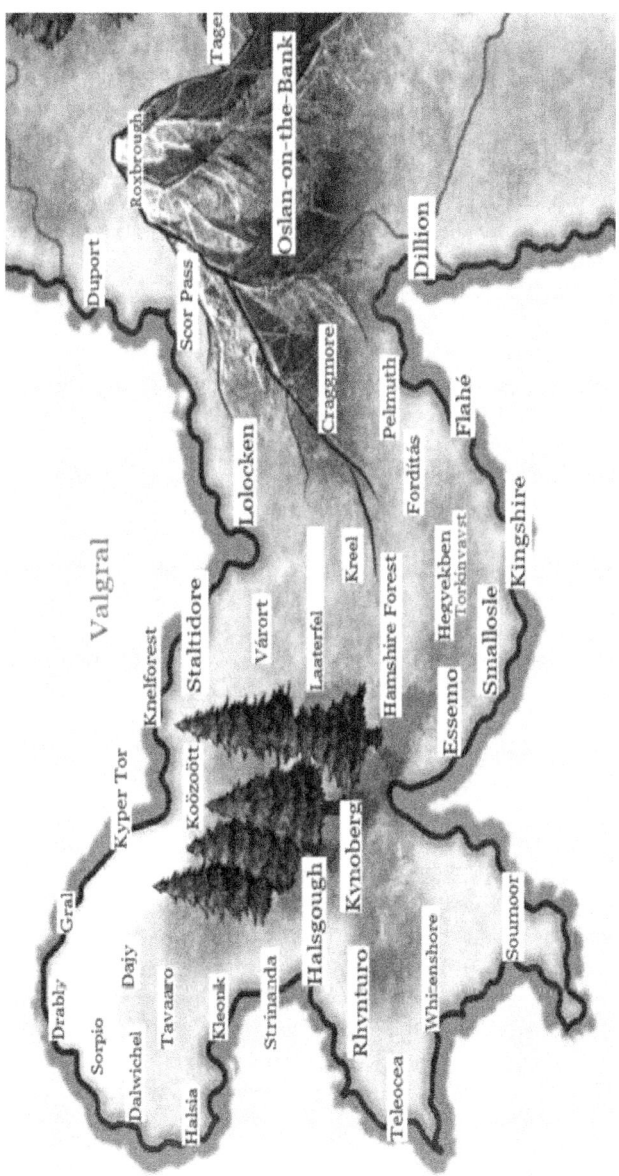

Major Roxbrough & Nik Gehenna

Foreword: by the authors of this novel.

I have been a fan of Nik Gehenna's work since his first fantasy novel *Mirror of Illusion*. I must confess that though I write science fiction, I cannot quite master the necessary style to create a good fantasy – Nik can. When the two of us met recently at a writing seminar, I was keen to exchange ideas with him, hopefully*, useful* ones. Strangely he had felt the same way regarding – my Science Fiction output. While I could not write fantasy, he felt the rigours of science should be left to the likes of me.

"You know what we should do? Should we collaborate? You can provide fantastic elements while I fill in with more science-based material".

To give the young man his due, (he is twenty-five, while I am his senior by more years than I care to reflect upon) he looked as though he was considering the notion before rejecting it. He pointed out that while we both had plenty of ideas for a new project, it would be impossible to merge the two when we write in very different genres.

No Science Fiction story ever had a dragon in it, he observed, while no fantasy ever had space ships and ray guns. How would such a merging of two very diverse mixes make sense? If he wrote chapter one, how could I follow with the next when I had already confessed that I could not create in his fantasy world? Similarly, if I did the first chapter, he could not follow with an addition in a genre that intimidated him with its rules of physics and grounding in the scientific.

I was about to concede the point and abandon the idea when his features lit up with the kernel of a notion. I demanded to know what it was,

"Just suppose", Nik offered, "That we both stick to our one comfort zone and write what we write best, but intertwine the twin storylines in such a way as to create a Science Fiction - Fantasy yarn".

"You mean you write fantasy while I fit my sci-fi into what you determine? Like a patchwork quilt, eventually, making something large enough to fit the bed"? I get like that when I am excited. Poetically Pythonesque, filled with analogies.

"Exactly so", my young co-writer-to-be acknowledged, "You start, what about the long-awaited follow up to *Invasion of the Zernoplat*"?

"Can you fill the alternative passages with fantasy"?

Myrrorball

"Who knows, let's give it a bash"?

Several months later, with numerous arguments and revisions what we produced is what follows in this book. The first Science-Fiction-Fantasy novel ever (to my knowledge) I hope it works. Also that you enjoy reading it as much as I tried to unravel the marvellously convoluted imagination that was Nik's

Major Roxbrough, Yorkshire, 2020.

I met Mortimer at a writing seminar in the third world of Yorkshire earlier this year I am from the south of England where civilisation has arrived. We have no worn clogs, nor kept whippets in the wardrobe for aeons. The old git was trying to teach others how to write as precisely as he does, with mixed success I might add. During the break, I found myself opposite him and congratulated him on some of his work. Particularly *Invasion of the Zernoplat.* He reciprocated by telling me how much he enjoyed my *High History of the Domisphere trilogy.* I suggested that we might have fun writing a collaboration. Of course, it would have to be a fantasy as I do not have the sort of scientific background to feel comfortable attempting the dryer stuff.

His response was a complaint. He could not write about dungeons, witches and magic swords. Was there a solution? If we did a fantasy - he would struggle. If we attempted straightforward sci-fi - I would not enjoy it. Neither of us would be at our best. Even as we talked it through a notion occurred. Why not write separate storylines but find a way of mashing then together into a clash of different worlds?

We agreed we had enough confidence and optimism to try it. The Major began the first few thousand words and then passed them to me. I immediately scrapped the very prosaic chapters, continued to number the scenes, simpler. We argued - the old git is set in his ways. Sometimes our debate grew so acrimonious I feared we would never finish the damned thing. After months of work and many cups of tea and many more disputes, produced something unique.

Myrrorball is not strictly Sci-Fi, nor fantasy, it is a Fantascience. I think we created a new genre. A young man with an old codger and new friend.

Nik Gehenna – Nyjord – 2020

Major Roxbrough & Nik Gehenna

PART ONE.

A FATE WORSE THAN DEATH.

Myrrorball

1.

What I am about to record on this e-reader is not something I would believe even though it happened to me. Yet I am a Science Fiction writer. Or at least I was – before it happened. I was putting the finishing touches to my novel '*Invasion of the Zernoplat*' when there was a slithering tapping noise at the office window. That was not so unusual as the cats like to come and go through that aperture. What was curious was that it was not one of my beloved feline friends. I found this out after I slid my keyboard back into the unit under the monitor. Padding over to the casement, undoing the latch. What entered did not resemble a feline creature to even the slightest degree.

I thought I would be allowing entrance to a friendly furry pet, not a slimy, cold alien!

It was Zernoplat.

Imagine an amoeba around three hundred millimetres long that is what a Zernoplat appears to be. I report this for the record with easy clarity because that was the creature I imagined for my *novel*. Thusly, one of three things was happening: I was asleep and dreaming, insane, or my imagination had become a reality. The thing about dreams is you know when you are dreaming. They are usually in monochrome, make little cohesive sense. You even know in the back of your mind you have gone to bed or settled on the settee. That a real Zernoplat existed was beyond reason, therefore, so was I. Help was needed: electricity, drugs, counselling. My lunatalistic hallucination then broadcast a telepathic thought straight into my demented brain,

'Thanks for letting me in, I have an important message for you, actually more in the form of cataclysmic directive'.

"You are not real", I retorted sternly, no use monkeying around with madness. "At this precise moment, *I* might not even be real. I've been working too hard, that's what it is, trying to get the latest book finished before Dexter takes me off at the knees. You are a character from that absurdity".

'I am sorry to dispute that erroneous statement, Nik. I exist. You, of all the people on your pathetic poisoned planet, should believe in my existence'.

"Because I created you in a Science Fiction novel"? I altercated, "How much sense does that make"?

'It is the reason I have decided to approach you. Of all the people of Soil, you should believe I am here'.

"Let us suppose for one second that I am not gah-gah billy bonkers", I reasoned (*reasoned? Was that even the right word*)? "How can a character in a novel, admittedly a thought-provoking and exciting novel at that, be real... I did not catch your name? This world is Earth by the by, not Soil".

'Same difference', the Zernoplat shrugged by way of explanation for the use of the nomenclature. It was more like an undulation of protoplasm than an actual shrug. *'Concerning your question, how do you think you came up with such an original and exciting novel, Nik? Who do you think put the notions into your brain in the first place'*?

"All right", I admitted to that twisted logic, "I'll buy it for the time being. If this is loony toony, it's quite entertaining for the moment. So what do you want and what is your pigging name"?

Myrrorball

'I am Hhrrhhoehhrrhooooingohh', came the mental broadcast inside that rat's maze of a dormant organ between my ears (my second-favourite organ of all time). *'Captain Hhrrhhoehhrrhooooingohh, but you and I do not have to be so formal, give me a nickname if you want? If it makes matters any easier for you'*.

"All right. I will call you Harry when it suits me to shorten your rather lengthy moniker. Right Harry, come on, hurry up, Harry come on (as Sham '69 liked to sing). I need to seek medical attention, so finish this little illusion before the white van comes with the nice men who will put me in a lovely jacket with extra long sleeves".

'You are quite sane, Nik', Hhrrhhoehhrrhooooingohh (Harry) my deranged chimaera insisted, *'Our existence was put into your brain because you are a writer of futuristic fiction. You were the best human to contact on Loam. Now, can I tell you what I came here to impart'*?

"Knock yourself out". I had lost the will to live. I could feel the life force draining out of my body. 'Quick nurse, the screens. He's out of bed again, Doctor'!

Repeat ad-nauseam.

'The dissolving gas you wrote about in your excellent novel...more of a journal when I think about it'.

"The one I imagined, that dissolved only humans and hurt no other life form, in my insanely-twisted diatribe of a book you mean"?

'That is the one, yes. In your novel, we used it to subjugate Ireland. A strange choice, we find the Irish hilarious, highly amusing accents. I digress, what I came to tell you is that in three months our entire fleet will arrive to bathe the whole of Clay in it. The world will return to the beautiful paradise it was before you upright monkeys fêtzalçlättered its ruin' [trans: Buggered it up. I aught to know, it was in my book].

I laughed. Well, I was not the full shilling.

"Not that olde-saga", I objected, "Surely my imagination can do better than that. It's done to death: Verne, Wells, Vonnegut, Dick, Adams - a few others. I know, in my novel, you required some fresh real estate, but there is no reason to commit genocide to get it. We could find somewhere for your armada. Why kill everyone? More to the point why tell me about it ahead of time? I can't do anything can I"?

'You can do nothing regarding the sterilising of Soil, that is true. I am here to offer you an unique opportunity though, Nik'

"Out of everyone on Earth, note I continue to use the correct name for the planet there. You are offering me an opportunity, what would that be then"?

'To live. Not on Loam, we have found another little planet for you - Rozhelia'.

"Let me get this straight then", I murmured to my apparition, "You intend to kill every living person on *my* world after relocating me to another"?

'Yes'.

"Why? Why me in particular. Of all the great minds, the wonderful thinkers on my world why select a lowly novelist to be the last remaining human being"?

'We like you. You did a good job on the novel. It is already a bestseller on Dweeb. Shame it will disappear momentarily here, but then we will soon establish our new colony I am certain it will do well then too'.

"Why cannot I – the great writer - remain here? Or be relocated to Dweeb, with you"?

'You would not like our company much, Nik. Those conquerors of your race that committed genocide. We have a little observational duty for you on Rozhelia Something to keep you plus the missus happily occupied'.

At that chilling moment, I realised, events, fantastic as they were, had conditions. If indeed I was knitting with only one needle. How come I invented a non-existent partner?

"Harry, you must know I am single"?

'Yes, now, but to agree to our little arrangement, we need you to hook up with a female of your species, to keep you ticking along. You have three months. Do not panic. I can help with the selected female's state of mind'.

"What are you going to do? Brainwash her into falling head over heels in love with me"?

Myrrorball

'Exactly'.

The half baked events took on a rather attractive mental diversion. I was having a sex-fantasy.

"All right let me get this straight in my mind then? Say I believe this for the moment", I began, believing it for the time being because it was the best bit and I wanted to credit it, "How will this glorious seduction work? I locate some rampant totty that turns up the thermostat on my boiler then you remotely give her the hots for me"?

'Excluding the rather prosaic colloquialisms, which we the Zernoplat, have mastered, thanks to our remote communications with your brain over the past few months – you have it in a kernel'.

"You mean nutshell".

'In three months, it will not matter. The only two surviving exhibits of humanity will be you and your chosen spouse'.

"On Rozhelia? How will I select the lucky, successful, candidate"?

'On your computer, go on your internet and find three females that take your fancy. I will then <u>prime</u> them mentally ready for your entrance into their lives'.

"I get three"? My hallucination was getting tasty.

'You get three chances to pick one. We are trying to be as generous to you as the period allows. At the end of three months, I will come and see you again. When you must then tell me which of the trio you intend to perpetuate the human race with'.

Undecided whether the events were taking place, or I was still turning the wheel even though Hammy had gone, I went back to my Lenovo. It was not a difficult task. I went on a trio of dating site, picked myself three luscious-looking prospects. The first to catch my eye was a twenty-six-year-old dentist from Russia. A green-eyed blonde (like me) with no children and single. I pointed her out to Harry, who undulated. Then I got a little more imaginative. It was *my* hallucination after-all. I chose Quianhua. A twenty-three-year-old dance instructor from China. A blonde and a brunette. Jennifer was, therefore, a twenty-six-year-old redhead who was something impressive in advertising. In the ordinary scheme of things, I would not have been in any of the three girl's league. I think it fair to note though circumstances were anything other than ordinary. I asked the Zernoplat how he would arrange my encounters with the girls.

'That is your concern', Hhrrhhoehhrrhooooingohh emanated into my seething mind, *'When you do meet them, if you intend to meet all three, then they will be stunned by how attracted they are to you, the rest is up to you'.*

"So I will have to travel to meet two of them"? I asked. Jennifer was at least in England. "I am momentarily impecunious, Hhrrhhoehhrrhooooingohh".

'Thirty thousand pounds sterling has already deposited into your account for sundry expenses', Hhrrhhoehhrrhooooingohh then informed me. *'Remain seated while I transmit Russian and Mandarin into your mind. It may prove useful to speak to your prospects in their native tongue'.*

"What if...". I began before a mental bolt drove through the language centres of my brain - like an ice pick. I believe my next words were,

"Gnnung Bwhaah", or similar.

When my tongue was talking sense once more, I asked, "What if it doesn't work out with any of them"?

'Oh we are determined to save a matched pair', Hhrrhhoehhrrhooooingohh responded, his thoughts striking me as cheerful. *'We have two back-up couples as substitutes if it proves necessary, but you are our first choice, Nik. After all, you are the author of Invasion of the Zernoplat'.*

"You are not called Zernoplat surely? I mean that part was me, was it not"?

'That part, as you rightly surmise, was your imagination, Nik. You could not pronounce our real nomenclature. To satisfy your curiosity, it is HhhâäàåâääåçêçêçêïïìïïìïìiggndgndÐñß¥þÞÝᴅ'.

If I believed nothing else, I did that.

'That is all for now, Nik. I will return when I deem it necessary. I wish you romance and good fortune. After

which you will be one of two human beings to live in another world. Before you ask, Rozhelia has ninety percent the gravity of your world (soon to be ours 'he was gloating') *and twenty-three percent oxygen, so you will feel very energetic and powerful. The part of the world we will send you to has a mean temperature of twenty-three degrees centigrade'.*

"If it's such a nice locale, how come you don't colonise it and leave us alone", I demanded – boldly given the circumstances.

'*You will find out*', came the strangely ominous reply, '*Whatever happens Nik, we must exterminate the vermin of Soil before they do any more damage, that, I am afraid, is immutable*'.

I had to agree with the inescapable logic. We had made a filthy place of what had once been a natural paradise.

2.

The logistics of the encounters I was then planning were the most difficult parts of the operation. Meeting three beautiful girls was something I, an ordinary-looking man of twenty-five years, would not have anticipated. Finding them would involve a little work on the net. Then I would be doing some travelling. I just hoped that what Hhrrhhoehhrrhooooingohh had done to their minds to make me '*hot stuff*' would be enough for me to '*seal the deal*' with them, all three of them.

There were three candidates, so why waste the opportunity? It would improve my previous score of conquests by one hundred percent. In my younger years, there had been Dawn, Jane and Mandy. The first two had been young and foolish flirtations that had only lasted a few months. Mandy had been different. We had dated for two years, but ultimately we had not had enough in common to keep us together.

I was not one for one night stands. Even though not superstitious, I did have a moral compass. Thanks to my late parents who had lost their lives on the M62, some years back. I suppose that was another reason the Zernoplat had selected me as a suitable candidate for their little zoo project. I was 'hooked'. If I was insane, I might as well run with it. I suspected that the fantastic events I am recording were happening. So it was time for Nik Gehenna, formerly introspective and introverted writer to come out of his cocoon. The butterfly that would emerge would be a love missile, a sex warrior – haha ha ha.

I went on the site, on which Jennifer had posted her profile, it told me she was living in Carlisle. Somebody had to, I suppose. There was only one thing for it, post a profile of my own on *Lonely Kittens*. *S*ee if my image alone would be enough to entice her into a rendezvous in the best restaurant I could find in the northern English town. That involved a search on google map.

I found Adriano's, an Italian dining room in a Roman villa style, showing images of Italy on terracotta walls and domed roof. 1 Rickersgate, Carlisle. Then it was time to post my profile on the site and *like* Jennifer.

My best shot of me was with bright light behind my head and wearing sunglasses. I found myself thinking that if the lovely redhead responded positively, then Hhrrhhoehhrrhooooingohh had given me a mighty boost. I liked Jennifer after filling in my details and then tried to put the whole thing out of my mind.

Impossible!

It was all I could think about. The world was going to be devoid of all humanity. Alien creatures were going to take it from us. I would be shipped off to a strange planet, with one hottie in tow. Not exactly something I could have contemplated in say... well ever.

I went to bed after making sure all the cats were indoors. It is in the darkness that they get run over, so I never let them stay out overnight. I had forgotten to mention them

Myrrorball

to Hhrrhhoehhrrhooooingohh. I would be pretty determined to take the little darlings with me. They were, in the absence of a partner and children of my own – my little kiddiewinks. Suffice to say, deep and satisfactory slumber eluded me. I heard the Lenovo chime and knew someone had sent me an email. As I was expecting nothing from just about everyone else in the whole world, I supposed it was a response from Lonely Kittens. Throwing on my dressing gown, I went into the office and turned on the monitor. Jennifer had responded:

**Thank you for your message. 🫖 would love to go to 🔔driano's. 🫖 am free Tuesday if you can book a table,
💍en.**

jennifer

Dinner was just that, dinner, even so, it seemed Hhrrhhoehhrrhooooingohh had indeed done something to the lovely Jennifer's brain because while I was a six on the attraction scale, she was a nine. Perhaps she was curious about my writing? I had put several details in my profile so who knew.

It wasn't going to take me long to find out.

I did not get a great deal of writing done over the next twenty-four hours. What was the point? My audience was soon to reduce to only huge single-celled chunks of protoplasm. If indeed they even wanted to read anything other than the book they had remotely written whilst borrowing my brain?

It did not take me long to pack for the trip to Carlisle. I decided to drive up, book into any bed and breakfast that looked reasonable. Of course, I would only stay overnight, as I could not leave the little rascals for longer than that. They had a litter bin, but the food would not last them longer than a day. I figured my journey would take

Major Roxbrough & Nik Gehenna

around three hours as I was one hundred and fifty-five miles from the county town of Cumbria. I would take the A1 then join the M6 at Kempley Bank Roundabout. I booked a room at the Hampton Inn, one of the dearest. Courtesy of Zernoplatite funds. It was a wrench to leave my pets. The first time I had done so, but they would not starve. They had their luxury toilet. I put my bag in the boot, off I went. Though I have a quite powerful car, I err on the side of caution when it comes to driving. The journey went without incident, the best sort. At the Inn, I unpacked my overnight bag, showered, changed ready for the date. I wore a white shirt with black tie, black trousers. When it comes to looking smart, the combination is unbeatable in my opinion. My only concession to casual was an oxblood leather jacket, again a timeless accessory for the smart-casual man. That was the best I could do. My thick blonde hair was side-parted and off the ears, my glasses the sort that John Lennon made so popular in the past. Girls could wear make-up to enhance their appearance, with me, what you saw was the real Nik.

I was early at the table, consequently sipping a glass of Black Tower when Jennifer drifted in a quarter of an hour late. She looked every inch the sophisticated woman-professional. Her white blouse and black business jacket complimented my choice perfectly. Rising to greet her and tell her how lovely she looked, she smiled and kissed the air at the side of my head. That was the way a young woman greeted men on their first meeting.

I will not bore you with the detail of our small talk from that point on. Suffice to say that by the body language, attention, smiling I was getting the distinct vibe was that Jennifer found me both attractive and captivating. She asked several questions about my writing, seemed genuinely intrigued. I found myself filled with ennui when she responded by going into a lengthy diatribe about advertising.

Still, if we were going to another planet, that avenue of her industry would soon be closed off to her. I waited until we were on dessert before opening up to her.

Myrrorball

"Remember the book I told you about"? I began, "Invasion of the Zernoplat, well that leads me to tell you something even more fantastic".

"A different work, or a sequel"? She asked.

"More fantastic than that. I was visited the night before last, by an actual Zernoplat, though that is not their real name of course".

"Why not, I like the name? You were referencing that Amerikan comedian wasn't you, what's his name, oh, you know, him who did the driving instructor".

"No, Jennifer, what I mean was that the single-cell protoplasmic lifeforms of the novel are actual".

She laughed delightedly, "I know they live at the bottom of ponds, don't they"?

"Not amoeba, Jennifer. Alien creatures three-hundred millimetres long, they live on their planet in the galaxy we call the Milky Way. They are going to cleanse the Earth of all human life in three months. Don't worry though, you and I are to be saved from that fate, by them, relocated to another planet".

"Phew, that was too close", Jennifer laughed, "You're going to put me in the follow-up, I'm very flattered, Nik".

"You don't understand", I persisted, "I'm serious, Jennifer the Zernoplat are real, their name is unpronounceable. They do exist though, writing the novel through my fingers", I tried my best to tell her, "They are the...

HhhâäàåâääåçêçêçêïïìïîìggndgndÐñßɎþÞÝ⚐', they are soon going to kill every living person on Earth except you and me".

I suppose when I reflect on it now the one response I got to this apocryphal declaration was the one I had least expected. Jennifer laughed,

"Oh, I get it the follow up is going to be like a sort of *Hitch Hikers*. You're branching out into comedy".

I began to feel frustrated and with it a certain amount of irritation,

"Jennifer, please listen to me? I'm telling you that the Zernoplat are *real*. They are real. They are going to cleanse the Earth of every living human except two. I have chosen you to be the second person".

Major Roxbrough & Nik Gehenna

Jennifer chuckled, This other planet then, is there hairdressers on it, beauticians? I mean to say, if a girl cannot get someone to make her look her best, then a girl would not go haha ha ha".

I was not getting through to her. She did not believe me. Then I asked myself, why would she? If I were her, would I believe me?

"I'm not joking Jennifer, the Zernoplat is offering us the opportunity to escape annihilation. I would like you to be the one to come with me. Put it this way, if what I am telling you is the truth, will you come? The planet is called Rozhelia"?

"Get out of town", was the response. Draining her glass, she asked, "Are we going to have some more wine"?

It dawned on me then. Though Jennifer was gorgeous and pretty sexy, she had a boring occupation, as far as I was concerned. Added to which she did not take me seriously. I switched to the topic of hobbies and interests outside work and it turned out that she spent her time in the beauticians or watching soaps on television. I was forced to reluctantly conclude that life on Rozhelia with Jennifer would be tedious indeed.

At the end of the meal, I gave her a peck on the cheek. As I made ready to leave her in a taxi she asked, as one pulled up to the stand, "Are you coming back to the flat for a night-cap"?

I mean to say, most chaps would not have said no, it was tantamount to turning it down. I was not most chaps. Not only that, but despite her obvious physical charms, I did not find Jennifer attractive, if I had Blitzkrieg mit dem fleischgewehr I would have respected neither of us afterwards. So I made my excuses, said I would email her in a day or so. Was gratified to see the disappointment on her lovely features.

Alas, Jennifer was decidedly off my list - to be the new Eve on Rozhelia.

Myrrorball

3.

Tula was a city in western Russia. Home to the Tula Kremlin, a 16th-century stone fortress, encompassing towers, cathedrals, a 19th-century shopping arcade. Not that the arcade was employed for commerce any longer. I have not seen it since my *little diversion*, but I do know the Zernoplat have no use for shops. The Tula State Museum of Weapons once had a vast collection of guns and army memorabilia. Obsolete following the gas attack, of course. The Samovar Museum had explored the history of the ornate tea urn, a Tula speciality. I made a point of visiting all these attractions before emailing Anastasya. I wanted to have details to discuss with her. In her tongue too. Then I arranged a meal at the Mark and Lev Restaurant a rare event in Russia - a 'locavore' restaurant where all the products used for dishes had been produced at farms no further than one hundred and fifty kilometres from the place itself. That involved a premium for the original concept. It proved worth every kopek. Her response to my invitation was expected, since my initial foray into matters romantic:

Спасибо за симпатию ко мне и виртуальный подарок Ника. Я хотел бы встретиться с вами на ужин в ресторане Mark and Levs. Да, четверг в 20:00 - это хорошо. Я возьму такси и увижу тебя там.
Анна ... х

translates as:
**Thanks for the sympathy for me and ⌨ick's virtual gift. 🚻 would like to meet you for dinner at the ♆ark and Levs Restaurant. Yes, Thursday at 20:00 is good. 🚻'll take a taxi and see you there.
辶🗝nna ... x**

Unlike the redhead who had fallen short of my expectations, Anastasya was both stunning and very attentive.

Major Roxbrough & Nik Gehenna

It intrigued her that I had learned Russian to find love in her country, but was also eager to relocate to England. My first experience had taught me not to mention the Zernoplat on the evening of the first date. The two of us seemed to desire the same dishes, although I chose firstly and she might have simply agreed to have the same as a move to flatter me. So we both enjoyed duck breast carpaccio with parsnip, pumpkin and salted tomatoes. It was truly delicious. For dessert, we both enjoyed baked milk ice-cream with rye gingerbread and wild strawberries. All the while - cleaning our pallets with Fanagoria Cru Lermont Cabernet Sauvignon. Afterwards, we had the cheeseboard and coffee.

I was very impressed with the girl who insisted on my shortening her name to Anna. Despite her profession, her pink frock was not especially expensive-looking, her jewellery only costume rhinestones. That was just the decoration. What did attract me was the lovely face, the light turquoise eyes and the platinum blonde hair, which was natural. Added to that rather nice packaging was Anna's personality, clearly a warm person, caring (hence her medical background) attentive - capable of holding an intelligent conversation on a variety of subjects. I think it fair to say that while she had been indoctrinated into liking me, I was bowled over by her.

I put her in a taxi, paid the driver and sent her back to her apartment, then returned to my hotel. I was stopping at the SK Royal Hotel Tula, where I immediately went on the internet and emailed missus Goldsmith my neighbour, to make sure the kiddie-winks were faring all right in my absence.

Myrrorball

It turned out that they were fine and the female Madam Yimin, was even on her knee purring loudly and missing me not one jot – disappointing.

I saw Anna three more times before she let me *seal the deal*. Thankfully that was as good as anything a French girl would have done. Anna was keen to please. I had not expected some of her initiatives, well not from a dentist anyway? We were laying in my very nicely furnished hotel suite, both slightly sweaty and spend from our horizontal exertions when I decided the time was right to come clean with the girl. After all, I had already come dirty, so why not?

In my grammatically perfect Russian, thanks to Hhrrhhoehh-rrhooooingohh, I accurately related my meeting with the
 Hhhâäàåâäåçêçêçêïï ïïïïggndgndDñßҰþÞҮ∆' and what it meant to our future together, if she wanted to have one. Unlike Jennifer, Anna did not interrupt, nor did she laugh. She listened to the whole narrative in complete silence. I had told her everything, she simply raised herself on an elbow and kissed me tenderly,

"It is time I should be going. I have surgery in the morning", she rose from the bed before I could respond, starting to dress.

"This is it"? I began, frankly surprised and speaking in Russian of course, "I just told you the most fantastic of fairy tales, and you dress to leave, would you like to comment on what I told you about?"

"Of course, when I have a sober thought. Do not worry, you are very dear to me, and I will write to you, sweetheart in the morning."

She left. I was alone wondering how the latest act of my little adventure would play out.

4.

Major Roxbrough & Nik Gehenna

I soon got my answer. Anna sent me a text:

Please to meet me at the Областной building this evening at 18:20
Anna x

That was all I had to work out. Why did the lovely Russian beauty want to meet me at the hospital? Did she have a revelation to reveal to me, was she suffering from some sort of malady? There was only one way to find out. I hung around for the intervening period, fretting over several possibilities before the time on my Casio digital watch said it was a reasonable time to get a taxi to the building of medicine.

When I got to it, I went straight to outpatients. Before I could enquire at the reception desk, I smelled the girl coming. She took my arm, kissed me gently on the mouth and informed me,

"You are just in time, I had to pull a few strings to get him to see you so quickly, but it will be worth it darling, you can tell him what you told me yesterday".

"Anna"? I was confused, "Are you well, the appointment is for me, what do you think is wrong with me, I'm..." The realisation hit me like a blow to the back of the head with a girlie-cricket bat. "Have you made an appointment with a friend who happens to be a shrink"?

"Dr Преображенский [Preobrazhensky] is highly regarded in his field. We are lucky to get to see him so quickly, darling".

"Anna, I am not mad, what I told you yesterday was actual, you and I will escape the mass genocide of humanity to relocate on a different world. I have no desire or reason to see a trick-cyclist, you had best go and explain yourself to your friend".

The beautiful blonde looked immensely saddened by my persistence, in what she considered to be a delusional state and said levelly,

"You are already very dear to me Nicholai, but if you won't talk with someone about your...difficulty, then I think you and I should go our separate ways. Come on?

Myrrorball

Come and just talk to the man, what have you got to lose"?

5.

I sent another email to Missus Goldsmith thanking her for continuing to look after the kiddie-winks and jumped on a plane to Xiamen [厦门市] Fujian China. Xiamen is a port city on China's south-eastern coast, across a strait from Taiwan. It encompasses two main islands and a region on the mainland. Formerly known as Amoy, it was an English-run treaty port from 1842 to 1912. Many Europeans and Japanese lived on Gulangyu. Now it was a vehicle-free island with beaches and meandering streets lined with old colonial villas. Very picturesque and hopefully equally romantic. I won't go into the boring details of selecting a hotel, all the rest of it. The upshot was that I sent my third choice a message of greeting and asked her out to dinner. I was learning from my previous mistakes, but I had also run out of options.

When I first saw Quianhua approaching the table, I was already seated in the Mingyue Xiamian [明月虾面] Restaurant, it is fair to say that I was impressed by her beauty. Impressed, yet in a different way to the two previous candidates, for she was exotic - full of eastern promise. She even walked like a beautiful woman. I arose from my seat, dressed in the usual way. Complimenting her low cut yet sleeved black frock, that clung in all the right places and left the rest on view. She wore a simple colourless crystal around her throat on a silver chain.

Major Roxbrough & Nik Gehenna

That was all the adornment she required. In the traditional way of the Chinese, her lipstick only covered the centre of her mouth, her eyebrows were real and not thickened. Her eyes held an almond promise of much. She was only one hundred and fifty-four centimetres to my one hundred and eighty-two, that made me feel protective from the off.

She offered me a slim hand, said simply,

"Nik".

"Quianhua", I smiled. Our romance had commenced.

I was negotiating the chopsticks in the very watery dumplings in equally thin gravy when she dropped a bombshell.

"You should use a western name for me. I would like you to call me Ann".

Too close for comfort, but I could not tell her why, so I nodded and smiled.

"I can tell you that is a dance teacher", I began in Mandarin where the phrasing is very different to what is indicated in the west, "You have the right shade [rough trans: the right figure for it]".

"Thank you", she smiled, a stunningly expressive indication of pleasant happiness, "I want to hear about your writing, Nik, what kind of book do you write? Why do you come to China? What do you want a Chinese girl to do"?

She was direct and not willing to waste time, excellent I was in the same frame of mind. I will paraphrase from this point onward for the benefit of any who are reading this e-account in English or translated Zernoplatite.

"My intentions are honourable...Ann", I assured her, "I am looking for someone to share all - for the rest of my life. When I saw your image on the dating site, I thought you one of the most stunning examples of femininity I have ever seen".

"Share the rest of your life with – where"? the girl was urgently desirous to know, obviously keen to get over to the western world and all its concomitant comforts.

I had to lie, too soon to tell her how I felt. I was desirous of neither ridicule nor counselling. So I told her -

in England. Then she pressed me for details of my writing. I told her all about my previous publications, leaving out my latest offering for reasons too obvious to state.

"Do you think you can make the adjustment needed to live with a girl who has spent her formative years in China"? She asked me then.

"I think so, why do you ask, what is it about you that you think I would need to adjust to, Ann"? I asked.

"When things don't go according to my plan, I may be surprised that it is Eastern-difficult, not what Western gentlemen are used to. I can say I disdain... Pessimism"!

I record that - exactly as she said it because I did not understand it at the time, alas now I do, but you can see why I dismissed it when she told me that. I did not fully know what I was getting myself involved in. Quianhua was beautiful, diminutive, exotic, even full-breasted. My defence - you do not get your mind into a deeply psychological debate as to the validity of a chance remark when you are keen to nail yourself a piece of prime-grade ass.

Nail it I did too. Quianhua did things to me that I will not put down in this record, for fear of causing you to blush dear reader (if you are there). Suffice to say I loved every sweat-drenched sexual minute of it. After just a week, we were hastily married following the Marriage Law of the People's Republic of China as adopted and amended in 2001 to introduce, synthesize, national codes of family planning. After five years of both marriage together with continual living in China at least nine months per year, I could have applied for permanent residence in the country. Quianhua could not wait to leave. I had no desire to stay after a bit of hasty sightseeing. Also in just over a couple of months, the only sentient race in any part of Mother Earth was going to be colourless undulating protoplasm.

It forced me to make a significant decision, that of keeping the tale of the annihilating of humanity from my Chinese bride until the moment Hhrrhhoehhrrhooooingohh itself told her what was going to happen and what her choices were. Of course, they were 'come to Rozhelia with me, or die hideously dissolved by fatal, if painless, gas attack'. I kind of figured she would go for the former of the two options.

I sort of suspected she might be a tad peeved at my deception too. As it turned out, I did not know the half of it!

6.

"Ann", I called to her, from the office, "Can you come up here for a moment please"?

Hhrrhhoehhrrhooooingohh undulated. Now I have seen some undulating in my time, but when it comes to Undulatertorätum, it does not come any better than Hhrrhhoehhrrhooooingohh can perform.

I will give her kudos for not screaming at the initial impression Quianhua had of her first HhhâäàåâäåçêçêçêïïïïïìggndgndÐñßŁþÞÝ◘' it was not favourable.

"What in Confucius' name is that lump of 他妈的败类 [you do not want to know what this means suffice to say it is not a pleasant expression] doing on the floor, Nik"?

'*Charming*', Harry observed, '*Was this the best of the three, Nik*'?

"Try to calm down, please, Ann, this is Hhrrhhoehhrrhooooingohh. He has something very important to tell you".

When Harry had concluded his information, Quianhua had but one phrase to say and it was directed straight between my eyes,

"混蛋"! [the sphincter between my buttocks] Then she stormed out of the room.

'*Forgive me for not understanding*', Harry broadcast into my brain then, '*But she is coming is she not? Otherwise, we will have to fall back on the other...*'.

"She's coming", I cut him short, "Give her till tomorrow, please, Harry. She'll come around, don't worry and don't forget you promised that I am allowed to fetch the cats with us".

Myrrorball

'In cages', Hhrrhhoehhrrhooooingohh shuddered. Not as good as his undulatertorätum, but still fairly impressive, *'Stout ones too'*.

I was beginning to get excited. I was going to go on an interstellar craft with a beautiful spouse and my four loving pets. Admitted Earth would no longer be an option for me, but Rozhelia sounded promising, it would be such an adventure.

7.

Vasnaar was not a man to take heed of the advice of others. No matter how sagacious or learned the advisor might be, Vasnaar was his own man. Gerner had warned that the ocean known as бесконечный [Beskonechnyy] for some reason lost in antiquity, was beyond his comprehension when it came to width. The King took no heed. Instead, he had promptly commandeered a schooner and set off further eastward than any mariner had ever ventured in the history of the world. The world, which was Nyjord, created by the Old Wise Gods, the Holy Ennead the novenary of creation consisting of five male and four female deities who between them had caused the birth of all things. They had made Angelus, who the uninformed called the Sun. They made the huge Blue Moon Goddess of Brahma which circled Nyjord, thusly bringing their number up to evenness, balance of the sexes. It had been said, that Shandor had created the moon just to annoy the black god Baalan, but only the Shandorites believed that to be so. The Baalanians, of course, denied it.

Even the Domispherek, the devoted priests of the Spherical God of Light had never ventured east of the Naavitaatul Ocean. Indeed some ancient sects had even maintained that the world was like a tabletop. Nought existed that far east, save for the edge. The Mage of Doras-Van-der-Garra-Plee had disproved that nonsense aeons past. Every clear-thinking man knew the world was a great ball spinning through the black sky, for they had been able to prove it by looking through the Mage Glass. A device of especially magical proprieties that brought distant objects closer. With such a thaumaturgical construct, magi had clearly shown that Brahma sometimes had one face toward Nyjord whilst at the other, she displayed her back. For the blue moon had countries and dominion just like Nyjord itself. Their shapes detected in the mage glass.

Determined by the witches of Woot, the only creatures who had ever visited Near Side from Nyjord's other face, most of which was the endless ocean depths – the бесконечный. Even so, in the vast expanse of that continual blueness were five island empires. The largest being the most westerly and called Woot. Woot was in a pairing, while over still further east was a trio of smaller dominion called the Triostrova. Two of the Triostrova were almost of equal size in terms of area and were: Severny to the north, Yug to the south and westerly of them both the tiny island of nebol'shoy.

None of these was of the slightest interest to King Vasnaar, however. Only the large island close to Woot was the one that fascinated him. Strangely called -The Fire of Saah, the dominion was reputed to be so fabulously wealthy it had more material abundance than any other realm on all of Nyjord. The reason for this was simple. The Fire of Saah was the largest mine, from which the Saahite quarried корунд [Korund]. Корунд was the most precious gemstone on Nyjord. A variety of a mystic mineral the mage-scientists called corundum, consisting of aluminium oxide (α-Al2O3) with trace amounts of elements such as iron, titanium, chromium, vanadium, or magnesium. The stones were blue, naturally occurring Корунд cut and polished into gemstones on the mage's isle, worn in their jewellery. They were remarkably hard. Denser than the hardest of steel. They were also the stone that Vasnaar's wife the Queen longed to possess more of, than any other living woman on the whole world.

What the Queen wanted, her King wanted to furnish her with. Thusly the quest was motivated by one emotion more than any other – greed. It was believed that the finest of Корунд was a bluer blue than the eyes of the goddess Shakita and that was very blue indeed. Vasnaar

Myrrorball

had gathered his most trusted men around him, provisioned the Zhirnublydok and set sail upon the most dangerous voyage any mariner had ever attempted.

There had been trials along the way. At one point the Zhirnublydok had been attacked by Progondax, fierce sea creatures that up till that point not all of the crew had even believed existed. Those truly hapless, who had confronted, to fight the terrible beasts brought up from the depths by a previous storm, had lost their lives doing so. Hideously mauled and ruined by the sea demons, they had thought themselves lucky when previously surviving the storm in which three crew were washed overboard and drown.

Vasnaar's final trial had been a very personal and excruciatingly painful one. With all the other dangers behind him, he had faced a tiny adversary that had introduced him to an agony he had hitherto never suspected could torment the flesh of a man and yet not kill him.

A tooth!

The king of one of the most powerful dominions on the world was brought low by toothache. An arrow had struck him in the throat during the Holy Wars of the Cross. Vasnaar had known pain at that time. He had borne it stoically, from that day forward worn a curious ragged scar on his neck that was a testament to his fierceness in battle and bravery at such a debilitating wound. For those in his more intimate circles, he also had a huge ragged strip of angry skin on his left buttock, where a Naav warrior had thought to end him by impaling him with a halbert. The man had died on the King's sword point for his trouble. Though in the bitter cold Vasnaar needed several cushions to seat himself comfortably, it was another impressive addition to his banner of sheer courageous moxie.

Neither of those two grizzly episodes - best forgotten were as anything. Not when compared to the pain the King endured with one of his molars, however. He threshed about in total agonised torment. His lieutenants hastily sent for the King's surgeon. By that time it was taking three of Vasnaar's strongest warriors to hold him down. He was close to blacking out. As he had endured such pain in the past, the sweet, if temporary oblivion of unconsciousness, was denied the warrior-king.

"Pull the damned thing, Surgeon", he bellowed through his miserable anguish. To his increasing horror though, the surgeon shook his head explaining,

"To do so would kill thee, My Liege. For malignancy and toxoid exist beneath the tooth and to pull it would allow such corruption into thy bloodstream, poison thee to death. Before the tooth can be excised the putrescence in thy jaw must be negated. I will go and prepare the necessary salve before I construct a drain beneath thy tooth. Before I return thou shouldst drink spirit until thy senses be dull".

It was a testament to the amount of pain the king was in, that he argued not one jot with his lowly surgeon. The man was his only hope at an end to discomfort. Even so, he little doubted that the cure would have its unpleasant aspects in extremis. Vasnaar was getting very drunk by the time the surgeon returned, with his potions and herbs he had created a noxious smelling paste, with which, to apply to the king's gum once the drain was in place. The instant the warm steel of the scalpel touched Vasnaar's inflamed jaw, he began to squeal and thrash about. The pain felt like a dagger plunging up through the skin behind his chin, driving up into the top of his skull. Finally, never a man to quit, the king of Valgral lost consciousness.

He awoke an indeterminate period later, bathed in sweat, still in great pain. He was carefully laid in his bunk. The clothing of the rude bed might just as well have had the ocean poured onto them, so drenched were they. For five long days of torturous misery, the king tossed, shifted, frequently wished that he might die. For in the oblivion of demise, there would be an end to his suffering. He fell into a feverish torpor, slowly emerged from it feeling much improved and ravenously hungry. When he climbed out of the cot to go and relieve himself, he promptly fell flat on his face. It was Gerner his scribe who found him, helped him back onto shaky legs. After doing that he helped him manage some thin gruel before he once more fell into an exhausted sleep. On the seventh day, with a very sore jaw indeed, he finally began to feel a little better. He knew then, why toothache often proved fatal to a man.

He could have been allowed a significantly longer recuperation period, events were not going to allow that. From his berth, he heard the lone cry from the crow's nest. Knew then that land was finally located. It was not necessarily their destination. They were navigating uncharted territory, they may well have reached their target at the first attempt. It could just as easily have been the southern coastline of Woot that had been encountered though. It was even possible that there were several islets in the бесконечный that were still chiefly unknown to almost everyone. For these reasons Vasnaar began to rise, only to sink back into the berth once he had thought through the various possibilities. As he suspected the scribe was the first to visit him. His face flushed with excitement so that he did not even need to open his mouth to tell the king what he was waiting to hear.

"My Liege. 'Tis the Fire of Saah, the Zhirnublydok has served us truly. We have braved the waters of бесконечный. Won thee a great victory, 'tis the stuff, of which songs will be sung from this day onward".

Vasnaar managed a weak smile, the truth of it was it was all he had vitality for. The infection in his jaw still coursed through his system, leaving him weakly torpid. He longed to close his eyes. Attain deep and refreshing slumber until his customary vitality returned. Instead, when he did lay down, it was to toss and turn restlessly, achieve nothing for his efforts. For a man who had been as vital, as active as he, it was frustrating in no small degree. It presented him with but one option though...wait. He could only delay until nature came to his rescue. His sadly present condition could not remain unbanished from his being indefinitely? Troubled by the response, Gerner then changed his tack accordingly,

"Forgive me, Majesty? Thou still labours 'neath the toxic cultures in thy jaw. Pray to forgive my momentary excitementation. What be thy royal directive, should we wait for vitality to return to thee, or mayhap a landing party to reconnoitre the coastline"?

"Sit", the king commanded, "Let us choose wisely from amongst our number and do as thy suggests? Advise me"?

Here was a matter that the scribe was eminently qualified to do so regarding. Seating himself, he rubbed at a bristled chin as he was want to do when cogitating over a conundrum. With a single raised eyebrow he observed initially,

"I should stay with thee for the time being, until thy current infirmity be a thing of the past. The party should be of a number successful to maintain self-protection in the event of antagonistic native presence, yet not so large as to incite resentment. I suggest seven".

"Wise counsel as ever, Master Scribe", Vasnaar could find no fault in Gerner's logic, "Continue, if thou pleaseth"?

"Prince Byno, thy eldest will be sorely aggrieved if thou dost not name him deputy in thy absence. Aside from which, he be ready, so give the command to him. He is fifteen winters, ready to take the commission".

"Go on"?

"Lord Kynoberg is one of thy most trusted senior lords, have him as thy son's right hand. Additionally have the party made up of lords, Lolocken, Staltidore and Flahé".

"Two more", the king sighed, already simply giving Gerner his attention was causing him fatigue that alarmed him with its intensity.

"Two more youngsters so that Byno does not feel alone in inexperience. Master Hersko, son of Flahé and Master Voong Staltidore's eldest".

"Not Nunne"? Vasnaar asked of Kynoberg's son, who was also on board.

Gerner shook his head sadly, stating somewhat superfluously,

"The vanquil (northern wind) continues to take most of the lad's comprehension. True he fights like none other aboard, with the bravado of one who does not fear death, but his ability to make sense of even the simplest of tasks

Myrrorball

at times may well make him a liability to the rest of the party".

"Thous speaketh truly and no mistake", Vasnaar admitted, before being forced to point out, "But his lordship will not take kindly to his disregard".

"Then name him thy bodyguard in thy son's absence", the scribe suggested. "I knowest that thou hast no need of one aboard the Zhirnublydok, but 'twill serve to placate his lordship"?

"Appeasement for my lieutenants, while I lay still 'neath the etiolation of this vile infirmity", the King moaned then, before conceding, "Very well Gerner, give the order in my name".

It was the measure of the king's loss of vitality that he did not change even one name in the suggested party. Normally, he would have done so just to underline his undisputed authority. He was resentful of his malady though. It was making him maungey. Gerner had seen his majesty several things: furious, affectionate toward the Queen, enmitous toward his enemies, proud of his children. He had never seen him maungey before, so he scurried away, glad to be feeling dismissed.

8.

The first person he encountered as he rushed through the ship was none other than, The Lord of the town of Lolocken. The latter was a veritable giant of a man. Almost 180 centimetres in height. With a barrel chest that attested to much of his 75 kilogrammes of bulk. His huge black beard and the angry scar across the bridge of his broad nose were further testaments to his former prowess on the battlefields. Still, the scribe was presented with a conundrum? How to tell the Lord of the landing party without raising his considerable temper. The reason being that Lolocken had little time for the prince, believing him a milksop and unworthy of his royal father's affection.

"His Majesty is not going to lead a landing party himself, but has chosen the prince to deputise for him", Gerner blurted, better to be direct, prevarication would only increase the Lord's ire. "You are in the party, My Lord".

Lolocken glared at the scribe and adviser to his majesty. The dark Lord was adept at glaring. Gerner waited for the tirade, but all the Lord of Lolocken then demanded was the names of the rest of the group to go ashore. Gerner delivered the requested information and then backed away. Lolocken turned and strode off in the opposite direction. It would be he who would organise the others. All Gerner had to do from that point onward, was to get the prince to the longboat. In time for the lowering onto the water.

"I cannot decide whether to wear the blue or the crimson, Gerner", Byno said some short while later. The foppish dandy was gazing at himself in the myrror. A tall piece of burnished bronze so buffed as to give a reasonable reflection of whomsoever gazed into it.

"If thou dost not choose and with alacrity, Highness, then the boat will go without thee", Gerner felt obliged to warn.

Noting that observation Prince Byno squawked acidly,

"If Lolocken leaves without me, I willst have his head so help me. Dost thou thinkest the purple be ostentatious? After all, I am a prince".

'*Or princess*', Gerner thought, amusing himself if none other, '*I wouldst wager thou would sit side-saddle if the choice were truly thine*'. Aloud he urged the dandy into royal blue and then placing his hand in the small of Byno's narrow back hurried him down the corridor.

"Art thou pushing me, Master Scribe"? The natty prince cawed,

"Indeed I am - Highness, urging thee to a successful quest in thy father's name".

"Ahaagh I see", it seemed to please the prince, "Come then let us canter and none mistake".

Gerner hurried after the son of the great king as he trotted toward the wooden steps leading up on deck.

Sure enough, when they reached the longboat, the others were all there and waiting. Lolocken gave one of his demon's-eye glares at the boy in the company of the scribe.

"We wait for thee, Highness and the tide be with us, thou art tardy", he roared. Lolocken had an impressive roar when the fancy took him. It did so with increasing frequency when in the presence of the prince.

Gerner returned oilyly, "Some last-minute instruction from, His Majesty, my Lord of Lolocken, good fortune in thy first foray into the new dominion".

It caused the tirade from the Lord of the Northern Town to desist. Two mariners began to lower the longboat with the employment of winch and tackle. A further four were in the boat ready to row for the shoreline, once the descent was accomplished.

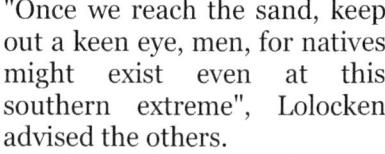

"Once we reach the sand, keep out a keen eye, men, for natives might exist even at this southern extreme", Lolocken advised the others.

Kynoberg objected, "Thou art not senior to myself nor the other lords in this party, Lolocken and thou willst not address us thusly - if it pleaseth thee".

Lolocken glared at Byno who then advised hesitantly, "Once we reach the shoreline, keep out a keen eye - men, for natives might exist even at this southern extreme".

Kynoberg could not resist commenting, "Wise and noble counsel, Highness twill be as thou suggesteth".

Staltidore shrugged to Flahé, who grinned at the internal struggles of politic between some of their number.

The water was clear as crystal and very blue, though some of that was the reflected face of the blue-moon goddess Brahma of course. As the sand drew closer they saw it was almost pure white, fringed with palms of a sort unfamiliar to them. Hugely tall wooden trunks of a strangely blued hue atop of which were expansive serrated leaves which were also startlingly navy. In their shading a variety of fruits and nuts that they did not recognise. All the bounty were various shades of azure too. If this was the Fire of Saah, then it boasted produce in abundance. It was also enjoying a lovely climactic mildness. Under their steel armour, all of them sweat freely.

When the boat ground softly to a halt, the men jumped out all save the mariners and Byno. The latter objecting to one of the rowers,

"These boots are kid and will not enjoy a dousing of saline. Thou willst carry me ashore".

"Shandor's Tits, Girl"! Lolocken roared, "Just get thy feet momentarily wet like the rest of us". The goddess of defence was the Lord's chosen. As such, resided upon his shield, so he knew the mammary glands in question very well. Even so, it was no way to speak to the prince, son of the king. Kynoberg rebuked him,

"My Lord, 'tis no way to speak to the leader of this expedition, thou willst apologise, right hastily, less thou incurs the ire of the rest of us"?!

Lolocken was a mighty warrior, but when he saw that the others were in like mind, hands creeping to weapons at Kynoberg's warning he muttered,

"Apologies, Highness, but we are most vulnerable on this open beach. Wouldst it pleaseth thee to show some alacrity"?

"Of course", Byno smiled pleasantly, jumping from the mariner who had waded ashore, "Let us be about our exploration of this strange realm then. Lolocken taketh point".

That brought a fresh wave of dissatisfaction from the huge Lord, for, in ventures with unknown consequence ahead, the point was the most precarious position.

Kynoberg smiled coldly, let his arm wave toward the palm-line and took one step backward as the bulk of Lolocken harrumphed and drawing his hefty broadsword, shield on the other arm, did as directed by the prince.

Myrrorball

9.

"Quianhua", I raced after her down the grey corridor. All was grey on the ship of the Hhhâäàåâäääçéçêçêïïïïìgg-ndgndÐñß¥þÞÝ⌂', or as I thought of them still, the Zernoplat. I had told my wife the night before Hhrrhhoehhrr-hooooingohh had informed me that the ship was arriving to take us to Rozhelia. She had barely spoken to me since and only then to let me know how furious she still was with me and my underhand shenanigans.

"About my nature, you have made a serious miscalculation, Nick.", she had said, "When I am sweet, I am as well-behaved as honey, but when I am angry, I am a Nozkavardé, so please do yourself a favour and stay away for a while. Quite a while."!

She had not been joking, I had spent my last night on Earth in the office with the kiddie-winks, while she had the double bed to herself. She refused to help me with the cages. We had boarded the ship that had landed in my back garden in great haste as the media, the police and finally, the army arrived. It was to no avail, the instant we six were safely aboard, Quianhua strapped into a strangely constructed seat with considerable webbing. The vessel roared back up into the sky, leaving my stomach back on Earth.

I was too busy deciding not to bring up my breakfast, or a lung or something when the armada swiftly followed. Why would I want to see the great banks of clouds of disintegrating gas that would hand the world of my birth over to the Zernoplat anyway? Abruptly the gravity fell from our beaten forms, then the pseudo gravity slowly replaced it, allowing us to undo the webbing.

"Let's go and see our cabin, then get the babies", I tried, Quianhua blanked me. Walked off in the opposite direction to the one we were informed would lead to the only human cabin on the entire vessel. Apart from we two, with our feline cargo that could not be freed into the corridors under any circumstances, there were only twenty-three Zernoplat on the vessel. Most of the systems were automatically controlled by immensely sophisticated computers. I went down the first of several corridors, over the next three and a half weeks, twenty-three days to be exact, this vessel would be home until we arrived in orbit around Rozhelia.

I have to confess with some degree of asperity that I did not relish the prospect of over three weeks of the girl's disdain. She was so beautiful and so desirable. She had wanted me like no other before she had learned she had been manipulated. Gold had turned into feculence.

I was not happy!

There was no change in my fortune or her attitude for the entire duration of the journey. The trip tended to be boring, once the novelty of being inside a spaceship wore off. I went in search of Hhrrhhoehhrrhooooingohh. Only to be told by his lieutenant Harahorahurrahaashume, that he was the captain of the vessel. Too busy to bother with one of the *limbed-passengers*. I had never been a freak before, but I was then. I was the one with grossly ugly appendages and translucent skin that stopped one from examining the internal structure without firstly cutting one open. Bored as I was - I was not going to volunteer for that particular procedure. There was only one other limbed freak aboard. She was not talking to me. With her inscrutable oriental logic, she must have thought that to be punishment. She was not wrong.

So when a suddenly different sensation gripped my gut, a thought entered my head for lieutenant Harahorahurrahaashume to go and get back in the take-off-landing web I was almost delirious with a combination of joy and relief.

"This is so exciting", I tried with the love of my life, the only human woman in existence at that point. All I received in reply was an almond-shaped stare of total antipathy. My body was then subject to violent forces, for a while, I was incapable of doing anything other than closing my eyes and wishing I was anywhere else. Finally, things settled down. A thunderous thump ran through the vessel. I knew we had touched down on Rozhelia. I was in a very select club indeed, one of a handful of men to ever tread on another world. Then I reflected sadly, I was not a member of that club at all. I was the sole custodian of homosapient life. I was the last man in the galaxy.

"How far have we travelled, Horace"? I asked of Harahorahurrahaashume, "Can you hear me, how far is it from Earth to Rozhelia"?

Harahorahurrahaashume's thoughts entered my head then,

'*We have spanned an area of space that would take light forty-two years to cross. The Hhhàäàåååäåçêçêçêï-îìïîìggndgndÐñß¥þÞÝ⚙' created drive, which we refer to as the Ðñß¥þÞÝ⚙-fotohajtás makes this possible. Do not ask me to explain it to your simian brain? Your race had not become capable of such science nor understanding. Even trying to think about the circuits and engineering*

Major Roxbrough & Nik Gehenna

involved may very well fry various parts of the simple organ in your bony cranium'

I was so glad I had asked.

I was then instructed to gather with the cat cages at the airlock. It would extend a ramp down to the ground on the outside of it. I knew this from embarkation. I had already been instructed that everything the two of us needed to survive would be in the *dome*. The building, bubble-shaped, hence its nomen was a marvel of Zernoplatite engineering know-how, inside we would be under no threat from indigenous lifeforms. With the knowledge of how to operate all the gadgetry inside, the Zernoplat had downloaded into our minds - survival techniques. Science ready for our research, the usage of impressive weaponry. In short, we had nothing to worry about. Between each six-monthly check the Zernoplatite vessels would make on us, expecting us to have data to supply them with upon such occasions.

I was to become a cross between Noah/Rambo/Attenbrough. Quianhua was there to get pregnant. She did not even look at me as the enormous hatchway hissed and then clunked out of the way and we began to descend to the strangely blue surroundings. Neither Hhrrhhoehhrrhooooingohh nor Harahorahurrahaashume was there to send us off nor wish us well. I have to confess that did not upset me. It was not easy to warm to a creature that looked like an amoeba and left a trail of slime in its wake rather like a mollusc.

We had just set foot on the turquoise blades that I already thought of as though it were grass. The ramp began to slide back into its enormous recess. We hastened away so as not to get scorched by the strange exhaust of the *Ðñβ¥þÞÝ⌂-fotohajtás* drive.

I glanced at a tablet, an interspace telephone/computer that was small enough to fit in my backpack and pulled up a map of the place that the Zernoplat had chosen to call Egszígør. We were only a kilometre's hike from the dome. So with two cages each, one in each hand and our backpacks in place, we set off in the direction I led.

Myrrorball

During the entire walk, I kept hearing the sound of rustling in the palms and serrated long leafed grass and knew what was responsible for them.

They were also the reason why the Zernoplat could not settle in that particular land. I had seen a holographic image of the creatures that were called Kézőrös. A species of warm-blooded animals about the same size as a cat that was native to Egszígør. A creature that would eat vegetation, but also meat if it could find any. Creatures that would happily feast on Zernoplat. The latter had not managed to create a gas that would dissolve *those* little buggers. I had asked if the Kézőrös were dangerous to Ann. I was told not to get too close to them and certainly not to get bitten by one as they had certain toxins in their saliva that would not agree with humanoid anatomy.

That was the sort of advice which did not need explaining to me above a single time. On that first day, I did not see one. Fortunately, they seemed as wary of meeting me, as I, they – fair enough. We reached the dome and what a marvel of advanced technology it was. From the outside, it looked like a large canvas and plastic tent. Once we got close to it though we could tell it would be far more durable than that. The white section were panes of some material stronger than brick. The transparent windows were of a structure many times the strength of glass.

Inside the temperature was a wonderfully controlled 19°.

Despite her determination to be in a foul mood, Ann skipped from one section of the dome to the other exploring delightedly while I released the kiddie-winks. There was no internal door. The sections divided by walls

only three feet in height, so it was a cross between open plan and divisions. I went to find the kitchen, the kettle and something which would approach tea, in that order. Then become aware that she had joined me.
I
"Everything works, how"?
Biting back a rejoinder that she had managed to speak to me, I gave her the simple facts, perhaps this was the beginning of the great thaw?
"According to Hhrrhhoehhrrhooooingohh a small micro-pile is buried beneath the bubble and will power all the conveniences for several hundred years".
"I cannot even say Hally", she noted rather bitterly, and you can use his real Zelnoplat name".
"I find your Chinese accent very appealing. I am making something that was in this container here, marked tea, I have no idea if it is the real thing, but would you like some"?

"I will take a sip of yours and then decide".
"I take milk and sugar".
"I will take a sip before you add milk and sugar".
"Not a bad notion, I think the Zernoplat eat cows, therefore, it might be soy-milk and sweetener, I'll let you know".

Mundane conversations were not something the two of us had enjoyed since Quianhua had been aware of our fate. It might seem peanuts to you, Dear Reader, but it was a start. I tried the finished drink. Ann reluctantly had a cup. Once I had added milk with sugar, I could tell nothing was what it purported to be, I would be able to get used to it, but it certainly was not Yorkshire Tea.

I went to the weapons locker I had been told about. Trained how to use of the contents. Took out a searpistol which I strapped over my shoulder in the holster made for that very purpose. Then I took out a blazerifle and turned to Quianhua who had been watching me.

"There will be three creatures that a small reconnoitre might involve me encountering, the two animals I am assigned to study and a hominid that I haven't, do you fancy a stroll"?

"I wasn't told anything, Nick, what creature, why I've been in the dark"? She asked in her strange Chinese phrasing that I understood as well as my tongue.

"I do not think the Zernoplat held you in the same regard as myself", I admitted to her. "To those asexual creatures who multiply by binary fission, you are little more than my companion. I am inviting you though. Can protect you more than adequately with the weaponry they have supplied us".

"How much do you know about these three creatures, can you tell me about them"?

The first is a Kézőrös", I began, "A ground arboreal cross between a rat, monkey and lemur, but not any of the three in any way, coming from this world Rozhelia. They are native to Egszígør, the name of this island. We have been left in the south of it. I can show you a map later if you want to see what it looks like. The diet of the Kézőrös' is omnivorous. They scrounge about eating just about anything. They would eat Zernoplat if the latter settled here, that's why we're here. To see if we can find a way of either teaching them to coexist with the Zernoplat or develop some means of keeping them in check".

"Keeping them in check being using gas on them", Ann observed bitterly, she was not wrong. I did not reply. She requested, "Go on"?

"The second main creature is a sort of reptilian birdlike predator, that eats Kézőrös when it can get its claws into them. The Kézőrös have learned a variety of ways of keeping out of sight of the Zürepüé. For that very reason. There aren't many Zürepüé, because they depend on the Kézőrös. They do not seem to eat anything else, so there is an ecological system in place".

"And the hominid"?

"Live up in the north of the island. They've reached a sort of stone-age level of advancement, they mine the ground for something, but the Zernoplat were not interested enough in what it was to be able to tell me. The most I could learn is that they have slightly blued skin. I want to explore the island and learn more about all three".

"Are the hominid men and women"?

"I don't know. The Zernoplat called them Kémerké. Which translates as blue humans, simply because they were unable to differentiate between them and us. There again they called you sárgembré which in their tongue means yellow-human".

"They taught you Zern"?

"Zernoplatite", I corrected, "Yes and they also taught me Kémerié the language of the Kémerké

"So you want to go out there, jabber away with blue stone-men is that it"? The air was suddenly so thick with the acrimony that I could practically taste it.

"It's my job to study all three of the creatures on Egszígør and give the Zernoplat detailed reports on a six-monthly basis".

"And what am I then", Ann demanded hotly, "An incubator, a breeding sow for you to spill your seed into, impregnate with relish".

"That is pretty much how the Zernoplat regards you and the reason for you still being alive", I admitted, she had to know the truth. "But I do not regard you so coldly, Ann, to me you are my life's partner, I'll treat you as an equal".

"Then know this, partner", the beautiful oriental girl began, "For the manner in which you deceived me - I hate you for it "!

10.

Lolocken was sweating profusely. He could smell his stink. He held up a brawny arm the rest of the party came to a grateful halt. Then the whining voice of, Prince Byno demanded,

"Why have we come to a halt, My Lord? I didst not order such".

Myrrorball

It was a measure of Lolocken's discomfort causing misery that he replied pleasantly,

"Forgive me, Highness, but my armour is heavy, also hot. I tire. Might we not utilise this natural clearing to our advantage? Take sup, food". He instantly hated the grin of wry amusement on Kynoberg's features at that point. Byno was no physical superman despite his lack of armour though. He too looked overly warm, fatigued.

"This natural clearing in the blue canopy be a perfect place for we brave warriors to sup, eat and rest awhile. Take rest my brave men lay down thy weapons for a spell".

'The only weapon thou was ever able to handle efficiently was between thy bed-youth's legs', Flahé amused himself with the thought as he flopped gratefully onto the azure grass.

"Should we not post at least one watch though, Highness"? Young Hersko, the Lord's son asked, "Lest the natives of this realm are abroad"?

Byno considered, nodded, his long straight-haired waving foppishly, as he did so,

"A worthy note of caution, My Lord. Stand too until thou art relieved".

Hersko's suggestion had not been in the form of volunteering for duty. He looked taken aback by the Prince's decision. He said nothing though, merely took up a position at the edge of the small clearing. The other six firstly caught their breath in the uncustomary heated humidity, then began to rummage in their bundles for something to eat and drink. Suddenly Hersko urgently informed,

"Something in the undergrowth just here, in the long blue grass".

The plants in question were not high enough to hide anything approaching one of the natives to the island, Byno ordered tiredly,

"Pray to investigate then, Thy Lordship"?

Drawing his hangar, the young son of a Lord did so. What happened next was like a farcical tableau. A bundle of fur, blue of hue suddenly hurled itself from the grass and Hersko yelled in alarmed pain,

"By the Domisphere it has me, oh, the pain"!

Lolocken darted forward, with a singularly decisive slash of his dagger, severed the creatures head from its shoulders. The ruined corpse fell away - pumping blood. The jaws of the beast stayed firmly clamped. Hersko still danced around in pain from the continued bite. Lolocken took his knife levered the jaws apart and let the head follow the body. While Flahé saw to his son's wound, which was impressive from so small a creature, Lolocken examined the dead animal,

"So this is what Gerner described to us as a Kézőrös is it"? he mused aloud. "Nasty little blackguard, given its size, but I doubt we have aught to fret over if this is the best the Fire of Saah can offer".

With the latter proclamation, he was in grievous error though, as he was subsequently to discover!

11.

So it was out there, Quianhua was not about to overlook my deceit any time soon. I was facing the choice of venturing out into an alien world alone or staying with a woman who currently despised me. That was not a difficult decision to make. I told her I would be a couple of hours.

"I will make something for dinner upon your return", she promised, "I am not the one you love any more, nor am I even a woman, I keep house for you like a good Chinese girl - that is all".

I had my weapons for companionship. It was too soon to let the cats out of the bubble anyway. I had never managed to teach even one of them to walk to heel! It was not long before I located a Kézőrös snuffling about in the long blue blades that I had named grass. The creature had rings of alternating navy and royal blue fur from head to hind. Gimlet blue eyes looked over an elongated snout. Its legs were short, thick terminating in huge grey hands with three fingers and a thumb on each. I went no closer to it than I had to, initially. I would only try to catch one with very thick cloves coupled with protective clothing

Myrrorball

because the snout had razor-like teeth in two rows, top and bottom.

As I ventured further I spotted another one up in a tall blue structure I refused to term trees. They were more like thick tuberous-fronds, The branches terminated in silvery leaves, the frond boughs infested with white fungi. Though it did not seem to be harming the plant, upon which, it lived. Some of the fronds were in flower, huge white blooms with yellow centres that looked like nothing so much as fried eggs. I, therefore, decided to name the fronds Avgófýllo [trans: egg frond] in the first entry of my journal to the Zernoplat. I was also thrilled to see a single Zürepüé, but it was high in the sky. I could not make out any features. There were no other birds. I guessed the Zürepüé had eaten them to extinction, at least locally. It was too soon to venture any further, not on my first day. Though I was armed to the teeth, I did not especially want to make our presence known to the Kémerké until it was possible to display that we were making no difference to their existence.

I did hear raised voices. I decided to cautiously investigate for two reasons. The first was that I doubted the natives could best me armed with such Zernoplatite weaponry as I was. The second was that the speakers were using a language I did not recognise. Even though Harahorahurrahaashume had assured me that Kémerié was downloaded into my brain. It meant only one thing. I was not the only invader on Egszígør. So I went down on hands and knees the searpistol in its holster, the blazerifle across my back. When I got close enough to hear individual words I crept very cautiously indeed. The others did not seem to care how much noise they were creating, making my comparative stealth so much easier. There were seven of them. All wore strangely fashioned iron armour. It must have been most uncomfortable for them, considering the heat and humidity of the place. The sort of metal protection reminded me of the Black Prince or other such figures of the 14th-century. I smiled at the unbidden thought of the Battle of Crécy. He who in the year 1356 on another chevauchée - Edward of Woodstock had ravaged Auvergne, Limousin, and Berry. Served the bloody French right for daring to have a 100 years war with good olde-England.

 These chaps before me were involved in some internally bizarre conflict amongst themselves. They were arguing, looking just like knights of antiquity. At least they appeared to be completely human though. How was it possible when the Zernoplat had brought me so far? Human life replicated so exactly. More to the point, why had I not been warned about the possibility of encountering them? The very question supplied the answer. The Zernoplat did not know about the humans of Rozhelia. Like the Spaniards entering the New World in our history, these Gothic warriors were also explorers from somewhere else on the planet. I could not decide if that were a good or bad thing. Would I have more in common with the ... I decided to call them Rozhelic, or the hominidical Kémerké. True I possibly resembled the former more closely, but would they present a greater threat to me? Perhaps they had ideas of conquest? Ann and I might represent an obstacle to their taking over the island? I needed to sound her out on that. To that end slowly reversing my course straight into my fourth encounter of the day!

12.

"Tarry for a minute", Lolocken suddenly boomed his demand for silence, "Something else is moving in that grass yonder".

"Probably another of those little blackguards", Hersko cursed, gritting his teeth at the pain, as his father tightened the torn cloth over his bleeding wound.

"It is something much larger", Kynoberg noted. As one all of them save father and son drew their various weaponry and slowly approached the direction of the sounds. What they saw filled them with varying degrees of horrified revulsion depending upon their ability to regard such things without not being shaken by them.

 It was tall, broad, in fact, barrel-chested. Pale blue by complexion with a hairless head on a powerful neck. In the face, a single, huge, bloodshot eye, long slit-like nostrils, above a pink mouth. The creature possessed no arms at all, no upper appendages of even a vestigial sort. The legs were stout, trunk-like, the feet appeared to have shrunken into them, barely recognizable as separate limbs. Noticing each of the warriors standing in front of it, the monstrosity opened its mouth, mumbled something in an unintelligible gibberish that may, or may not have been, foreign language.

"Shandor's excellent breasts but that shagger is one ugly creature", Lolocken cursed with relish, even though he knew it would offend the Prince. "Shall we put it to the sword, Highness"?

"Certainly not", Byno was outraged, "Why would we do such a thing, the beast might well be a peaceful herbivore. As for it being short of comeliness, so art thou, Lord Lolocken.

"What is it mumbling"? Staltidore wished to know, "Be it of some rudimentary intelligence, can it see much from that eye".

"We need Gerner here", Voong noted, "He might even know what the blue mumbler is".

"Blue mumbler", Kynoberg chuckled, "Thou hast just named the creature, young Lord Voong, methinks we should call the beast a Blue-Mumbly".

"What about that rotten little critter that bit Hersko then"? Lolocken demanded, "What are we going to call that? Or are we sticking to the name Gerner gave it"?

"The Kézőrös' are already catalogued by our scribe". Byno declared. "You will not change their nomenclature, My Lord. As Hersko is injured and needs the inspection of the scribe, we should turn around. Curtail our expedition for today. My father may well feel enough improved to lead one himself, on the morrow".

"We could send the young lordling back with his father and proceed further a pace", Lolocken argued.

"Or we could obey the expedition leader, our prince, my Lord", Kynoberg added darkly, it became plain to Staltidore then that there was no love lost between the two nobles of the northern towns of Valgral.

Major Roxbrough & Nik Gehenna

Lolocken shook his head as though in bemusement, but he allowed the foppish dandy to lead them back toward their vessel. At the shore, they used a piece of burnished bronze, utilising the brilliance of Angelus to signal the ship to send out the longboat once more. Within an admirably short period, it was back, scraping the white sand and the seven of them climbed aboard. One of the mariners asked how the foray had gone. Byno informed him that the king would be the first to hear the detail of their report.

Within minutes they were grazing the side of the schooner, clambering aboard. Byno instructed,

"My Lord of Kynoberg, thou willst come with me to see the King, my father, lest I leave out any detail of our first brief foray onto the Fire of Saah".

Lolocken scowled but said nothing. He went in search of Lord Rhynturo, one of his drinking comrades - Lord of the Western Port.

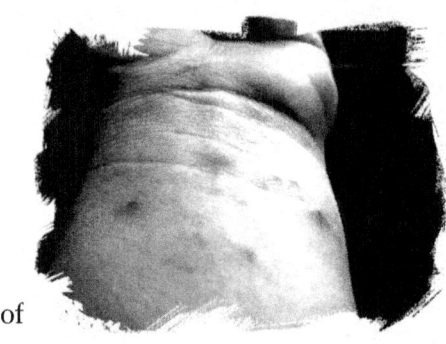

Vasnaar had gained more strength and was seated in his bunk, which was a vast improvement. He had taken one of the scribe's special powders with his soup. It was giving of a great benefit. Together his son, with occasional additions from Kynoberg described the incident of the first foray. When they got to the young man's injurious encounter with the Kézőrös, Gerner excused himself, going in search of him. To attend to his wound before it started to fester. He found Hersko reclining in a bunk, claiming that,

'My hand throbs something rotten and none mistake - feels much worse than it looketh'!

Gerner rinsed his hands in a bowl kept for just such a purpose and requested that he see the injury. Upon removing the hastily created bandage though, the scribe stared in wonder at the young man's wrist.

"There are no bite marks here", the scribe told father and son, "As thou seest the skin be unbroken".

"But I didst bleed and profusely and the wrist pains me, Gerner", Hersko objected.

As if to qualify his son's claim, Flahé nodded, "He speaketh truly, Master Scribe. Question the others if thou doubtest, but they will confirm testimony"?

"I doubt not thy words", Gerner agreed graciously given the circumstance, "The wounds be healed Lord Hersko! Thou canst go about thy business untroubled by the incident. I have no explanation for the throbbing, nor the curious lividity of the skin around the site".

"The blueness will fade in time"? Flahé demanded.

"We be forced to wait and see", Gerner hedged his bets, the entire debacle was beyond his experience. He never sought to display ignorance.

By the time he got back to the king, his son together with Lord Kynoberg were both gone.

"We shall go on the Fire of Saah on the morrow, Gerner", Vasnaar informed the man of learning, "With thee in mine company we shall get more answers than riddles I fancy".

"Thou art still weak, my Liege", Gerner was troubled that Vasnaar was trying to do too much too quickly.

"Ifin I dost not get free of this timber gaol on the morrow I fear my mind might go the way of Nunne. Speaking of the young Lord, he will be with me, though his mind be addled, his arm be strong. He be as worthy a bodyguard as any".

"Who else, Sire"?

"Lolocken, Rhynturo, Hersko to point out the creatures to us and finally Lord Halsgough".

"Halsgough, Sire? A curious choice, for 'tis known the two of thee harbour nought but enmity toward one another"?

Major Roxbrough & Nik Gehenna

Vasnaar grinned, Halsgough will take the point, I certainly hope he dost not receive an arrow in the throat".

Gerner smiled. The king was indeed on the mend.

13.

The creature was taller than me. I am 183 centimetres. Tall, broad, with a mighty barrelled chest. Its skin tone was a curiously livid pale blue with a bald head not even a fringe of any growth around the upper neck or base of the skull.

It was not tonsured, though. It was on top of a powerful neck. In its face, a single - huge bloodshot eye. The nostrils were little more than elongated slits in the front of the blank face.

Beneath them was a pink mouth. The alien possessed no arms of any sort, no upper appendages, even vestigial ones. The legs were stout, like the trunks of young trees, the feet appeared to have shrunken into them, barely recognizable as separate limbs. I could see toenails on the front of the base of each leg, rather like those of an elephant scaled down in size of course. Seeing me with its single eye, as I almost walked into it, the bizarre creature opened its mouth. Uttered something incoherently. Yet another language that I had not been taught, by the Zernoplat teaching system. It thusly came across as unintelligible gibberish that may or may not have been a foreign language. It might have been what it sounded like to me – gobbledygook.

"Hello", I said, I've got a right imagination when I get going. "I am not going to hurt you (unless you start something then watch out buster, I've Zernoplatite weaponry in my arsenal). Who are you? What are you? I am a man. I'm Nik".

The blue creature prattled on with some sort of palaver but did not attempt to harm me or even move toward me on those impressive lower (and only) limbs.

Myrrorball

"I not understand", I mouthed, I was getting less loquacious. "Do you require any assistance? From me, can I help you"? Quite how I was going to do so when the two of us could not understand one another was beyond me. I had not the foggiest idea of what else to say.

I decided to get personal, "What is your name". I pointed to my chest and said, "Nik".

How the blue column was going to reciprocate, I had not thought through. You can only point with the appropriate mechanism to whit – fingers. So I pointed at myself and repeated my name and then pointed toward the column for it, the answer I got was,

"Mmmuurghhnnghmm".

I may have spelt that erroneously, but you get the idea. It was time to get creative,

"Pleased to meet you them Mervin, how's it hanging"?

Another faux pas, because a closer inspection revealed the fact that poor Mervin did not have anything *to* hang. In fact, for all - I knew Mervin might well be a Mervina or, saddest of all a Morv [agamogenetic]. I also needed a name for the genus of the animal before me and settled on – Blevastís (trans: blue gibber). Our gripping conversation exhausted I finally said,

"Well it's been a real blast Merv (seemed a polite compromise) but you know how it is, things to do, aliens to encounter? I can't stand here jawing with you all day. The little woman is fixing me up some poisoned noodles, so off I have to go".

I backed away, turning when I knew the Blevastís could not reach me in a rush before I had drawn and fired my pistol, then went back the way I had come. I don't know what made me turn half-way toward the bubble, but when I glanced furtively over my shoulder, Merv was shambling after me. I tried to shoo him away (yes really), but he kept on following. Or she? Who knew? Maybe she was in love or what not? Anyway, the shooing did not affect it, indeed with taking the time to do so I made less progress back to the bubble. Which meant Merv was closing the gap between us. As I was unprepared to shoot the very first Blevastís I had met, I let the dogging trail continue until I got to the front airlock of the bubble.

Major Roxbrough & Nik Gehenna

When I got inside Quianhua greeted me with the cheerful rejoinder,

"What's that bloody blue is dazzling blue?" [trans: What the bloody blue blinding bluery is that].

"Oh, that's Merv", I even amazed myself at my casual tone, "Pet number five, he's a Blevastís, don't worry he'll sleep in the laboratory and the lab does have internal walls and a stout lock on the steel door".

"You are a special case. You know that Nik", she observed then, "We've not been on this miserable alien world many hours. What happens? You already started bringing specimen home".

"I *am* a special case", I agreed. It is always an appropriate way of deflecting sarcasm, act as though you are taking it literally.

What's for tea, babe"?

"Don't lie babe to me, this deceptive British asshole", she cursed in her Chinese which I had once found so endearing. "Go washy-washy your hands".

I went washy-washy my hands. After all, it was the hygienic thing to do. It could have possibly have saved our lives, what with the Coronavirus and all. We had left in the middle of it, but the following Zernoplatite gas had made that little snuffle, look like chicken-feed. The food was good, It was tempting to invite Merv to try it. I sensed Ann was not in the right frame of mind for entertaining that evening. Call me empathic, I know.

"What are we going to do this evening"? She suddenly surprised me.

"I thought we could watch a holographic film? Hhrrhhoehhrrhooooingohh informed me that the list of available titles is almost inexhaustible. What do you fancy watching"?

Ann seemed to consider this, finally replied, "Red Cliff".

Whatever I had been contemplating was banished by that choice. What a belter to watch holographically in a three-dimensional presentation?

"Good choice, your turn tonight", I conceded. We watched the film together on the settee, Ann - careful not to touch me the whole time. I sensed she was ever so slightly starting to thaw toward me, but a nice shag was decidedly not on offer that first night. I was spent by the time I looked in on Merv anyway, soon to be sleeping soundly, an invisible but impenetrable barrier between the lovely Chinese beauty and I. To add to my punishment she chose to sleep nudey. 'You can looky, but no touchy', she seemed to say to me, the rotten sow. Not that it bothered me as much as she was hoping, the minute my head hit the pillow I started to doze. Within seconds my brain had turned out the light on any future thoughts.

Strangely the conversation I dreamed was going to turn out to be auspicious.

"I don't care what it does or doesn't do. It makes me creepy, can you take it out of our house"?

"Or else what"? I suddenly flared. My Chinese spouse was beginning to get on my nerves. Curiously a show of anger worked toward the desired result far better than if I had once again been reconciliatory. The girl suddenly pursed her lips when she did speak, her eyes filmed with threatening tears.

I woke then, turned over, the conversation was gone.

14.

When I checked in on Merv the night before, unsuccessfully asking him if he wanted any supper, Mrs Mimms must have sneaked in for the night too. When I opened the steel door to the laboratory, it was to see something that made me grin from ear to ear. Merv curled up as foetal-like as his bulky and featureless torso allowed. In the crook of that bizarre blue hollow, Mrs Mimms curled up with him fast asleep. At the moment I carefully lifted Mrs Mimms from Mervin's lap, a curious mewling sound came from him - rather than her, he had begun to worm his way into my affections. I'm such a soft git at times. I was intrigued, he had a mouth but never seemed hungry and as far at that went, I never saw the corresponding exit one needs if one has an entry point either? He did not seem to be suffering from malnutrition. The reason for that came to me in a flash as

I prepared this report for Hhrrhhoehhrrhooooingohh. Mervin was a plant! He had to be. His only form of nutrition came from the rather large and bright sun up in the sky. He just soaked up moisture by osmosis. A plant, capable of communication through sound waves. I had yet to learn his language, but I could not dismiss the fact that he could…mutter). The only question was, how did Mervin reproduce?

I put these hypotheses to Quianhua at breakfast, her response was less than stimulating,

"No matter what you think, just take 'the something' out of my house? It will make me creepy. [What ever you think, just get the thing out of my house it gives me the creeps]".

Strangely my patience was at an end with her, despite how gorgeous she was, she was beginning to get on my nerves. I lost my temper. It had the opposite effect to that when I had been previously reconciliatory,

"Or you'll do what exactly, leave here? Good luck with that"!

Her lovely almond eyes filmed with unshed tears at that moment and she observed quietly,

"I apologise for the demand. It isn't the way I was taught to speak to my husband. Please forgive me. However, the Blevastís makes me nervous, would you mind keeping the two of us apart at all times"?

What could I do, she had defused my anger with one remark (the bitch),

"Very well Quianhua, apologies for my outburst. Please try to remember that I am on this world amongst aliens too you know, the only human I know is you".

"You should have told me sooner though", she observed head bowed.

"Then you might not have come to Rozhelia. That would mean you would now be dead. Would you rather be dead than spending some time with me, Quianhua"?

She took a second or so to shake her head, I considered that a victory and was not going to bludgeon her into submission on day two of our new life together, so I said simply.

Myrrorball

"I am going out again researching with a chem-kit, do you want to accompany me this time"?

"The Kézőrös frighten me, just the thought of their little alien bodies, the Zürepüé or the Kémerké, I hate Egszígør, Nik, I want to go home".

"Egszígør is home now Ann", I was forced to observe, "I'll take Mervin with me. I don't want you in the bubble alone with him".

"Fine, please be careful, I've been reading the library files that Zern puts into our computer, which is very dangerous for our new world. I don't want to find myself here alone. Despite everything, I don't want anything to happen to you."

I smiled at her, left her to her maunge. I mean to say anyone can sulk right but she was starting to toe the mark? So I collected my newest pet, nicely armed once again and the two of us set off. It was too soon to let the cats out until I knew how dangerous the local fauna could be regarding them. It was driving one of the three males – Gentry, barmy, but he had his toys. Also his bin. It was better than violently fatal death. I know that's poor grammar, yet I read it once by the BBC. The other two cats were Mr Choon and Colin. They would stay in for as long as I wanted, so lazy were they.

Mervin was not capable of a great deal of speed, which was just as well because I was sweating like a darky on a rape charge after we had gone but forty paces. I know that at one time that observation would be perceived as racist. As it was a good olde-Yorkshire saying where I had lived. Thanks to Hhrrhhoehhrrhooooingohh, there were only two human races left anyway, mine and my Chinese Missus. If we did have children, the resultant strain would be a lovely new race and a single one at that.

Those reflections caused me to wonder about the Kémerké and the Rozhelic. Would it be possible to diversify the offspring a bit better? I was already beginning to have a list of questions for Hhrrhhoehhrrhooooingohh the next time he chose to 'drop-in'.

I hesitated in my stroll to pick a blade of grass, all the better to examine it. Just my luck, the serrated edge of

Major Roxbrough & Nik Gehenna

the stipule sliced the very crease of my index finger. Human, oxygenated blood flowed liberally for the first time on the alien world as far as I knew. It was serious because it was the first time I was haemorrhaging on Rozhelia. Hastily I scrambled in my backpack for the tiny first aid kit that I had at least had the foresight to pack before the two of us set off. For his part, Mervin was useless. He just stood, stared with his single bloodshot eye, mumbling incoherently to himself. At least he did not faint at the sight of blood, with my painful finger I would not have fancied trying to lift him back onto his stumps if he had keeled over. We proceeded on a pace, then had to stop as I had a small piece of gravel in one of my boots. It may have been minute, it gave me hell though. It took me five minutes to get the lacing sufficiently loose enough to pull the boot free. How on Rozhelia had it managed to get where my fingers could not? Not only that, but we were also on a patch of grassland, there was no gravel in sight. I even entertained the notion that Quianhua had deliberately placed it in there during the night as a cruel and crude form of contraception – as it was making me limp! The ever-present sun was not blocked by even the wispiest of clouds. It soon forced me to start on my water ration. Hhrrhhoehhrrhooooingohh had advised us to abstain from drinking out of streams or rivers. At least - until we had been on the world for a month. We were taking some sort of tablets that were slowly building up our white cell count so that at the end of thirty days or so we could cope with the resultant microbes when we did so. There were underground storage tanks beneath the bubble, more than we would need in the meantime, but carrying it was the main problem when going into the field.

I noticed Mervin doing his best to steer a course through the still dewy bluegrass as much as possible. That explained why he did not drink, at least not through his mouth. It was this action which incidentally introduced me to a second life-form on Egszígør. The Blue-Mumbly's huge feet suddenly threatened to crush a **Kézőrös** which had been sleeping in the grass, with an excited chitter it scurried out directly in my path. Its beady little eyes regarded its first-ever human being, for two precious seconds, it was like a rabbit in headlights, frozen in a combination of fear and fascination. Or was it? It suddenly chittered furiously, puffed its blue fur out rather like one of my cats trying its best to look twice its natural size, double its ferocity. For my part, I saw the razor-sharp teeth, tiny but numerous and had no desire to engage in any form of combat what so ever. So we remained frozen regarding one another until the creature ambled away. It seemed I was not even impressive enough to merit a scurry. I felt somewhat deflated by that. After all, it was only three-hundred millimetres in length and would have only weighed about 5 kilos if it was a gramme.

What was fantastic compared to the rather disappointing stand-off though was Mervin's reaction to the Kézőrös. He took to giving a type of keening howl of abject terror and his flesh [if it was flesh and not fibrous pulp of some sort] quivered from the top of his bald head to the base of his elephantine hooves. He was plainly in morbid dread of a creature that looked mostly like a lemur on steroids. I thought about it as I tried to calm him down, wondering if perhaps he was - a she, after all. For it was rather like a young woman climbing onto a chair to avoid a mouse. There seemed no way such a tiny thing could do any real damage to something as large as a Blevastís.

"Keep your hat on, Luv" I tried a nice Yorkshire phrase to try and calm Merv down. It amused me at the time even if the humour of it was lost in translation. The only thing that did, in the end, was to simply wait for the Blevastís to realise the Kézőrös was gone. I finally got her to settle down. Placing her under the boughs of some Avgófýllo. There I picked up a flower from above, sealing it into a neoplas-bag, placing it in my bundle for analysis later on. Scrutinized, it looked nothing like a fried-egg.

Too late to change the name of the blue frond-like structures by then though. I still liked the nomen, so it was not going to be changed. What I did find of interest were more fungi growing in the deep shade afforded by the Avgófýllo. They looked entirely like Terran mushrooms except for the fact that they were very brightly devoid of any pigmentation in even the smallest of degrees. So I named them Agarispo, a contraction of the name given to white mushrooms on Earth – the Agaricus bisporus. They looked so invitingly edible that I was tempted to nibble one, for about a half a millisecond

that was. We had a diagnostic bench in the rear of the bubble, but I was not about to start acting in a way that might induce its useage sooner than was necessary. As for Merv, I now thought of her as decidedly plantlike and would not have an alimentary canal of the sort we find in animals.

"Time to move on, Merv", I said once I had cooled down a bit and sipped a bit more water. I had also eaten a bar that the Zernoplat had left us in the kitchen cupboard imaginatively called - *Nutrient*. It had some sort of nut on its pathetic wrapper, which may or may not have been an almond. I could not taste it whilst eating it, but it seemed to do the trick, I remembered the higher oxygen content in the air and slightly lower gravity. I was, therefore, ready to set off once more on our journey of exploration.

It was an eventful one.

Suddenly from out of a canopy, we could barely see, due to the Avgófýllo foliage a dark outline swooped from the air and landed not too far from where the two of us had been resting. The instant sound of a soft thudding issued from the undergrowth, a high pitched scream of terror and morbidity shattered the peace of the morning. Ignoring Merv's reticence in approaching the cause of the commotion, I threw my blazerifle from off my back. Advanced like the commando I had never been. Rounding a clump of Avgófýllo saplings I immediately found the reason for the horrible commotion. A Zürepüé had plummeted down from the sky to land on a Kézőrös. It was tearing at it with a teeth-filled upper and lower beak. The little blue rat-monkey was screaming as strips of fur-covered flesh were being ripped from it whilst still alive.

I might not be the most compassionate of chaps when told of the human apocalypse, this was something I could not stand to observe. Raising the blazerifle to my shoulder, I thumbed off the safety catch, as if I had been using the weapon all my life. The rest was not difficult for the rifle had telescopic sights. Easing the trigger to a squeezed position after hearing the rifle whine its immediate charge my first shot neatly decapitated the flying reptilian. A second one put the ruined but still living carcass of the Kézőrös out of its misery. There was movement behind me, it was Merv. She was shaking as much as she had first been when seeing a living Kézőrös, after almost trampling it to death. It seemed the Blue-Mumbly or Blevastís was a pretty peaceful individual. She did not even like seeing her enemies vanquished.

The next item of note was when I replaced the rifle onto my back. The action caused the cut in my finger to remind me of its existence. Tentatively I pried up the edge of the plaster I had applied to see something which did cause me concern. I could barely see the cut, which had closed up. It had been quite-narrow anyway. That was not the problem, what was, the skin around it had gone a pale blue of hue, as though starved of oxygen. Not a bruise, more like skin discolouration. My finger seemed to be exhibiting the early stages of cyanosis. I know many conditions can cause one's skin to have a bluish tint. For example, bruises and varicose veins can appear blue. Poor circulation or inadequate oxygen levels in the bloodstream can also cause the skin to turn bluish. I was on an alien world though, what seemed innocuous on the face of it could have deeper implications if left untreated. It was thusly time to turn back and seek the advice of the computer in the laboratory at the rear of the bubble. As was usual with all journeys, getting back did not take half as long, even though I had to keep waiting for Merv to catch me up. At that point, I was becoming convinced that if I had to attribute - sex to the Blevastís. She had to be decidedly feminine, so I changed the nomen of the curious Blue-Mumbly to Merla.

Quianhua was surprised at the alacritous nature of our return and asked in a pleasant tome,

"You were not gone as long as I expected, is anything the matter"?

"Just a small injury", I told her, "Nothing to worry about I hope"?

"You hope? What sort of injury? Show me"?

Self-consciously I pulled off the plaster and explained as I did so. "It was only a small cut, but I'm not sure I like the look of the skin around it considering I only did it a couple of hours ago, what would you think if it was *your* finger "?

"I'd be mildly concerned. I don't think you should be going blue like that. What are you going to do"?

"How much were you taught about the lab back there"? I nodded in the appropriate direction,

"I had the cap-thing placed on my head so that I know how to use it", she confessed, "Even though you did too would you like me to scan your finger for you"?

"Please Quianhua and thank you".

"Come on then let's see if we can find out if you need the Xiǎo húndàn cutting off", she grinned.

It was ironic. It was taking the possible loss of a digit to motivate her to be civil to me. It was not even the right finger!

The three of us went into the laboratory,

"Don't worry about Merla, she's like a Labrador-puppy, follows me around and just as harmless".

"Merla, I thought you'd named it Mervin"?

"I decided that she was a female. If she is sexual at all, which is possible she is, female".

Myrrorball

"That's a great deal of superstition with no facts. You should put her through the scanner following your excise of this blue finger".

I chuckled, having always been a fan of black humour. It seemed the Chinese liked it too, or at least the last Chinese woman ever.

Quianhua picked up a small device that looked like a tub of tablets with a top that was serrated around its circumference. From the base of it was a cord of wire in insulation, which disappeared into the side bank of the operating table. She activated it by depressing a button in its side. A slight humming type of spinning noise was heard as she waved it briefly over my finger. After turning it off, Quianhua went over to the console and began to type far faster than I ever could. On the 380 millimetre screen, a series of equations appeared. The girl read them with interest. Doubtless, I could have de-cyphered them too, as she was willing to help, I let her do so.

She turned to me, "Come and look. This is what healthy blood looks like when scanned by the diagnostic device". She then showed me a second image, "This is what the blood from around your wound looks like".

"I'm infected, on a massive level, just by a tiny cut from the bluegrass"?

"Your finger is", Quianhua corrected, "The effect is

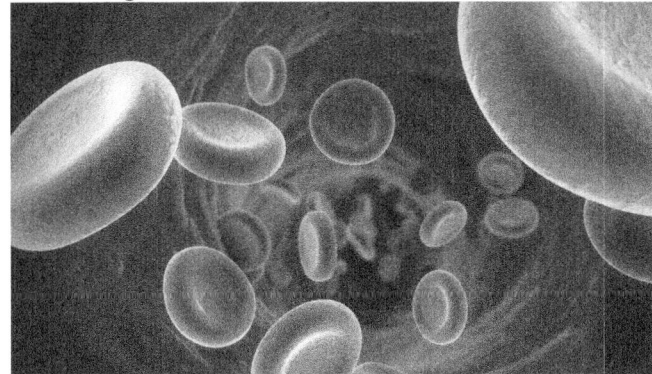

currently localised. As you know blood travels around every vital area of your body. Within hours all your blood cells will have been invaded unless we can do something to stop it".

Major Roxbrough & Nik Gehenna

"Can we"? I was beginning to feel alarmed, "There must be something otherwise why would Hhrrhhoehhrrhooooingohh & Harahorahurrahaashume have brought us here, if the place was so toxic to humans"?

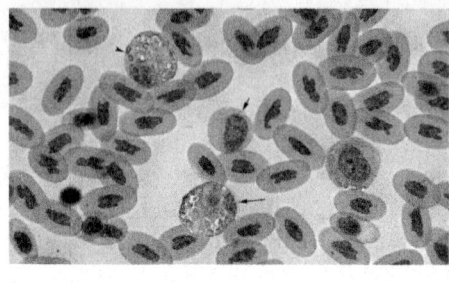

The girl consulted the screen and nodded after a mercifully brief interval.

"They knew this could happen and have labelled the toxicity as dilitírio dilitírio".

"Dilitírio dilitírio, I have a new disease"?

"No, it means, roughly translated - Rozhelic poison. It would seem you need to take only two tablets of antígialitikó. It will kill the invasive cells of your dilitírio. They will be dead by the time you take the second tablet".

She went over to a section of the lab that looked like an apothecary, sought out one of the large white tubs there. Unscrewing it, she took out two tiny white capsules and handed them to me,

"Two-hundred microgrammes of Antígialitikó", she informed me with a smile. "It seems the Zernoplat have also given it an English trade name just for the fun of it, called Poisease".

"And when I wrote about them I gave them no sense of humour", I grinned. I immediately swallowed the first capsule. "Thank you, Anna, I would have managed on my own. It was much more pleasant having you doctor me".

"Don't tempt me with phrases like that", she then objected, "There have been times when...".

"I get the picture, but how many times do you want me to say the same phrase over and over? You know why I did it? You know what the alternative would have been"?

She nodded, "That's what I've been thinking this morning. I'm prepared to make a concerted effort to forgive and forget, Nik. There is just one other problem though"?

"Whatever it is, we can work through it together. Tell me what it is? I will do everything I possibly can to help"?

"I'm not sure that you can", I was informed sadly then. "You see Nik, I hate this place, I hate Rozhelia"!

15.

Vasnaar looked up into the morning sky and breathed deeply of the salient-tangy air. It made his jaw ache where the tooth had been pulled. Not as much as when the evil fang had still resided in his gum though. With deliberate sloth, he made his way to the longboat where the landing party and rowers were patiently waiting for him. He was their King. It was therefore expected of him, that he would arrive late, then be first to leave. Most of the selected nobles and warriors were quite happy with that arrangement. It was tradition after all. The Lord of Halsgough was not. He was not a patient man at the best of times. Lean and his otherwise mousey-brown hair beginning to show signs of grey at the temples, he waited in a growing state of frustration. An irritation which it amused Vasnaar to see at every conceivable opportunity. The king of Valgral, distant Valgral across the бесконечный [Beskonechnyy] Ocean who had come in search of Корунд, which was was a more azure blue than the eyes of the goddess Shakita and that was very beryl indeed.

As he had then improved from the malady of the tooth, it was time for the king himself to lead expedition number two onto the isle - Fire of Saah. He clambered down into the shallow hull of the boat, taking a spot beside Gerner. The latter looking less than charmed at the prospect of encountering strange animals and natives. Bound by duty to his monarch which took precedence over his duty to protect his wrinkled hide. Nunne grinned and nodded, Nunne grinned a great deal. When he took one of the oars though, he showed at least one of his admirable traits. He was immensely strong if not very quick-witted. Lolocken was beside his only friend, Lord of Rhynturo. The final duo that made up the septemviral were also seated together, the scowling Halsgough and the rather wan Hersko.

"How is the hand now, my lord"? Gerner asked of the young lordling.

Hersko replied carefully, "It feels a bit insensate, Master Scribe, as though the weather were frigid and the vanquil was playing athwart it constantly".

The vanquil, so frigid it chased away the mistral amid winter. Gerner frowned, the prognosis of his learning was lack of circulation, yet the young son of a lord looked healthy apart from slight paleness. He lied,

"That is not a bad sign. I willst give thee a physical upon our return to the Zhirnublydok".

The longboat was soon crunching into the beach. The seven who were to make up the search for...anything of interest climbed out and waded to dry sand. In the warmth of Saah, it would not be long before they were dry, so they were heedless of their wet legs and feet. Gerner had a board, upon which, was a stretch of parchment, ready to draw at least the crudest of maps but due to the thick undergrowth he would not be able to add any useful features it seemed.

Myrrorball

"Take point Halsgough", Vasnaar ordered with just a shade too much relish. The Lord of that town of Valgral did so without as much as a murmur. He did not betray his inner consternation before the others.

'One day though. One day...'!

According to what Byno had reported to his father the first expedition, brief as it had been having struck northerly from the shoreline, so he took them in the same direction. Wondering as he did so if that young fool Hersko would manage to get himself attacked by some sort of blue rat-like creature again. Perhaps this time it would be the empty-headed Nunne?

Even unhelmed, with partial armour the heat soon became oppressive. The Lord of a cold northern-town on the other side of the world even grew weary of carrying his sword. He sheathed it, to risk attack but conserve energy.

When returning to Valgral, if they ever did – alive, Halsgough resolved to mount an uprising against the crown. The western lords had endured eastern oppression and mismanagement of their funds for far too long. If anyone had the foresight and rhetoric to stir them up, it was he, Lord of the town that gave him his title. A banner that he acquired from his father by right of succession and not bestowed by the crown as was the lordship of Oslan-On-the-Bank. Halsgough had estimated that he could gain enough support for an insurgency to raise troops equal in size to the Crown's. The west against the east and he calculated that the west would prevail.

His thoughts were rudely interrupted by a flash of blue fur darting across his chosen pathway. In a flash bright steel was in his hand.

"What be delay's reason", the king demanded from behind him almost at once. "We need to progress further than Lolocken with the lad did yesterday".

As the huge dark Lord of that nomen scowled, Halsgough explained,

"Something didst scurry athwart my pathway Majesty, I hesitated to draw glaive and willst now proceed".

"Wait"? Vasnaar commanded, instantly halting the western Lord, "Rhynturo, thy arbalist, have it primed and bolted. Take the point and if another such hapless vermin dost cross thy purpose let the bolt fly. For I wouldst see one close up, if dead"?

The ally of Halsgough merely nodded. Placing a booted foot on the bowed section of the weapon he hauled back the lever that pulled the cord taut, then fitted a feathered bolt one depression of the release trigger. A deadly arrow would then fly at the unsuspecting Kézőrös. Indeed it was not many moments later that the troupe all heard the twang of the weapons release and a squeak of astonished fatality shortly thereafter. Rhynturo promptly strode forward, holding the carcass aloft by the bolt that had impaled it. A bright blue of fur, the grey of skin, sharp of snout.

"That is the curs-ed creature who sank teeth into my flesh yesterday"! Hersko declared with ire and then suddenly plopped down onto his backside as though instantly exhausted. Although Gerner would have loved to examine the rodent-monkey or what-so-ever it was, he went firstly to the youth and asked,

"What be the nature of thy infirmity, My Lord".

"An ague dost possess me, Scribe", the young son of a Lord protested. Gerner scrutinised the youth. Suddenly jumped to his feet revolted by what he saw.

Myrrorball

"What be the cause of thy abhorrence, Gerner", Vasnaar demanded, keenly, having observed the tableau curiously.

"Look at the lad's hand? The one 'pon the end of his formerly injured wrist, Sire"?

Vasnaar did so. His eyebrow rose in Ancelottite astonishment. The rest of the nobles gathered around the poor addled Nunne was the one dim enough to make the verbal observation that none other deemed necessary.

"He only has three fingers! Where has his little pinky gone"?

In an exhausted stupor, Hersko looked in that direction to see that the simpleton was right. Where his little finger should be was a perfectly healed scar.

"Shandor's sweet tits"! Lolocken cursed freely, "Where has it gone? One cannot simply lose a finger without noticing or with no pain. If the Majax had taken it, we would have seen".

"Then it must have been Ogglenooré, for He is invisible", Rhynturo concluded, being an Ogglenonial and follower of the god of theft it was a logical conclusion for him.

Gerner was a Mazormazurite, a follower of the god of healing Mazormaruri but he doubted he could heal the lad. How did one even begin to treat something that was simply gone? With them, all equally distracted Nunne suddenly yelped and cried out,

"Majax' teeth, one of the little blackguards have just bitten right through my boot".

The lad wore only kidskin footwear as he was not trusted to carry anything other than a dagger and wore no sabaton on his feet. Gerner suddenly looked nervously about him. He too wore only boots. If the Kézőrös were getting bolder for some unsuspected reason, then he too was in danger of suffering a bite. Vasnaar immediately made a decision,

"Halsgough, escort Nunne, Hersko and Gerner back to the shoreline if thou pleaseth. I told the mariners to tarry till our return, yet get the lad aboard the Zhirnublydok and right hastily, so that medication can be administered. Then direct the longboat back to these shores and accompany the mariners".

Major Roxbrough & Nik Gehenna

Halsgough nodded. While his ire boiled at the thought of being reduced to ambulatory duties that were beneath his dignity. The king oblivious to the mental protest simply instructed,

"Take point Rhynturo, thy crossbow once more in readiness, methinks the three of us will proceed a little further".

Rhynturo, the huge Lolocken and the king left the quartet and continued into the blue canopy of strangeness.

16.....

The medication was probably the best I had ever taken. 100% effective and speedy, damn but those Zernoplatite chemists knew what they were doing. There again chemistry had always been their thing, *their bag*, to use now extinct vernacular. It had been with atom and molecular change that the protoplasmic invaders had descended upon the birthplace of man and like the Hvergelmir (Old Norse: bubbling boiling spring) brought the *Prose Edda*, written in the 13th century by Snorri Sturluson back to life or rather a death. Where liquid from the antlers of the stag Eikþyrnir flow. The first spring had been in Niflheim, one of three major springs at the primary roots of the cosmic tree Yggdrasil (the other two Urðarbrunnr and Mímisbrunnr). Within were a vast amount of snakes and the dragon Níðhöggr. The second appearance had been from the planet Dweeb, or Zern or Zernoplatinatia if one prefers, the last one humanity ever witnessed.

Only two people survived (if the story is to be believed, after all, the claim came from a dubious source) I was one of them. My finger looked healed. I felt fine. Just like the weather. Time to see if I could persuade Quianhua to come out of the bubble, free her of her self-isolation and join me for a blue stroll where all was teal, turquoise and ultramarine.

She declined, no matter - I had another companion and one that said far less to me, she said nothing to me that I could understand, but there you go. One phrase she repeated over and again came out as,

"Mielőtkézőrös megharapolna, Kémerké voltafertő zéstaren dszerbönve, ésngem késztetve".

Repeated ad-nauseam. So much so that I finally typed it into the computer and asked Zernogle to translate it into English. Now the thing about translating a language, is that there is more to it than simply changing one word in one - to the other. I used to wonder why certain materials proved to be - badly translated? One of these reasons was a phenomenon known as polysemy: the many meanings that a single word can take. For example, in English, the word *'plain*' can take on the following meanings: ordinary/undecorated: a *plain* white shirt easy/simple to understand: *plain* English a level area of land: great *plains*. In other words, one had to know which sense of the word, was the one that was needed.

So when I fed the garbled words that Merla kept mumbling to me. It came out as a translation that only a local would have been able to make sense of. What she was saying to me was,

"In previous times when by the spy, spoiled for sitting and being forced".

Another Blue-Mumbly/Blevastís would have made perfect sense of it, after spending a couple of years with me to learn my speech patterns and meanings. Damnation, there is never a Blevastís interpreter about when you need one. The only person who could learn Kémerié properly was me. I had the word-for-word knowledge in my brain as downloaded into it by Harahorahurrahaashume. Now, I needed to learn meaning, syntax, colloquialisms and so forth. On the plus side, I had the time, but it would have been nice to have been able to chat with Merla.

So the oddest of all odd couples that ever existed, left the bubble that day. Keeping a keen eye out for nasty little simian rodents, flying reptiles and the most remotely of the trio – natives. I had not given a great deal of thought to the would-be conquistadors, because it seemed to me that Egszígør had them hopelessly outclassed. Indeed even I did. They were no match for a fully charged blazerifle. I made sure that I never left the house with mine in any other condition. Occasionally I heard the flapping of something overhead, but the Avgófýllo foliage usually meant that was the only impression I received, it was not possible to see the sky. I was thankful for the resultant shade. It would be considerably hotter underneath the unfiltered sun and not only that my skin would burn pretty rapidly like all Caucasians, of which I was now the only one. The accompanying scream of some Kézőrös who were being dined upon sometimes accompanied the downward gusting fluttering swoosh, but more often it did not. The smaller ground dweller had ways of hiding or getting out of the way when the Zürepüé came hunting. Meral and I rounded a patch of Agarispo, that I still did not know if I could eat, when beyond them flared out into an expansive clearing.

At the far edge of it, three figures seemed frozen to the very spot, very possibly at our appearance. One was a huge fellow who looked especially fierce-some, with his barrel chest and broad shoulders. One of the other two was clearly in a far greater earning bracket, for his armour and accoutrements were of much more intricate design. The trio was the conquistadors (as I had taken to thinking of them) not the local natives I had yet to encounter. I knew this as images of the locals had been downloaded into my memory. Of these strangely Gothic warriors, I concluded Hhrrhhoehhrrhooooingohh and Harahorahurrahaashume were ignorant. Otherwise, why not educate me regarding the possibility of encountering them? For maybe five or six seconds, neither the warriors nor I moved. Before they decided I represented a threat, I decided to try and make a gesture that would be regarded as friendly. I had the superior firepower and the time to employ it if necessary. I did not know how many the trio represented, yet why would they start a confrontation merely for the sake of it?

I raised both my arms palms outermost and then called gently,

Myrrorball

"Hello strangers, we are friendly, are you"?
The trio glanced uneasily at one another and then began to discuss what had just transpired, speaking rapidly, indicating their nervousness. I dressed in one of the Zernoplatite silver jumpsuits possibly it was this above all other considerations that confused them mostly.
The one who I had thought of as the knight, sergeant or some such then spoke slowly. In a language, I had never heard before,
"Menem a nyelv edbes zéli'Való furcasa vaghonnan jöttélj"?
To my utter astonishment Merla then suddenly mumbled,
"I be going to get the tongue out of the tongue. Thou art strange thou comest from somewhere that only gods for a walk to take".
Bless her large blue hide. She was translating for me. It made more sense then when she was mumbling her strain of barbarian too. I could read between the lines with what I had heard relayed.
The warriors could not understand what I had said and thought me a deity, fallen or otherwise. I turned to Merla,
"Tell them I am from a foreign land far away and have no designs that conflict with their purpose here. Tell them I will keep from this area of the island and will trouble them no further, ask them if they agree"?
Merla mumbled and the leader gasped in open-mouthed astonishment and then observed, as translated by the Blevastís,

"Azdja, what kind of blue-eyed flock art thou talking to"?
"Merla is my friend".
The reply was getting confusing "Ill met thee with one of them earlier, dlems, that might be talking to none".
I got it they had encountered the Blevastís before and been unable to understand them, or even to get them to talk and wondered why Merla did so and so hopefully.

Major Roxbrough & Nik Gehenna

The conversation went on in this lengthy fashion for some time until causing us consternation, the leader began to walk slowly toward us. It seemed he wanted a closer look at me. He did not draw his sword and even lay his shield on the bluegrass so I tried my best to look unconcerned.

He tapped his chest and said after translation, "King Vasnaar".

I responded in like fashion giving myself the title of major, well why not? I didn't want him thinking he was conversing with a humble pen pusher. He asked me in his language.

"Finding hast thou plenty of корунд [Korund], Lord Major"?

"корунд, I am afraid I do not know what that is, where I come from there may not have been any", I responded honestly enough. I am not seeking anything here other than a study of the Kézőrös, Zürepüe and Kémerké".

"Kémerké"?

Warning bells rang when the king echoed the last of the mentioned trio. The phrase unknown to him and possibly it should remain so. I thought of the Aztecs at the hands of the Conquistadors and immediately back-peddled explaining them away as a third life-form on Egszígør and nothing more. He had not heard the term for the island either which was not especially surprising as they had not encountered the Zernoplat. He referred to the island as Fire of Saaph. Then once again asked about the Russian sounding term which I gathered was some sort of product or mineral or the like. I told him I had not ventured far and was only recently arrived on the island and that seemed to satisfy him. We agreed that should we accidentally encounter each other again we would treat one another with respect and then the king turned and rejoined his two knights.

"I think I would like to hurry back to the bubble, Merla", I admitted then, to my trusty companion and interpreter. "I've got a feeling that Quianhua will be most interested in the detail of today's little excursion".

Myrrorball

She listened to me with a rather intense look on her inscrutable features, I could not quite understand what might be going through her mind. Then she observed when I had fallen silent,

"We need to decide on just how much help we should give the Kémerké if what you suggest is true, look what happened to the Aztecs. These Rozhelic will exploit them at best, what was the name of that stuff you said they were looking for, again"?

"They asked about корунд which Merla translated into Korund".

Quianhua went over to the console and typed in the word, Zernogle came up with the following: Corundum alumina mineral Al2O3. The name of the mineral derived from Sanskrit *Kurivinda* - meant ruby. Noble varieties included rubies and sapphires. корунд, a crystalline form of aluminium-oxide, typically contained traces of iron, titanium, vanadium and chromium. It was a rock-forming mineral. It was also a naturally transparent material that had different colours depending on the presence of transition metal impurities in its crystalline structure.

"They are after precious stones", the researcher informed me, "And we can guess who they think will provide the labour to mine them for them"!

"Do you think we should try to make contact with the Kémerké"? I asked, "Take sides when it is not anything to do with us"?

"We live here, do we not? If this island becomes one huge mining site, it will affect us as much as the locals".

"Do you desire to be a part of this, Ann"? I wanted to know, "Do you want to leave the bubble for the first time since we arrived here on Egszígør"?

"I suppose I might have to", She delighted me by conceding.

17.....

Major Roxbrough & Nik Gehenna

The trio rounded a thicket of the blue trees before the undergrowth suddenly beyond them flared out into an expansive clearing. At the far edge of it, a bizarre duo of figures seemed frozen to the very spot, very possibly at their appearance. One was a mumbler with his limbless torso, strange featureless head devoid of any hair whatsoever. The other was clearly in charge of it. He wore the strangest garb the warriors had ever seen. It was a bright silver yet not metal. The weave was practically indiscernible. It could only have been the stranger that Byno had given an account of previously. For perhaps five or six seconds neither the duo nor Vasnaar moved, this made his warriors also remain stationary. Before Vasnaar could decide that the stranger represented a threat, he made a gesture that would - could only be friendly. He raised both arms palms outermost and then called gently, albeit in a bizarre language the like of which not one of the trio recognised. Vasnaar doubted even Gerner, had he been present, would have understood it.

The King glanced uneasily at his two nobles, "Suggestions my Lords"?

"He seems peaceful, Sire, perhaps a gesture from one of us will diffuse the tension of this situation"? Lolocken suggested.

"A worthy notion", the King agreed, "It should be I of course". He then spoke slowly, but obviously to the strange figure,

To his total surprise, the mumbler then spoke and to the stranger, was it translating for him? Vasnaar wondered if the Silver Figure was a god. The godling or stranger from a bizarre and distant shore then spoke to the mumbler. The tall, bloated form addressed the King directly,

"Nik is from a foreign land far away and has no designs that conflict with your purpose here. He will keep from this area of the island and will trouble you no further, do you agree to this arrangement"?

Vasnaar gasped in open-mouthed astonishment and then observed,

Myrrorball

"Majax, what kind of man art thou who canst teach a mumbler to speak, we thought them mute"?

"Merla is my friend", the mumbler relayed from the Nik.

How was it that the Nik could understand and converse with the Blevastís?

The conversation continued for some time and lengthily but soon began to cause Vasnaar consternation,

"Stay here the two of thee", he ordered his nobles before deciding boldly to approach the Nik. To better scrutinise his countenance. He did not draw his sword and even lay his shield on the bluegrass seeing the Nik doing his best to look unconcerned.

Vasnaar tapped his chest and told the Nik his name, then learned he was, Major Nik. A military godling then or a warrior from a foreign clime. It was time to inquire about the Корунд

"корунд", the mumbler repeated, "I am afraid I do not know what that is, where I come from there may not have been any".

Instead, he seemed to be studying the Kézőrös, Zürepüé and Kémerké.

"Kémerké"? Vasnaar asked, the phrase unknown to him. The strange silver Major explained that the Kémerké was simply a third life-form on Egszígør and nothing more.

Vasnaar had not heard the isle thusly called. Most of the near side knew it as the Fire of Saaph. Once again he asked about the Корунд. He learned in response that Major Nik had not ventured far and was but recently arrived on the island. That satisfied the King. He did not intend to share precious stones with anyone - save for his own family. It was agreed that should the strange Major and Vasnaar's expedition cross one another's path, in the future then they would treat each other with respect. Vasnaar turned and rejoined his two knights. He waited until he had returned to the schooner before contemplating what he had learned. The reason for that was simple. Only Gerner's opinion was of any real importance to him. He sought the scribe out post-haste, but Gerner had something of his own to report.

"Sire, there is something you should know about Nunne, 'tis of exceeding import".

Major Roxbrough & Nik Gehenna

"Before that, I have something to tell thee", the King was not the most patient of men.

Gerner dared, "Yet what I wish to impart endangers every one of us, Sire, including thyself".

"Very well, what is it", the King demanded, annoyed.

"The bite of the Kézőrös be far more deleterious to us than a simple wound, an infection that it produces is toxic. That is the reason Hersko lost his finger. I do not believe the loss will stop there either".

"Why"?

"Nunne's foot has taken on a livid hue, just as the other lord's wrist. I will keep careful watch, but if what I suspect is about to happen dost occur 'twill start with the loss of a toe – a different beginning that will ultimately prove to reap the same result".

"Which will be"?

"That two of our number will gradually transmogrify into Blevastís"!

"Blue-Mumblies? Thou art telling me that Blue-Mumblies are people"?

Gerner nodded, "Exactly so, Sire. Like Hersko and Nunne, but further along from the effects of the toxicity of Kézőrös' bite".

Vasnaar was reflectively silent at the news of this latest threat to himself and the success of the expedition. It was the scribe who dragged him from his reverie with the question,

"Thou hadst something to tell me, Sire"?

Vasnaar relayed an account of his meeting with the Nik who was also a Major. When completed, it was the scribes turn to look reflective.

Myrrorball

PART TWO

SAVAGE IN A SAVAGE WORLD

Major Roxbrough & Nik Gehenna

18.....

Moaab hastened through the village in search of the virázető [leader, guide, chief, manager, etc:] Aznodib

"What reason for your hastening", the ever-present and annoying Kalmoac wanted to know. The latter was annoyed. He was not selected to scout that day, the virázető having bestowed the honour upon Moaab in his place. Moaab could not resist answering, he never could,

"Can I find Aznodib with your direction", he asked in the Phrased speech patterns of the Kémerké, "Or will you reveal nothing of assistance".

"I would do so if privy to the reason for your hastening", Kalmoac grinned. He was finishing a leg-of-dog. Some of the greasy meat was still sticking between his feral-yellow teeth.

"Lead then", Moaab reasoned, "In doin so you will hear the detail of report"?

It was an opportunity to good too miss as far as the ever-curious Kalmoac was concerned and he threw the leg bone into the fire, wiping grease from his fingers, onto his rawhide pants as he did so. Moaab followed him, to find the virázető smoking a pipe full of yohán. Down by the river, carelessly watching two of his young wives beat the daily laundry.

"Moaab and Kalmoac, two of my best young scouts. Bringing to me, why so"? Aznodib desired to know. "Tell hum-drum is to be replaced by a report"?

"And thusly - it is". Moaab replied and told the virázető of the meeting he had seen in the clearing earlier. The encounter between the Silver-wraith and Blevastís on one side of the expanse. The metal-clad newcomers on the other. When he had finished, Aznodib asked,

"The import of wordage, did you hear"?

"One word to my ears drifted", Moaab stated, "Корунд! Корунд our precious eyes of the goddess Shakita. All seek, all desire, the Silver-wraith had heard of them not. The metal-clad told him of them".

"Did he also want"?

Myrrorball

Moaab slowly shook his head, "He was ignorant of our goddess' eyes. He expressed no desire to possess – curious in itself".

Aznodib pressed, "But not to the metal-clad"?

Moaab nodded, "Not so them, a desire was their evidence in strength. Like the empty belly before the feast".

"We must know them in strength compared to Kémerké", the wise virázető decided. "Both to go and count their strength".

Kalmoac was glad to nod along with his rival. The two young natives turned to leave and do Aznodib's bidding, but he delayed them with another inquiry.

"The vast metal town that floated could in the sky? When of that, did you today see? The clear gods that are like water and are not like water, they who crawl without legs or arms but puts their thoughts into heads of us"?

"*HhhâäàåâääçêçêçêîïîìïîìggndgndÐñßҰþÞÝ◊*'   were gone", Moaab was pleased to display the memory that those water that was not water had broadcast directly into his mind. Those who had thoughts that he could not conceive the meaning. Those who had drawn vast knowledge from the minds of **Kémerké through their god-like powers of thought alone. The town that could fly had roared into the azure canopy of** Egszígør some time past and had not returned. Moaab was privately glad the gods who were water and were not water had not returned. He did not like their impossible shape. The way they made his inner mind itch with their extraordinarily atrocious tactile tentacles of inquisitive intrusiveness. When the town that could fly had defied logic and rose from the ground with a terrific barrage, the young buck had found that he was relieved. Hoped that lives in the mining town of Shad would return to normal.

Major Roxbrough & Nik Gehenna

That was unlikely given the appearance of the silver-wraith and the metal-clad. The last few weeks were filled with strange events.

"Scout after eat", he informed his closest friend and fiercest rival then.

"Already I eat", Kalmoac objected, "Setting out I will rightly".

"Probably, wrong direction", Moaab observed in amusement, forcing the other to wait while he had also had a bit of fried dog and some berries, washing everything down with beer. Kalmoac paced, his impatience forcing him to do so, allowing for nothing else of use. Moaab took as long as he dared without making his tarrying look deliberate. He rose and instructed superfluously,

"Come Kalmoac, I can tarry with you no longer, we have to observe the metal-clad".

The other gasped out a breath of exasperation but did not fall into the trap of making a contradictory remark. Picking up dagger and bow, he followed his rival dutifully. Like feline creatures of a type, they slunk through the undergrowth beneath the Avgófýllo. Making as little sound in their passage by practice rather than design, for what then happened was not something they could have reasonably been expecting. They suddenly happened upon not one but two silver wraiths. The second was curiously feminine, with a complexion that did not look very healthy. Instead of a mixture of pale coral and fuchsia, like the man's, he with facial hair of the hue of corn. The female's skin-tone seemed to be ever so slightly xanthic. Her eyes did not seem to open as widely as was natural. Yet despite these mutations, she was comely with her long hair gleaming with vitality and health. Before Moaab or Kalmoac could react in any way, the Wraith spoke, in Kémerié.

Myrrorball

19.....

"Greetings. Do not be alarmed, we are from far away, but our mission is a peaceful one", I told the startled duo.

One of them, who I later learned was called Moaab asked me hesitantly,

"Do you live"?

Quianhua giggled at that, saying in Kémerié, "We are not ghosts if that is what you are thinking. We are simply from a distant land – a very distant land"!

The two local natives gazed at my spouse. It was plain they found her attractive even though she would have been the very first (and last) Chinese girl they had ever encountered.

Moaab asked Quianhua, as I was momentarily forgotten, "Our Szorkráló [a cross between a sorcerer and medical person] knows many things. Conversed with the ones who were water and yet were not water. Learned of all the dominions on Near Side, what is the name of *your* land"?

Quianhua returned candidly, "I lived in China. I am Quianhua. Here is Nik, he lived in Yorkshire. Does your Szorkráló know of them"?

To our surprise, Moaab nodded, "Those who were water and not water told us of you, told us you were here to learn our ways and would not harm us".

I had a flash of inspiration, "You met the Zernoplat"?

"The town of iron came down from the sky and those who were water and yet not water, who crawled without legs or arms, yet put their thoughts into the Szorkráló's head came, the HhhâäàåâääçêçêçêïïïïïïïggndgndÐñß¥þÞÝʘ".

"We were brought here by the Hhhâäàåâääçêçêçêïïïïïïï-ggndgndÐñß¥þÞÝʘ", I told the only native who seemed willing to converse with us. We are a friend to them, they to us [if you're going to lie you might as well tell a zinc-plated whopper]. Now we have a word of warning for both your virázető and your szorkráló. There are others here on Egszígør, others who would exploit and enslave the Kémerké. We have come to warn you about them so that you can prepare for their appearance in your village".

"The warriors encased in metal"?

"You have detected them"?

"Moaab saw you talk to them, with the mumbly. Moaab did not know that the mumblies could speak and be understood".

"Merla is a very special mumbly", I smiled. "It would seem you do not need our advice after all then? We will trouble you no further and go back to our habitat".

"Please come with us and meet the virázető"? Moaab requested then, his gaze barely leaving Quianhua's features for an instant, "The rest of our village would like to meet the silver-fold also".

"What do you think"? I asked Quianhua, "Do you wish to explore a little for our sponsors"?

To my surprise, she nodded. Perhaps she was hoping to make me illogically jealous? If she was, it was not working. She would not be upgrading by showing interest in one of the rude savages of Rozhelia, that was certain. I had already donned a button camera and had both visual and audio data streaming back to the bubble. The excursion suited our benefactor's purposes very well. I was mildly annoyed that they had not told us that they had already met the native populace of Egszígør. There again, I supposed they could enjoy their little mysteries for what they were worth - vicarious at best.

It turned out that Moaab's companion was not mute, was named Kalmoac and judging by the way they spoke to one another I detected an undercurrent of rivalry between them. Not that I had any reason at that point to want to exploit it, but I filed it away, lest such a situation did arise in the future. We were soon entering the village, which was surprisingly close to our bubble and immediately gathered a curious crowd in our wake. The children, though light azure of skin tone, were like those anywhere. They were soon dancing about us chattering excitedly all the while. Their lack of fear was a cause for concern if they viewed the conquistadors in the same way. If their parents were trustingly curious by nature, then the village would be at their mercy. It did not concern me in the slightest that what I was doing was not something the Zernoplat had advised. It was the right, moral thing to do.

We were ushered to a tarpaulin dwelling several times grander than those that surrounded it and told we were going to be given an audience with the head honcho. Moaab ducked inside the opening flap ahead of us and announced our arrival, then straight inside we went. Introductions were speedily made, the virázető was Aznodib, while his szorkráló went by the nomen of Hízlatan. I bowed to them both. It seemed we had been expected. For the szorkráló was already in the virázető's company. Scouts had detected our arriving before we had done so. Quianhua managed to curtsy before the Chief who clapped his hands. A signal for local fare, which was then brought into us. The girl and I exchanged a glance. We did not know if we could eat any of it without heinous consequences, possibly even fatal.

"We are yet to be able to assimilate local food, great Virázető", I admitted, "But appreciate your social generosity in the offering of it".

I hesitated for a second, for the slowly turning ball at the apex of the tent suddenly distracted me. A ball of hammered facets of copper so brightly burnished as to be like the mirror-balls. The type one used to find in discotheques in the sort of filums I had seen starring John Travolta. It brought a somewhat whimsical smile to my face I have to admit. Never was there a less incongruous locale for a disco than in that very place.

As another young female member of the tribe entered with a tray of sweetmeats, I was distracted from the ball of copper. The sweetmeats were conveyed by a figure of very sweet-meat of a different sort. The young woman noticed me staring at her, promptly smiled an open expression devoid of nerve nor shyness. I found her pretty, shapely in her clothing, such as it was - served only to tantalise better than if she had been nude. What followed was rather amusing and gratifying in equal measure. Seeing my obvious attraction to the girl, immediately reciprocated, Quianhua suddenly took my arm and threaded it through hers. Even strained to reach my cheek, kissing it gently, urged,

"Keep your mind on the matter in hand, Darling, think with your big head. Tell the Chief here what you came to inform"?

The shapely native girl was not to be so easily outdone though and approaching said in a delightful sing-song tone of sweetness,

"I am Pelua. You are from the sky, are you"?

"Yes he is", Quianhua answered for me before I had the chance, "And so am I, his woman".

That was an improvement, I had a woman it seemed? It did not seem to phase the girl, Pelua, one jot. She continued to give me her almost undivided attention during our conversation with the Chief and his Witch Doctor. At least that was how I came to regard Aznodib and Hízlatan, even though their official titles were virázető and Szorkráló respectively.

Between us, Quianhua, who had suddenly grown far more vociferous than over the past few days -rivalry eh? She told the native Kémerké what we knew of those who had arrived on their shore by ship. Only to discover that they were already aware of their presence and planning to do something about it. I suddenly realised that this could put me in a rather sticky position with Hhrrhhoehhrrhooooingohh or Harahorahurrahaashume or both. I was meddling in local affairs, not acting as a dispassionate observer.

My job was to provide documentation, scientific observations of the Kézőrös and the Zürepüé. The Kémerké mentioned as an afterthought. What I was doing was far more than simple observations, certainly as far as Pelua was concerned anyway. I suspected Quianhua was having a similar effect on the hormones of some of the male natives. It was time to get out of Dodge.

Myrrorball

I made our excuses. Despite the abrupt ending to our visit, which my Chinese wife found irritating, we left Shad. That which involved me taking Quianhua by the hand and almost dragging her from the place forcibly. It seemed she was on some hitherto unsuspected cycle too!

20.

That night my Chinese wife, the one who had treated me to the delights and depths of her disdain since we had landed on Rozhelia, suddenly changed into something far more... acceptable. I had just slipped into bed after typing my report into this e-reader when she dived on me. I'm certain almost two buttons on my jammies were casualties as she urgently tore them off.

Hey Ho, who worries about buttons when one is being raped and ravished by their beautiful - randy wife? I use the word rape advisedly because what happened that night never had involved consent from me. I had no choice in the matter. I would have put up a concerted fight had it not been for the fact that I was enjoying every minute of it. I also remember thinking that if this was as a direct result of visiting the Kémerké town/village/settlement, then we must do it more often. Having my brains shagged out by Quianhua was, to put it mildly, great fun and very satisfying.

As I lay in a pool of my sweat afterwards having been cruelly and selfishly used I remember remarking,

"I would not have done anything with the native girl you know, Darling".

"Nor I with the handsome warrior", Quianhua returned with a wicked smile, "Who knows what sort of xìjùn they might have given us". She then promptly turned her back on me, my usefulness at an end and began to snore a satiated sound indicating deep refreshing sleep. So I did the same.

It was not long before the exact nature of the fascination we had for the Kémerké became apparent. For Merla and I were taking a walk the following morning, the Blevastís seemingly far more sluggish than usual when who should we suddenly encounter on our route than Pelua. This time the girl decided to waste no time informing me of her desire,

"Come and lay with me, warrior-of-silver-from-sky"? She demanded as she undid her leather brassiere, "Spill your warm seed inside me and give me a silver-warrior who is like the gods who are like water but not like water"?

"Begone brazen hussy", I demanded suddenly feeling like I had been couch-casted into some sort of medieval farce. Though the process would have undoubtedly had its pleasant compensations, I was not a prize stallion to be put out to stud when it suited...anyone. Did the Zernoplat know this was going to happen? I guess that they did. If you are reading this Hhrrhhoehhrrhooooingohh, humans are not like the beasts of the forest.

They do not procreate through driving necessity. They have to feel a deep affection for one another (mostly, the good ones anyway) before they start bumping their less attractive bits.

Fortunately, Pelua had irritated, inflamed gods from the sky. A good job we had skedaddled from the village post-haste.

The next morning I told my confidant all about the gymnastics of the night before, ending,

"Would you credit that"? Before realising that some things were very much amiss with Merla. Strange changes were happening to the Blevastís. She was stationary, an action which had left her several places behind where the wanton incident had just occurred.

"Are you all right"? I asked my favourite alien as I retrod my steps in retreat to see how she fared. Merla had fallen

Myrrorball

silent. So I got no verbal response. I put my hand on her blue skin for the very first time, to hell with contamination, this was a friend. Anyway I suspected the laboratory, come clinic, would have suitable antidotes for the contraction of local germs. Merla felt fibrous, an inappropriate way of describing the sensation of touching her. I would more accurately describe the feel of the Blue Mumbly's skin as – woody.

"What a simpleton I was!

The realisation hit me like a cricket bat around the back of my ear (either one, it did not matter). I knew in a flash of insight what was happening, what had happened. You probably knew too, Hhrrhhoehhrrhooooingohh? You wanted to see if I could work it out for myself. I had also deduced why you together with your other HhhâäàåâäàäåçêçêçêïïïïïggndgndÐñßȲþÞÝ◘' chums could not migrate onto Egszígør. It was the most bizarre lifecycle any man could ever witness. Cyclical, alien, sort of beautiful in its brilliance. The Kézőrös fed on the fallen fruit of the Avgófýllo, that flowering frondy-tree that bore fruit that looked to my eye like fried eggs. From such fruit, strangely transformative toxins, or chemicals depending upon one's point of view, flooded into the Kézőrös' bloodstream. Once inside the strangely hybrid monkey/rat/lemur, it did no harm at all. If the Kézőrös bit any other of Egszígør lifeforms, that toxin then entered the hapless creature's body and began to transform it into a...Blevastís! The victim slowly transmogrified into a blue-mumbly. Once the entire process was complete, the mumbly then could not mumble any more. It lost even that ability. It also transformed from an animal into a plant. Then the final piece of the puzzle had fallen into place for me. Merla had never eaten, never drunk. At least not in a way animals did. The reason was her change from one life form to another, from animal to plant. What did plants ultimately do? They *rooted*. Absorbing nutrients and moisture from the soil. To reproduce, they grew flowers, which fell to the ground and fed any animal that chose to consume them!

Avgófýllo-Kézőrös-animal-Blevastís-Avgófýllo, it was a bizarrely wonderful cycle. I would wager every penny I

Major Roxbrough & Nik Gehenna

did not have that Merla had taken root. Her trunk would shrink to feed her underground petioles until they could then feed the peduncles that would grow from it. Those branches would bud twigs which would, in turn, throw out-shoots that would become flowers and the whole cycle would start again. It was alien, but I found it very impressive in its wonder.

20.

"We have tarried long enough", Vasnaar told his gathered lords. 'Tis now time for action, the village we seeketh lies just northerly. 'Tis my intention to attack and subjugate it in a single penetrating raid. For this action, I intend to leave just a skeleton crew aboard the Zhirnublydok. We will then strike and subjugate the local savages, subsequently putting them to work in their mines, for us. Questions"? Almost inevitably it would be a western Lord who would object to the scheme. The King expected Halsgough to say something derogatory, but it was Koözoött who rose slowly to his feet. Koözoött whose town was practically the one which separated the two factions within the kingdom of Valgral.

"Sire", He began solemnly, "I have no desire to butcher a few savages. I am a knight of honour and will face any equal enemy on the field and have done so at thy side as thou knowest, I, therefore, request to form the party that remaineth aboard in thy absence"?

Vasnaar was disappointed, he had thought the Lord of Koözoött pro-crown. It seemed that though he had never supported the western lords in their frequent demands, he had sympathies with them in some small or great regard".

"Very well, My Lord of Koözoött, thou canst stay on the schooner with Halsgough, are there any others who cannot stomach the thought of subjugating a few mindless savages"?

There were, every Lord that had a seat in the west, slowly each of them asked to remain behind; Rhynturo, Kynoberg, Stianda, Halsia, Dalwichel, Tavaaro and

Sorpio amongst them. Practically half of the Lords the King had instructed to accompany him to the Fire of Saaph. If left a goodly force, even so, he would lead: Staltidore, Lolocken, Flahé, Fordítás, Craggmoor, Hegyekben, Kreel and Laaterfel being the ones who had powerful seats. None as strong as his own, Kingshire. He turned to Gerner, who was standing beside Oslan-On-the-Bank,

"You will stay aboard, Scribe. To continue thy ministrations on the young lords who are in grave danger of losing yet more limbs. I leave Oslan-On-the-Bank, general in mine absence".

Gerner slightly nodded his approval of that choice. The most eastern of the Lords present and after Kingshire itself possibly the strongest. The selection was met with an undercurrent of disquieted murmurings - good, that was what Vasnaar had hoped for.

"Now, we go", he told them, those who would be in his force hurried to their quarters to get weaponry and other vital accoutrements. Each Lord had with him aboard a compliment of some twenty or so guard. Fighting men who were regulars rather than pressed townfolk, the savages would be no match for them, so they assumed! Three longboats took them ashore, they then assembled behind their King.

The monarch chose Staltidore to lead close to ten-score of warriors. Armoured and armed, they feared none, yet were careful to watch out where they trod and not to encounter any Kézőrös. Staltidore knew approximately where Shad was to be found. The party cut directly north from where the schooner was moored. None of them could know just how close they came to stumbling upon the dome, the bubble in which the Terrans resided. Missing it by a matter of a few metres. Major Nik was even closer than that, but hearing the passage of such a huge force (comparatively), he wisely secreted himself in the undergrowth until they had passed him unnoticed. He ardently hoped his words of warning to the virázető of the Kémerké would prove to be of some benefit.

So it was.

An arrow suddenly whistled through the fronds, to plunge straight into the eye of one of Staltidore's best men. It embedded itself deeply, striking into the hapless warrior's brain. The Lord of the Town grasped him to halt his fall and let him descend gently into the bluegrass. By the time he had done so, the man was dead. Everyone in his wake was in a state of confusion. More arrows hissed their way into unfortunate targets. Vasnaar cried,

"Find them, put them to the sword", even as the trained warriors struggled to comply though, more of their number fell in the unremitted hail of the deadly ambush. Then the Kémerké made a tactical blunder, instead of staying in hiding, letting further arrows fly, a series of braves suddenly whooped savagely and attacked the armoured men directly. Some of the attackers were armed with cudgels, others, short one-handed axes. That was not sufficient when up against an armoured warrior with sword and escutcheon. That was more to Vasnaar's liking. He quickly lined up the warriors into a defensive phalanx. A wall of steel that the braves of the Kémerké dashed against, bounced off, many mortally wounded in the process. The attack floundered, failed and shrank back into the forest. A few less experienced and foolish warriors ran into the thicket in pursuit, they did not come back.

"Orders, My Liege", Staltidore requested of Vasnaar, "We have wounded, the savages were lying in wait for us. Their resistance, at their village, will be even more determined. Should we proceed with half thy force, or return to the western Lords and press them into thy cause"?

Lolocken added, "Twould be better to regroup and with double the numbers, Sire"?

"Very well", Vasnaar could see the sense of the advice, "We return for the benefit of those who are wounded, require the ministrations of the scribe".

Myrrorball

They about-faced and were soon on the shoreline that had become all too familiar to them. The longboats were gone. A signal must be given to the schooner. Unfortunately that no longer lay at anchor in the deeper waters of the shore. Of sight of the Zhirnublydok, there was nought!

21.

Gerner knew there was trouble the moment the door opened and Halsgough strode inside determinedly.

"My Lord", he began politely, "Art thou ill, a malady mayhap. Otherwise, may I ask why thou art present in the quarters assigned for the sick"?

"I just came to tell thee that thou willst soon feel the anchor being weighed and the vessel getting underway", Halsgough informed the scribe matter-of-factually.

"The King gave thee no such directive", Gerner observed icily, "Where dost thou think to take the schooner and what has my Lord of Oslan-On-the-Bank to say to this deceitful manoeuvre"?

"Oslan is now our prisoner", Halsgough informed, a grin of little good humour on his features that displayed a habitually stern countenance.

"What - thy perpetrateth be treason, My Lord", Gerner noted. "If thy scheme, what-so-ever it might be, fails, then thou willst lose thy head".

"I knowest", Halsgough surprised him with the weight of such a grave admission, "That be why we cannot fail, must not – fail. Scribe, I harbour none ill will to thee, do as bidden and live. Defy my orders on this vessel and thou will die as surely as any other man".

"Where art thou taking us? Back to Valgral to pursue rebellion in the king's absence"?

"Nay", Halsgough shook his head, "To the northern tip of this island. From said, we will mount our attack on the King. We will not return to Valgral till the eastern Lords are brought to heel. Then shalt the King lay mouldering in his grave".

"I be preoccupied with looking after Hersko and Nunne. Thusly can I take no part in thy machinations, nor afford any to oppose it", Gerner reasoned, placing his safety in doing so, "Doest, My Lord of Oslan-On-the-Bank need any attention in this regard"?

"He may have need of an scalp wound stitching and some of thy dubious pastes applied to it", Halsgough conceded, "I will have him brought to thee".

With that, he took his leave. Gerner went to examine Nunne's foot. The remaining toes were flattening out. Each slowly but inexorably being absorbed into the bulk of a broader yet less pronounced foot. Nunne had spent most of the last twelve hours sleeping, so the scribe turned his attention to Hersko who had wisely held his tongue in the presence of the Western Lord.

"Let me see thy hand"? The scribe come physician asked.

Hersko held out a shortened hand on a shortened arm with only three fingers remaining.

"If I werest whole I would stop Halsgough", the Son of Flahé told him with gravitas. "Do you not have some potion or powders that could incapacitate the vile treasonous hündin"?

"Not enough to render them all as sleeping", Gerner considered, "He does not act alone, half those who sailed east are with him".

"Will they kill my father"?

"It will depend on how the insurgence doth proceed", Gerner returned honestly. "One thing be certain my lord, thou art in no fit state to consider any action of thine volition".

"We shall see about that", Hersko returned, "Once this vessel lays anchor at the north of the island I intend to affect an escape, go and warn the King His Majesty, what is afoot".

"Thou art in no state of vitality, no position to contemplate such".

Before Hersko's intended position could further be debated, the door was rudely thrown open. Announcing the entrance of he who then stepped inside, Lord Oslan-On-the-Bank. One side of the Lord's features were crimson with his gore. He looked about him miserably, the expression suggested one of disappointment in his capture, rather than concern for his injury. Behind him, sword drawn Lord Sorpio, Baronet of that smaller town, guarded him warily. Gerner barked,

"I will not have drawn weaponry in this place, leave us, My Lord? Twill be easier to simply bar the door than stand there like some mute blackguard. Once his Lordship of Oslan has been attended to, I willst call out to thee, now go"?

Sorpio did not so much as hesitate but left the four of them to their devising. Gerner indicated a high pallet to his Lordship of the most western dominion in all Valgral.

"Gratitude", began the unusually tall, blonde knight. Margrave of that mountain town. "I was set upon by many and could not sustain defiance indefinitely".

"None here will criticise thee, my Lord Margrave". Hersko noted, "I'll wager the enemy did not subdue thee without injury".

"Two of Sorpio's men are dead because of me", Oslan-On-the-Bank admitted but without satisfaction, "Valgraln killing brother, tis not fitting for them".

"Tonight, once the ship be at anchor I intend to escape the ship and go warn his Majesty what is afoot, art though with me, My Lord"?

"Readily", Oslan-On-the-Bank nodded, causing a fresh trickle of blood to run down the side of his handsome countenance.

"Hold still now while I apply some bark to the cut prior to sewing it up"? Gerner demanded.

"Hoot and pish to the tree bark, Scribe", Oslan-On-the-Bank objected, just sew the edge and be done with it".

"There will be pain, a considerable amount of it".

"Pain and I be comrades in arms, Gerner", Oslan-On-the-Bank laughed in dramatic and projected fashion, "A most notable coward, an infinite and endless liar, an hourly promise-breaker, the owner of no one good quality be that Halsgough. We shall be away from that starveling, with elvish-skin, dried neat's-tongue, bull's-pizzle, and nought of substance but stock-fish".

Major Roxbrough & Nik Gehenna

"Well said my Lord", Hersko enthused. "If we could but slay him on our way yonder then I for one would feel that my blue demise will not be in vain".

"The Lord concerned would indeed infect mine own hand were I to soil Iniquitous in his back-toaded liver. If thou willst needs destroy the fool, 'twould not be worth the jeopardy. For he be well guarded by fops and manningtrees. A wise man knows well enough what monsters one maketh of such as he. Yet time will come when the sand runneth into his lower glass. Thence shalt the dark hand of retribution tear vile effluvium from his ruptured gullet, yet rightly to have end to him".

Gerner was about to furnish words of caution. However, the voluble Lord of Oslan-On-the-Bank was not yet done,

"The trunk of humours, that bolting-hutch of beastliness, that swollen parcel of dropsies, that huge bombard of sack, that stuffed cloak-bag of guts, that roasted Angelus-burnt ox with pudding in his belly, that reverend vice. I long for the day Iniquitous tears at that father's ruffian, that vanity in years. I wouldst that his black blood boils in the bluegrass of this place of strangest commodity, pursed with debate".

"It sounds as though the gorbellied, ill-nurtured, ass-fed be due his comeuppance with none mistake ", Gerner mouthed dutifully, "Now hold still my Lord? Let one who wouldst as bringest thee succour do his work".

22.

"Thy orders, Sire", Lolocken demanded with relish seeing the King's dilemma, "Whither shall we goest from here"?

"As I perceive our current situation we have but the one choice", Vasnaar returned, worrying his still sore gum with the tip of his tongue. "That is to seek out the silver-wraith who goest by the nomen Major Nik and seek his assistance".

"Where dost thou thinkest the schooner be gone to, my Liege"? Fordítás wondered for them all.

Myrrorball

It was Craggsmoor who conjectured, "Halsgough be up to some devious manoeuvring, but I doubt he would think it possible to return to Valgral and have none explanation for our whereabouts".

Kreel observed, "He could tell those who asked that we fell in battle".

"Just the eastern lords and none fatality in the western? Twould be unlikely in the extremis and doubted by many", Byno observed. For once his words were not met by sneered amusement. "My royal Father gives wise instruction. I can lead us to the dominion of, The Major Nik, for I have good suspicion as to the location of his strange abode".

"The Prince shall take vanguard", Vasnaar agreed, able for once to find industrious occupation for the young lad.

"Be careful of the Kézőrös", Byno instructed as he began to lead the warriors, "Their bite continues to corrupt the flesh of two of our comrades, Mazormazuri protect them, Azdja taketh their teeth and tiny hearts".

It did not take long for the fop to find the bubble-shaped dome structure, the entire gathering marvelled at its facade of wonderous material. It had lain not far from the shore that the schooner had dropped anchor.

"What now, My Lord Prince"? Hegyekben asked with considered politeness. It seemed that Byno had suddenly been elevated to a higher position in the estimation of the gathered force. One of the *small-lords,* little more than Alderman of the village of Torkinvayst suggested,

"I would like to volunteer to approach the structure? Ask for aid of the strange warrior from a distant clime".

"I will accompany thee", Byno astonished the others. He matched Torkinvayst stride for stride. The latter's village lay south of Hegyekben and north of Smallostle and was noted for the production of sweet beer when the season was just right.

The duo reached what looked like a white doorway and the prince self consciously hammered upon it with an urgent staccato.

23.

Major Roxbrough & Nik Gehenna

Quianhua and I were having a pleasant luncheon (amazing how a good sorting puts the humour back into a girl) when there was the least expected sound the two of us could have imagined echoing through our dome. Someone or something was hammering at the door!

My first thought was that Pelua had become emboldened with lust (after all, I always was a love-missile). About to make her desire even more difficult to ignore, were such remotely possible.

Thusly it was me who gained my feet ahead of my spouse, "I'll get it, be ready with your blazerifle though, just in case"?

"In case of what exactly"? Quianhua demanded not unreasonably.

"How the blood-blue-blindingness do I know"? I can be quite potty-mouthed when in the grip of stressful situations. If I had been allowed a considerable number of guesses as to who was at the door, I would not have chosen correctly, chiefly because on the other side of the locked and coded barrier was someone I had never met before. What a someone too...wow.

The phrase *hot-squaw* came into my mind as I regarded the stunning beauty who was nearly wearing a pair of braces instead of a blouse and a ridiculous Indian headdress of feathers. Her glistening breasts were magnificent. I aught to know, over my few years of mature adulthood, I have made that part of a woman's anatomy one of my studiously vocational subjects of keen interest. The fact that it was a warm day on Rozhelia was causing her to sweat. The mammaries in question were not only spectacular in shape and firmness but also glistening. She was facially beautiful too, even if her skin did have a slight azure tinge to it. Kémerké then. She smiled at me, that did it, whatever she wanted, if I had it, she could possess it utterly, without condition.

"Can I help you"? My enquiry was my admittedly feeble greeting under the circumstances.

"I am – trader", she began hesitantly. "You are Silver-Wraith, would you like to trade with me"?

I would have liked to do many things with and too her, so I nodded. She produced a small leather satchel, which hung upon one of her divine bare shoulders. Rummaging about in it she pulled out a tiny hessian pouch, held closed by a simple cotton drawstring.

"I am Leoma, what would you like to give me for this special recipé", she asked me, smiling mischievously.

"Well had I reasoned I knew what I would like to *give her*! She had reasoned along identical lines too. There was still the annoying germ question, which I was working on, but had yet to reveal conclusive results. I could only tamely reply,

"What have I, that you would like in exchange"?

"That", she pointed to the silver chain around my neck, from which a black and white ceramic mandala hung. It had cost me about ten pounds from China of all places. Even so, the pouch did not look like it could contain much of value. On the other hand, she was gorgeous, so as quick as, Spring-heeled-Jack, I removed the chain. She turned asking,

"Put it on me"?

Ruddy-hell, that was some temptation. Quianhua did not appear to be coming to the door to see what the delay was. I behaved myself though. I am ashamed, chagrined to say. The instant she had the low-value trinket, she danced away and called after herself,

"Enjoy, it will help you to *know*".

What on Rozhelia did that mean? I went back into the bubble. Quianhua was seated on the settee looking quizzical.

Major Roxbrough & Nik Gehenna

"I was beginning to worry, have you made another friend? Another one of those tall blue aliens, what happened to the first one anyway"?

I had not told her about Merla. She had never liked her, so I had kept what I knew to myself.

"It was a Kémerké trader", I tried to sound casual, just wanted to swap me this little pouch for the chain I had around my neck this morning".

"What chain and what little pouch".

"It's of no consequence".

A suspicious gleam suddenly sprung into her almond eyes, she asked, "It wasn't that native girl was it, what was her name, Pelua"?

"Absolutely not, you can put that blazerifle back in the cabinet. The trader has gone now. I'm going into the lab for a while, what are you going to do with yourself"?

"Clean up the pots, then I'll join you", she promised and let me go into the rear of the bubble alone.

I strolled into the back of the habitat and then finally decided to look at what dubious native concoction was in the pouch. Emptying a tiny amount into my palm, I detected a sudden aromatic tickling the back of my nasal cavities. The snuff was in the form of tiny black grains that looked like how I expected gunpowder to appear. I knew it was snuff from its visual and olfactory information. Plus the fact that my great grandfather had used it, leaving down our male line - his treasured box, in which a tiny amount had remained. I had never taken the tobacco nasally before, but this was Rozhelia snuff, or maybe I would be better thinking of it as *snufz*. Intrigued I poured a tiny amount into a dish and sent it into the diagnostic slot of the Zernoplatite computer to see if I could safely try it. After all, it had cost me silver and my favourite mandala ceramic.

To my surprise, the computer soon informed me on the monitor that the stuff was: polycyclic aromatic hydrocarbons, benzopyrene, tobacco-specific nitrosamines (NNK, NNN), aldehydes, carbon monoxide, hydrogen, nitrogen, toluene, phenols and of course nicotine (4-Aminobiphenyl). In other words, tobacco plus an added aromatic. With one added ingredient that was flagged up as being unique to the planet or the mixture, the addition of phenothiazine derivative which the computer chose to label phenoquadrazine. I had to look up the former to understand what the latter might be. Phenothiazine was a class of agents exhibiting antiemetic, antipsychotic, antihistaminic, and anticholinergic activities. Phenothiazines antagonized the dopamine D2-receptor in the chemoreceptor trigger zone (CTZ) of the brain. Potentially preventing chemotherapy-induced emesis. The agents had peripherally or centrally antagonistic activity against alpha-adrenergic, serotonergic, histaminic, and muscarinic receptors. (NCI). In plain English terms, it was an antipsychotic.

What then was phenoquadrazine? Surprisingly the computer had an answer for me: Phenoquadrazine, a chemical building block. Phenoquadrazine could be used as a reactant in the synthesis of arylmethylene aldehydes. Acetoacetates in the presence of sulfonamide as a catalyst via one-pot pseudo-five-component condensation by treating with mercaptoacetic acid and aldehydes or ketones. It could also be used as a precursor for the preparation of selective carboxymethylated products by reacting with dimethyl carbonate in the presence of a bronsted base salts as a catalyst.

So what would it do to my body? What would it do to my mind? I typed the direct question into Zernogle. The immediate reply: the introduction of phenoquadrazine into my cerebral cortex would open pathways that would facilitate increased understanding together with the ability to reason and calculate by accessing parts of my mind that up until that point had lain dormant. That sounded far from bad - it sounded good, like an intelligence boost. The computer said it would not harm me, probably the opposite. I was sorely tempted to try it right away. I typed in once again requesting possible deleterious results from snorting a small amount of snufz (the name had stuck with me). I was informed that chances of any damage of any sort were as close to zero as could not be feasibly computed. Leoma had said I would *know*! How could I suspect such a lovely and seductive

creature of having any thought of harm toward me? The answer was I could not. I was so curious that caution went out of the window (those that incidentally did not open as it turned out). I placed a miniscule portion of the flecks onto my hand and holding the other nostril closed, snorted the snufz directly into my sinus cavities. From there, up into my cerebral cavities.
Whoosh!
Leoma had promised me *knowledge*. Though it was difficult for me to credit the natives with such an advanced formulation concerning the snufz, the product did what it said on the tin. For the first time in my life, I felt that I *knew*. My mind was especially lucid, the figurative cobwebs had been blown away. I could concentrate more easily. Work out mental problems that had previously confused me. Finally, flashes of insight came to me that I had no normal right to suddenly perceive.
Boundless energy seemed to course through my being and I rose from the seat, to rush outside and simply observe. I saw so much more. The Avgófýllo were no longer just fronds or blued fibrous trunks. Embedded within them were figures, I instantly knew the impressions within them were of those who had been before the transmogrification of an animal to plant. Some were warriors, others, women of various ages and shapes. It was not just visual information that was flooding the newly created synapses in my brain either, but I had become an instant meta-physicist. I was in possession of knowledge that I could not conceivably know any logical way other than by insight. The most pertinent example of this was the fact that I knew without a shred of doubt that the snufz had been supplied by Hízlatan. I determined, as a result, that a little meeting between the two of us must be undertaken at some point in the near future. I went back inside knowing it would not be for long. A party of Valgraln were on their way to the doorway of the bubble having been left stranded on Egszígør by those who sought to undermine Vasnaar's powers of his majestic rule.

Myrrorball

24.

Byno waited nervously for the hatchway to the iridescently albescent bubble to yawn open. The duo did not seem to wait very long at all, had the white-wraith seen them approaching? He opened the entrance to the wondrous domain and smiled pleasantly,

"Prince Byno", he astonished the duo, "Alas I can be of little help to you, for I am not certain if any of the provisions within are digestible to natives of this island. Indeed it might be the case that they would poison you".

"Thou knowest my identity"? The prince gasped, "How canst this be when we have ne-er been formerly introduced, not, to mine knowledge. Has any mentioned detail of me to thee".

The Major – Nik tapped the side of his nose with a forefinger, a gesture unknown to the duo, before telling them with deliberate mystery,

"I know a great deal. I have certain powers that it would be best for you to acknowledge. I know the Valgral are a warlike people bent upon conquest. I advise your father, The King, to rethink his strategy in that particular".

As the Silver-wraith had thusly addressed them, two other figures had slowly detached themselves from the main bulk of the waiting party. One was Byno's father, Vasnaar, the second - a minor lord from northern Roxbrough, whose title was Ispán. At the sight of the latter, the Silver-wraith's eyes took upon them an amused whimsy, he remarked,

"Roxbrough, who is the Ispán and also novelist, who is both and who is neither. You even resemble him in no small degree".

Roxbrough looked understandably nonplussed to be addressed thusly and returned in a bemused fashion,

"Alas, Major thou has advantage o-er me, I perceive not the meaning of thy proclamation"?

"It doesn't matter", the Wraith grinned sardonically with his curious phraseology, the stilted manner of his speech, "I know what I mean. I find it funny, curiously that you don't - makes it even more amusing".

Major Roxbrough & Nik Gehenna

"Major Nik", Vasnaar cut into the confused-convoluted diatribe then with no small amount of impatience, "We be in need of thy chivalrous aid, canst thous be of any assistance to the King of Valgral"?

"As I've just told your son", the Wraith observed, "The only help I can be is in the form of advice. I have no supplies that I am certain will not harm you".

"What be the manner of thy advice then, Major from a distant realm"? Roxbrough dared. For it was not customary for an Ispán to even give utterance when in the presence of his Majesty. The Wraith replied,

"Make peace with the Kémerké, before Halsgough does. Your two factions are just about evenly matched. It is the natives of Egszígør who will ultimately hold the balance of power".

"They did render some of my force unto death. Had the desire to put still more to that fatal fate", Vasnaar objected, "And now thou thinkest to have me smoke the yohán of peace with them"?

"If you don't you can guarantee Halsgough will", Major Nik smiled. Still regarding Roxbrough. the petty Lordling, with continued amusement. His eyes suddenly took on a sparkle of insight that almost brought a real glow into them. He asked in his curiously alien speech, "Wait? I will have something to show you and some vital information in a second. Do not try and enter the bubble, please"?

Vasnaar turned to the Ispán, "The alien Major, he seemeth to hold thee in curious regard, when he doth returneth, thou art now the spokesman for the party".

Roxbrough bowed his head, returned smoothly, "Thou dost me great honour, Mine Liege. Be assured of mine utmost diligence 'pon all occasion".

The Major from a far place (a very distant localé indeed it seemed, more so as more of the party met with him) returned after a brief interval. In his curiously pinkish hand, he held a piece of velum of extreme quality, Upon it was the work of a wondrous cartographer. He displayed it toward Roxbrough, who stood his ground. Allowing the Wraith into intimately close proximity with him without so much as a tremor.

Myrrorball

"This is Egszígør, that you call the Fire of Saah", Major Nik began,

"We are here", he pointed to a place covered with alien runes, that he could doubtless decipher, but alone. "This is where you landed, and here the town of Shad, which you unsuccessfully engaged in a skirmish with before returning to your landing site".

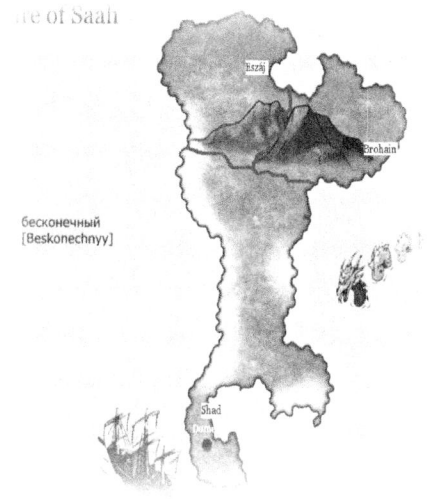

"You observeth that event"? Roxbrough desired to know. Then did the Major from distant place give an enigmatic grin and returned with contrived mystery,

"In addition to being a Major, I am also an Augur. I have the power of prognostication without a hint of adumbration".

"So thy title shouldst be Major Visionary Nik".

"That title rightly suits me", the Wraith-in-Silver - seemed delighted with it. "Now back to the map, you will know something of the tribes who live in the mountainous north I guess, the Benszülöt over here in the west and the Akerányó in the east".

Roxbrough glanced at Vasnaar who frowned, such knowledge was not for everyone. In the past, bitter pitched battles had occurred between the three tribes of Egszígør. The Kémerké had only driven the vanquished up into the mountains with the greatest of cost in men and materials. Major Visionary Nik seemed to know of these things. His powers of prognostication were broad, to thusly be respected. Roxbrough merely nodded. The King noted how well he had taken to his new position within the group. The Visionary went on.

Major Roxbrough & Nik Gehenna

"Halsgough has landed here at Brohain, where he is meeting with the Akerányó. He desires to smoke the yohán with their virázető. I think you can reason why"?

"New allies, with which to start a conflict that will result in his Majesty's demise", Roxbrough gasped.

"Correct. It is then, part of the rogue's intention to do a similar deal with the Benszülöt. You let him get the jump on you, then he'll subjugate Egszígør for his devices, the Корунд mine will come under his control. You'll find yourselves slaves working within its deeply constricting confines. That is why you need to go to Aznodib and forge an alliance with the Kémerké".

Vasnaaar merely nudged the Ispán of eastern Valgral in the ribs to prompt him to ask,

"Major Nik, who art also Visionary and sorely wise, wilt thou ally with us? With the Kémerké? Willst thou aid we unhappy warriors and his noble Majesty? For to do so will result in the realisation of his gratitude which will and can be expansive".

Vasnaar then added solemnly, "A dukedom, Major, aid us to put down the rebellion of the Eastern Lords and thou canst choose from their seats and rule for thine life and bestow the title through hereditary passage down to thy offspring".

As he was making such a gesture of grand design, who should appear in the doorway of the curious castle but the Major's woman? Exotic in extremism she was, with her complexion of purest saffron and her wondrously mysterious copper eyes that were the shape of almonds. She also possessed an admirably generous bosom that drew the admiring glance of every warrior present, even Byno.

"What's going on"? she demanded, her tone filled with urgency, her contractions as alien as any utterance the Visionary ever employed.

Turning to her, the Wraith/Major, the prospective duke, spoke in a tongue so alien, so bizarre, as to be beyond the perception of any present. Roxbrough fancied even Gerner would have been nonplussed.

Myrrorball

"他们希望我帮助他们进行内部起义,这很容易使整个岛屿崩溃。 [They want me to help them with an internal uprising, which could abruptly bring down the entire island].

The two of them seemed to jabber until wocky. Roxbrough was nudged once more, by his ruler.

"Pray to excuse, Major/Visionary Nik, but is the good lady to accompany thee, whence can we get about our mission"?

The Major seemed amused by the question. His woman, beautiful as she was, scowled. It was plain she spoke Valgraln as well as the alien tongue reserved for her and the Major.

"The good lady", she began, referring to herself in the third person, "Is reminding his Visionariness here that we have been set a task by the *HhhâäàåâäåçêçêçêïïìïììggndgndÐñß¥þÞÝ◊*˙. They are the creatures who the Kémerké refer to as those who are water and not yet water".

"Those who are water and not yet water", Roxbrough repeated keenly, "A riddle, I am a great devotee of such. What be water and yet not be water hmm".

"It isn't a brain teaser, Roxbrough", the beauty flared, "On your kingdom do you have slugs - shell-less non-terrestrial gastropod molluscan"?

"Csiják"? The ispán guessed, "We have them in Valgral. Here I suspect the Kézőrös will have consumed them unto extinction".

Byno was regarding the ispán with a novel admiration, the confident way he was able to address a noble lady so intimately without a hint of self-consciousness.

"Those are the little buggers", the *lady* in question noted, "Well imagine transparent ones this long (she held out her hands like an angler), you're in the right general ball-park".

"We have encountered parks – none, My Lady", Roxbrough returned confused, "Certainly none with facility for pastime involving balls".

"And yet you manage to spew it out of your pie-hole with great dexterity", the alluring woman observed. The latter conundrum noted by the Visionary

Major Roxbrough & Nik Gehenna

"Quianhua you're not helping now! Regardless of our directive from Captain Hhrrhhoehhrrhooooingohh, if we do not help these Valgraln, the natural habitat of Egszígør will suffer damage in one way or another. The *HhhâäàåâääåçêçêçêïïìïïììggndgndÐñβ¥þÞÝ⚙*'n grand experiment could be spoiled by this Halsgough chap. We should help His Majesty here to stop him if it is within our powers".

"His Majesty be the noble, the right liege for the crown", Roxbrough persisted, "And questing in his name be an holy obligation of right and true warriors, such stuff as would bring forth legends and songs are on the cusp of being conducted".

"You're full of it", the beauty observed. Causing Roxbrough to bow stiffly at the waist, declaring,

"Gratitude, My Lady".

"You can't even insult these clods", her ladyship then complained, "Do what you think is best then, Nik, I don't believe you've listened to one word of advice I've offered you since we got to this primitive place"!

"Advice is what it is, My Love", the Visionary returned, "An opinion or recommendation offered as a guide to action and conduct, with the option to ignore if not desired".

"Yes, well all right smart-ass. Go with your new admirers, I'll stay here and maybe even do what the *HhhâäàåâääåçêçêçêïïìïïììggndgndÐñβ¥þÞÝ⚙* told us to do, study flora and fauna".

"Very well", the Silver-wraith that was Major and Visionary both smiled pleasantly, "**Ispán Roxbrough, you and I will take point and go to Shad**".

Vasnaar said nothing, though he was King, he did not relish the prospect of catching an arrow in the eye.

As the strangest of alliances proceeded, a weird occurrence began to take place. Roxbrough explained hastily to Major Nik.

"Tis the Kayved 23, this way, My Lord. Hasten if thou pleaseth"?

Behind them, one of the warriors had begun gasping for breath and frothing at the mouth.

Myrrorball

"Cave head 23", The alien Major mispronounced the distemper, do you mean Heineken Virus, Roxbrough"?

"Kayved, my Lord Visionary, not the appellation thou sought to bestow. Thou hast not the vile affliction from wherest thou came"?

"It's likely that it is something similar as a virus can travel through space, on the tail of comets for example".

"Vile Rust, My Lord Visionary and comb nets".

"Virus", the Visionary corrected, "A virus is a disease, pestilence, malady".

"Ah, thou art not in error, Kayved 23 be the virus then, the twenty-third wave of it that scythes through our people each time Angelus fades with the cold season. Comb nets"?

"Comets, the white glow that occasionally appears in the sky, with the flowing tail".

"Frosted Mortis, sometimes called the Bleached Seraph. 'Tis they who bring the ague and the Vyrust"?

"Yes", the Visionary agreed, "The Frosted Mortis comes down from the dark sky and attacks people. What will happen to the warrior who is gasping"?

Roxbrough said leadenly, "He gasps no longer, my Lord Visionary, the Kayved 23 be merciful in its rapidity. Aimuur has now gone to meet the gods".

"Good job I've had every shot at the *HhhâäàåâäåçêçêçêïîìïîìggndgndÐñß¥þÞÝᴧ*'s dispensary".

"The *HhhâäàåâäåçêçêçêïîìïîìggndgndÐñß¥þÞÝᴧ*' shot thee, my Lord Visionary"?

Call me Nik", the Wraith requested of the Ispán of Roxbrough, "The shot I am referring to was by a tiny arrow through which medicine could be administered into my bloodstream. I hope I am immune to your virus. What of the rest of you, will it scythe through you like the Grim Reaper"?

"According to Gerner the Scribe, many have a natural immunity to the virus...Nik. Be the grim reaper one of your deities"?

Nik shook his head, "Just a figure from superstition, Rox, forget about him".

Major Roxbrough & Nik Gehenna

"And thy gods", Roxbrough was curious and most loquacious when he got going, "Who dost thy people worship"?

"The greatest source of worship in my dominion was for money", came the sardonic reply, "The lint and metal pieces that were used for barter, do you have them"?

"Thou meanest coinage"? Roxbrough guessed, "But how can coinage be a god, tis not alive"?

"And therein lies the source of many of my people's woes", Nik observed with a sigh. "Let us not talk of such depressing matters though, Rox. Tell me about the missus, and are there any little Roxette's dashing about in Valgral, is it"?

Roxbrough smiled in remembered affection as he admitted, "The Lady Roxbrough be greatly fair of feature and form. I be the envy of greater Lords than me for the possession of her".

"Now hold up", Nik interjected, "There are no greater lords than you, Rox, me-olde. I will put that matter to rights and right soon. Hey Vasnaar, come up here a second, please"?

The troop ground to an expectant halt and the King, not far behind the leading duo approached demanding,

"What be the import of this delay, my Lord Visionary"?

"I find I am in the company of only an Ispán and would like you, at my respectful request - make Rox here a higher Lord than any save you".

Vasnaar nodded, a request was coming from the Silver-Wraith. He knew Roxbrough to be a competent Lord, so he agreed without hesitation,

"Perhaps a Császárim [Imperial Marquess], would that be lofty enough to keep thee in the comfort of companionship, my Lord Visionary".

"Császárim suits me down to the ground, Majesty. Do you need to tap him on the shoulder with your sword or some such little ritual"?

Vasnaar glanced at the ground and then looked bemused before returning, "Roxbrough, formerly Ispán, at the bequest of the lord Visionary of... of...".

"Yorkshire", Nik supplied, the King went on.

Myrrorball

"York-shire, I hereby elevate thee to the title of Császárim and the title be hereditary for all thy descendants. Art thou satisfied, My Lord Visionary of York-shire"?

"Perfectly", Nik returned, "And as you are the King, Majesty, you can call me York, but none of the other Lords can, all right".

"Tis graciously accepted as long as also the prince can use the same nomen – York"?

"Agreed", the Visionary of Yorkshire had a sense of humour that the warriors of Valgral had yet to discern.

The troop through the forest continued. Roxbrough said at once,

"Gratitude, Nik, I be in thy debt for what thou just hast done for me and mine".

"That's all right", Nik was magnanimous when it did not cost him, "We're friends. That's one of the things friends do. Wait till you tell the little lady that she is no longer an Ispánette, but now a Császárimissus".

"That wouldst be Császária and Ispám, Nik. How be it that I cannot call thee York also"?

"Nik is for buddies", Nik smiled, "While York is more formal, you and I are buddies, that's close friends, all right"?

"Agreed then... Nik".

"So before we get to Shad, tell me about the Roxette's, the bread-snappers, the little lords and ladies that you and the Ispám had before her elevation to the new title"?

Roxbrough swelled with pride. He informed the man from another place, "My eldest son be twelve summers, he be called Rox. I have another son called Bruff. He has seen ten summers. Then there are the girls, Zen and Iarr, nine and seven and both as fair and graceful as their mother".

"Who was called Zeniarr before you wed her I'm guessing"?

"Zenia", Roxbrough informed, "But tarry, Nik, I believe I saw sudden movement up ahead, let us fall silent and proceed with caution"?

Despite his vast knowledge and strange weaponry, the Visionary seemed more than willing to follow the advice of the newly created Császárim. From behind some foliage, two figures stepped forth in unison. The duo seemed to be vying with one another as to who presented the most exceedingly strange appearance. One was a man seemingly made of metal, the other a huge upright frog, carrying a spear and wearing clothing. Their appearance froze Roxbrough with indecision as to know quite what to do. When the frog spoke, his wide head indicated that he was addressing the Visionary.

25.

"Greetingth, Nik, I thee you have finally managed to friend the localth", the manbian observed with his long-short tongue.

"This is getting ridiculous", I complained, "I created manbian in one of my stories, you cannot possibly exist nor, for that matter can you, 23".

The silver android did not show any emotion on his face. It might be because the android I was addressing at that moment had yet to have an emotivorous chip installed into his system.

"You two are from the 33rd and 71st centuries, how can you be here? Not to mention the somewhat disconcerting detail that I created you - in my writing".

Roxbrough interjected, "Nik, what be this strange tongue thou speaketh with the aberrant duo. Be they the enemy, or friend to, His Majesty"?

I switched from English, or at least the English I spoke. It was the same language both 23 and the manbian referred to as Standard. Back to Kémerié, I assured the Császárim,

"I am attempting to find out. Please wait while I converse with them". Then to 23, I demanded,

"Have you come to aid or to hinder"?

The android replied in orotund tones, "Help. As for our reality, you must remember that the *Hhhâäàåâäää-çêçêçêïñïïñïggndgndÐñß¥þÞÝ◊*' have mastered the fourth dimension. What you wrote was not fiction, Nik, but history, future history".

"I am being monitored then, by either Hhrrhhoehhrr-hooooingohh or Harahorahurrahaashume or perhaps both of them. I wonder if I ever wrote anything imaginative at all? Or if all my supposedly good ideas were broadcast into my brain by the *HhhâäàåâäääçêçêçêïñïïñïggndgndÐñß¥þÞÝ◊*"?

"It doeth not matter", Mr Genks observed, "I am, Mithter Genkth by the way. What matterth now ith that we help make Egthzígør a thafe plathe onth more".

"Let me tell his majesty that you are allies then"? I asked. There was no use denying their reality any further they were standing before me. I felt like I had fallen down the rabbit hole or perhaps more accurately into the kingdom of the Jabberwocky. When is an eel liked to a light bulb?

I turned to Vasnaar and told him that the duo was also part of my dominion. That they had come to help, but could not speak the local tongue. I could have told him virtually anything seeing as 23 and Mister Genks could not contradict me. Even then the King demanded,

"What strange manner of world dost thou inhabit when armour canst have a life of its own and the beasts of the field are as men, able to walk upright and converse in strangest of the tongue"?

"One that suits my powers of Visionary", I told him with what I hoped was an enigmatic expression on my face. It seemed to satisfy him for the moment. I then turned back to the new arrivals.

"All right fellows, you're in. Though why Hhrrhhoehhrrhooooingohh thought I needed you, I don't know, I've got this entire situation under control".

Now I have been known to say obtuse things from time to time. I have been guilty of not letting ignorance get in the way of my having an opinion. When I said I had the entire situation under control, it might well prove to be one of those occasions.

26.

"You will do it Gerner, or thy hide will decorate the main-mast. Your freshly skinned body will feed the progondax", Halsgough declared. It was plain, by his tone, that he brooked no objection to his demand.

The scribe observed, "I will need time to prepare the necessary potions. Then I will have to consult the Liberex Respondoss".

"I give thee sixty arcs of Angelus [an hour] Halsgough offered magnanimously, if thou hast not readied thyself by then, I will hand thee over to the baronet and thou knowest his particular if deviant specialty"?

It was Nunne who answered, "The Herékprézet"!

Halsgough smiled, "The Herékprézet [a device placed onto the testicles and then turned by a key until the organ turned into little more than gory paste]. So be ready to either manifest the phase-door or sing to the eastern lords in soprano by sunset peddler of potions, speaker of riddles".

With that, the malign noble flounced out of the room spectacularly, as his hair was long and dark, lent itself to just such a dramatic gesture.

"Thou art knamerült [trans: knackered, debilitated, enervated]", Nunne offered not especially helpfully.

"What does the kutyavialt [trans: roughly means unnatural son of a dog or lower breed creature] want with the sorcerous aperture into the ether"? The firmly

Myrrorball

chained Oslan-On-the-Bank wondered. The key to his chains being around the Lord of Halsgough's neck.

"There can be only one reason", Gerner groaned, "He desireth to bring something or someone of unnatural powers to aid his machinations".

"What art thou going to do"? Again the Margrave desired to know.

"As I am quite attached to my jewels, I have little choice", the scribe conceded, "The last poor unfortunate that Sorpio worked on died of shock before he had admitted his crime and sought contrition for his misdemeanours".

"It has to be a necromancer", Oslan-On-the-Bank assumed, "He thinks to tip the scales against the King with unholy assistance".

Gerner nodded, hurrying over to his phials and ampoules, reaching for the previously mentioned grimoire.

"Like as not thou art, not in error, my Lord Margrave, but my choice is none at all. I have to do as directed. Otherwise, I will ne-er serve my King again".

Oslan-On-the-Bank nodded, "I see thy dilemma and wouldst not trade places with thee for a gold pig. I concur that thou must aid the vile Lord of the West, hoping to oppose him another day. Proceed, scribe. While thou art about it be there anything that could be utilized to free me"?

"I couldst manufacture an acid so powerful as would dissolve the iron", Gerner began thoughtfully, "But twould also proceed then onto thy skin if the administering of it were not precise. Alas and alack I have no time for the present though, My Lord, the doorway into Abaddon will take me all but the time allotted".

"A future project then", the Margrave conceded, "Thou has thy ministrations assigned, my friend and none mistake".

"I wouldst also like to find Calamitosus for thee", Gerner referred to the Margrave's semi-sentient broadsword, once the property of Abominorv. It had been confiscated by Halsgough - for obvious reasons.

Major Roxbrough & Nik Gehenna

Hersko suddenly rose slowly from his gurney, "I will aid thee in that respect, My Lord Margrave", he offered, "None will suspect me, the Eastern Lords will maintain their distance as I pass through the ship. They believe I shouldst be isolated, that I should be a metre from them, lest they do not end up residing a metre 'neath the ground".

"Thou art not contagious", Gerner objected.

"Aye", the faintly blue Lordling agreed, "Yet ignorant of such are they, so off I go and do my bit despite my malady".

"How will thou explain thy movement through Zhirnublydok", the Margrave wished to know.

"Hunger", the Lordly returned. Slipping through the door, he was soon absent, leaving Gerner to begin reading. Several moments later, the wick of their lantern giving off pungent smoke of near exhaustion. He dived to his feet. As Nunne slowly lit four candles, the scribe began mixing potions from his stock of chemicals. To protect himself from any possible injury he had donned an expansive leather apron, together with long black rubber gloves that reached to his elbow.

By that time he was almost ready to begin the proclamation that would manifest a phase-door. Halsgough returned. In his company, the baronet, seeing the bench, upon which, Gerner had been working, nodded his grim approval. For his part, the diminutive and sinister Sorpio gave issue to a dark scowl of disappointment, given aid by his swarthy complexion and almost black hair. It was the reason for his sobriquet – *'The Raven'*.

"Well, Peddler of Mummery, Vendor of Imprudence, hast thou finally maunged something of use to those as has ambition"? Halsgough wanted to know, even though the answer was obvious, "Or am I to hand thee over to the pernicious embrace of Sorpio's bosom"?

"Thou hast an aggravating penchant for the melodramatic, Eastern Lord of Rascality", Gerner verbally jousted before being forced to confess that a phase door was a distinct possibility.

Myrrorball

"Then maketh one and right swiftly", Halsgough demanded. "I want Banustib bringing to me".

"Banustib"! Gerner gasped, "Has the stallion bolted the stable without a saddle, Lord"?

"I know full well what I be about, Scrivener. Now do as commanded lest the Raven gets thee as his latest toy".

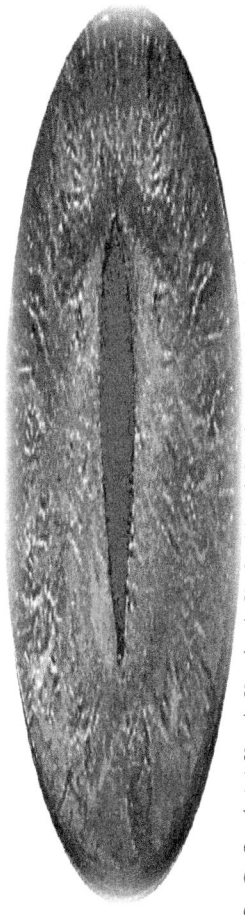

Gerner's shoulders slumped. Into a small bowl of blue china, he poured the concoction on which he had been working. The fluid had a silvered, mirrored appearance and when gazed into looked more like a mirrored-ball than a flat-topped surface, an optical illusion. It was snabbertox, a broth-like elixir with myriad mystical properties. Gerner began a litany of pishogue and cantrip, which when phrased in a certain way ensorceled nothing less than a phase-door into the ether. The room grew suddenly cold. The candles flickered as though blown by an unseen draft. Which was indeed the case. Before the expectant attention of the Lord of Halsgough a shimmering quality in the centre of the room suddenly widened into a violet iris. The ellipse spread into something much wider. At the foci of the doorway, a black light shone with such intensity that it was blackwhite. From out of the lustred glitz, a woman suddenly stepped. The phase door imploded with a malign bang, Gerner slumped in exhausted debility.

The woman was eerily beautiful in some menacing fashion. Her eyes were unnaturally large. Her hair as dark as the Raven's, her ears pointed, the crimson slash that was her mouth demanded,

"Who brought me here? What wantest thee with Banustib the Beautiful"?

Major Roxbrough & Nik Gehenna

Halsgough stepped forward and informed her,

"I was the one who gave the order, beldame and by the code that thee and thine operate, thou must now do my bidding until such a time as I will be fully satisfied and am the King of Valgral".

The dark beauty gazed at Halsgough for a moment and then smiled, before returning, "Thou seeketh power and thinkest Banustib the Beautiful can aid thee? So be it, my powers of theurgism shall be lent to thee until thou achieveth thy ambitions".

Halsgough laughed a wicked laugh. Sorpio revelled in the mischievous tone of it. Mischief was afoot, with the addition of the carline, the foot had just become booted in steel.

27.

What art thou doing abroading, Hersko", Teleocea demanded, "I am none wanting to be turned into a mumbly such as thee will be. Get thee hence".

"Keep the metre from me, isolate and contacting will thou nought", Hersko returned. He was pleased to see Teleocea hurry away and the instant he was no longer being watched, slipped into the schooner's armoury. It was easy to find the sword - Calamitosus. The silver pommelled blade shone even in the below-decks illuminations which were scant. Taking the sword by its sheath Hersko snatched it up and ran back to the cabin set aside for the sick. Even through the casement of its sheath, he fancied he could feel the semi-sentient power of the blade coursing through his veins. He hoped it might stop the malady he laboured beneath. Alas, that turned out to be a vain desire. Bursting into the room, he handed the weapon over to its rightful owner.

Myrrorball

"Gratitude, Lad", Oslan-On-the-Bank acknowledged, then to Gerner, "Put acid from memory, Scribe. I now have the means of mine liberty".

With a single swish of the enchanted hanger, the Margrave carved the left bracelet of iron from his wrist. Two more well-aimed swiped and his anklets were similarly cleaved in twain. He held out the Toledo to Hersko and requested,

"Thy right hand be more accurate than mine left, if thou pleaseth, my Lord"?

"What if I misjudge"? Hersko wanted to know.

"Then my right hand shall be as thy left is becoming, but not azure of tinge", the Margrave observed with dark humour.

Hersko nodded, wielded the sword of the Rainbow Demon. The final fetter was cleaved from the Lord of the Mountain Town.

"For my aid, I ask a single boon"? Hersko demanded then, whilst handing back the fabled sword to its rightful owner.

"If 'tis within mine power", Oslan-On-the-Bank was never one to duck an obligation.

"Take me with thee, witherest thou goest, thy might be grateful for a second blade while e're I can still wield one".

"Come with me and right welcome, Lad. Yet the lividity progresseth"?

"I can make up some powders for the Lord to take that will tarry the progress of the corruption", Gerner offered, "I will have to stay here with Nunne".

"Tarry - not halt"? The Margrave asked.

Gerner nodded, "Mayhap by going with thee, he will find an answer, on Saah itself"? The scribe proposed.

"If we get off Zhirnublydok and still find ourselves alive", Hersko wondered.

"If I fall, 'twill be at the cost of many", The Margrave promised, armed with Calamitosus none doubted it. "Shouldst thusly transpire, thou has chance to take the sword from my fallen form, make the western wretches pay a still higher cost lad".

Major Roxbrough & Nik Gehenna

"Wager 'pon it", Hersko promised, who had lost two fingers to the toxin of the Kézőrös but thanks to Gerner's concoctions his vitals were far from becoming Blevastís.

The scribe-come-surgeon handed the younger of the duo a packet. The recipient promptly tucked into a jerkin beneath his breastplate.

"Ready, Lad"? Oslan-On-the-Bank asked, throwing a bundle containing food and drink onto his backplate. Hersko nodded and picked up similar supplies. Their intention, to travel down Egszígør, become reunited with their King. The door eased ajar, none was present in the corridor beyond. In one hand the Margrave carried a small arbalist. Two of them were up on deck before anyone spotted them, for it was the hour of Walpurgis being 23:00. It was said of Warrior Walpurga that he battled: '*pestilence, phleege and the scrogies, as well as witchcraft*' every night at that hour. It was most unwise for mortal men to be abroading if not necessary. Thusly the lone guard that was on watch learned to his cost the wisdom of such caution when one of the Margrave's bolts burst his windpipe. He staggered, fell choking, soon quite, then very – dead.

With all the quietude that the poor lad could manage with the block and tackle, Hersko lowered a longboat into the water. Even as the duo was about to clamber down into it, a light sleeper belonging to Sorpio climbed up the steps to gain the deck. He, wanting to see what the squeaking of the pulleys was about.

The very same gory bolt that Oslan-On-the-Bank had torn free of the corpse embedded itself in the man's eye - piercing his brain behind. The Margrave caught the corpse before it could thud onto the boarding. Lowering it carefully and then rushing to join the young lordling. Together they untied the longboat once it was on the surface of the ocean and taking an oar each, began to row for the shore with exaggerated care to remain as quiet as possible. Once they were out of earshot, they bent their backs to it, began to make encouraging progress.

Myrrorball

"See up in the night sky", Hersko noted between gasps, "The Blue Goddess Brahma smiles down upon our endeavour, we are the blessed".

The Margrave chuckled at that, "Thous thinkest thyself to be blessed by Brahma, Lad? Be that why thou art turning the same hue then? Once all limbs are gone what dost thou think to do with a goddess"?

Hersko's features grew glumly at that observation. The duo made silent progress until reaching the shore. With much effort together with mighty heaving, they tugged the boat from the sandy shoreline into the blue canopy that seemed to cover the island. Once it was truly hidden, Hersko demanded,

"What now, My Lord Margrave? Do we start in the sable cloak of the forest? Or get our heads down till dawn"?

"Twould be folly indeed to enter a place proliferated by Kézőrös in the dark, Lad. We shall sleep in turn, while the other sits watch, we do not need a fire for the clime be truly mild, so whoever sits watch shall have the crossbow. I will take first watch, then wake thee when Brahma has run half her arc".

28.

"You're pretty arrow-proof, 23", I said to the android, "And you came to help, so please aid us by going ahead and telling Aznodib we are on our way to come for a peaceful parley concerning a matter of importance to both our forces. If he displays any scepticism refer him to the szorkráló, Hízlatan and tell him that I am enjoying the snufz he sent me via Leoma".

The use of that narcotic is not advisable", the android returned in his spookily non-emotive tone, "Do you know what it contains, Nik"?

"I do", I found myself annoyed at the prospect of being interrogated by a mechanism, "I have conducted a thorough analysis on it and am satisfied it can do me no injury. Perhaps in your time, the composition was changed. In future I would appreciate it if you call me, Major, too, Nik is for my closest of friends and I do not wish to start any rivalry between the locals and yourself, we have enough to contend with".

"Very well, Major understood fully on both points". The android then darted away with a velocity that I would barely have been able to credit for something made of heavy metal before Hhrrhhoehhrrhooooingohh came to visit me that was. Since that moment, I found I could suspend my disbelief just about any time I needed to, which was becoming a frequent occurrence.

We had barely proceeded a couple of hundred metres further when the android returned. In his wake was a female Kémerké I had never seen before, but just like Pelua and Leoma before her, she was very easy on the eye – very very easy in fact. Perhaps it was me? There was maybe something about their azure skin their skeletal arrangement that I found most appealing. When I suddenly turned to regard the reaction of the Valgraln though I saw that was not it at all. The newcomer was yet another beauty by any standards.

23 was oblivious to such considerations, he announced in his curiously even tone,

"Major Nik, this is one of the Kémerké scouts sent to guide you and your honoured party back to Shad, her name is Cassiti".

The girl smiled at me with both her lips and her eyes. In the twinkle of the latter was the unspoken message,

'Well visitor from far away, I'm up for it - if you are'.

Myrrorball

Here was another young woman with raging hormones hoping to be the first of her clan to give birth to a half Kémerké, half star-child. Alas,

the process to achieve that ambition would be in the usual biological fashion. I was certain, without even asking, that Quianhua would not understand my altruistic reasons for obliging one, or several of the hotties. Such a pity, several delightful creatures gagging for it and me shackled to one single woman. I told myself what a woman though - coupled to the fact that we had so very much in common. Well, we came from the same planet. She was the only chick of Rozhelia who could make that claim (to my knowledge, I could no longer take just about anything for granted). All that delirious mental lumber had sailed down the river of my mind in the merest of instances leaving my mouth free to greet,

"Welcome Cassiti, allow me to introduce you to King Vasnaar, Majestic Ruler of these collected warriors who all hail from Far Side and their land is called Valgral".

The girl cupped her right hand into her left, then raised it to her forehead, dropped it to her chest and then let her arms spray wide.

The King acknowledged this salute of respect (presumably), with a tight nod. He demanded to know what I had told her. The fact that neither side spoke both languages put me in a very pivotal position. Added to that 23 and Mr Genks could not converse with either side, only me. The android seemed to have managed quite well with signage when contacting the Kémerké. Perhaps they thought him another alien like me? Or another warrior like the Valgral? For silver did seem to be the new black on Rozhelia.

"You are the silver-wraith who rode the tail of the Frosted Mortis through the black sky before coming down to Egszígør", the girl then smiled charmingly, "I am in the middle of the six days leading up to, ovulation, the egg in my body is waiting for you to fertilise it. It would be my sole honour to carry the first of the Kémerké/Bleached Seraph offspring. Not only that, but I am practised in multiple techniques for giving a brave pleasure, I can...".

Miss Cassiti", I cut in, "Honoured as I am by your amorous attentions, there is a matter of graver urgency to all the Kémerké at this time...".

"No, no", she cut me short that time, "Hízlatan advises we women of the tribe that...".

"I will be having a word with Hízlatan when we are escorted back to your village in kindly fashion if you please"?

The girl then realised she was trying to get a fish to swim upriver against a fierce current and returned with a delightful smile,

"Of course, Frosted Wraith, who is the Nik, please to follow me? I will take you to the Szorkráló"?

She looked as good from the back as the front. Behind me, I could hear the lewd laughter of some of Vasnaar's warriors. I fancied there were several in the company who would have gladly fertilised her eggs, given a chance. It forced me to caution against fraternisation,

"Majesty", I began, "These natives of the Saah are friendly and naive, please caution your men against mistaking such for an amorous invitation. Should an incident occur that could prove to have unfortunate consequences, then all our machinations will be undone and what you lose could ultimately prove to be Halsgough's gain".

"Understood, York", the King returned gravely, "My warriors will be schooled, to keep *all* their weapons in check once we meet the locals".

His choice of wording made me smile, but the two of us understood the importance of a useful parley with the

Kémerké. I was also thankful that there had been no further incidence with the Kézörös. Császárim Roxbrough had told me of a couple of injuries to the Valgraln before they became two factions and I doubted either of them would be very hominid for very much longer.

29.

When Angelus slowly heralded roseate dawn by climbing above the horizon, the two of them never saw anything of its splendour. The ever-present Avgófýllo hid the spectacle from their eyes. They ate dry rations. Hersko took one of Gerner's powders and then they arose ready to start their northern trek.

"Halsgough did not think to follow us in the darkness", the young Lordling remarked as they began their journey.

"He has matters of greater import than to take the time and energy spent chasing down the two of us, Hersko", the Margrave observed. "The fact that we can get to the King, perhaps a few hours before he does is what will prove vitally important tactically. I just thank Anaadi [goddess of fortune both good and bad] that she smiled upon us when influencing the King not to fetch horses to this side of Nyjord. The Eastern Lords could have ridden us down, even in this thick forest".

"I did not take thee for an Anaadit, my Lord", Hersko observed.

"I follow none of the gods when I am maungey and all of them when it suits me, Lad", Oslan-On-the-Bank grinned.

"Well me thinks this be the forest of doom rather than the forest of fortune", Hersko objected, "For it contains the Kézörös and its bite will ultimately prove mine undoing".

"We know nought for a certainty, Young Man", the Margrave argued against such defeatism, "Thou knowest the maxim of the Valgraln – '*Ne'er Retreat' Ne'er Surrender*', a battle be not completed, till done"!

Hersko tried to smile but found that he could not. His arm ached. He had pins and needles in the three remaining fingers of his blue hand. He never complained about it for it would not be the noble nor knightly thing to do, but it worried him. He found himself contemplating his mortality more each day since the attack of the hellspawn creature with bright blue fur. Oslan-On-the-Bank was a fit, a vital warrior in the prime of his life and Hersko, though, younger, felt drained by his malady. He thusly found it difficult keeping up with him and was almost pleased when the two of them were ambushed. The Margrave went down fighting three warriors until a stone-headed axe knocked him senseless enough to be overpowered. Hersko had the good sense to surrender when faced by natives that seemed to exude from the forest itself. As blue as his arm was, all over their bodies. With blue-black hair, some even had white stain daubed on their noses, a sort of warpaint. The duo was quickly bound tightly by the wrists. Hands, behind there backs, led by ropes through the undergrowth. Hersko reflected bitterly that for a warrior so skilled, with such a reputation as the Margrave possessed, he seemed to fall into the clutches of his enemies with startling regularity. Perhaps he was not the right custodian for one of the six swords of the Rainbow Demon Abominorv?

  They were taken into a village consisting of rude huts of wattle and the various bindings that could be made from the Avgófýllo, not that Hersko could know them by that name - as given by Nik. To him, they were the fronds, nothing more. The duo was taken to the largest of the huts and thrown roughly to the compacted dirt ground. Once they managed to scrabble up to their knees, not an easy manoeuvre when one's hands were not free.

  They saw a young and very striking woman eyeing them critically. She asked them something in a strange language. They were unable to satisfy her curiosity. The more Hersko looked at the strangely azure complexioned woman, the more he grew enamoured of her. She wore a ridiculously large headdress of bird feathers, evidently taken from avians from a different island as there were none on Fire of Saah. Her skirt was woven from frond fibres. She was naked above it, bare-breasted and seemingly uncaring of the fact. As some sort of staff of office, she carried the most ornate spear that could never have been any use in actual combat. It would have been too cumbersome for effective use in battle. With it, upon various occasion, she chose to prod either the young Lordling or the Margrave - when they failed to understand her signs, her gesticulation.

Her comely if narrow features were adorned with white body paint, broken up by a livid design that must have taken no small while to apply. After what seemed like hours of intense questioning, neither side had learned much from the other. Hersko knew that the ludicrously young woman was the virázető [leader, guide, chief, queen] of the Akerányó. A rival tribe to those in the south of the island. The village was called Brohain, the woman, Sahbaj. She, for her part, had learned a good deal more about them, thanks mainly to Hersko himself.

For his part, the Margrave remained sullenly silent, refusing to cooperate in any small degree. Once the virázető grew tired of them, they were led to a stout timber cage where they were freed of their bonds. Yet closely watched by several well-armed warriors until the door was securely fastened on the outside. The gap between each timber trunk was forty centimetres, any escape was thusly impossible.

"Thou shouldst have told her nothing of the Western Lords", the Margrave complained once they were alone. "They may be in opposition to the King, but they are still Valgraln. Thou might bring these savages down upon them. They might destroy the Zhirnublydok, then where would we be"?

"I have no love for Halsgough", Hersko confessed, "Nor will I be leaving this island, My Lord-of-the-Bank. Thou forgeteth I will be a Blue-Mumbly by the time thou art setting sail".

"She did not seem especially animous toward us in truth", the Margrave confessed at the mention of the younger man's ultimate fate. Mayhap thou can eventually strike up a useful dialogue with her. Yet I fear not before Halsgough arrives".

"He might miss this village, in which case we could do with northern allies. I wonder if the King has decided along the same line of reasoning".

Oslan-On-the-Bank surprised him by ejaculating, "Pah, the King thinks of only one thing, the acquisition of yet more Корунд for his bitch the Queen"!

Hersko was shocked and then amused, finally burst into ironic laughter, the two of them were still laughing when the door was opened once more. Two warriors came into the area of confinement holding bowls of food.

"They do not seem harsh captors do they"? the Lordling noted, as he nodded his thanks to the native who gave him his. They backed out, the door was once again securely fastened. Oslan-On-the-Bank squatted down onto his haunches, began to eat the steaming meat,

"Thank Shakita [goddess of food, drink and good health] 'tis goat's meat".

They dined in studied silence. After a while liquid followed, a type of fermented milk courtesy of the same animal. The third time the warriors entered, they indicated they wanted only Hersko. Oslan-On-the-Bank hastily advised,

"If she wants servicing, my young stripling, be certain to ride her well for the both of us"!

Hersko was dragged without, wondering at his imminent fate. There could be much worse consequence than being expected to deliver what the Margrave suspected. Torture a quest of harsh endurance, death, slowly being transmogrified into a Blue-Mumbly. When he was hurled into the hut of the virázető the second time, the beautiful woman was not alone. In her company was the most aged and ancient man the young Lordling had ever seen.

Myrrorball

The lividity of his skin was the darkest of any Hersko had previously witnessed. It was lined, like old leather. His silver beard had not even the faintest trace of colour. As Hersko slowly gained his feet, hands tied behind him in the usual fashion, the ancient man held his hands together, pointing upward, all his fingers into a unified shape.

He spoke in a voice like the dry sirocco rustling the previously fallen leaves of the autumn before.

"I - Szorkráló, Himmelwhahu, understand"?

"You are the surgeon come sorcerer here? Thy name be Himmelwhahu"?

The Szorkráló nodded his aged head. His neck so frail Hersko worried it might topple from it at an instant, again the voice devoid of any moisture or vitality,

"Why you come to Brohain"?

"To warn thee of others that will follow in our wake", Hersko intoned slowly pronouncing each word the best he was able. "A warrior with deleterious designs for thy people is just behind us. His name be Lord Halsgough. Thou must not be taken in by his words of sweetness filled with utopian promises of riches and better times for thee and thy tribe. He speaketh untruly. He be rapscallion dissimulator, his fables are not to be given credence".

The Szorkráló nodded once more. Though his speech was stilted he seemed to understand Hersko well enough, he then demanded,

"What of thee, Herky? Thy companion"?

"Tis Hersko", the Lordling corrected, "My nomen be Hersko. The man in my company be a Margrave of Valgraln, he meaneth thee and they tribe none harm also. 'Twas thee who captured us, we wouldst continue southerly to find our king before Halsgough attacks him to steal his throne".

"Halsgough seeks allies"?

"Aye. To do unholy battle 'gainst the Valgraln in southern Saah".

"And the Kémerké"?

Major Roxbrough & Nik Gehenna

For the first time in the strangest of conversations the young Lordling had ever taken part in, he seemed to have lost his way.

"I knowest of none such beast, only the Kézőrös, Zürepüé and thou Akerányó"?

"We Akerányó", the Szorkráló explained patiently. "Down beneath mountains Kémerké – not Akerányó".

"Aha, a different tribe, thou art not brothers. I see. There has been conflictual in the past then, has there - truly"?

The Szorkráló nodded. All the while the two of them had been talking, Sahbaj had remained patiently silent, her patience seemed about to expire as she suddenly spoke to Himmelwhahu. In the language of the natives. The Szorkráló nodded and turned back to Hersko,

"Her virázető desires knowledge of Kézőrös attack how long past"?

Hersko told the venerable fossil what had happened. Then waited patiently while the narrative relayed to the beautiful chieftess. She listened intently and then gave the Szorkráló some sort of directive, judging by her tone and mien. Himmelwhahu asked Hersko,

"Know what will happen"?

Hersko nodded, responded bitterly, "I will become an Blevastís eventually".

"You want this"?

"Abaddon, no", Hersko returned with feeling, "Who would want to become an Blue-Mumbly"?

The old-man did not react in the way the Lordling expected when he pointed out,

"Yet then Avgófýllo (or a word to that effect). Avgófýllo holy state, the journey over, enlightenment".

Thou meanest the Mumblies take root in the ground and become the fronds. Thou thinkest that enlightenment? Why wouldst I want that, why wouldst I desireth to become as an plant"?

"Peace, accord, reconciliation, unity with all".

"Thou makest it sound truly fine. I have yet to live my manly existence, it cometh too soon".

The tribal relic turned back to his ruler, relayed the last scrap of information. The woman smiled before giving the

Myrrorball

venerable Himmelwhahu a directive. The latter rose from his cross-legged repose. Hastily he untied the Lordling's bonds. Went next to an area in the hut that contained a bench and some curious pots and bowls. He began to mix something odious. As he did so, he explained over his shoulder

"I make medicine, you take. You take when I say, then you become as was before".

"Thou meanest thou hast a cure for the malady. I can be restored to a man. What about my two fingers"?

"What gone – gone. Yet all else be fine".

"Pinkey and ring, goodbye", Hersko retorted sadly, "Yet rest of body, hello".

The foul brew that the old-man finally placed beneath Hersko's nose was so odious, as to make his gag reflex an immediate problem.

"Take", Himmelwhahu instructed pushing the bowl against the youth's chest. "Drink. Drink all. Leave not".

Hersko did his best to breathe through his mouth, then poured the vile concoction into it as swiftly as it would leave the container. It had a slimy, stinging mucusian astringency to it. He found the piquancy revolting, almost spewed it forth right away. He did not desire to become a Blue-Mumbly though, nor a frond. If such was the case, which he still found very difficult to believe. It was more likely an Akerányó folk-lore legend or village myth. Yet he swallowed. The brew seemed to burn his throat and guts as it passed into his stomach. He felt salty-after-tasting. Wondered what his chances were of not projectile vomiting all over the old-man, the hut and the beauteous virázető. It was the latter part of the reflection that forced him to hold onto what he had put into his already poisoned system.

"Tomorrow, another dose", the Szorkráló dismayed him with the information. "Then final day - day after".

"Three doses willst cure me"?

"Three doses remove lividity, cured then".

Hersko had much to tell Oslan-On-the-Bank upon his return to their captive cell, only he did not then know the full story.

Major Roxbrough & Nik Gehenna

30.

The person I wanted to meet, was ardently keen to have an encounter with, was curiously absent from our first meeting with Aznodib. I was practically grinding my teeth in frustration. I was keen to forge an alliance with the Valgraln and the Kémerké. It was not until I had been acting as a translator/negotiator that a notion struck me. 23 was an android. As such, he would have a memory bank that was as close to eidetic memory as made no sensible difference. He had been listening to the talk and soaking it all up. Surely he could then deputise for me while I requested to see the Szorkráló?

"You can speak Standard, Kémerié and Rozhelic by now surely, 23"? I challenged the android whose creator had not attempted, in the slightest degree to pass him off as a human being.

"I know", the typically logical reply was pretty much what I expected.

"Then I am going to ask you to deputise as the translator between Aznodib and Vasnaar for a while while I ask to speak to the Szorkráló – Hízlatan".

"Why"? The android dared.

"What in Hades do you mean by why, you walking tin-can"? I demanded. Who did the mechanism think he was?

"For what? For what reason, cause, or purpose? On account of which"? The machine thought to elucidate.

"I know what the ruddy word means", I told him, "What I mean is what is it to you? I am the Visionary, the Silver-Wraith, the Nik who is also Major. You came to offer assistance, so do so, clear"?

That would have settled his circuits I figured if nothing would. I was wrong. It seemed androids in the 71st century had more about them than filling in for cash registers.

"I was requesting additional data in the event of an unforeseen occurrence", 23 pointed out. "One of several which may or may not have resulted in jeopardy for you, that was part of my remit, if the request for data irritates you then I can always retire to whence I transported from and...".

"Brilliant! That's all I need an android with attitude. Don't get reesty on me 23? Carry on being my assistant. To do so, I need you to act as a translator in the current parley. If I hit any snags I will use one of my superior items of weaponry, does that satisfy your curiosity circuitry"?

"Not especially, but as a favour to the *HhhâäàåâääçêçêçêîñïîìggndgndÐñß¥þÞÝ⌂*', I will continue to assist for the time being".

"You are too good to me".

"Not so it is the *Hhhâäàåâääçêçêçêîñïîìggndgnd-Ðñß¥þÞÝ⌂*' who hold most of the power in this quadrant of the galaxy. In your lifespan, you will not get to witness much of what they do".

"Well, in that case, you and I will have to have an illuminating little chat sometime".

"I am more than a little sceptical that your substratal cerebration could countenance the astronomical compilation of data that my anamnesis circuits store"? 23 observed impassively.

Way to call a guy a *thicky*? Especially considering I was very likely the brightest hominid on the planet.

I started for the door of the hut, felt a second presence in my wake, turning to expect to see Roxbrough, it was to find Cassiti dogging my steps.

"Do you have a few minutes to spare, Frosted Mortis Wraith"? The girl asked sweetly, her eyes telling me far more than the words.

"Listen baby", I began in an Amerikan gangster type drawl, "You'd need longer than that to see to all my requirements – capisce"?

"I do not fully understand, but I suspect you think we should take a greater leisurely pace over the process, this is not a problem - I am willing. Can you stay in our village overnight"?

"I am devastated to have to inform you that I cannot", I drawled, "I have to get back to the little woman you see, the wife, my mate".

Major Roxbrough & Nik Gehenna

"I see", she did not, "But it is not customary for a brave to have but one compliment, is it? The Kémerké can have...".

"Cassiti", I cut in hastily, "Quianhua is from the Bleached yet Golden Seraph tribe, they are monogamous".

"Mono-game-urs", the girl had evidentially not come across the word before, there was no equal to it in Kémerié. "This means what exactly"?

"The practice of having only one mate. I follow the same guide".

"That is so selfish", the girl declared then, suddenly quite vexed. "The bull or the stallion can sire hundreds of offspring with the herd, why do you harbour your seed in such an aloof way".

The truth was not working. It was time to manufacture something that would get the admittedly delightful creature out of my hair. Or perhaps that should have been to negate interest in the contents of my trollies.

"I am from a race who has few seeds", I told her, grimacing inwardly. When all have *'been sown'*, my fruit dries to a wizened husk, then I die. I only have a few seeds left. Such is the way of the Wraith".

Cassiti looked shocked and then reflective. "The firing of your seeds eventually kills you"?

"It does. Now before I die can you take me to Hízlatan"?

"Come this way", she was instantly all business, I liked her, sometimes marriage can be such a bind. Strangely I wanted a chat with the Szorkráló even more. He was in his hut, well if you're the Szorkráló you have to have certain advantages in status I'm sure. When he looked up at me, the girl melted away. Abruptly I perceived *the knowing* - in his eyes.

"Have you been using your snufz", I asked, a strange greeting but there you go.

He nodded. I found his tacit initialism rather irritating,

"I've come for some answers, Matey. I *know* now, but I know less, what is real and what is not"?

"Sit", he instructed. I let my legs cross the best I could upon one of his fine woven carpets. Then I waited. He asked me in a deliberately labyrinthine fashion. "You ask me what is real and what is not. I ask you, that to know that - what *is* real"?

"Real is: true; not merely ostensible, nominal, or apparent, existing or occurring as fact, actual rather than imaginary, ideal, or fictitious being an actual thing, having objective existence, not imaginary".

I was rather pleased with my definition. The Szorkráló then shot me down in flames,

"When the moment is gone, '*real*', is just a memory, it exists in reality no greater then what is in your head, Nik. All is in your head. All is real in memory, yet all can be so much fantasy. If one believes something to be reality - then so it is to you. Are you here with me in this tent? Or are you still labouring behind your keyboard in your office? Is the world now the dominion of the HhhâäàåâääçêçêçêïïìïïìggndgndÐñßɎþÞÝ⌂? Or is it in the grubby hands of those impertinent upright monkeys still? You dare to call them humans. Some have other notions"?

"What are you telling me, that my life, my existence is nothing more than words on a page. That none of it is real as far as I am concerned"? That gave me a feeling of abhorrence-tinged dread like none other I had ever felt.

"Did you lock the heavy iron gate with the huge key on the chain of your belt yet still need the electricity to make it truly done? Did you talk to Johan who picked up the smooth metal and wiped the oil from it with a rag before placing it in the huge steel jaws of the machine? Are you any more real than your memories? Are they real at all? Is any of us here? Or, are we the product of another mind creating us for his amusement? The amusement of any who choose to read those recoded in the computer or the book"?

"How can you, a savage, in a savage world, know about computers"?

"How can you, man, have reached the stars when they are thousands of light-years away"?

"How am I going to get any answers from you if all you do - is to answer in riddles"? I demanded then.

Major Roxbrough & Nik Gehenna

"I have not sought to confuse you, Nik. You should continue to have your mind expanded with the snufz. That is if you truly want to *know*. In a lot of cases, ignorance is bliss. The youth who sits and rocks back and forth to constant voodoo-nigger-bullshit pounding away each section with the same tempo - is happy in his moronic way. Alternatively, the philosopher is always asking why. Why this, why that, why anything, why nothing? Which would you rather be.? You can quest for answers. Or you can let the threads of fate simply take you, like the unthinking twig in the river's tidal course".

"All I want to know is if I am on Rozhelia, or if I am in some asylum making Ribble noises, grinning with drool trickling from the corner of my mouth and my pants soaked with my piss"?

"There are far more alternatives than that. You could be the character in someone else's fantasy? You could be the Wraith that even death had not stopped his eternal mind from thinking. You could be in my imagination. All this...". He waved his arms in the air to indicate the world, "...could be nothing more than a microbe in the belly of a huge beast. The galaxy in the cell of a table leg that resides in another galaxy that resides in ... so on, ad-infinitum".

"Your answers are not answers at all", I complained.

Hízlatan smiled knowingly and remarked, "That is because, in the field of questioning you choose to converse with me in, every answer leads to yet another question. The answer can only truly be in you, Nik. The ultimate answer".

"The ultimate answer"?

"To the ultimate question"?

"Are you going to tell me what the ultimate question is"?

He nodded, "It is - why am I"?

"Why am I? Not What am I? Why am I what"?

"Exactly", he smiled as though he had given me some marvellous insight into *my* reality".

I rose without another word and left his hut despondently. I had gone to him for answers. All he had given me in response were questions. As I reflected on

Myrrorball

what he had told me, however, I realised he was right. There was only one question. None had ever satisfactorily answered it. Slowly I reached into the pocket of my jumpsuit and pulled for the little pouch that held my supply of snufz.

Major Roxbrough & Nik Gehenna

PART THREE

KNIGHTS IN DARK SATIN.

Myrrorball

31.

"I be pleased for thee, truly I be", Oslan-On-the-Bank told the younger noble, "But my chief concern must be to escape. I do not see the Akerányó, or more likely the virázető doing this for thee and not expecting something in return. Our quest be to find the king, forewarn him of the rebellion Halsgough plans, for forewarned be forearmed".

"Then what wouldst thou have me do", Hersko almost wailed, "Abandon cure for the sake of duty"?

"Thou must reunite me with Calamitosus and thence we shall part ways for a time, mayhap for an considerable time".

Hersko nodded and knew in his heart that he and the Margrave he admired so must follow different paths. He determined to find and steal Calamitosus. There seemed only one way of doing that – to inveigle his way into Sahbaj's affections and trust and then betray it.

The question uppermost in his mind was, did the virázető have any amorous designs for him? He reasoned that she must otherwise why give him the antidote to the Kézőrös' poison?

When the Szorkráló Himmelwhahu came for him the following day, he let him get a short distance in front before veering off, attempting to duck into a different hut and lose the old isangoma. The attempt was instantly detected. Himmelwhahu looked greatly ired,

"That is the wrong place, lordling. NEVER go into that hut ...ever! Do you understand"?

"I understandeth that certain areas of the camp bc off limits to one such as I, I became confused, apologies". Hersko returned with urgent alacrity. Noting the hut, full-well with compelling intrigue. Just what could be so important in that particular hut, that the mundunugu did not want him to find its contents. Could it be a semi-sentient sword by any chance?

Major Roxbrough & Nik Gehenna

He was soon before the lovely Sahbaj once again. This time he asked the wangateur,

"Tell me Himmelwhahu what be the Kémerié word for beautiful"?

The Szorkráló grinned before replyying, "It is gyönyoroűs".

With that gem of information, Hersko carefully Approached the leader of the tribe. In just such a way as to cause no alarm, taking her hand, he placed it to his lips before looking into her curious features, saying,

"Gyönyoroűs".

It worked like a charm would have done, the woman smiled, practically a simper, so pleased and complimented was she. It was offset by the second dose of the foul-tasting slime that was Hersko's cure.

"I wouldst converse with Her Majesty through thee is such be permitted", the lordling finally managed after forcing himself not to throw up that which would cure him.

"I will ask if her royal personage has any desire to do so, warrior", Himmelwhahu returned. The Lad waited until he saw the young woman smile and nod.

"Very well", the wangateur conceded, "What is so vital that you would have it conveyed to, Her Majesty? Apart from the fact that you find her comely, that is"?

"Tell her I admire her village, her braves and that they be a testament to her royal powers and purpose. Ask her if my Lord of Oslan-On-the-Bank may be released, for he has none thought of harm for the tribe. Rather he seeketh to be back in the company of his King. Reunited to warn him of the infamy of one Lord Halsgough - who seeketh rebellion against the crown"?

Himmelwhahu was relaying the message, Hersko hoped accurately. A brave suddenly burst into the royal hut. By the tone and mien of the Szorkráló, it was easily discernable that he was rebuking the brave for such a rude entry. Hersko still illiterate in the language was

Myrrorball

forced to watch a tableau act out that he suspected the cause. The brave babbled something the virázető then gave him an urgent directive. The intruder left with the same sort of velocity, with which, he had initially intruded.

Hersko demanded of Himmelwhahu, "Halsgough if I be not mistaken"?

The isangoma nodded and then asked, "Have you any sway over them"?

Hersko shook his head, "I was their prisoner, as was the Margrave. If thou giveth him back Calamitosus, he may help defend thy village against the invaders"?

"They might only be seeking allies", the mundunugu tried half-heartedly, why should they injure anyone"?

"These be the eastern lords of Valgraln", Hersko warned, "They will firstly conquer, take their pick of the women, enslave thy warriors and then press thee into their service. They will use initial deadly force to ensure continued obedience. Her Majesty raped unto near death for her beauty and thou will be put to the sword".

"Why will they kill me"? Himmelwhahu had lost all his self-confidence at Hersko's proclamations.

"As thou art not of our faith, our observance of the nine gods, thou follows practises of thine own. Thusly thou shalt be burnt as an heretic, burnt unto death - to the ground"!

"One moment", Himmelwhahu had a hurried conversation with the lovely virázető. For her part, she assumed a grave expression at the content of the colloquy. Replying hastily and it seemed to Hersko in a royal directive. For Himmelwhahu bowed, looking up demanded of the Lordling,

"Come with me, make haste, my young Lord".

"I am not a Lord yet", Hersko replied as he hurried after the Szorkráló. I am ...".

"You are an Úrrh", Himmelwhahu interjected, "That is a Lordly Warrior of the Akerányó. Your inaugural ceremony will have to wait until after the battle".

"Battle"?

"The warriors are closing in on the village. We need you to help defend it"!

"Release the Margrave. We will need him if thou intendeth to oppose Halgough, even then...".

The Szorkráló suddenly called over a brave who was running past and gave him what seemed to Hersko to be a quite complex instruction, before turning back to the newly created Úrrh,

"It's done. That warrior I just ordered to do so, is now on his way to your Margrave's sword and then to the cage".

"Why then are we not going in the same direction"? Hersko demanded not unreasonably.

"At the behest of, Her Majesty, I have something special for you", Himmelwhahu informed and stopped suddenly at the very hut he recently warned Hersko not to enter under any circumstances. Throwing the door open, the Szorkráló stood to one side and bid Hersko enter, with a grand wave of his arm. The latter did so hesitantly, for the gloom was subfusc, not possible to see much in the interior with ease. As Hersko blinked in the dimness, willing his eyes to begin perceiving the gloom he found to his surprise that all it contained was a small frond-wood table at its centre, nothing more. Upon the table was a container covered with a darkly decorated piece of substantially robust fabric.

The Szorkráló, suddenly in his element, sashayed into the room, placing himself behind the table. With a dramatic flourish that any magician would have been proud of, he drew the cloth free at great speed. It revealed the sort of green-glass dome that fitted over the rare, expensive mechanisms for measuring the passage of time. An useless device in Hersko's opinion. One could gauge the time by the position of the sun Angelus during the day. The stars and their constellations at night. This domed molten-sand cover was not over a clock though. It protected something far rarer and magical. Hersko slowly crept closer to examine the curious artefact the better. He was surprised to see what appeared to be an amber-glowing hand. The extremity floated above the base of the enclosure seemingly without any support of a device.

"What stoppeth it from falling, what be its purpose", the Úrrh asked of the Szorkráló.

Myrrorball

"Power", Himmelwhahu replied tacitly, then more verbosely, "Power, that goes back to a time before we roamed Rozhelia. When mysterious creatures walked holding sway, over our lands. Who knows, perhaps they were like the *HhhâäàåâääçêçêçêïîìïïìggndgndÐñß¥þÞÝ*∆? None can say for the detail is subfuscated by the vast aeons that followed. The Vandei Motestas knows nothing of age though. Its weird vitality is eternal. So I believe".

"Vandei Motestas"?

"It is in the ancient tongue we know which we called Øsinelv. That was the language of the creatures, I alone of the Szorkráló am the only one who has ever managed to translate any of their languages. That was Vandei Motestas – Hand of Power.

You can possess the hand, Hersko, newly created Úrrh. It can be magically fused to your wrist. You will once again have ten fingers, not only that but the Vandei Motestas will make you a great Úrrh. Possibly the greatest warrior lord of Akerányó ever".

"But I still have two hands", Hersko objected, "How will the Vandei Motestas be fitted to my body"?

"Not to your body, Úrrh Hersko, to your wrist".

"But, for that to be possible...".

"I must strike your hand from it with an axe"!

32.

I be a patient man", Halsgough told Gerner, "So patient indeed that I be willing to explain the situation to thee once more, afore handing thee over to Sorpio. I will ask thee where the Margrave thinkest to flee? Thou will tell me in all truth, with none subterfuge. Shouldst I detect in thine mien or word, then Sorpio will begin his work. My Lord of Sorpio is an artist. He painteth his canvasses in blood, pain, yet he be no butcher. Every pang of agonising terror that thou willst endure before telling me what I want to know will be his chorus to an unholy symphony. The end of it be that thou will tell me what I want to know, Gerner, so why maketh matters difficult for thyself and unsavoury for me. Of the three of us, only Sorpio will enjoy his artistry. Be the matter now clear in that rather keen mind of thine"?

"It was before", the scribe admitted, "I will not repeat mine answer to thee, there be no hope for thy understanding if thou dost not accept the truth of it".

He had told Halsgough that he did not know where Oslan-On-the-Bank or Hersko were going. It was strictly true, for the forest was dense and not easily navigable. The duo could end up just about anywhere in its dull confines.

Halsgough sighed, "Very well my lord of Sorpio, I hand him over to thy dark ministrations, maketh him howl, scream and cry, but maketh him talk".

The short and swarthy lord of the western town stepped forward eagerly. He was a man who took great pride and no small delight in his work. Swiftly he removed the scribes kid-skin boots, then taking hold of his breeks hauled them down around his ankles. He cooed to the master of recording, the keeping of data,

"I could start with thy toes, Scribe. Thence - were we not pressed for time proceed to what I knowest be thy valued 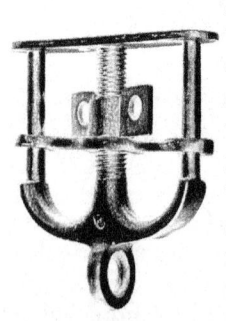fingers. For they caress the quill when thou doest thy most important occupation". He snatched at the scribe's scrotum dragged it forward, with a dexterity that even Gerner was forced to admire, had the right one in the herékprézet even as the scribe struggled futilely against the ropes that bound him firmly to his chair.

Gerner's testicle was clamped tightly as the cruel Lord spun the winged nut that tightened the bar onto it. It was then that Sorpio made the mistake that would cost him his eyes. He asked,

"Knowest thee, Pen-pusher how easy it be to crack a nut. Something thou must value even greater than thy extremities"?

"Thy pardon"? Gerner requested, sweat running down his glistening forehead, "I failed to perceive, the blood seemeth to be roaring in mine ears"?

Sorpio grinned, leaned forward to repeat his sadistic taunt afresh.

Gerner bit down on the capsule he had secreted between two teeth, lodged in the gap that he had cunningly created when the offending premolar had given him so much tasking, two years before. The capsule promptly split as it had been designed so to do. Powder within Gerner's mouth spat into Sorpio's glistening eyes. The cruel glint instantly replaced by sudden foaming of acid, some of which scorched Gerner's lips, but it was worth it to see dribbling gore run down the sadist's cheeks and hear his screams agonisingly,

"My eyes! My eyes, the nozkavardé has blinded me".

Halsgough acted swiftly. It was far too slowly to save Sorpio's vision though. He barked to two of his men,

"Water, fetch the boiled and sterile water quickly, rinse out the Lord of Sorpio's eyes".

"Take this infernal device off me, or thou shalt be next", Gerner bluffed. He had but one capsule of the acid which had been totally spent. The bluff worked, Halsgough was not bright enough to realise that the scribe had not used wizardry to blind Sorpio. It had all happened too swiftly for him to follow.

He undid the herékprézet tossing it contemptuously into a corner, while Sorpio continued to scream. By the time Gerner's bonds were undone, the men returned with the water. The acid copiously flushed out of Sorpio's sockets. There was nothing left of the eyeballs. His face contained nothing but two angry pink sockets.

"Thou thought to take my balls, so I took thine", Gerner said to the whimpering blind-man who would never shed another tear. Then the scribe turned to the rebellious, Lord of the West, warned,

"If Nunne and I are not rowed ashore within thirty-arcs of Angelus, thou will be next Halsgough"!

Major Roxbrough & Nik Gehenna

Halsgough ordered that the scribe together with his lone patient were hastily conducted in just such a manner. To his surprise, Gerner added,

"Have Sorpio's wrists shackled behind his back and a slave collar placed around his neck. I willst take him with me, like the blind-dog that he now is. My bundle will have salve to ease his pain, maybe, now he be blinded he will see more in the fullness of time"?

33.

Quianhua and I were enjoying the last few fluid notes of *Magnetic Fields* when there was a pounding on the door. I cut the power to the Yaqin valve amplifier by the antiquated metal toggle and shrugging to my wife went to see who it was.

I was not expecting to be surprised. I was not. Yet another comely member of the Kémerké was waiting to speak to me. She had the most striking silver hair, a fitting crown to her pale blue comp-lexion. I was disappointed when she did not offer herself to me though, rather, she began,

"Visionary, have you seen anything of Tru-eti Varzslatoj"?

"I do not believe I have met that individual, are they male or female and what might your name be"? I enquired.

At my proclamation of ignorance, she looked mightily crestfallen and explained then,

"I am Lurlene. Tru-eti Varzslatoj is not a person, what sort of Visionary would not know the particular of that"?

"My sort evidently", I confessed, "What then is it"?

Tru-eti Varzslatoj is the magical city - all on Egszígør seek, it is the best place to be, but it is almost impossible to gain access into it".

"So difficult that even your Szorkráló does not have any knowledge of it, it would seem".

Quianhua appeared at my shoulder then and almost snarled,

"Not another one, another bitch on heat, tell her to koof-off".

"She's seeking Tru-eti Varzslatoj", I explained, reddening at my spouse's profanity and rudeness.

"I bet she is", Quianhua still did not understand, "What is it, when it is in the bedroom? Some bizarre and revolting sexual position these savages like to use. I bet it involves their ass in some perverted way"?

"It is a magical city of some sort and exists somewhere on this island", I explained patiently thanking what-ever gods were currently looking down on us that the girl was speaking in Chinese. Lurlene was looking at us although we were two gods having a conversation in an alien tongue of deitic standard and wonder.

I turned my attention back to the comely native-girl, "I cannot help you concerning the location of the city, so you should leave now, Lurlene. We both watched her sashay back into the undergrowth. Quianhua observed with not one jot of sincerity,

"I hope she doesn't get bitten on the ass by the blue-furred little Kézőrös".

Get inside woman", I cried in mock anger, "Lest you feel my wrath at your despicable behaviour, the result of it being, I have to severely admonish you"!

Squealing in delight, the Chinese girl ran back indoors.

34.

"What in blazes be it now"? Halsgough demanded in a foul temper at being rudely awoken from his slumber

Blazes be the right expression with none mistake, My Lord", Teleocea blurted on the edge of panic, "The Zhirnublydok is on fire"!

Halsghough was instantly wide awake and struggling into his breeks,

"Fire! How"?

"Some burning arrows were fired at the sails. Once the alarm was raised, the men began to take steps to put them out a second rain fell on the deck. One of Rynturro's guards fell, mortally impaled by one. The men are fighting it now, but 'twould seem it be a losing battle".

Halsgough was gripped by dread as he let Teleocea hurry him into his armour, without the schooner the King would be marooned on the Fire of Saah. Yet so would he! Who would usurp him? The ironic name of the island was not lost on the Western Lord, at that point either.

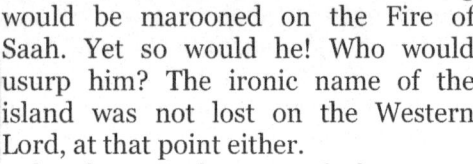

The duo raced up on deck. It was obvious from little more than a fleeting glimpserama that the flames had taken with such ferocity that the vessel was doomed to a fateful conflagration.

"Get as much in the longboats as possible"? Halsgough demanded with a roar of impotent fury, "Even if we have to cling to the sides and paddle ashore ourselves".

His orders were acted upon with speedy efficiency. Yet once such a fire takes hold of timber, it progresses very rapidly. Much was abandoned, lost to save their skins. The five longboats that remained were getting close to shore when more arrows rained down on the eastern lords and their men. One hit Lord Kleonk in the shoulder at the joint between his pauldron and gorget. He slipped beneath the waves, lost to them. The rest employed their escutcheons as best as they were able.

"Banustib, do something", Halsgough roared, but of the witch, there was no sign. A voice the rebellious leader did not recognise cried,

Myrrorball

"She turned herself into a gull and flew from the ship as soon as it was obvious it was going to sink".

Halgough turned in the direction where the Zhirnublydok had lain at anchor. All that he could see were the raging flames of the dreaded conflagration. It forced him to huddle, soaked beneath the protection of his shield, the metal on his body threatening to drag him in the same direction as Kleonk at any moment. Mercifully he felt his booted feet hit shale and knew they had made the shadows. It was still a deadly business dragging themselves onto the beach when at any moment they could get an arrow in the vitals. Firing into darkness was a wasteful enterprise. There were no further casualties, as soon as they had pulled the boats onto the sand. The attack ceased.

"Shall we go after them, My Lord"? Halsia enquired.

"Art thou out of thy mind, Halsia", Halsgough rebuked, "Chase after natives who have lived all their lives in these very woods, in the dark. What do you think would happen thence"?

"The natives have not lived in these woods all their lives", a female voice contradicted him, Halsgough whirled around and observed acidly,

"Good of thee to fly back to the coup, Witch, didst thou enjoy thy fish"?

"The natives who attacked and burnt the schooner have not lived in these woods all their lives", Banustib repeated, "They are the Benszülöt from the west of here, the sworn enemies of the local Akerányó".

"Why was I not informed of their incursion into this territory ahead of time? Oh, thou peddler of pishogue and mummery"? Halsgough fumed.

"I learned such myself when flying over the land, as an gull. This but recently. The warpaint of the Benszülöt is interestingly different from that of the local tribe, in that...".

"Well whoopedy-nemözökülés-do", Halsgough cursed, "Thank the gods for thy edification, Witch".

Banustib's dainty mouth twisted in distaste at the crudity and she walked away.

Major Roxbrough & Nik Gehenna

"It might not be advisable to ire her, My Lord". Rhynturro advised Halsgough then, "The Witch may be our only chance at getting off this island – ever"!

35·····

Quianhua faced me her eyes, her lovely almond eyes filmed with unshed tears and asked,
"Do I have a right to know what is going on, Nik"?
"We both do", I told her honestly, "And a great deal of what I know, you know Anna".
"Then tell me the rest"? She demanded not unreasonably.
"And I want this endless troop of young women who are only after one thing, to stop coming here. Can you at least fix that"?
I nodded, "I'll speak to Hízlatan, that part of it can be easily sorted".
"And the other part, I want the whole story"?
I told her the story so far as recorded in this e-journal. As I suspected, it brought forth a further series of enquiries,
"You've been taking a drug, whilst here with me"? She looked more wounded than ired, which bothered me more, curiously.

"Snufz is no worse than snuff really" I tried to wriggle out of it, but my Chinese wife was better at interrogation than to let that one pass.
"You told me yourself it has mind-expanding properties additionally. So what do you know or think you know that you haven't told me"?
"This is going to sound lame", I began falteringly, "The truth is the more I learn, the greater number of unanswered questions I found myself facing. The

Myrrorball

vagueries of philosophy started to torment my lucidity, such clarity became confusing".

"I don't know about lame, it certainly sounds confusing".

I leaned forward and grasped her upper arms, they were somewhat undefined, slender. I found that appealing,

"That's just it, Anna, it *is* confusing".

"Tell me then", she urged after a slow and gentle kiss, perhaps I can lend some clarity to your bewilderment"?

The Császária – Roxbrough. The name is beyond coincidence. I know an artist and author by that same name. What are the chances of that? We are on a distant world, light-years from our allegedly devastated planet and one of the first locals I meet has a name that is very familiar to me through association"?

"It is a powerful coincidence, but can still be just that. What else"?

"The Zernoplat – HhhâäàåâäääçêçêçêïïïïïïggndgndÐñß¥þÞ-Ýʌ, are they real? Are they the creatures who put the notion of a novel into my brain, or...".

"Or what"?

"Are they just a race of impossible creatures from a rather fanciful novel, so *are you and I*"?

Quianhua laughed, but at the edge of her humour was a tinge of trepidation

"You're suggesting I'm a novelist's creation Nik, that you and I are only a collection of words on a page. That cannot be true. I *know* I am real"!

"But of course you would say that – in the book. That is the cunning of the author and the author is Roxbrough".

Quianhua took my hand and pressed it to one of her impressive breasts,

"Does that feel like words, Nik, do I? When we do it, does it feel real to you"?

"Do you not see, the very fact that I *know* real cannot possibly be at all - proves to me that all can be an illusion"?

"That is so much bull", Quianhua scoffed, "If what you say is true then nothing is real except the knowledge that we are...are..."

Major Roxbrough & Nik Gehenna

"Are, full stop", I finished for her. "Except for the fact that we are. Nothing else can be proven or disproven. The world could be just like we left it. We could be on a HhhâäàåâääçêçêçêïïìïïìggndgndÐñßɎþÞÝ◬ vessel having stimuli fed directly into our comatose bodies, abducted just for the amusement of them. Or we could be in some lunatic asylum somewhere living in our dementia. When I say we, I mean me of course, you could be part of an entire simple delusion".

Quianhua started to look alarmed, "You're frightening me now, Nik. Are you certain you are not beginning to lose sight of reality"?

"Either that or beginning to understand it too well", I told her gravely. "I think the only answer is to play this thing out".

"This thing"? She echoed. I could hear her scepticism, "What *thing* would that be Nik"?

"To find out once and for all what is and what isn't", I told her more calmly than I had felt in a long time. "To go to Tru-eti Varzslatoj of course, ask whom-so-ever is custodian there, what is going on".

"The city, the one you didn't even realise existed until only moments ago? You want to abandon the safety and comfort of the bubble now and go in search of a native myth"?

"It's a quest", I told her, "Our reason for being here perhaps, something that Hhrrhhoehhrrhooooingohh & Harahorahurrahaashume very well may have put us here to pursue".

"They put us here to find a way of combating the Kézőrös so they can move into yet more real estate", the girl objected, "Not to go off on some hair-brained scheme of personal curiosity".

"Did they though"?

"Is this what snufz does to the mind, gets you questioning everything and then when you've done so questioning the questions"?

"Yes".

"In that case tell me what we need I'm coming with you, who will look after the cats"?

Myrrorball

"I'm sure one of the local native girls can be persuaded to do that for the Frosted Mortis Wraith"? I grinned, "As for Mr Choon, he's coming with us".

36.....

"What are you about, My Lord Császária", Mr Genks asked as he entered the hut set aside for several of the nobles – guests of the Kémerké.

Roxbrough was bending over a low table almost in posture. Not a position he could have maintained for long without discomfort. Besides the parchment a pot of ink, into which, the Császária's quill kept dipping to load.

"I thought I might keepeth a record of our daily events, something for the queen to read upon our return to Valgraln", came the grunted reply.

"Why go to such a tedious effort? When the Visionary could type it into the computer for you, in a fraction of the time"?

"I knowest not the terms *type* and *computer*, though many believe that the Domisphere may be one of the latter. Why would the Wraith who slippest away when best it does suit him, give aid to me anyway"?

"Why would he not"? The manbian returned with certainly mysterious amusement. "One good thing has come out of the introduction to the Kémerké, you with they combined are now a fearsome defence against the rebellious lords and any they press into their cause.

Roxbrough considered that and then suddenly scowled,

"I would give an princely sum to know the very detail of Halsgough's machinations. More importantly the location of the Zhirnublydok".

Both of them fell instantly silent when 23 abruptly entered the hut. Roxbrough found it strange that the manbian was never comfortable in the presence of the android. Not that he fully understood the nature of the mechanism himself. To the Imperial Marquess, 23 was nothing much more than a very elaborate trebuchet or scaling tower.

Major Roxbrough & Nik Gehenna

A device created for a specific purpose. Yet the automaton could convert the language of the Valgraln into Kémerié and the only other with such power was the mysterious Visionary, the Wraith who had disappeared once serious discourse was underway between Vasnaar and Aznodib.

Roxbrough closed his eyes and kneaded the eyeballs with the ball of his thumbs. Writing by tallow usually gave him a headache. The words began to blur after a while. Forcing him to continue at arm's-length. How did that make sense? He could see distant objects better than those closer. Surely physically, it was against logic? It was the type of conundrum one would normally deliver to the likes of Gerner. Roxbrough missed the scribe. He had enjoyed many a double-candle night discourse with the keeper of records. He wondered what he was about at that moment, or if Halsgough had executed him on some vile trumped-up charge?

37.

"Hurry, Blind Raven", the scribe, virtually spat, jerking the chain connected to the maimed Lord's metal collar with savage satisfaction. For his part, the former master of Sorpio merely whimpered, hastened to do as commanded. His eyes were on fire, yet he had no eyes. The phantom pain was real to him. In the front of his head. In his face. Impossible to try putting from his mind. Admittedly he would have given the scribe indescribable agony, but once he had talked, he could have survived quite happily as an eunuch. This! This was so much worse, his career, his nobility – all gone in one hateful lone savage instant. He was reduced from a noble to a beggar An beggar and an slave to the nozkavardé who had mutilated him. he most outlandish of triumvir stubbled through the darkness and Sorpio almost hoped a Kézőrös would be disturbed, or were nocturnal and would bite him. He could know peace as a blue-mumbly. The instant the thought occurred to him, he rectified it, he hoped the scribe would be the one bitten. Yet then he would be in the forest with two mute creatures - sightless. Perhaps it would be possible to commit suicide painlessly? Halsgough did not seem to have sent anyone to follow, recapture and bring the hateful Scribe to justice. The rise of the Western Lords was experiencing difficulties before even the initial plans had been enacted. It seemed the gods were with the king. The gods – was that the answer to the blind raven's predicament? He had never been a superstitious man but needs must and so on. Mazormazuri was the god of healing – Sorpio began to pray. He promised the god everything he possessed to regain his eyes. His lands, his hereditary title, his precious collection of torture instruments, the castle at Sorpio. He promised the rooms filled with grand possessions, the fine horses in the stables, the woman who had been his faithful wife for the past nineteen years, the two virgin daughters they had bred between them. Mazormazuri was a male god, a couple of comely virgins might very well be to his liking.

'Mine daughters are thine, Mazormazuri - do with as thou pleaseth if thou canst only restore mine sight', the Blind Raven was prepared to sacrifice anyone and anything he could think of to achieve his selfish design. It seemed as though if Mazormazuri even existed he was not especially tempted by the offer though, for an answer- was there none. It was a double shame. The first being the Raven stayed blind, the second being if he ever got off the island, back home he would have two weddings to find the coin for. His foot caught in something then. Before he could reflect upon how miserable he was, he went sprawling into the undergrowth, something sharp slicing the back of his left hand.

"I'm injured", he said as the weight of the chain suddenly slackened around his neck. He had the good sense not to cry out. The local savages could very well be within earshot.

"Hold still while I bandage the gash", a voice commanded, it was the tone of the scribe. Certainly the most hated enemy Sorpio had ever opposed. Circumstance forced him to civility though, so he asked in the mildest way he found he could force himself,

"I do not supposeth thou wouldst consider removing the heavy chain from my collar"?

"Of course I wouldst consider it", Gerner returned, "Whence thy contrition has served an useful period".

"And just how long must my humiliating penitence last, Scribe"?

"That canst only be determined by thee, Blind Raven. There be conditions, I will convey so that thou might commence work upon them with right alacrity. One, thou art no longer lord. Lord of Sorpio, or noble of anything. Thou art slave, thou nomen be Blind Raven. Two, thou shalt not address me as, Scribe any more, I am Akodó [Master, Owner, Predominant etcetera]".

The Raven ground his teeth. It was to his credit that he gave tongue to nought - despite grave temptation.

"When thou has mastered those two simple disciplines, then we can see about affecting thee a better existence", the Akodó told him and suddenly dragged him to his feet. He was physically more obdurate, vital than the former, Lord of the Western provinces, had given him credit. It would have been interesting to have tortured him to death, see how long his vitality could have kept death's freezing talons at bay.

He followed, the metal chafing the skin on his neck raw within twenty arcs of the blue moon goddess. At one stage

Myrrorball

Gerner handed the chain over to the dimwit. Thusly increased his humiliation, to be led by the neck by an imbecile.

Suddenly the sound of swiftly moving foliage, bare feet hitting undergrowth caused him grave panic. It quietened before he could succumb to it and he heard his new owner speaking hesitantly to someone in a tongue he did not recognise. The cursed savages! Gerner had known how to communicate with them all along and had cruelly kept the knowledge to himself. If the Raven ever got his hands around the scribe's throat....then he began to listen. It became plain by the amount of repetition that was being used, that both sides of the parley could not fully understand the other. He felt a breath on his cheek and Gerner said to him with an intimacy born by proximity,

"We have been intercepted by the Akerányó. I have accepted their kind offer to dine in their company, maybe rest for a while".

"Was it not they who thou couldst see attacking the ship as thou dragged me into the forest"? The blind Raven wanted to know and then remembered to add, "Akodó"?

"No, Blind Raven", Gerner sounded smug, "That was the other tribe from over to the west 'twould seemest, the Benszülöt".

"The Benszülöt are out to slay us all"?

"They have no desire to welcome visitors from distance shores 'twould appear. Doest not fret, the Akerányó have already advised me on how to avoid them. Instead of heading for the spine of the island up into the mountains, we are to hug the Western coast and travel firstly to Sélifalu, that way the danger will be avoided".

"How will that reunite me with the other Western Lords"?

"Why wouldst thou want such, Slave? What use wouldst thou be to a rebellious warrior like Halsgough? Dost, thou think he would treat thee well"?

"Will Vasnaar treat me any better"?

"Thou art now my slave and will enjoy my protection. Ifin thou dost work diligently in all tasks I give to thee, thou hast no need to fear the king or any noble of all Valgral".

"I understand thou hast some powers...Akodó, but where were they when thou fell captive to Halsgough but so recently"?

Before the scribe could answer, from amongst the foreign jabbering the blind Raven heard a familiar voice cry out,

"Gerner as I dost live and breathe, how didst thou manage to get here, be another attack imminent"?

38.
The day before...

"All right. I am ready". Hersko stretched out his disabled hand, the one with two missing fingers. He laid it on the wooden block. Himmelwhahu had told him there would be initial blood loss and pain, a great deal of pain. The Szorkráló would snatch up the Vandei Motestas. Using his powers of office - mould it to Hersko's ruined wrist. In that theurgical action, the veins, the arteries would be sealed, the power of the hand would also negate all pain. The feeling would flood into it, the extremity would feel like his own. Feel like his - but more.

"Get on with it Himmelwhahu before Halsgough gets here, or I change my mind".

The blow when it came did not cause any pain, had the Szorkráló completely missed? How incompetent was he"? Hersko looked down. His hand lay on the compacted earth-floor of the hut. From his wrist arterial blood was spurted at every beat of his heart.

Pain began.

It was unbearable. The scream that tore from Hersko's throat would have hurt if he could feel anything other than the throbbing agony in his ruined arm.

Abruptly it was gone!

The Szorkráló had moulded the Vandei Motestas to his wrist as quickly as it took to grasp it from its case and push it toward the warrior's ruined arm.

It felt good!

It was a feeling that was...wonderful. A sense of well being, energy, elation flooded into Hersko's body. He heard himself laughing as he held the Vandei Motestas up before his gaze. It shone with saffron light, the majority of it a conflagration at the palm. Crackling shards of flameian iridescence ran up his wrist almost to the elbow. He drew his sword.

"I can take on Halsgough alone", the Úrrh of the Akerányó declared, an almost unholy glee in his voice – his eyes.

Himmelwhahu looked slightly nervous for the first moment since he had been initially in Hersko's company,

"Warrior Lord of the one true race of Egszígør", he began, "It will take a while for you to become familiar with the intensity of the hand of power. Might I suggest...".

"Suggest pfuwaggest", Hersko laughed, "Lead me to them, they will be decimated pretty quickly by Calamitosus in the fist of the Margrave of Oslan-On-the-Bank and by my new sword-arm".

Himmelwhahu hurried after the intoxicated youth. A brave ran up to the Szorkráló. Jabbered a hasty report before running back into the darkness, Himmelwhahu sounded relieved as he observed,

"It is already over, Úrrh Hersko, bearer of the Vandei Motestas. The men from the Far Side have been repulsed in this instance. They have melted back into the darkness"!

39.

"Gerner, thou managed to escape, with Nunne also. What be this shambling creature dragged in chains, surely 'tis not the Raven"?

"The Blind Raven now", the newly self-appointed Akodo returned, "And therein lies a tale. I wouldst wager thou has one of thine own also, Young Lordling. There be something magical in thy wholesomeness, the glimmering of thy restored hand"?

"That there be, that there be", the Úrrh – Warrior Lord of the Akerányó smiled, "Come with me to my hut and we shall bringest one another to the present in the telling of them, then we go to meet the virázető of this tribe. A beautiful Queen.

"And the Margrave", the scribe wanted to know. "The two of thee left together, where be he right now"?

"With good fortune, on his way to the King", came the hopeful response.

40.[i]

"We will set off on our quest tomorrow", I told Quianhua, who was all ready to make the trip that instant. Leoma was on her way to look after the cats for us. I tried not to think of Leoma. It was not easy. Suddenly the notion of an apocalyptic short-story entered my head. The first such motivating me to write fiction since meeting Hhrrhhoehhrrhooooingohh had interrupted my career, my life, everything. Of course, I had to write it down – then, while the inspiration for it was still raw - fresh.

I ignored the Chinese' look of deflated disappointment, hurried to the keyboard – this keyboard, so here goes...

Myrrorball

PART FOUR
CORONA DANCE

Major Roxbrough & Nik Gehenna

40.ii

The Corona19 had been something of a disappointment if one had been expecting the end of the world. In the end, it was true, thousands were dead, but on a global scale, thousands out of eight billion was a spit in the Pacific Ocean. The banks and their underlings, the politicians breathed a sigh of relief, thought that was that.

It was not.

Fourteen months later, with all the sporting bodies thinking everything would soon be back to normal and they could once again begin making obscene amounts of money, the first case of Heineken20 was detected. Another epidemic was feared. This time it was no fizzling failure of a pandemic re-named epidemic though, this baby was muscular. It was no respecter of position, wealth or even health. Corona had been the practise run, now the real plague began. In five hysteria filled months one billion bodies had been drowned in their phlegm. A whopping 12.5% of the world's population were being piled high in the streets, after being doused in petrol, committed to open cremation. It had been the only way to get rid of the dead and keep the deadly plague to a manageable level.

Men were resilient though, after all, had he not endured two world wars, the Black Death, Spanish Flu? Everyone thought the Heineken20 of 2021 had been the ultimate test.

They did not know the half of it!

Sport - had become a pastime once more, the industry that had been entertainment was merely amateur. Few films were made, due to budgetary restrictions. Actors went back into the theatres. The industry managed to limp along, backed by considerable influxes of cash-loans from the world's top governments. The slump began to flatten out. Just at the point where things were beginning to look better, the planet was smitten with a further double-whammy. In Korea, an outbreak of Stella21 coincided with Budweiser22 in Mexico. The already frail

Myrrorball

infrastructure of the world could not cope. The health services could not either. The death toll was impressive. No one thought men could endure two plagues at once. It was the first instance in modern history where the death toll exceeded the survival rate. The need for police state type patrols became necessary to stop the looting, the acts of violence, the senseless rapes. The Rangers were created, firstly in England and then every other country in the world followed suit.

The population shrank from seven billion to one hundred thousand million, 86% of the entire global population was dead. Cannibalism became a necessity to those left behind. The animals were unaffected, but so few were left to husband them. Hopefully, the various *Germ-Raids*, as the entire four years became known were over? How could another attack reap so much havoc when so few were left behind? Whole areas of the world were almost devoid of humanity at the end of it. Africa was an animal paradise once more. The Middle East, a deserted wasteland. Canada and Russia contained only the very hardy, the extremely stubborn few who refused to be beaten by lack of food and foul weather. Amerika was no longer the United States. There was not a big enough population to merit having States at all. Australians, refusing to ever stay indoors no matter what the circumstances, were gone. The Aborigines had won back their land the hard way, but it was an eventual victory. In Europe, where the majority of the world's population remained gathered together, the industry collapsed. Agriculture became the leading one in a bid to feed the remaining populace.

The final thousand million who remained were hardy, enduring and tough, surely nothing else could attack them? Even if it did, people were too thinly spread over great distance for it to finish them all off. The planes, trains, cars and ships were a thing of the past. There was none to extract the oil from the otherwise useless sand.

When Phleege23 arrived, those left alive almost shrugged. How could even the worst virus ever possibly infect everyone, when hardly anyone did not live alone? Of course, some couples existed. Some offspring were even born. That was when nature decided to play its part. Ensuring the leading species of mammal on Earth would not even be killed by the phleege. The mutants grew in number. They were immune to infection it seemed.

There was barely any need for rangers any more. The population of the entire globe was a mere five hundred million. Of them, the latest estimates were that 23% were the newly arrived mutants. Various stories sprang up regarding the latter. Hideously deformed, said certain agricultural myths. Achingly beautiful, contradicted others. Still, a third legend was that they could pass themselves off as human, but had strange internal differences that protected their lungs. The Germ-Raids had all attacked the lung for some reason. All had killed in the same way as a severe form of double pneumonia.

None of this made any difference to Froxbrough, he had been a Ranger since '21 and had seen just about everything any man would wish to see and avoid in his lifetime. He had observed incredible acts of kindness and self-sacrifice. Witnessed depravity, cruelty and downright indifference all to an equal degree. He had shot looters, hauled rapists from the quivering bodies of their victims, before casually castrating them, eaten human flesh, started mass funeral pyres. He no longer had rank, for his Major had been dead a year by then, so he had assumed the in-the-field promotion by short wave radio from Central - before they too had fallen silent. He was a Major with no troops to give orders. A man with not a single subordinate. Nor superior, nor comrade. The day he came across the bubble, he had been thinking despite every attempt to keep his mind a complete void. He had been reflecting that he was lonely. A tired, dirty figure, friendless. With even fewer enemies [ha ha ha], not even a single acquaintance. The pack on his back had grown alarmingly light, no supplies in there much any more. The blast rifle on his shoulder was correspondingly heavy. The creature, known once as man-kind, had finally reached Mars in '21, the last-ditch attempt to avoid the wave of plagues. The colony had died out almost at once with no Earth infrastructure to supply them with vital oxygen and other essentials. Professor Hoyle had brought back the lichen, DNA spliced it with just about anything it would splice with and created marvellous food supplies that were no longer needed or could in the main be farmed. Why bother growing crops with all the effort and attention and finally so little actual nutrient value, when there was always fresh meat on the menu?

When Froxbrough saw the startling albescent bubble pristine in its whiteness, he thought it merely a mirage, or perhaps insanity was beginning to nibble at the edges of his fraught sensibilities? He was in what had once been Romania. Now simply part of Gerasia, which stretched from the far western-coast to the deserted city of Moscow, governed, if such a term still applied, by the German Emperor. Not that it mattered, farmers had become nomadic and finally settled where the soil was most rich and fertile. Froxbrough checked the charge in his rifle. It could cope with almost any eventuality. He crept forward, hunched into a position that made of him, a lesser target. There was no need. No fire suddenly started up. No one wanted him dead.

Almost at the point when the Ranger was about to reach the front hatch-shaped opening, the airlock of sorts swung aside. A grizzled man of a broad chest, large biceps, was standing in the jamb.

"It's a Ranger", he cried over his shoulder to someone inside, then turning back toward Froxbrough seemingly oblivious to the possibility of danger, greeted,

"Hello, Ranger, come inside, you're a welcome sight. We don't get many visitors nowadays".

Froxbrough approached warily and concentrated on the man's eyes. It was always evident in the eyes, the intent.

The farmer was exuding friendliness, Froxbrough breathed a sigh of relief and almost collapsed as he gave in to the fatigue.

"My name's Jethro", the farmer clapped Froxbrough on the back. A cloud of dust pluthered from his tunic-jacket. The ash of the cremated dead, the filth of the living. Froxbrough went into the comparative gloom, blinking, willing his eyes to accustom themselves to the drop in illumination. Within, standing almost at attention behind a farmhouse table were two women. It seemed to Froxbrough that they were mother and daughter, wife and offspring.

"This is Matilda", Jethro waved at the ruddy complexioned somewhat rotund spouse, "My wife. This, our daughter, Kasee. Even though he was aware that he was staring at the latter, he could not tear his eyes from her. She was the most beautiful girl he had ever seen. Or at least the first young woman he had seen in four years. Adrenalin charged through his body making him heedless of the earlier fatigue, his hormones, that had lain dormant for so long flushed a charge of raw desire through his groin. He smiled and coughed to cover his excitement.

"You must be desperate for a bath", Matilda, the mother noted, she had smelled him. "We keep a fire going even though the pumps no longer work we have a well, plenty of pales. I'll fill the tub with some hot water for you. While you bathe I can launder your clothes in our boiler? In the meantime, you can wear some of Jethro's, until yours are dry again".

Tears of gratitude filled Froxbrough's eyes as he asked, "Why, why are you doing this for me? You know I'm a Ranger, but nothing else, I'm a stranger to you".

Jethro returned, "A Ranger helped us more than once, when the *Crazies* roamed, this is our chance to repay, accept what we are offering, humble as it is, it is what we can spare".

"I'll accept the help in the spirit, in which, it's offered then, thank you". The words seemed to stick in Froxbrough's dry throat. It had been a long time since he had vocalised any thoughts.

He let Matilda lead him to the bathroom. Waited while pails of water were brought steaming into the room and poured into the tub. Great clouds of fragrant steam filled the bubbles, salts had been added into the bath - before the water. He began to strip off his crusted tunic. Matilda waited by the doorway, seemingly careless if she saw him nude. A farmer's wife, uncaring about such things, she did not seem to notice. He kept his back to her as much as he could. For the sake of his own crumbled modesty. She picked up the muddy, dusty grime-filled fabric, replaced it with clean clothing on a hard-backed chair beside the sink - left. Froxbrough took a keg of soap, a jewel in an oasis of desolation, began to use the friction sponge provided. The grime fell away underneath the onslaught. It revealed the body of a man. Who knew, perhaps one of the last on Earth? He used to encounter people every day. No longer, the distance between them grew exponentially.

He climbed reluctantly, eventually out of the brown water, picked up a towel of soft cotton, rubbing himself briskly. The clothes fit. Like him, Jethro was a goodly size, built from muscle honed by years of hard physical labour. Thusly mightily refreshed, keenly hungry, the Ranger left the bathroom, Matilda was waiting without,

"I wanted to clean it", he apologised, "But could not find the materials".

She held up a fist, cloth, cleaning cream. Smiled indulgently, "Go and eat, talk to Kasee, she does not enjoy the interaction with people as a girl her age should, especially men".

Did the woman know what that was doing to the Ranger? The olde-familiar tightening of the groin, the feeling of upwardly roving heat? Surely the two of them were not being set-up? Yet on the farm, there would be no production without birth. Froxbrough would gladly, eagerly, sweatily contribute to the gene-pool given the parents blessing.

When he seated himself at the table, he was stunned to see the girl had applied make-up, changed into a scarlet low-cut frock. She smiled at him and licked her lips as her father placed a plate before him,

Major Roxbrough & Nik Gehenna

"It's not real beef I'm afraid, nor even real potatoes nor carrots. All of it is that new *lichprod* stuff, but we have enough to spare. You're welcome to it".

Froxbrough's mouth watered at the aroma. The taste was somewhat disappointing. It had a type of green-leaf undercurrent to the individual flavours that seemed to lend them all a disconcerting sameness. He was famished though, gulped it down, even agreeing to a second plateful.

"For dessert, we have lichapple crumble, unfortunately, made with lich-flour, but the real thing goes to the one percent", Matilda apologised, back from her cleaning duty. "Don't just sit there Kasee, pour our visitor a cup of lichcoff".

"The one percent"? Froxbrough asked, suddenly aware that he had not given them his name, nor had they asked for it. He was busy doing his very best not to stare down the girl's billowing frock, as she leaned over the table. He was sure her breasts would be divine.

"The same one percent that there always was", Jethro seated himself opposite the Ranger. A green tube was sticking in the corner of his mouth. His eyes had a look about them of one who was enjoying a joint. "The one percent who have ninety-nine percent of what there is, while the rest of us have the other one".

Froxbrough nodded, no sense in getting in any sort of philosophical debate with anyone who had been so kind, even if he disagreed with their point of view. It was not worth arguing about anyway – what *was* any more?

The dessert was sweet, though unfamiliar, welcome. After dried ranger rations, he had eaten like a prince. He tried one of Jethro's snufzcigs but had to put it out, the aroma was not to his liking. It seemed to rapidly give him a dry throat. Jethro chose to view the action as one of complete exhaustion which was not far from the truth anyway.

"It's time for the good soldier of law and order to get some well-earned downtime I think. You'll have Kasee's room for the time being. You have to stay until your uniform is ready to wear once more, I don't want to hear any arguments".

"I could not possibly put the girl out of her bed", the Ranger complained, his mind racing as he did so.

'No reason why we can't cuddle up together in it though'. "I'll take the settee or maybe even somewhere comfy in the barn".

Jethro laughed, "This is a working farm, Ranger. Go in the barn if you must then you're likely to get an angry hoof in your nethers. As for the settee, we're up at dawn and don't retire till darkness. You need several uninterrupted hours of sleep. Don't worry about Kasee, she'll get under the stairs in a camp bed we have for times such as this. It hasn't been used for, for...for years. It will be something of an adventure for the girl. Isn't that right, Kasee "?

When the girl spoke for the first time, it was in a voice that Froxbrough could not possibly have anticipated. Low, guttural, not fitting to her visage in the slightest degree. It was not even an attractive contralto. It was the sort of voice that comes unused to a throat. Froxbrough wondered briefly if he sounded like that to the Romanians, even though they were conversing with him in Hollywood.

"I want you to have my bed", she told me. Her body moved sensually from side to side as she spoke. A lithe movement like the hypnotising snake.

"That is extremely kind of you", the Ranger heard himself simper, "And in that spirit, I will accept it at least until I have had one good day's sleep at any rate".

'And if you want to slip beneath the sheets with me later on, then I will show you more about animal husbandry than you ever dreamed possible', he thought - as an undercurrent.

Jethro watched him climb to his feet indicated the desired direction with a nod of his greying head. Curious, he did not look quite old enough to have a daughter who appeared to be in her mid-twenties. Perhaps the fresh air and the outdoor life had much to recommend after all?

The room was a woman's decorated in saffron and coral hues. White bedding with a tiny rosebud motif. Too many pillows, girls loved their pillows. Froxbrough threw off the loaned clothes and slid into the gloriously fragrant, soft envelope created by his own body. He almost instantly attained the fluffy period between sleep and doziness when the door opened. Kasee slipped inside. Though the action seemed devious, her parents were still up and awake. Whatever was going to happen was with their blessing. She sauntered over to the Ranger who watched her with burning eyes of frost and passion. Then her soft, almost pneumatic lips were on his. She asked in a whisper to disguise her voice,

"Do you want it, Mister Ranger"?

"What do you think"? He managed to croak, "Do you know how long it's been? Do you realise how much you're affecting me? You who are...".

"But do you want it"? She repeated, breaking in upon his babbling, "You have to say the words, you have to tell me"?

"Get in here. I'll tell you with more than my mouth", he managed, feeling himself hardening. She was still fully dressed, not in the bed with him, yet he was consumed with urgency.

"Not until you tell me, in your own words that you want it", she licked her lovely pink, promising lips.

"I want it", he gasped, "Jezzis-H and all the dead saints I want it, get in bed with me. You'll see, hurry, or you might even be too late"?

She pushed him across the bed so she could climb in beside him, strangely powerful,

Must come from humping milk churns all day', he thought to himself, then her lips were on his and the throbbing in his member was almost painful, but in an ecstasy of ache. He began to rub his hands over the dress. It was not the same as if she were naked, so he demanded,

Take it off, take everything off"?

"Everything, you want me to remove everything"?

"Goddammit get naked, Babe, take off everything"!

The scarlet dress of fake promise came over her head firstly. With it the foam inserts. There were no breasts, they consisted of a flat chest without so much as raised nipples. Before he could even try to hide his disappointment, the wig was pulled free of the bald head. Carelessly tossed onto the carpet. It was quickly followed by the teeth, a full set, top and bottom. Placed with far greater care onto the old chipboard bedside unit. As she half-turned, he saw the external lungs, slowly inflating and deflating, on the outside of the body. Powerful organs, leather-clad, resistant to a virus of any type.

Froxbrough would have said something, tried to make the best of a terrible situation, but beneath the covers, the labia opened. A tentacle lashed out from the opening in the vagina. Needle sharp injectors fastened onto the tumescence in his groin yet he felt no pain, for they included a local anaesthetic which gushed through their hollow points into him. Then the writhing thing that was what the mutant fed through began to activate its powerful suction. The blood in Froxbrough's engorged member was greedily consumed firstly. It was not enough, nowhere near enough. Kasee continued to feed until all that lay beside *her* was a chalk-white husk of a corpse with not a single drop of blood remaining inside it.

Slowly, regretfully, she slid out of bed satiated. Sexually dissatisfied of course. For men could never hope to mate with the female mutants. Men were doomed, slowly to be devoured, until they were gone. Mutant females would exist until their source of sustenance failed. They would adapt then, farm the cattle, breed the bulls too. They would survive. Earth was theirs.

Major Roxbrough & Nik Gehenna

PART FIVE

BLOOD RAIN AND THE TOWER THAT ATE PEOPLE

Myrrorball

41.

"Are we going today. Or are you going to spend all day in front of that ruddy computer"? A sing-song voice suddenly cut into my reverie.

"It's all right", I assured as I slid the keyboard back under the monitor (how many times had I done that, on two different worlds no less), "I've finished what I was working on, a sort of alternative history for our world. It didn't work out much better for us in that thread either".

Shaking her head in a combination of frustration and disbelief that I could waste my time that way, she noted,

"Well, one of your wet dreams has just come out of the undergrowth, the slutty looking one that's going to look after your pussies while you think about hers".

I chuckled at that. It was rather amusing. I did not know until that point that there was such a thing as Chinese humour. We picked up our bundles, put the lead on Mr Choon and went out to speak to the pneumatic native. Quianhua immediately nodded to her and then walked off. No sooner had I managed to make a quick exit from the alluring creature than another of the amorous natives appeared at the edge of the clearing,

"Cassiti what are you doing here? I thought we had established that I can't... that we are to remain apart"?

"That is true. I accepted your words, but I have been sent by Hízlatan, to watch over you to help you".

"To help him out of his pants the first chance you get more like, "Quianhua was on form that day. I found her jealousy rather flattering if truth be told (which I always do - tell the truth, that is).

"Help the two of us how Cassiti"? I asked carefully.

"As a guide through the heart of the forest, which is strange to you. To protect you from attack".

"Attack"? The two women had engaged in conversation at that point. I let it run its course.

Cassiti nodded, "The Kézőrös can bite, this has many complications (I knew full well about them), while the Zürepüé has been observed swooping down on the unsuspecting upon rarer occasion and always seem to go for the eyes".

Major Roxbrough & Nik Gehenna

Quianhua shuddered at the thought of having her sight damaged and then astonished me,

"Are you protection enough then? Should we not have a more substantial escort"?

"We would benefit from greater protection that is very true", the hot native girl admitted, "All the male braves are committed to helping the King of Valgral though, but I have sisters, cousins, even nieces who could join us if we went through our village"?

Quianhua glared at me as though it had been my suggestion, then said evenly,

"No nieces, I draw the line at that, maybe a cousin or sister or two. Lead us to the village, while I keep a close eye on the Visionary - here".

I understood the double entendre only too well. It may prove a feast for the eyes, our trip to the magical city, but that was the only desire I was going to have satisfied. While I strolled off to see how the alliance was progressing, The two women, who seemed to have established grudging mutual respect for one another, went to find more female escorts for myself and my spouse.

Hízlatan found me almost at once, which was no surprise. "You go north soon", he stated rather than asked, "As do we, the Valgraln are keen to subdue the rebellion and in return will leave our island, to return much later with payment for our aid".

"And what might that payment be like"? I found myself asking somewhat cynically,

"Weapons and a small amount of gold, which we will exchange for a consignment of Корунд".

It looked like the wily king had finally secured what he had come for in a roundabout way, good luck to him with his Корунд that was a bluer blue than the eyes of the goddess Shakita and that was very blue indeed. I was not much further into the conversation when a quartet of beauties seemed to be walking toward us. One was the wife, who was still very fetching despite our *bondage*! Another was Cassiti, in their company were the latest recruits, the standard was maintained!

Myrrorball

I was introduced to Cassiti's sister. The resemblance was easily discernable. Busty, beautiful - but rather stern-faced upon our first meeting. Her name was Tergiss. The other girl was called Kharnivool. A cousin who looked  even less delighted to be joining our company. It seemed that the Valgraln provided the young women with as great a distraction as I? They were not particularly overjoyed at being dragged away from them. In my case, there were several reasons why it was not going to happen, Quianhua not the least of them.

I made a hasty farewell to the Valgraln, something which took about twenty minutes. Then rejoined the rather serious group of young women

"Is everyone happy to come along, Cassiti"? I wanted to be reasonable.

"The men are leaving tomorrow anyway", Tergiss suddenly chirped, "And they are not Frosted Mortis Visionary".

"Who is to be protected but not molested", Quianhua added darkly.

Tergiss held her hands to her forehead, the customary sign of supplication. Kharnivool remained sullenly silent, which suited all of us as it was to turn out.

We finally managed to set off after all the preparation. I found myself wending through the undergrowth. I had never been so far north before, Quianhua certainly had not. It soon became necessary to carry Mr Choon. His six kilogrammes began to make my arms ache after about ten minutes. The silent Kharnivool approached, took the black and white cat out of my embrace, into her own. Still, she had said nothing, but she was helping, so I let her have the animal.

We stopped for lunch. What with my typing the short story, it was not long into our quest. Everyone was hungry though, eating heartily. The native girls had brought their fare. For we were unable to sample one another's as I had still not gotten around to testing everything. The reflection caused me to wonder when Hhrrhhoehhrrhooooingohh would make the first of his checks in on us. It would be amusing if he chose to do so while we were not there. I wonder what his reaction would be?

Filling their stomach's did not seem to make the new arrivals any happier. Tergiss could have been stunning had she smiled a few more times, while Kharnivool also had the potential to be pretty, if she could lighten up a bit. I suspected the two had been chosen by Quianhua and Cassiti as neither of them saw them as a threat. I being too closely kept under the watchful eye of my dear darling wife to be a naughty boy, behaved as was desired. I still did not know if I could catch some unpleasant microbes off any of the native girls. I realised  I had wasted my time somewhat at the bubble. Certain matters I should have given urgent attention to - I had completely ignored. Were our rations to become exhausted on either the trip outwards or its return, that would present us with a problem. My only consolation was that my morose Chinese partner had done even less. It did nothing to assuage a feeling of growing guilt though at the prospect of the imminent inspection from the HhhâäàåâäåäåçêçêçêïïïïïiggndgndÐñßɎþÞÝΔ.

Hhrrhhoehhrrhooooingohh & Hara-horahurrahaashume would ask,

"How're tricks then, Mucker, how's it hanging (or words to that effect)"? and I would be obliged to reply,

"I've done bugger all"!

When the attack came, therefore, I was very preoccupied, distracted, so I reacted accordingly – to wit – in slow motion. It was one of those Zürepüë swooping down toward us with malign intent in its reptilian eye. I had struggled to get the blazerifle from my shoulder to a firing position when two arrows whooshed into the air in unison, closely followed by a third. I never found out which of my bodyguards I should have admonished for tardiness, in all the confusion. The main thing was, the Zürepüé let out a horrible caw of pained astonishment and promptly plummeted to the ground into a seriously fatal heap. The crashing creature caused two others to come scurrying out of the blue-grass. This time I was the fastest. I burned the Kézőrös with one slightly splayed protracted blast. When I turned to see the native girls, they were even more ashen-faced than the wife. The blazerifle was something that filled them with trepidation Rightly as it should as well, it was an awesome weapon that I was glad none on Earth had ever had available to them. I suppose the closest thing would have been a flame thrower which was as dangerous to their users as to those who died horribly in their gouts of petroleum fuelled conflagrations. The stink for the three corpses – the blaze had spread to the dead reptile - was not an especially pleasing aroma and the five of us hurried away from it. No one spoke for the rest of that first day's light. Not a word. We created a camp as dusk threatened to suddenly plunge us into complete darkness. The canopy would never allow twilight.

Quianhua looked as exhausted as it is possible to be just before collapsing, she threw herself onto the ground, the minute we stopped hiking. I created a fire by carefully judicious use of my rifle. The natives began a stew, from various ingredients in their knapsacks. For me it was Nutrient and pineapple juice [according to the carton label and it tasted like it, to my taste-buds]. While Quianhua had fallen into an exhausted doze which I would not rouse her from except to lift her into a sleeping bag later. Our sleeping bags had a type of mesh outer cover which I suspected would protect us from Kézőrös' bites. The natives had no such convenience. They owned a woven blanket apiece, would sit-watch in rotation throughout the night.

Major Roxbrough & Nik Gehenna

I felt dirty, we had encountered no streams, in which, to wash. Even though I had been promised we would cross a river or two, in the course of our journey. So I did the best job I could with three sanitary wipes courtesy of the Zernoplatite bubble and then settled down into my bag after Tergiss had helped me with my spouse. I was just wondering if I could ever get comfortable on the mound of palms and grass packed under my bag when a doze claimed me. Before I could descend further into nice peaceful slumber a mortal scream rent the night. Waking us all with a start. Tergiss was instantly beside me,

"It's only a Kézőrös, being hunted by a Zürepüé, or an even bigger Kézőrös". She explained in a tone designed to put me at my ease, [as if?].

"They are cannibalistic"?

"Are not most animals"? Tergiss assumed a kneeling position. She seemed glad of the distraction from keeping watch. A boring duty, even at the best of times. I knew, from my service days.

"What about the races who live on Egszígør"? I asked, "They do not eat their enemies do they"?

"Legend has it that in ancient times it was the way", she admitted openly, "That was quite some time ago though. Although I only tell you that in confidence when describing the Kémerké and the Akerányó. The Benszülöt, I would not be at all astonished to discover that they still do it when needs must".

"And how close will we be going to their territory"? I asked reasonably.

Tergiss smiled, she had white teeth that glowed amber in the fire-light against her swarthy complexion. She was possessed of, a very pleasant smile.

"Why that is up to you, Visionary, you are the one who's knowledge is supposed to be our guide".

Great! I had no idea at that particular moment. Fortunately, I had my little pouch of snufz with me. I was not using it at that time, saving it for just such an occasion as when needing insight into the location of a magical city.

The girl offered,

Myrrorball

"In two more days if we keep making good progress we will pass east of the village of Acleegása. We can replenish our supplies there. The people are friendly to we of the Shad. Unless you would rather we keep a straiter line to the river"?

"The river"? I was not looking forward to having to cross any bodies of water, never having been a strong swimmer, "Is it deep – the river"?

"The Ganglo is shallow but has a strong current. I think it easier to get across then the Gilgolium though, which is calm but deep and which the Vízarapákellemetlen roam the depths of".

"Vízarapákellemetlen"? I echoed, dread beginning to rise within me, "What might they be"?

"They are like the fish but not fish, a lizard but not a lizard, they eat what they can get. They are long like snakes. They are nasty. A full-grown adult male can grow to a metre in length, they have a bite radius of...".

"I'm soo glad I asked".

"Your tone does not indicate sincerity", Tegis observed, then a lascivious expression came over her face, she observed,

"Your first-woman sleeps deeply tonight, Visionary"

"She does", I observed regretfully, "And I need to also otherwise I will be slowing you down tomorrow".

"You would sleep better if you were fully tired and satisfied, truly drained", she observed.

"I am all of those things Tergiss and wish you good night now", I hated myself for turning *it* down. What man would? It took me ages to get to sleep.

I awoke to a curious sound. A cawing issue that sliced through the rising steam of the early morning forest".

"What is that"? I asked the girl whose back was to me. It was Kharnivool, I expected no answer, but when she did speak, she had a rich contralto voice the like of which few women possess.

"The sound of the Œrdimahdá".

"Another type of animal"?

"A flightless bird. Birds that could fly are all gone, hunted by the Zürepüé, but the Œrdimahdá has a beak as large as the reptile. Talons that even Ghema could not make appear as anything other than wicked".

"Ghema"?

"Goddess of beauty. Our gods are not the gods of the Valgraln".

Of course, they would not be. Why did I not suspect that? More research for the Zernoplat, but would any of it be of interest to them. Like Earth before it Egszígør, or Nyjord as the Valgraln called it, it represented nothing more to them than real estate. I found that I was urgently desirous that you HhhâäàåâäääåçêçêçêîîĩĩĩggndgndÐñß¥þÞÝ⌂ would not be able to develop a gas that would kill the Kémerké? The Valgraln neither nor even the other races on the planet. I was rather morose at the thought that you eventually would.

Did you have the right? Where you not already guilty of mass genocide? I could not stop you though? Could I heckers-like, how futile to even hope I ever could. You'd chosen to save me, just only me plus Quianhua. You'd placed me into what represented nothing more to you than a zoo. A temporary one at that. I resented that. I didn't like the fate you had given me. Did I hate you, my saviours - it's fair to say I felt no warm fuzzy feelings for you? There again, you probably didn't like me that much either. If Tru-eti Varzslatoj was truly magical could it possibly contain something I could use to drive all you HhhâäàåâäääåçêçêçêîîĩĩĩggndgndÐñß¥þÞÝ⌂ from the shores of Egszígør forever?

[note to self - remove this section before submitting it to Hhrrhhoehhrrhooooingohh]

We breakfasted. Quianhua managing to tuck-away an impressive amount of rice, which we'd boiled up over the fire. Even though I tried to spice mine up a bit with chopped up scrambled egg, I could not then fry it. We only brought a wok, no oil, so I munched it quickly as I found it exceedingly bland. It amused me as we prepared to break camp how various members of the party snook off into the foliage one at a time to do what they needed to do. Then my guts told me I was going to have to do the same. Fortunately, Quinhua had insisted upon bringing two rolls of tissue, for the use of. Otherwise, I would have had to learn how to wipe my ass on leaves. The way the Chinese wife of mine guarded them against the notice of the natives though, one would have thought they were fashioned from gold! I reasoned as I walked that day, that it was time to find out what I knew, from what I *knew*. I started with, could we eat local food if it was cooked properly? The Œrdimahdá sounded like a large chicketurk. The local girls anticipated managing to kill one, claiming that its flesh was delicious. So I tried to meditate whilst on the march and kept asking myself the same question over and again, repeating it in my head like a mantra,

"Can we eat Œrdimahdá? Can we eat Œrdimahdá"?

I found that I could discern between actual knowledge, gained on Earth from what I had acquired beyond. That which I chose to term *Instinctual-Knowledge*, gained during the use of snufz. We had acclimatised to Egszígør. To the air, gravity, the airborne microbes. Eating Œrdimahdá would do us no more harm than when one first goes abroad, trying something one has never eaten before. In other words, the worst we could expect might be the squits for a few days. Not death though, unless very unlucky indeed. Armed with that morɜcl of comfort, I suggested that the native contingent of our party hunt for something that would make a right tasty supper. Their enthusiasm was infectious. They even wanted to press Mr Choon into service.

Major Roxbrough & Nik Gehenna

"He is feline. The game is avian. It should be something he leans toward naturally", Cassiti reasoned, so who was I to argue?

"Just keep him clear of the Kézőrös" I warned, "I think they might be more game than he could manage".

Indeed they would be", Tergiss agreed "Kellemetlen little swine".

"So that explained part of the Vízarapákellemetlen's name, it meant nasty in Kémerié.

What brought a smile of amusement to my countenance was the speed with which Mr Choon bounded off when carefully placed down onto the ground. He had not shown that turn of speed in... ever when I came to think about it. He was one cool cat, did not rush for anything or anyone. Already fifteen Earth years old, I suspected the lighter gravity, coupled with greater oxygen content would give him such a boost as meant he would live for an age yet. Quianhua looked at me and smiled,

"That's given them something to do, now then how are we going to entertain ourselves while they are gone"?

"If you're suggesting what I think You're suggesting then I don't think I've ever done it outdoors", I objected.

She chuckled, "Never *been on safari*? You don't know what you're missing. Come here, Husband"?

So I came and later on I came again.

42.

"I am not certain that you realise what your hand can do Úrrh – Warrior Lord of Akerányó Hersko". Himmelwhahu told him. "It is not a weapon. It has no powers of attack".

Hersko was crestfallen. He glanced down at the limb in question. The glimmering had subsided yet he instinctively felt, that with effort, he could soon bring it back. Up to the same level as it had been when first attached to his wrist. Now that the lambency had reduced it looked like it had been carved from ice. Or water that retained a shape, or green-mage-sand with the green hue removed from it. It had no colour, if held up to the sky, almost disappeared, was transparent.

"If I cannot use it to attack, then what use is it"?

43.

"We have wasted enough time with this simple village," Halsgough told the gathered nobles and their guards and warriors. "Were we in Valgral and this was a town, 'twould already be, fallen. Ransacked, the survivors enslaved or put to the sword".

"And the rape and pillage, Majesty", Tavaaro grinned, "Forget thee not how Sorpio used to love the rape in particular".

"The Blind Raven be gone", Halsgough barked, "He be no longer an asset to mine cause so best to forget him. Now, this village, Brohain, 'tis time to take it. We have been repulsed once, but not a second time. Keepeth shields raised against their arrows, which must be depleted somewhat, strike down any as resist. Our initial attack will be cruelly barbarous, only once the spirit goeth out of them will we begin to take prisoners, understood"?

The men nodded, one in the company of Kynoberg dared to point out,

"We are not as great in number as an invading army though, my Liege, if...".

He never finished his whining, Kynoberg cuffed him roughly about the jawline with a mailed gauntlet,

"Silence poltroonardly cur, they are but a bunch of naked savages, not armed men, thou will doeth as thy king directs and without miserable complaint".

"There", the king nodded, "That be an end to it, let us advance".

The warriors fanned out. To eat up the space between where they had been given their final instruction. Then onto the edge of the village. The first native they met was not expecting them. Unfortunately for the invaders though, he died noisily on the point of Teleocea's blade. At the betrayal of their position, the Western lords and their men broke into a controlled trot, one which they knew they could sustain until ending in the centre of the village. Several villagers got in their way in every instance it ended in their deaths. The Western Lords did not lose a man. A sudden rush of perhaps twenty natives then caused a pitched battle to ensue.

Rhynturo found himself faced with a tall brave carrying a stone-headed axe. He let the fool attack, the head of the stone weapon crashing against the boss of the steel escutcheon, then sliced the back of the warriors Achilles with his sword. The native grunted in pain yet did not cry out. The Western Lord admired his courage as his next thrust rammed into the fallen native's chest-bursting his heart. Halsgough still carried the lighted brand, even though it was daylight. He touched it to the first hut he reached, the beginning of the end arrived for the village of Brohain.

"Stop this", a voice they all recognised, suddenly issued before the advance, "These people are not thine enemy, they are the Akerányó. It was not they who attacked thee, that was a different tribe, the Benszülöt from across the mountains over to the west".

Halsgough stepped forward, "We will kill no more, and burn no more houses if thy and they surrender".

Hersko grinned grimly, "To what fate, Usurper".

Halsgough considered that, returned with his brand of reason.

"The men will be pressed into the service of the next ruler of Egszígør, myself. The women will be required to provide comfort for my brave men. Alas, thee will have to die, son of Flahé, for thou art guilty of several counts of sedition. If thou now layeth down thy pitiful arms though, I will make they end swift and painless, I swear as the new ruler of this Fire of Saah".

"Thou art not returning to Valgral"? Hersko looked mystified.

"The Zhirnublydok is gone, sunk after being set alight by thy native friends here. None of this land any longer have the means of navigating the бесконечный [Beskonechnyy] Ocean. We be here to stay, Hersko, though not thee of course - Little Lordling".

Myrrorball

From behind the Úrrh, another familiar figure then appeared, Halgough's features twisted in animous hatred,

"Gerner, so thou art lurking here under the protection of a callow youth, it will, alas, end badly for thee, I cannot make the same agreement with thee as I just offered him".

"Retreat and task us none more", the Scribe returned sadly, "We must all end our days on the Fire of Saah, thou hast nought else to fight for, Halsgough".

"On the contrary, I have an island empire to build. Once it be accomplished then I canst consider the other island of Far Side. For they might be in reach of canoes, or we may yet build another vessel".

"Another vessel", Hersko scoffed, "Without plans or carpenters". He then pulled the arm that had been behind his back and pointed it toward the frozen warriors. Frozen but only waiting for a word from the Western usurper and they would spring into deadly action. Halsgough, the Western usurper in question - gazed at Hersko's hand.

"So, Scribe, thou art capable of some wizardry after all. Thou has managed to assuage the perniciousness of the Kézőrös' bite. Although thy Lordling's hand now looks rather insubstantial. Like all thine potions the effect is less than completely satisfying".

"Twas none doing of mine, Usurper", Gerner countered, "The extremity thou seest pointing accusation at thee be the Vandei Motestas".

"Enough twaddle and hogwash", Halsgough then roared, stirring his men in readiness to continue their attack, "Dost thou yield now, or after many more be dead"?

Gerner said quietly given the situation which was rapidly becoming serious,

"I suggest the moment be upon us, Úrrh Hersko, do it now".

Before the astonished scrutiny of the gathered Western Lords, the young man with the hand that had no hue waved it about in some vague and random pass. Both he and the Scribe seemed to take on themselves a shimmering haze. Like an object on a summer day when the heat is rising from the hot ground. They continued to do so until they vanished from sight.

Halsgough was the first to regather his wits after a pause of several moments,

"Continue the attack, find them, bring them to me, subdued and bound", he demanded. The invaders advanced with yells of ired animosity. Halsgough waited, suspecting what might prove to be actual, fantastic as that would be. Koözoött returned firstly,

"The natives, My Lord, we found them gone"!

44.

"Where are we"? Sahbaj asked.

Gerner was cynical, "Not where we were. In a different place".

"I do not like it", the virázető complained, "It's unnatural, it fills me with trepidation, I mean look at the grass, it is not the right colour? Whoever saw grass that was not blue before".

"In Valgral", Hersko answered her gently, "The grass be green like this. A fine emerald carpet neath the feet of they as would run through it in joy and wonder".

"Is that where we are then", Sahbaj demanded, "Have you brought us to your realm, Úrrh"?

It was not the newly created warrior lord of Akerányó who answered her. He did not know the answer. So the Szorkráló stepped forward.

"Úrrh Hersko did not think of his domain, My Ruler, but took the advice I humbly offered him for his first use of the Vandei Motestas. He would not have been able to flex his new capability so far in just his first attempt".

Sahbaj turned to Himmelwhahu, "If not Valgral then where, Szorkráló"?

"This place is still Egszígør, my Virázető".

"How can that be the case", the virázető was beginning to lose her temper, "When the grass is green instead of blue, we cannot be where you claim"?

Myrrorball

"Let me explain"? Himmelwhahu began, "I suggest we return to these rather strange huts. Locate yours before I do so though, Virázető".

"How can one of them be mine? How can this be our village when the grass is green instead of blue? Look at the Avgófýllo? Fool, did you ever see brown trunks on them before? Green leaves instead of silver? Are the Avgófýllo like this in Valgral, Hersko"?

He shook his head, "We call them trees, Virázető. They look like trees, yet they still bear the fruit of the Avgófýllo, see the white petals with the yellow centre. No tree on Valgral ever looked as they. I humbly suggest we find somewhere to meet and listen to the Szorkráló".

He suggested it because he did not know where the Vandei Motestas had taken them any more than Sahbaj or for that matter, Gerner. So they wended their way through the tuft topped huts, created from strands of pale-coloured straw, rather than the palms which seemed absent where the village resided. On the way, they encountered many natives wandering about trying to find where their homes were too. One directed them eventually to the largest, the grandest. They knew they were approaching Sahbaj'. On the way, Gerner seemed to have located Nunne and the Blind Raven. Together the sextet entered the hut of the Virázető of the Akerányó.

"This is my place"! Sahbaj gasped, "Filled with everything I am familiar with, how can that possibly be"?

"Once I have a goblet of wine, I will tell you all I know", Himmelwhahu promised, the ruler clapped her hands, bringing retainers who saw to it that her desire was soon satisfied. By the time all of them were comfortable with refreshment available to them, the Szorkráló began. Where were are is actually Egszígør" he told them, "Just not our Egszígør. Have you ever held two mirrors pointing into one another so that they form myriad reflections? Like the myrrorball, but turned inward upon themselves, each image in the burnished metal getting smaller but proceeding on indefinitely. That is what we Szorkráló call the Zlátamvilájg or if you prefer myriad worlds. I see by your looks of incredulity that you find the notion fantastic. There was a time when I was a mere apprentice that I felt the same way. I thought there only one world, but it is not the case. Our world has reflections. The reflection of another Vandei Motestas, powered by the vitality of our Úrrh. It has enabled us to cross the barrier between one such, to another. That is where we now find ourselves".

"But which is the original"? Sahbaj sounded deeply shaken by the Szorkráló's revelation, "Which is the real world if we have been living on nothing more than a reflection"?

"Perhaps none of them", Himmelwhahu returned, "Or perhaps all of them, it rather depends upon one's point of view does it not"?

"No", Gerner argued, "What thou proposeth maketh none sense, one world must be *the* world"!

"Why"? Himmelwhahu asked simply, "You assume everything must have a source and by definition, therefore, an end too. If that is the case, tell me where the beginning of a circle is, where its end"?

A circle be only existing in two dimensions", Gerner was proud to show his knowledge, "Yet we exist in three: near and far, up and down, east and west".

"Then what of north and south", Himmelwhahu asked.

"Thou playeth with words for thy superior sport methinks, Isangoma", the Scribe grimaced, the only way north and south differ from near and far be syntactical".

"Very well then, let us examine the dimensions another way", Himmelwhahu reasoned, "What of the dimensions of yesterday and tomorrow, do we not exist in those? If we do, then we have four dimensions. Yet the reflections in the two in-turned mirrors have only three. The beginning, the real and original world existed perhaps yesterday, while the final reflection will not exist until tomorrow. Thusly when tomorrow arrives, it becomes today and the final reflection of tomorrow replaces the reflection existing in today. Similarly, the first world no longer exists in yesterday for yesterday has become the day before, the new original is, therefore, the one that replaces it. The word for this constantly changing reality is Œöröç in Akerányól. In Valgraln it is eternal".

Myrrorball

"Blasphemy"! The Blind Raven suddenly burst unbidden into the tutorial, "Only the gods are eternal, the isangoma should burn to the ground! Virázető, I demand to be the one to place the torch at the base of the kindling"?

"One moment", Himmelwhahu looked amused rather than irritated by the once lord of Sorpio's outburst and subsequent demand, "I will go to the stake right willingly if thou can answer me this - blind man. If only the gods are Œöröç, then where did they live when the world did not exist, if it too is not Œöröç"?

The Raven spluttered, "What dost thou mean, Isangoma? They lived above the world, that is common knowledge amongst the priests".

"How could there be an above if there was nothing beneath" Himmelwhahu wanted to know, "Is not the term above relative to space which is below it"?

"It was above the...", the Raven could not escape the illogical corner of the landscape of a conundruma that the smooth-tongued Szorkráló had painted him within.

Himmelwhahu then asked the others, "Why is a Raven like a writing desk"?

None could answer, nor ever would. None could remember where the question had originated, nor how olde it was, none ever would know that which was unknowable.

There were four answers:

'Because it can produce few notes, tho [sic] they are very flat; and it is nevar (backwards) put with the wrong end in front.

Because while one has flapping fits, the other fitting flaps.

Because one is apt for writing books, the other better for biting rooks.

Because a writing desk is a rest for pens, while a raven is a pest for wrens".

None of the company knew the answers. They thought Himmelwhahu was merely making a riddle for the blind man and at his expense.

It was Hersko who finally brought the conversation around to something more tangible and less ethereally abstract.

Major Roxbrough & Nik Gehenna

"Then we shouldst go exploring this new world and see if this Brohain be more or less suited to us. For if tis better than the reflection we left then surely tis a solid notion to stay here"?

"I will make that decision", Sahbaj replied determinedly.

45.

The natives returned whooping like Apaches (pronounced A-pash-ees) pleased with their kill. Their success at bagging two Œrdimahdá aided by the indomitable Mr Choon meant that Quianhua and I struggled to keep up with them that day. In the evening, gathered around another campfire courtesy of the blazerifle the smell of the rotisseried Œrdimahdá made all of us drool in anticipation.

"You'd better be right about this", Quianhua warned me. "If it turns out that the Œrdimahdá is poison to us and I wake up dead, then I'm going to kill you"! Chinese humour - inscrutable.

I had watched Cassiti pluck the two large fowl, Tergiss gut them and Khanivool search for a stick that would serve as a spit and not burn through before the roasted paltry were fully cooked. It was a class in how to survive in the wild.

When my bird came, I had insisted on breast, on a plate. The women tore into legs, there was just enough for each of them, but I had always been a breast man.

"We can reach the village of Acleegása tomorrow if you'll allow us to replenish our supplies", Cassiti told me with a mouth greasy with bird (don't go there).

"They cannot be, low at this point though, or do you seek to swell our number still further"?

"It would not hurt to have more in our company, considering what we may encounter. Also, I have distant family in the village, as has Tergiss and Kharnivool and we would be pleased to warn them about the threat of the Western Lords and the allegiance of the King and our virázető".

"'What we may encounter'? What are you anticipating"?

"Kézőrös, Blevastís, Zürepüé, Vízarapákellemetlen, the Western Lords".

"The Blevastís is surely no threat"?

"Most are not", the girl conceded, "But occasionally one of those with the fájdamütés can be lethal".

"I know I am going to regret asking this but what on Egszígør is a Blevastís with a fájdamütés".

A fájdamütés is an elongated limb on the end of which is a stinger. For reasons we Kémerké do not understand, every tenth or perhaps less often, Blevastís has one. If a fájdamütés stings you, then you turn into a Blevastís".

"So like nature to have a back-up system", I observed, "If a Kézőrös bite does not change you, then the fájdamütés will".

"A Kézőrös bite does not change you into a Blevastís", Cassiti observed with a frown. "True its bite can be very unpleasant and quite serious if in an unfortunate place (I did not ask) but it does not change one into a Blevastís"?

"It does the Valgraln", I then had information to impart to her, rather than it constantly occurring the other way around. "The Kémerké and other tribes indigenous to their island have built up an immunity over time to the toxin in the ground-animal. So the Blevastís has developed a secondary way of perpetuating themselves. Do you know what happens to the Blevastís after a certain adolescent period"?

The girl nodded, "They take root and become Avgófýllo".

I should have had a conversation with this girl a while ago I realised then. "I think what you are suggesting makes sense", I finally conceded, "Tell me this though, why is it so easy to recruit when I do not offer payment. If it's because you know me as The Visionary, then that allure will not exist for the Acleegása"?

"Acleegáás", she corrected almost absently, "A native of Acleegása is an Acleegáás".

"Got it. So what would the motivation be to join us"?

"Why adventure of course", she smiled, she had a lovely smile - very nice, "Life can be dull at times in the village. An endless rota of hunting cooking, cleaning, what we will be offering is a break from routine".

Major Roxbrough & Nik Gehenna

"Is that why Tergiss and Kharnivool enlisted into our happy little band".

A cloud crossed those handsome features, "Ah, no, that was not their desire at all".

I did not need to ask what was, the fact that I could not act upon it was beginning to make it tedious.

"We will do as you recommend then", I finally agreed, "We will take a small detour to include the village of Acleegása. I stretched the ache out of muscles I did not until that moment realise were protesting. I found myself drained, satiated and exhausted, slept the sleep of the dead that night. I don't mean the living dead. I slept like a corpse fresh in the crypt, cool, peaceful, beyond care - excellentio.

Dawn brought with it, more mist. The promise of yet another mildly pleasant day. I informed the others of our new route. All seemed pleased by it, even the wife. Perhaps she thought it might be interesting to meet yet more new natives. It was growing increasingly hot and humid as noon approached. When we were suddenly intercepted by male natives, who were clearly of the same racial group as the girls of Shad. It was a relief to have an escort into the centre of Acleegása. Of course, our first stop had to be a visit to see the virázető [leader, guide, chief, manager etcetera] and the right-hand woman to her, the Szorkráló [a cross between a sorcerer and medical person]. Both were female, both were physically lovely, but I was beginning to get used to attracting attractive females. Neither of them bore comparison with Cassiti. Neither Quianhua nor I had suffered any ill effects as a result of eating Œrdimahdá the night before, so when we were offered food and drink, I accepted both without reservation - big mistake! The local brew was called Llúglé. It had the aroma of rum, a kick like a mule and could lay out a corpse if one drank enough. We lost a day!

46.

Myrrorball

They decided to create a group of seven an Algonquin. Consisting of the: virázető, szorkráló, Scribe, Úrrh, Blind Raven and two of the most fearsome warriors in the tribe. The latter being a huge broad-chested native by the name of Nagiyat and a much slimmer, yet speedy guard to the virázető - Veekon. Both looked eminently capable and gave the non-native contingent confidence that they were relatively safe. They had barely gone a few hundred metres in a direction determined by Hersko when they heard the sound of sawing and hammering. Curiously they wended their way toward the mysterious construction. Two guards suddenly bared their way, demanding to know who they were, what they were about, they spoke in the local tongue. It was easy enough to understand their words and their duty.

Sahbaj stepped forward. With certain grandeur she told them who she was, little expecting the reaction her proclamation received.

"Sahbaj The Mysterious, returned to us", noted one of the guards, "Tell me Majesty have you taken up residence in the abandoned town"?

"Abandoned town"? the virázető echoed.

"Olde-Brohain, which has lain empty since you mysteriously disappeared decades in the past".

Gerner wished to know, "If the abandoned town be now called Olde-Brohain, where be thee from, warrior-guard"?

The guard pointed vaguely behind him, returning honestly,

"Why Brohain-Minor of course. I've lived there all my life".

"Let us pass"? Sahbaj demanded then, "I want to see you building your new town".

The warrior's features creased in a misunderstanding at that, he returned,

"The town was finished long ago, Majesty, before I was born".

"Then what be the sound of construction that fills our ears with its clamour", the Warrior Lord of Akerányó wished to know.

The two guards exchanged an incredulous look, then the one who had done all the talking thus far told them,

Major Roxbrough & Nik Gehenna

"It's the tower that you started and never finished due to your disappearance, Majesty. We have since renamed it, *The Tower That Ate People*, due to the various disasters".

"Take me to inspect it", the lovely virázető commanded. She found herself escorted toward the noise.

"What be the reason for the nomenclature"? Hersko asked as they entered the clearing. Beyond was a tall wooden tower, stretching precariously up into the sky. Behind the at best rickety construction a town that mirrored Brohain. At the arrival of the party, all construction abruptly ceased. Several workers gradually gathered around the Algonquin.

Finally, Hersko got his answer,

"The tower has been responsible for several deaths over the last few years, it eats the living. Not literally of course, but eats them it does".

"What be the reason for it"? Gerner enquired. It was Sahbaj who answered,

"Why to reach Sholdistan, of course, to bask in her shadow on her blue domain".

"Sholdistan"? Hersko was naturally lost. The Scribe explained quickly,

"Sholdistan be Akerányól for Shandor, who created Brahma. They are attempting to reach her".

"But...", Hersko was waved to silence by his scribe, who knew better than to argue over matters of superstition. The Scribe knew well enough that the distance was too great to reach in such a crudely pathetic way, but the Akerányó were allowed their beliefs and dreams.

"May I approach", the Scribe asked of the gathered throng. They parted like a spring tide before him. Allowing him to go much closer to the precariously balanced, unstable structure. In the absence of iron or steel, there was no recourse to nails, so the tower was constructed by the carpenters, furniture makers, shipbuilders, cabinetmakers, joining pieces of wood together. Wood glue had seen employment (animal-hide glue), but that was not enough to ensure solidity. Glue alone would never hold the huge wood poles at the base of the tower. Therefore, mechanical fastening had been utilised to give the finished piece - strength. The answer to that problem was the same as had been used for centuries - pegged construction. Pegs or round wooden dowels had been passed through the joints in boards, providing a 'bridge' of strength between the two pieces while helping to hold them together. Depending upon the design of each particular piece, pegs had been employed in conjunction with other joining techniques like glue or a mortise and tenon. Higher up the sides of the tower increased strength with rope and some canvas shielding from the wind. Therein lay the difficulty though. It also made the tower heavier at the top than at its well-founded base. It was easy to see what would happen once it became windy, the tower would pull itself down under its mass, little wonder it had eaten people.

"How many towers have you built", Sahbaj asked the gathered workers of timber. A timber inci-dentally that would not have been available in the reflection from which they had come. Frond bows would never have had the integrity necessary to create a tower half the height, being too lightweight and too flexible by far. The guard who had initially spoken to them seemed to have become their spokesman. He answered on behalf of the workers

"Why, we are still working on this one, Majesty, so the answer is - one".

Major Roxbrough & Nik Gehenna

"Her Majesty means how many times hast this structure failed and had to be started anew, from the wreckage of the previous endeavour".

"Ah, I see, this tower has seen twenty-two attempts before it - to reach Sholdistan".

The Tower that Ate People was the twenty-third. There would doubtless be many after it, for what they were attempting was not physically possible.

"I think it might be time to meet your virázető", Sahbaj murmured then, the answer she received surprised her,

"You are our virázető, Majesty, only the Szorkráló Iglenedes rules in your absence".

Vandeveble

A Szorkráló who would not recognise the young virázető, but would remember her grandmother.

47.

Imagine the biggest headache you've ever had in your life. Then double it, that was how bad my head hurt after Llúglé-frenzy. Inside my cranium, an evil little gremlin was kicking something soft cuddly, like a house-brick. It kept crashing into my brain. I had to tilt my head at one point because it knocked it out of whack and it took me several tries to get it back into its recess. When I rushed out of the hut to throw up in such a way as kept my considerable dignity intact, it banged like a nozkavardé! I had to pick my eyeballs up - after dusting them off slip them back into the pain-drenched sockets. I would never-ever-ever drink spirits again - at least not until the next time anyway. Going back into the less pain-soaked shade I found Cassiti, the little moggy looked as bright and chipper as always, the rotten mare.

"What is wrong with you"? she inquired, "You are not ill, are you, Visionary"?

"I am guilty of over-imbibing", I readily admitted, "But I do not deserve the resultant punishment, none deserve the pain and the bitter taste I am currently experiencing. How has the recruitment gone"?

"I have enlisted the joining of four male warriors to accompany us to our destination", she told me. "You should come and join me in greeting them before we set off into the forest". I did not want to. So I did. That will teach me to overindulge. I was more than fully prepared to punish myself.

Thirty minutes later, according to the gold Casio that still resided on my left wrist, even though it needed constant adjusting, I was introduced to four strapping young fellows. They went by the names of, Vandeveble, Chavayda, Mesoloras and Collari. The first of these was the impressively muscular and rather severe looking Vandeveble. I had confidence that he could tackle just about anything we encountered on our expedition. Chavayda was considerably senior to him. Though less vital, just as strong, able to offer sage counsel, additionally.

Mesoloras fit in between the two. Younger than Chavayda, not as strong as Vandeveble, but said to be a keen shot with a bow, a worthy addition to our troupe. I liked the look of him, as serious as the others but in his eye a little twinkle which hinted at better humour, improved mien. The last of the quartet, Collari was the hardest to read of them all. Had I not been told he was a warrior, I would have thought of him as a Szorkráló. He had that mysterious look about him. He was getting toward the mature age of his life expectancy too. Perhaps the older duo thought to find something in Tru-eti Varzslatoj that might turn the clock back on their ageing process, who knew? The girls seemed glad to have all four of them along though, so I had no objections and a group of ten, we were now a decad if one included Mr Choon, had much more chance of surviving adversity than a smaller number of mainly - females. The women I noticed, spoke less on that first morning, as we proceeded northward once again. It seemed they had genuine respect for their male cousins. I certainly had no objection to quiet females and found the quartet to be good company in varying degrees.

I found there was something about Collari that I could not quite put my finger on. I did not think I would ever put my life in his hands. In that respect, I had no doubts about Vandeveble or Mesoloras, as for Chavayda I thought he might be slower, certainly weaker. Collari remained the mystery, so it was he I sought to walk with him, to question him.

"Tell me Collari", I began logically enough, "Why did you desire to come with us on this quest, what is it in Tru-eti Varzslatoj that you desire to find"?

"I could ask you the same question, Man-from-Far", he returned unhelpfully, "What do you search for"?

"I asked you firstly. Perhaps I will give you my answer once I have heard yours"?

"I do not know what I seek. Perhaps I will when I find it. My journey is one of hope, not having all the answers. I do not have enough. Maybe in the Tru-eti Varzslatoj, I will find some of them. Fundamental questions, like why are we on the world, are the gods malign or benign, what do we have once this life is over? Are your questions greatly different"?

I looked at Collari with different respectfulnessity when I had heard him talk. He was a thinker at least. His existence was so much simpler than mine, yet my questions were just as simple, I told him so. Leaving out the fact that I had the distinct impression that my world was very possibly the creation of an authors mind, which he would not have understood anyway. I could not rid myself of the notion that the name Roxbrough was inexplicably pivotal in everything that was happening. Yet I had cheerfully left the Császária with his King. In a subsequent battle, he might very well perish. I could have told Collari that the more one knew, one only realised how little one knew. Yet I doubted he was capable of appreciating such paradoxical thinking. The irony of it was, that up until a few short days ago in real terms, I would have been guilty of such septicemic myself. So we continued on our way, shooting the breeze, as the saying goes.

48.

"It is going to topple over it will come crashing down. Some of the workers in the timber will be hurt possibly even killed", Iglenedes agreed.

"Then there is no point to it", Himmelwhahu sounded angry, "Why would you allow them to continue working on it, when you know it will fail, will always fail".

"How would you have me explain it to them", his reflection asked. "Would you have me crush their faith, tell them there is no such god as Sholdistan. That it is futile to try and reach her"?

"Of course not", Himmelwhahu conceded, "Without faith, we are as the beasts of the field, the plants of the forest. We live, we continue, we reproduce, but without purpose. Faith is the only thing which makes this world seem real. The promise that it will lead to something better, in the presence of divine beings".

"Then how should I shatter their delusion, or is it an illusion? Perhaps the day may come when we can reach up into the sky, reach the blue moon goddess and meet her"?

"That would be magical. The whole tribe would have to be mages".

"Or more knowledgeable. Yet if this tower was duly abandoned they would not be building on past attempts, they would not have the *foundation* of progress".

"It seems a high price to pay for memory. For some to die prematurely so that in generations to come more advanced than us can do what we only dream of doing".

"The stories of the Tower that Ate People will endure, because of the cost in material and lives. Only through struggle will progress be maintained. Take away the need to struggle against the seemingly insurmountable, then the result is contentment. That breeds stagnation, we become like the Kézőrös and the Avgófýllo existing only to exist. No, my reflected friend, I accept that you have been on the other side of the barrier, you must accept the tower. Let the tower fall and stay fallen. The ultimate result will be the loss of the Vandei Motestas' facility too".

"I do not see how one equates to the other, but I accept that you believe it to be the case", Himmelwhahu admitted, "But you must know that this virázető is not the one who left this realm years ago, nor the descendant of one".

"It makes no difference". Iglenedes returned, "The tower is what it is. It is hers".

The group slept in the one building that night, for safety, though they had no idea safety against who or what. The following morning Hersko and Gerner took a pleasant walk toward the tower. Even as they approached, the sound of urgent activity reached their ears. The sound of sawing - pegs being hammered home, winches hauling bulky bundles of planking dangerously high into the sky. There was a southern wind gusting quite briskly across the island when the duo reached the site it was to see the Tower that Ate People swaying quite significantly.

Gerner predicted, "It will be down by evening unless the wind drops. They wouldst need far more material in it than that, to make the base truly massive, if they ever hopeth to make it stable enough to gain more height".

"Even then wouldst it fall short of the objective"? the Úrrh desired to know.

"By my math tis not even one-eighth of the way to Brahma", the scribe predicted confidently. It was confidence ridiculously inaccurate. The highest the tower had ever reached before tumbling back to the ground was 85.4 metres while Brahma was 384 million metres from Iysador or Nyjord or Egszígør, dependent upon who one asked.

The winch that the Akerányól were using was straining and squeaking as a team of muscular braves hauled on the rope that slowly sent the bundle higher, then still higher.

"It giveth them a purpose", Gerner observed sardonically.

"Aye, but an futile one", Hersko underlined, "Tell me scribe, shouldst we stay here or move to another plain in the myriad of reflections".

"We are under no threat here, twould be senseless to rush a decision in either way. The virázető seemeth content to stay, so we are under no duress. Dost thou ask because thou wishes to aid Vasnaar"?

"We do seem to have abandoned him".

"Yet without the Zhirnublydok we are forced to make the Fire of Saah our home, the only question be which island. I believe the King would understand our position, not expect us to reach him. Especially thee, Warrior Lord of Akerányó. Whence last he knew of thee thou was in danger of becoming a blue-mumbly. Now thou hast responsibility to Himmelwhahu and his people, be that not so"?

Hersko nodded, satisfied that he had asked the right questions. The duo fell into silence for a time, simply watching the futile endeavours of the carpenters and their highly unstable construction.

49.

"How long for exactly"? Halsgough demanded. Kyper Tor shrugged before replying,

"Tis impossible to be precise in matters of this nature, My Lord, but I would hazard more than just today".

"And they shadow our progress"? Kyper Tor nodded.

Very well, we shall not wait for an attack, but take the initiative", the Usurper declared. "Halsia, on the morrow thous shalt continue on our present course but with only thy guard, the rest of us will double back, swing around, then attack them from the rear. I advise thee all to use caution and courage, men. These are not the mild-mannered Akerányól that we wouldst have easily enslaved, were it not for a vile, traitorous son-of-a-dog Hersko. These are the more warlike and adept Benszülöt. Do not underestimate their prowess in battle".

"They will be no match for a trained warrior armed with good Valgraln steel", Lord Drably declared confidently. It turned out his rash-bravado was the undoing of him. He was the first of the assembled Western Lords to die, his brains dashed out by a stone-headed axe.

The battle was ferocious, bloody. The Western Lords wore armour though, carried weapons of steel, yet the Benszülöt were swifter and more agile for not having anybody armour. Drably fell in the vanguard quickly replaced by Lord Gral. The latter carried the morning stars in place of a sword and from behind his shield, he rained down blows on any who dared to oppose him. Each time the terrible barbed club of iron thrust outward, Benszülöt fell with blood crushed skulls or hideously fatal injuries to bodies and extremities. It became obvious to the general of the Benszülöt, that the Lord who was meting out such a heavy toll on his braves, had to be disposed of quickly. With no further loss to his forces either. He directed every one of his archers to aim for the well-protected dealer-of-agonised-death. Well drilled, the archers fired almost as

Myrrorball

one. Several barbs rattled ineffectually against Gral's raised shield, two of the others were deflected by his armour. To make it flexible, it had to have joints, that was its ultimate weakness. One arrow avoided the Lord's cuisse, landing in his thigh, piercing a blood vessel. Another struck just above Gral's vambrace, rendered him harmless, for his morning stars fell from nerveless fingers. Not that he had much time to mourn its loss. A stone-headed axe immediately found its way over the top of his escutcheon, tore his eye from his head. As he fell a second blow took off the back of his helm and skull beneath. He fell dead into the gory blue and scarlet undergrowth.

It began to look as though the Benszülöt would win the day, take a terrible toll of the numerically inferior lords of Valgral...until Banustib earned his pay for the rest of Halsgough's lifetime. The Benszülöt were forcing the Western Lords into a grudging retreat when they were momentarily distracted by the swooshing chitinous sound overhead. From out of a sky that would have been dark with them, were not the canopy obscuring their view, the Zürepüé plunged. Heedless of the frond palm-leaves in their way they launched themselves at the Benszülöt. They snapped with razor-sharp beaks, raked with equally deadly talons. The Benszülöt panicked, as well they might. Distracted, those who were not killed directly by the avian threat were easy pickings for Halsgough's revitalized men. The enemy was driven back into the forest with heavy losses. Once achieved, the Zürepüé immediately took to the air once more, in an instant were back in the realm from whence they had come.

Major Roxbrough & Nik Gehenna

The Benszülöt had received a bitter lesson, at grave cost to Halsgough's remaining Lords though. His force had been weakened. He could not help but wonder if he still commanded sufficient armed men to be able to overcome the admittedly less warlike King with his more reasonable compliment?

50.

The thing I need to impress upon you Hhrrhhoehhrr-hooooingohh & Harahorahurrahaashume is the strangely alien beauty of Egszígør. Now I know what you did to Anglesey in my novel. Although it turned out to be your minds that were directing my fingers, the digits in question were undoubtedly mine. I proof-read and edited what you had made me type. So I know what you do to terrain given free rein. You strip it down to the bare bedrock, turning it into an expanse of flat grey desert. Where is the beauty in that? Unless one finds an austere attractiveness in a stark, barren flat land with no features of any note? I imagine the whole of Dweeb is like that. The only living creatures left alive on a bare ball of rock being the Hhhâäàåâäåäåçêçêçêîíîïïîîïggndg-ndÐñß¥þÞÝ∆ undulating across its featureless surface. The Zernoplat the reaper of whole worlds, the beings who ultimately lay waste to...everything. Have you the right? Have you the right to exist to perpetuate at the expense of every other living creature in the galaxy? What will you do once you have filled the Galaxy with cold featureless worlds covered on every available metre with clear, cool cytoplasm? Will you move on to the next one and then again? Is that to be the end of the universe when all is Zernoplatite?

Myrrorball

Back to Egszígør. It is a land filled with wondrous attractiveness. Once one grows accustomed to azure grass. The Avgófýllo is the main feature of this comely scene, with their cerulean fronds, their glittering argent foliage in the shape of tiny palms. They give the light that reached the ground, cool tone, but they are beautiful. Even if they do cut out the face of Angelus most of the time. Added to this are the wondrously bleached domes of the Agarispo – white mushrooms [Agaricus bisporus] that proliferate the ground although the Kézőrös seem to devour them with relish. I suppose the Zürepüé keep the monkey-rat-marmoset-like creatures in check sufficiently to allow the survival of the fungi.

I followed the others as they wended their way through the lovely forest and the quote drifted into my head,

"'Mielőtkézőrös megharapolna, Kémerké voltafertő zéstaren dszerbönve, ésngem késztetve", then the strains of a sublime melody drifted through the fronds and to my ears. So canorous was it that I was instantly frozen into a statue of appreciation and delight,

"What is that euphonious harmonic"? I asked Chavayda, who happened by chance to be closest to me at that particular moment.

"We approach musicalium", he began, as though that was explanation enough. Realising his error, he added, "musicalium is the village in Egszígør where the musicaliuvista live".

"The musicaliuvista [note to Hhrrhhoehhrrhooooingohh - the 'm' is always lower case, the musicaliuvista of musicalium are modest above all other considerations]"? I asked.

Chavayda added, "They are the tribe on this place, they create the dulcet, the concordant for the pleasure of all other tribes. Come, we approach them, they are playing the simple pleasure of it right now. When

Major Roxbrough & Nik Gehenna

they meet us though they will push themselves to even greater heights of resonant conception.

I let the others lead me, mesmerized by the symphonious strains caressing my ears. There were the musicaliuvista, each one playing a different instrument. I suspect that the HhhâäàåâääåçêçêçêïïìïìïggndgndÐñß¥þÞÝ⌂ have no music (at least I did not write any into the novel so I presume that creatures without ears would have little or no need for it). Let me describe each of the seven instruments that were being so adeptly employed to create the miraculous refrains.

The first was a blown tube of hollowed-out wood that I would liken most to a clarinet. I learned later that the local name for it was the százél. The százél was from a family of woodwind instruments. It had a single-reed mouthpiece, a straight, cylindrical tube with an almost cylindrical bore, and a flared bell. A person who played such an instrument was called a *százélist*. Where the harmonics of the composition were close enough together to produce scales of adjacent notes as opposed to the gapped scales or arpeggios of the lower register. The parts that required virtuosity were known by the term *százé*. Which, in turn, came to apply to the instrument itself. It was, therefore, the *százélist* that helped themselves by playing particularly difficult passages on the instrument.

Accompanying and complementing the melody of the százél was a wooden űszlóda A wooden flute-like pipe played sideways in a similar fashion to the modern metal instrument I was more accustomed too. The űszlóda was an aerophone - a reedless wind instrument that produced its sound from the flow of air across an opening. By varying the air pressure an űszlódang [player of the űszlóda] could also change the pitch. Causing the air in the flute to resonate at a harmonic, rather than the fundamental frequency, without opening or closing any of the holes.

The sound the two made together was ethereal and faintly angelic. Above the two of them playing an octave higher was a third and final woodwind, the diminutive oktáva. The composer of the lilting piece had doubled the űszlóda part, adding sparkle and brilliance to the overall sound because of the aforementioned one-octave transposition upwards. The player of an oktáva was an oktávanaran.

This delightful trio was then complimented by the lushness of strings. The most easily recognisable instrument of all those being utilised by the musicaliuvista was the rather primitive but obvious three-stringed hárohúro. The local version of the violin, but not played under the neck but in the crook of the arm, the one doing the fingering, while the bow sawed away on the rather thick strings. It sounded to my ears like a deep-noted violin or a high-noted viola. The hárohúrost [hárohúro player} was making very mellifluous notes from it indeed, underlying the woodwind to superb effect.

Major Roxbrough & Nik Gehenna

The instrument itself was a skilled piece of work created from contrasting hues of wood that shone back the light

with the layer of varnish that had been patiently applied to it. A series of accompanying chords were underlying the melody. This was due to the next musicaliuvista who was playing what looked like a three-stringed guitar, or lute.

Called a terjhárohúro, the terjhárost player plucked the strings of the unfretted instrument which also had a neck, a deep round back enclosing a hollow cavity, with sound holes in its body. Its strings ran in a plane parallel to the sound table, attached to pegs or posts at the end of the neck, which had the usual turning mechanism to enable the player to tighten the tension on them. The terjhárohúro was plucked or strummed with one hand while the other hand '*fretted*' on the neck's fingerboard.

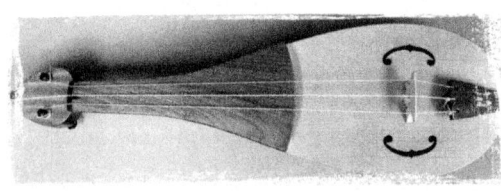

The final chords beneath all others were coming from the penultimate musicaliuvista squeezing and pulling apart a gomdoza. The gomdoza was Unisonic, meaning that each button produced only one note, whether pushing or pulling the bellows. It could be freely played in any key, usually with identical fingering patterns.

Myrrorball

Beneath all six instruments which were making such a relaxing and seductive sound was the simplest of drums keeping the rhythm. A taught skin stretched over a wooden enclosure, tapped by the fingernails of the ütésona, which was the name of a musicaliuvista who played the ütéso.

We reached the musicaliuvista, who were all female, to  my surprise, though why it was unexpected, I cannot honestly say. They smiled at us and continued to play to the end of the piece. I learned then that a group of seven was collectively called a hétész - seven musicaliuvista from musicalium. I began to clap, something none of them had experienced before, but they understood the intent behind the gesture and smiled, inviting us to lunch at their village. I have always wanted to be able to play a musical instrument and wondered then if my newfound knowledge thanks to the snufz would include such a bestowed skill. As I followed the musicaliuvista, I did find that after borrowing each in turn from the friendly natives, that I could be  an accomplished ütésona. It was not going to be the most fantastic revelation of the day. Something was to happen that would stretch even my imagination to the utmost bounds of credibility.

Together all seventeen of us went back to the village known as musicalium. At the centre was the strangest structure, next to the Zernoplatite bubble - that I had seen on the island. It looked not unlike an old World War II concrete bunker in construction and configuration.

Major Roxbrough & Nik Gehenna

Several things impressed me about it. One that I doubted the musicaliuvista had worked out how to make concrete and secondly the strange, seemingly random markings etched into the conglomerate before it had set. The natives seemed to pay it little heed. Why would they, it must have been in their village for a very long time, judging by the layers of dirt and moss that covered its crown? It had no business to be on Egszígør though. I was forced to wonder how many times you had visited this planet Hhrrhhoehhrrhooooingohh and if you had conveyed the whole story to me?

We were conducted to a specific hut, the construction of which was far more complicated than anything the Kémerké possessed. Timber formed the walls and overlapped for much better thermal properties and waterproofing. The Kémerké merely filled the abutment gaps between planks with a mixture of mud plus more dubious adhesive mixture. We were led to the most splendid, once there met someone called the Composer. In the village of musicalium, the Composer was treat like an Emperor.

At first, nothing extraordinary took place. We were given pork, fried agarispo, roast œrdimahdá and some sweet tubers, not unlike potatoes that the natives called arulis. Afterwards - was fruit, which was very similar to mangoes, but the greatest of shocks was the beverage. With considerable ceremony, accompanied by a singularly special tune played as the native brought it in on a tray were several cans of a carbonated energy drink called Orang-U-Can! Industrial technology required to produce such a drink was way beyond what the locals of

Egszígør could command. Both contents and can itself. It was also a play on English wording and describing a creature that I doubted existed on the planet. How could it possibly have existence, in the world we inhabited? It also contained instruction on the can which would be nonsensical to the natives and proclaimed a measurement that they would not comprehend either. It was a startlingly orange hue while two of the letters were in royal blue. I had not heard of the energy drink which I tasted. I found it to be similar to most others, particularly sweet, with a specific taurinean aftertaste. Curiously it had no hint of orange in its flavour, but then I presumed the company produced a selection of soft drinks, one of which, would have. It had no place existing on a world that had reached no further forward in civilized progression than the Gothic period. I asked the Composer about it, he explained,

"We still have several cartons of this almost magical elixir, which we reserve for special occasions, this seemed to be one such as that. We welcome you to musicalium".

"But where do you get them from"? I asked, "You must know that the technology required to produce such a product is beyond any on this island"?

"I have not heard the word teck-knowledgey", he admitted. Stumbling over its alien sound to his ears, "But if I understand your meaning then you are right. We cannot create the wondrous beverage. We are simply the custodians of the ever-dwindling supply".

"Where did you find this caché"? I asked

"In the *Fortress* of course".

"The Fortress"?

"You must have seen it on the way into my humble abode, it dominates the village, lying as it does directly in the centre of it"?

"You mean The Bunker? The concrete structure? That is where the pop is found"?

"Bunker? Pop? I have no knowledge of these words, Visionary"?

Cassiti had introduced me with great pomp. Just before we had been invited to dine with the purveyors of pleasant melodies.

Major Roxbrough & Nik Gehenna

"Is it a sacred place to you"? I asked him then, "Or would I be permitted to take a look inside".

"It will be my pleasure to *conduct* you on a brief tour, but only you will be allowed inside, Visionary", the Composer told me then with a certain amount of observed irony in his pun. The others looked a tad disappointed but accepted my status as the Visionary. After having a brand lit for him and then a second for me to hold, we entered the bunker after a huge stone was rolled out of the way by three strapping male musicaliuvista. The action caused fresh images to spring into my mind - Lazarus rising from the grave, the tomb of Judah Ben-Joseph being discovered robbed - by the two Mary's. Then I found myself smiling for according to my ever faithful Casio it was Friday, April 10$^{th.}$

Good Friday on Earth, an Earth that the Jewish prophet had given his life - to save all mankind. Only to see it ravaged and ruined by the HhhâäàåâääçêçêçêïïïïïïggndgndÐñßҰþÞÝ⚠. There again perhaps the HhhâäàåâääçêçêçêïïïïïïggndgndÐñßҰþÞÝ⚠ would have their superstition? There own HhrrhurrashubenWhaahooarÐñßҰþÞÝ⚠ who had been nailed to a granite block for acts of sedition? I somehow doubted that Hhrrhhoehhrrhooooingohh, being as you had no hands nor feet nor any discernible extremities through which, to drive any form of attachment.

How many Zernoplat does it take to change a light bulb?

None, the Zernoplat see in a completely different way to stereoscopically equipped creatures. They do not have the fingers to put the light bulb into its bayonet fitting anyway.

The tallow illumination of the torches we carried caused chiaroscuro shadows to dance, shimmering on the lithic

Myrrorball

walls of the place. I have to admit to being excited in an anticipatory way. What on Egszígør was I going to find apart from a carbonated energy drink? How in the cosmos had it gotten onto this strange world?

The interior was lined with row after row of shelves and benches. It looked like it had originally been constructed for scientific research rather than some military usage. I walked over to the items thick with dusk, laced all together with heavy grey webs of what could only have been an arachnid.

"May I touch things, Composer"? My enquiry did not exactly echo, but the ambience of the circular enclosure was very live. Why would it not be? The walls were nothing more than whitewashed concrete. A cooly unyielding surface which absorbed few sound waves.

When I was permitted to delve, I did so eagerly. A voice from outside called into me later,

"Visionary, are we staying in this village overnight? Because if we aren't, then we should make use of the rest of the day's light".

It was Cassiti, I glanced at my Casio and pressed the little button that would illuminate its face, I had been in the bunker two solid hours!

"Staying overnight"? I returned, unable, or rather unwilling to leave the treasure that was inside the concrete construction. I had already explored the following:

Chemicals in row upon row resting in wooden racks and sealed with rubber bungs, a spirit burner and an array of various glass containers to do experiments. Evidence of live eggs, seeds ready to be germinated, then... who knew what had happened to the ones that had sprouted? Stacks of recorded media in the form of open magnetic tape, some digital medium in the form of memory sticks. Amplification, valve-driven, devices for reading the sticks, playing the tapes. Several pairs of loudspeakers, the sort using magnets to reproduce sound-waves. Stacked tins of Orang-U-Can, the company producing all manner of foodstuffs and drinks, the musicaliuvista had barely scratched the surface of the supplies. A generator, fuel for it, secondary units for everything including components in the event of the first failing. i-pads, a tower PC with monitor, keyboard, mouse.

Those were the items I could recognise. Added to that treasure trove was:

Bottles of fluid with names I could barely pronounce like isoproprylalcoC_3H_8O(C_3H_7OH, $CH_3CHOHCH_3$, (CH_3)-$2CHOH$) very catchy, ligandC_{23} H_{22} F_3 N_3 O_2 and NaClOsodichlorgen, another winner. Hundreds of sticks of various shapes, fittings, boxes sealed in strange plastic that I had not the time to open. Tools, spanners, pliers, a hammer. Others which seemed to be electrical of nature, the use of which I could not imagine, two soldering irons, files containing thin sheets of neither paper nor metal yet also seemed to be like both. Metallic zip-sealing packets in bright blue with no writing or indications of usage on the outside. Strange little clamps, packs of ciggies that looked like they had a lighting mechanism of their own on one end.

It was like being in Ali the Muselmänner' cavern with all that he could have wanted, which characterized Sunnite orthodoxy, i.e. the idea that there are no such things as causality but that god performed every occurrence in the world, meaning that everything including men and even HhhâäàåâäåçêçêçêîïìïïìïggndgndÐñß¥þÞÝ⌂ simply undergoes the workings of god and do not act on their own. I presumed fate, or abandonment had declared the Moirai of the Bunker.

I finally ceased my investigation of the place when my torch guttered out plunging both of us into pitch blackness. The Composer's brand had already become exhausted. I had not noticed, while outside, something I had become oblivious too, it had grown dark.

The Bunker had forced me to one inevitable conclusion - Quianhua and I were not the only humans ever to set foot on Egszígør. The controls of some of the equipment had been etched in English with variations, the graphics being like:

THAT WAS THE WAY MOST PIECES OF EQUIPMENT HAD BEEN ETCHED, SOME OF THE PACKAGES LABELLED

Myrrorball

What was impossible was actual. Men, from Earth, had been on this world, before us. How? The technology to cross vast expanses of space did not exist in 2020. The only vagrancy that did have the capability was the Zernoplat. It seemed Quianhua and I were not the only exhibits to have been imprisoned into their little menagerie. There was another theory, I hesitated to entertain it, but it was there in my mind, the men who had reached Egszígør were from my future. In some bizarre way, they had travelled space. Been warped backwards through the fourth dimension to arrive on the world ahead of the two of us. If that was the case, then how did they exist? Had not the Zernoplat wiped them all out? That led me inexorably to theory number three, parallel worlds, the reflections of a mirror, the ball of the multiverse. Quianhua and I were humans from one layer of the multiverse. While the men who had landed on Egszígør centuries in the past were from an Earth that was vastly in advance of ours. One in which Catholicism had not held back scientific progress a thousand years. In other words, one in which Judah Ben-Joseph had never become the Saviour and Paul the first pope. The cosmos was like a mirror ball, each reflecting section another version of the collective whole.

My head was spinning with conjecture as the Composer led me outside. The very individual I met waiting for us was the one who could only serve to make me even more confused!

"Mister Genks"! I gasped as the manbian observed me with his disconcerting globular eyes, "It's a pleasure to see you, Sir, but do you mind if I ask you what you are doing here"?

"I ruthed ahead to make thertain you and the otherth are all right", the being who was half-man half amphibian lisped with his impossibly long tongue.

His appearance presented me with an instant opportunity to possibly satisfy one of my theories.

"You are from Earth are you not, Mister Genks"?

"Ath I have told you before yeth, I am from Earth". Came his mystified reply.

"In what year, Sir"?

Major Roxbrough & Nik Gehenna

His arched green brow wrinkled in consternation and he returned honestly, it seemed to me,

"The year wath 3287 if memory therth me correctly, why the interetht in the year"?

"I ask because I am from the year 2020. In that year, according to Hhrrhhoehhrrhooooingohh, every living human was sought out and exterminated. Dissolved away to nothing by their alien gas. In order that it might be colonised by the Zernoplat".

"I thee, that doth prethent a thertain paradocth. If what you have been told by your HhhâäàåâääçêçêçêïîïiîìggndgndÐñß¥þÞÝ⌂ ith true then how can I exitht"?

"You say my Zernoplat, was the Zernoplat who brought you here not the same"?

Mister Genks shook his huge amphibious head and replied, "No, 23 and I were brought to Nyjord by Hhruuhhum".

"Of course, you would be enrolled by a different Zernoplat even they do not live eleven-hundred years I don't expect. We should discuss what could have happened in greater detail over supper.

"You are thtaying here"?

"Just for tonight if that is all right with you, Composer"?

The native was looking awestruck by Mister Gents, who had arrived while we were in the Bunker. None of the musicaliuvista had dared to escort the manbian, obviously struck Muselmann by his appearance. He managed a mute nod. We returned to his hut, where he then proceeded to chastise the other musicaliuvista for not making him aware of the hybrid's presence in his village. We were all treated to a fabulous concert during supper, the manbian looking especially moved by the pulchritude of the haunting melody.

"It ith reminithent of the Winter Thymphony by Tchikovthky", he murmured.

"And the beverage"? I asked, holding one can aloft.

"Ith from the Orang-U-Can Corporathion", he beamed, "I worked for them for a while, until my stint on Venuth ended".

Myrrorball

"Venus, that hellhole, how can mankind bear to live in such an unrelenting storm of acid and boiling heat"?

"Venuth hath been terra-formed", he told me, "Ath hath Marth, the Moon and Callithto and of courth parth of Nyjord".

My head was buzzing with the difficulty I was having trying to reconcile *his* facts, to what I knew. In his history, the Zernoplat were defeated when they had reached Earth. It seemed mainly through the actions of one man, who was called Quinn. The very *hero* I had created in my novel. Yet the subsequent events after the novel, the history as known by Mister Genks then forked off into two very different branches.

Unless?

Had Quianhua and I both been lied too?

Were the two of us placed in the Zernoplatite zoo just for their entertainment and Earth was safe?

Did it matter? If I demanded the truth from either Hhrrhhoehhrrhooooingohh or Harahorahurrahaashume, they could tell me exactly what they wanted. I could disprove none of it. I seemed in the position whereby I was living a Zernoplatite reality, what-so-ever they chose to shape it. I felt like a character in one of the novels I had written myself. I didn't like the sensation one bit. It was like being Virgil, Scott, or Captain Scarlet. I had no real control, not even over my limbs. I wanted to be a real boy, not one made of wood.

Why is a pig, like a vacuum cleaner?

Because while one wallows in filth, the other sucks it up.

Because they both eat any old muck put in front of them.

Because while one makes sausages, the other seeks the source of dust for ages. Once you have read this, oh you mighty HhhâäàåâäåàåçêçêçêïîĩiĩiggndgndÐñß¥þÞÝ∆, know that I am tired of being manipulated (or should that be 7ernipulated). Give me back my original reality, even if it means I will not know what I now *know*!

51.

Major Roxbrough & Nik Gehenna

It had been 03:23 hours when the sound of the world crashing into something tore them all rudely from their slumber. Himmelwhahu had told them, even before Iglenedes had arrived to explain,

"That would be the latest construction, brought down by the wind and smiting the surface of our world".

Iglenedes then arrive while the blind raven whimpered uselessly in the corner.

"The Tower has just fed once more", he told them. "It is too dark to do anything. The wind is blowing out the lanterns, so I would ask for your assistance in the light of morning if you are agreeable"?

"We shall help in any way we can", Sahbaj promised,

"Nice of her to volunteer us for manual labour", Gerner objected under his breath. He had not spent a lifetime thus far in a constant study to commence employment as a shoveller of dirt or lifter of weight.

Hersko grinned, turned over and went back to sleep. When they got to the sight of the tower the following day, it no longer looked like an organised construction. Rather, it resembled exactly what it was, a shattered and splintered huge mound of broken timber. The Brohain-Minorette set about organising several work crews. Giving them specific tasks, which they did with admirable efficiency. The grim part of the industry was that it soon began to reveal crushed and maimed bodies, some alive, others corpses.

"We must set up an emergency infirmary", Himmelwhahu beseeched Gerner. "What the two of us know that extends into medicine can help these poor misguided fools and then afterwards we can start to point out to them the futility of the tower".

Those natives who had not been buried under the collapsed structure were already starting to repair planking removed by their comrades. Began to shape them back into something serviceable for yet another construction.

"Worry not about another tower, "Hersko said to the two learned men of very different worlds, "I believe I can

Myrrorball

affect a solution that will halt progress for some considerable time to come, if not forever".

Neither of them asked what the young man's notion was, but each had their private suspicions. Decided they did not want implicating in any future investigation.

Sahbaj ordered that one of the huts was especially employed for the purpose the duo intended. The reflected Szorkráló Iglenedes began to organise those from one facet and soon found himself with twice the resources when the virázető instructed her faction to pull together with them.

Within an admirably short time, the infirmary was selected, scrubbed out and kitted with cots and what simple medicinal equipment the Akerányól possessed. The maimed and wounded started to be brought in on hastily created wooden pallets courtesy of the carpenters. It was an example of what could be achieved by an autocracy. The regime where none thought to oppose the word or will of the lone governing body.

While Iglenedes assigned himself the task of setting broken bones and employing splinting to hold the reset limb immobile, Gerner did the stitching of soft tissue wounds. Himmelwhahu had the messiest but just as vital job, of removing foreign bodies from those who had been pierced in various places by varied parts of the Tower that Ate People.

Hersko was outside, watching the workers of wood starting to catalogue recovered piles of lumber. He slowly shook his head from side to side several times at the futility of an enterprise that would only ever yield the very same repeated result.

It was during that period that the real tragedy occurred though. One of the Akerányól, one of those who had travelled through a barrier between the actual and the reflected, must have made a chance remark to one who had not. A native of the new reality. The recipient found an exception to it. An argument broke out. A third party got involved, no doubt supporting one of the two initial protagonists. The debate became elevated and enlarged. Within several disconcerting moments, a full-blooded exchange of words was raging through the men gathered around the debris of what had been the Tower that Ate People only the day before.

Before Hersko could decide what cause of action to take, or even if he should get involved in what was after all a native dispute, virázető Sahbaj appeared from out of her hut, began to demand details. Who could know afterwards if she had stayed inside if the debate would have escalated into a deadly fought battle, but that would only have been possible to conjecture with the benefit of hindsight? One of the natives to the reflected layer of the multiverse must have picked up a small stone, for suddenly one flew through the air and struck the virázető on the temple just above her right eye.

Almost at once, a thin trickle of lilac blood ran from it. The natives of the same layer as Hersko went from ired to enraged. Though there was confusion, raised voices, no single one could calm the storm. Weapons appeared as though by some malign legerdemain, blows fell, returned, a battle ensued. One of virázető Sahbaj's followers must have found a torch from somewhere because the fighting only started to lessen once the huge pile of timber took to light. A massive bonfire threatened the entire village with its inferno.

"Get containers"? Hersko managed to bellow over the clamour, "Anything that can hold water, we must try and control the conflagration, or everyone's homes be at risk".

Many ignored him, doubtless still intent upon revenge for fallen comrades. Perhaps to simply kill as many of the opposition as they could. In desperation, Hersko drew his sword, but a voice behind him stayed his hand,

"Úrrh – Warrior Lord of Akerányó, sheath thy weapon. Lest the battle rages on as the fire causing many more to be slain", It was Gerner who had emerged from the infirmary, motivated by the sound of clamour, the cries of fresh deaths. Iglenedes appeared from behind him and seeing the virázető turned an even paler sky-blue with shock and horror. Hurried her back into the place of healing. Many were dead before the battle, very much like the consuming bonfire - burned out. Those who had survived were left to regard the smoking ashes with a mixture of horror and regret. That was when Himmelwhahu addressed the sooty, smeared faces that were tear-streaked from the smoke and the anguish.

"What has happened here today must never be allowed to happen again", he began. "Let those of you who have lost loved ones cast the hatred from your hearts, for we are all Akerányól under the one virázető. No longer must we regard ourselves as those who lived here from before early times, those who came by the grace of the Vandei Motestas, we are all brothers and sisters".

Hersko knew that he was not though. He knew on that day that he would not be able to stay in Akerányó. For if the original tower builders now resented their newly arrived cousins, how long would it be before they had even greater enmity for he who had been responsible for bringing them to their village? Not only was he guilty of doing that, but he was also alien to the Fire of Saah. He determined there and then that he would use the Vandei Motestas at least once more. It would be to cross the substantial lines between one layer of the multiverse and another.

52.

"It has been brought to my attention that the man who be also an frog is now absent from our ranks", Császária Roxbrough, the Imperial Marquess noted, to the warrior who was always garbed in steel. "If any knowest where he be then it be thee, the twenty-third knight of a distant realm".

"I am no knight", the steel man returned, "I have explained to you many times before, Roxbrough, I am an artificial life-form, an android.

"Thou hast been made a knight by his Majesty", Roxbrough also repeated, "Knight and Roid, thou art both".

"Not roid", 23 explained, "And-roid".

"I believe I didst address thee so-est, Knight and Roid - 23. So the man who be a man and also be a frog, whither hast he goneth"?

"Not to your enemy, if that is what you fear", the Knight and Roid returned, his voice ever-patient, even if his circuits detected a slight raising in temperature every time he conversed with the Császária, the Gothic Advanced Lord was so ...obtuse. "I was not the manbian's keeper. He and I were brought here by Hhruuhhum and Herrwhohuurel in a spaceship. Not to look after one another, so much as to keep an eye on, the one you thought of as having some sort of powers as a seer".

"The Visionary didst indeed have such qualities. Along with his mode of speech, which was more like thine. His mode of dress which was also...".

"I grew tired of him", the knight of Roid interrupted. "Indeed I grow tired of this planet and most of those upon it, there is not enough to keep my circuits vital. I think I shall have to investigate ways of escaping it".

"In the ship that sails the spaces"?

23 did not quite sigh, but his eyes dimmed slightly. He almost slowed in the already tardy pace set by the king. It was not great, the day was warm, their armour had heated up like body-radiators. The Császária was speaking again,

"Couldst thou employ the ship that sails the spaces to take us back to Valgral"?

"The ship was not mine. It belonged to the clear vermin that call themselves Hhhâäàåâäâåçêç-êçêïïìïîìggndgndÐñßɎþÞÝ◬. They seem to be more advanced with their technology than even my settlement on Mars".

"Could you get word to Maaz, tell them of our need"? Roxbrough tried.

23 demanded, his components struggling despite his internal cooling system being on maximum, "How Császária? How would you suggest I do that when the settlement in question is millions of light-years distant and also more than a couple of thousand years distant to if what Nik told us is true. He informed us this was 2020. Mister Genks and I were brought back thousands of years into the brutal and primitive past, the two of us not even the same amount".

Myrrorball

The Császária became lost in some of the phrases and explanations of the Roid. For the main, he seemed to have learned the language of the Valgraln. In an impressively short period to boot. Yet he clung to too many words of mystery and foreignness. It did not help when conversing with the king's nobles. In fact, of them all, the Császária was the only one who ever actively sought the knight of Roid out. The others found they could not warm to a man who refused to remove his armour at any time, yet did not seem to hum at the end of a day's marching like the rest of them.

"That be truly a shame, therefore", the Császária finally conceded sadly.

"As you say, Császária, a shame it is - indeed". The knight of Roid remarked.

The two of them had been the vanguard that day, suddenly the column of men seemed to concertina to a shambling halt at the sound of commotion and incident up ahead. Knowing the knight of Roid had both acute vision and hearing, Roxbrough merely drew to a halt, asked,

"What be reason for the sudden delay, My Lord"?

23 did not bother to correct the Császária for possibly the thousandth time. If Roxbrough wanted to call him a lord or a knight of Roid, he was growing complacent at the inaccuracy. Instead, he informed his companion,

"His Lordship of Voong had just trodden upon a Kézőrös in the undergrowth, the creature bit his ankle".

"I must go make an end to it then, tis the least I can do for his Lordship". Roxbrough drew his sword. The emerald in its pommel twinkled as it was grasped by a fist of iron, the blade being named Evilartus.

"There is no need", 23 returned at once, "That dubious honour went to the Lord of Staltidore. I believe it was the twelfth bite since our journey began. If this toll continues, you will have few men with which to meet the threat from your Western Lords".

"I loathe this dominion", Roxbrough spat then, "I curse it to an grizzly end at the hands of Parasprio"!

Finally a nugget of information that excited some interest in the android,

Major Roxbrough & Nik Gehenna

"Parasprio", he echoed.

"One of the ten gods", the Császária explained. "And in many ways the one that causes fear to spring into the breast of the bravest of warriors. Parasprio be the goddess of death"!

"She may be indeed visiting us sooner than you anticipate", 23 explained suddenly, "For unless my auditory receptors deceive me we are approaching a huge body of water. It would be the river Ganglo, that Hízlatan warned us concerning".

"The swiftly moving but shallow river of the two. The one which does not contain so many Vízarapákellemetlen"?

23 found himself nodding to the primitive Császária, observing as he did so, "I find it curious that for a force that arrived here over the surface of a vast ocean, that so few of your knights profess their inability to swim, or feel comfortable in the water ".

"The mariners didst bring the Zhirnublydok here, the one which Halsgough and his western cronies have stolen from his Majesty", Roxbrough returned, "Tis the armour that drags us down, surely thou has the same problem, Knight of Roid"?

"I can walk upon the bottom of any body of water. My nyloplanyon inner skin keeps my circuitry dry, my durilium-steel exoskeleton is stainless, so I do not fear oxidation".

Much of what the Knight of Roid told Roxbrough was beyond his understanding. He did pick up on one vital point though. "Thou walkest along the bottom, how dost thou breathe"?

23 would have sighed, had it been one of his affectations, which it was not, he patiently repeated, "As I have told you before, my Lord, I do not breathe".

Myrrorball

"And as I returneth in the past", Roxbrough *did* sigh, "All men must breathe".

"You are right", 23 admitted, "If I were a man, I would need to do so. It continues to delight me that I was not created from flesh, bone, blood. I am a superior being to you and your king in many ways, Császária, myriad ways in point of fact".

The debate, if such it was, ended when the troop reached the shore of the river. Natives from Acleegása under the direction of Hízlatan, the Warrior Lords, their guard from Valgral, together with the lone android began to wade across. The traverse went not without incident. Voong already weakened, distraught over his recent injury, one which would lead to dire consequence unless the troop were reunited with Gerner, slipped. His centre of gravity suddenly left his body. He lurched to the opposing side to try to righten himself. It proved his undoing, he fell headlong into the water, which was swiftly moving and one hundred and fifty centimetres deep. Lord Kreel was the closest to the flailing, drowning knight being pulled down by all the iron on his body. Kreel snatched at the moving, drowning comrade as the current pulled him away from the others, into deeper water. He caught the body by his flailing gorget but was instantly pulled along with him, losing his balance in the process. Fordítás and two of his men went to go to their aid, then suddenly yelled and began slashing into the swiftly moving water with their swords. Hízlatan yelled,

"Migratory Vízarapákellemetlen! Get out of the water"!

There was a general panic as everyone began to rush for the opposite bank. For several seconds all was confusion, loss of coordination. When the entire troop finally made the opposite side of the river, to be standing dripping wet Vasnaar demanded,

"Who remains with me, of my Lords, who didst we lose"?

Voong, Kreel, Fordítás and Hegyekben had drowned. Along with several guards belonging to all the Lords, only half a dozen of the Eastern Lords of Valgral remained alive to serve the king and his son, Prince Byno. Along with Császária Roxbrough were: Lords Staltidore,

Lolocken, Flahé, Craggsmoor and Laaterfell. Even with their remaining guards, those who had served the Lords who had been killed, they would be numerically inferior to Halsgough plus the rest of the rebels. Was it not for their Kémerké allies?

"Thank the gods for the assistance of Aznodib", Roxbrough murmured.

23's eyes glowed slightly brighter at the observation.

"According to Hízlatan, the next village we shall encounter on our journey northward will be Kimmerfalucska. It is to be hoped that their virázető feels the same way toward those who suddenly appear in their land".

When the first attack came the following day, 23 received his answer, rudely. The natives of Kimmerfalucska, known as the Kimmerfal, were warlike and very territorial. There had been no attempt to parley, to open negotiation of any type. They always attacked, furiously, in a very coordinated fashion. The day was not exceptional in that regard. The first wave of arrows and spears killed half of the Kémerké. Meanwhile, the Valgral sheltered behind their shields in the dətbağası formation. The dətbağası being a shelled reptile that hugged the coastline of Naav, it was how the formation, had earned its name.

With howls of demented fury, once the bulk of their missiles had been exhausted, the Kimmerfal threw themselves against the travellers. Immediately overwhelmed in the vanguard Craggsmoor fell, his skull shattered by a stone-headed axe. His brains gushed out onto the blue-grass of the forest floor as Lolocken called,

"Form into a slowly retreating formation, give ground as they come, but continue to resist".

It was a practised tactic of Valgral. Unfortunately, the Kémerké had no concept of it. Despite the desperate instructions of their Szorkráló, many ended up slain by the Kimmerfal. The latter seemed as happy to fell a retreating man with a fatal blow to the base of a skull, as face a native or warrior head-on. Their intention was genocide, such was obvious - the battle could only end in one result. Genocide - for the loser.

Though far fewer in number though, the Valgraln were seasoned warriors, better protected, far better armed. Roxbrough's sword was soon crusty with brains, flesh and dried gore. Both his arms ached abominably. One from the wielding of Evilartus. The other from holding the weight of his escutcheon for so long. The tide of the battle turned though, after two hours of grizzly hand to hand combat. Some of the Kimmerfal, sensing they were going to be defeated, began to turn, ready to run back into their domain. That was the point at which Hízlatan turned his heavily depleted force, ordered them to a chase. He was going to exact bloody vengeance on those who had reaped such a heavy toll on his men. All the Valgraln were too heavily weighted to be swift enough to run after natives, but the Kémerké clubbed down any who were getting away.

The battle ended abruptly, with a suddenness that caught everyone by surprise. All that was heard for a moment, was the heavy breathing of those who were trying to force enough air into their taxed lungs.

"Staltidore"? The king finally gasped, "Who survives"?

"My lords: Flahé, Lolocken and Laaterfell", came the wheezed response, The Imperial Marquess additionally and the guard who still live".

"Count them", Byno demanded.

There were only forty-seven left alive,

"We have the Knight of Roid still", Staltidore added, "And Hízlatan with twenty-three of his Kémerké braves".

Vasnaar turned to regard the inscrutable knight of Roid, "Didst thou fight them, Sir"? He demanded.

23 slowly nodded, "Those who attacked me personally".

"I see no weapon about thy personage", the King persisted. In response 23 held up his hands, once gleaming, then covered with body matter, he stated simply,

"I needed none against ill-coordinated, poorly armed savages".

That seemed to be the end of that matter as far as both parties were concerned, Lolocken stepped forward then,

"Before we find the Zhirnublydok to challenge Halsgough for the captaincy of it, my Liege, we need further allies. We will not find them in Kimmerfalucska, it seemeth".

Why thank thee, My Lord", Vasnaar sounded particularly sardonic, "For enlightening us all by stating the sikmişil [profanity, not necessary to trans] obvious.

53.

"It looks deep indeed, my Lord", Teleocea observed, "There be no way we can wade o'er it. We need some type of craft. Tis a pity we left the landing canoes behind.

"Whilst fighting off the Benszülöt"? Halsgough was not impressed by the reasoning of one of the Lords still loyal to his cause. In the frequent battles with the warlike tribe from the west, their number had been depleted gradually. The Lords: Halsia, Rhynturo, Teleocea, Kynoberg, Tavaaro, Kyper Tor and Koözoött survived, many of their men did not. They had shrunken to a force that would struggle to destroy the King.

"Banustib"? Halsgough suddenly roared, "Where are you, Witch"?

The admittedly attractive female that most of the men rightly feared came forward.

"Was that the voice of my dear lover", the once-male mage desired to know sweetly. She was deliberately embarrassing the lord of Halsgough, for though he had lain with her and copulated to their mutual satisfaction it was common knowledge that the witch was a transsexual. By becoming involved with her that made Halsgough a çirkliçinçirkinisi [one guilty of dirty-ugly, sexual practice]

"Enough", Halsgough tried, though he already expected the process to be a futile one, he was not master of the witch, if anything it was the other way around. "Hold thy tongue till I give the permit to speaketh".

"That was not what thy urged me to last night, sweetmeat", Banustib grinned lasciviously, "When mine tongue approached thy...".

Myrrorball

"Silence witch, or so help me...".
"Thou willst do what exactly"? she spat.
Sensing a drawn weapon behind her, she suddenly changed her tack, smiling, apologised,
"Thy pardon, master of the west, I forget myself sometimes when in thy presence due to our evenings of intimacy. How may I serve My Lord 'pon this day"?
"The same aid I always require of a witch", Halsgough blustered, "With depraved magic of course. We need to get over this river, bring us craft which will enable our passage"?
Banustib looked nonplussed, "Truly though asketh that of me when the material thou requires be all around"?
She felt something thin and very sharp pressed into the small of her back then,
"Speak plainly, Witch", Halsia urged unpleasantly, "Lest I stab thee in this forest and in the liver".
"I speak of a raft of course", came the tired response, "Cut down some of the fronds with the two war axes still in our possession, then use dirks to cut creepers and vines to lash them together. There be no use for enchantment when natural materials are to hand. With my mental acumen together with thy laborious attention, we will get o-er the river without the need for my services".
"Do it", Halsgough ordered. It proved the work of but ninety arcs of Angelus before the expansive craft was launched. The men precariously balanced upon it. The Sihoa was deep but slow-moving, it was also home to the deadly Vízarapá-kellemetlen. Halsgough chose to believe that it was pure chance that the first to be dragged from the raft to be devoured alive was pure coincidence. For it had been Halsia who had threatened to stab Banustib in seriously fatal fashion. Tavaaro, together with several guards suffered the same grizzly fate before the western lords' raft bumped against the far bank. Halsgough glanced at those who remained with him, lords: Rhynturo, his closest ally, Teleocea, Kynoberg, Koözoött and Kyper Tor, would it be enough to face the might of the King?

Major Roxbrough & Nik Gehenna

54.

"I believe this to be folly", Gerner argued not for the first time. "Stay here with us", he begged.

"My mind be decided", Hersko returned, "Come with me, Scribe, tis not too late to change thy mind. The virázető has more than enough wise counsel to help her continue here. Himmelwhahu, Iglenedes, both will give her the sort of advice she needeth o-er the coming months. Thou shouldst desire being reunited with our King. To see if the Margrave of Oslan-On-the-Bank survived, found him"?

"So many lives put in jeopardy for the greed of our ruler", Gerner argued. "What price Корунд now, Úrrh Hersko. We have not seen any blue stones bluer than the eyes of the goddess Shakita, very blue indeed. So azure perhaps as to be beyond the possession of mortal men".

"Our mission has changed", Hersko admitted, "Yet our fate should not be to stay here and to rebuild the Tower that Ate People".

"It will not be thusly", Gerner agreed, "The triumvirate of the advisory council be determined that such will not be the case. We can build a home here though, we need the Warrior Lord of Akerányó in Brohain Minor".

"I cannot stay, I hope to achieve that which I most desire. To reach the Tru-eti Varzslatoj of which we learned, the magic city that lies in the mountains of Thol".

Gerner could see that the young warrior was resolute so he suddenly traditionally gripped his forearm,

"I feel my destiny is best played to a conclusion, here. Good luck then, Hersko".

The two continued to grip one another firmly for perhaps three seconds. The Úrrh closed his eyes in concentration before waving his arm, the arm upon which the Vandei Motestas resided. He seemed to shimmer. With a sucking pop, then vanished.

55.

Myrrorball

I lay on my back with hands behind my head, glanced up at the ubiquitous blue canopy that almost constantly blotted out the golden globe of the sun. Our journey had been much easier in many ways, once we had taken what we desired from the bunker. The Conductor had not been overly concerned, most of the items were beyond his understanding. We had only taken what we needed, just as importantly, could carry.

Strangely the day was much cooler than those we had grown accustomed to. Not that it concerned me overly, for the onesy that the Zernoplat had supplied me with had a tiny control on the left wrist. I could adjust to warm or cool dependent upon that which I required. Not for the first time I wondered if Hhrrhhoehhrrhooooingohh or Harahorahurrahaashume had arrived at the bubble by then to find Quianhua and me - gone! What would their reaction be? I hoped them capable of irritation, the murdering kutyavialt. I no longer possessed the desire to study the Kézőrös, Blevastís, Egszígør, Zürepüé, Kémerké or anything on Rozhelia. I no longer desired to cooperate with you - Zernoplats!

You had told me that the posting was for us to study the place, but what you had effectively done was to place us in your living zoo, as you had with Mr Genks and the curiously ominous android. I did not want you to slay the living obstacles in your path to colonizing yet another world. I did not even desire that the Kézőrös be harmed. I was recording my thoughts into one of those futuristic pads I found in the bunker by then. All I had to do was speak to it, the typing appearing on the little screen. Strangely I hoped you would never read this though - ever. I hope you never found me? I did not care if we ever saw one another ever again. I rose to my feet and contemplated the river before us. There were several things we could do. Cut west and walk along its western bank as it flowed northward for several days. That would only mean delaying having to cross it though. The Acleegáás; Vandeveble, Chavayda, Mesoloras and Collari assured me thy could create a raft in short order if I did not fancy wading through the water which would have

Major Roxbrough & Nik Gehenna

come up to my waist. That seemed the sensible choice because they could not assure me that there were no Vízarapákellemetlen lurking in the shallows. So I ordered it done.

An Œrdimahdá gobbled in the distance and at the edge of the river, I saw my first dətbağası - a sort of blue turtle, but not the type Sting sang about, these were far more beautiful. A rainbow of hues was reflected from their lovely shells. Collari had told me there were several species of bilıque [fish] to be found in the river Ganglo too.

Quızılbalığ [salmon-like], Otsæzan [very like a carp] and the Cənukamsi [like an anchovy] were plentiful in the rivers of the island and saltwater version could be found in the ocean off the coast. As I was allergic to fish of any kind, I would not be eating them. My period-of-study had been placed on hold for the time being.

I was in a peaceful state of mind, despite the much cooler day. My suit was lulling me to sleep when a lovely face appeared above my line of vision. My wife told me the raft was completed. A shaft of the light from Angelus had managed to avoid all the foliage and was currently behind her head as she told me. It gave her long brown hair a halo effect, I realised how lucky I was to have such a wonderful creature adore me. I even then did not realise until much later, just how important she would become to me. Nor how much she would be able to enhance my existence. I jump ahead of myself  though. We reached the far bank of the river without mishap, continued on our way. I detected that the natives were getting very restless, sought out Vandeveble to question, as he had the least guile amongst any who we had protecting us.

Myrrorball

"Why is the mood suddenly cautiously sombre"? I asked him directly, he admired straight talk, replied honestly at once,

"We are getting nearer to the village of Kimmerfalucska, the people there, who are called the Kimm-erfal, do not take kindly to incursion to their territory".

"Will they see such a small group as a threat to them"?

"Possibly not, your weapons are curiously unknown, but the rest of us are armed. The Kimmerfal have been known to attack firstly, then ask questions afterwards".

It was not long after that conversation that we came upon the scene of carnage. There were some hastily dug graves concealing who had been attacked by the locals, while their dead bodies had simply been left to rot out in the open. Already the smell was the unmistakably sickly sweet odour of decaying flesh.

Mesoloras observed, "The graves will contain those you described to us, those who were your friends. Probably the Kémerké too. They won. Otherwise, they would be out in the open, the Kimmerfal took back to Kimmerfalucska, to create a pile for a sacred funeral pyre".

"Some of these could be our kin", Tergiss murmured, brothers, fathers, cousins, uncles".

We cannot defile any graves to find out Khanivool pointed out, "So we must wait until the day in the far future when we return to Shad".

I turned from the scene it had depressed me considerably, in those shallow graves were the bodies of new friends, or supporters, in either case, the innocent.

That night I decided to take some more snufz, I don't think I was searching for answers, I just wanted to escape reality for a while - a recreation. Whether the pinches were unusually large or my tiredness made the *hit* more impactful I'm uncertain. All I know is that I thought I had initially blacked out I had not, instead my mind had left my body. The feeling became suddenly wonderfully specific. I was in my body in terms of my level of consciousness, but also out of my usual form. I floated out and above myself and looked down at...me asleep.

I was having what others call an *Out of Body Experience*. Where should I go? As melancholy had gripped me earlier. I decided I needed the comfort of nostalgia. Could my mind make something visible that perhaps no longer existed? There was only one way to find out. I floated upward at an alarming velocity, was soon free of the gravity of Rozhelia. I halted for an instant, observing the entire planet, the huge secondary one that the Rozhelic thought of as a moon but was actually a secondary binary spinning on its axis and also orbiting the primary. Together both orbited a star which they called Angelus. I had not fully learned of this celestial arrangement, but on a level that was impossible to explain, I knew what I was looking at was authentic, that was certain.

Time to go in search of the planet I had spent the majority of my life on. How could I be sure of the correct direction to travel? If all was an illusion, (as Errol Kennedy had proposed) then I did know. I might be deluding myself, but I wanted a glimpserama of my homeworld. I desired to remember next week.

Searching for a destiny that's mine,
There's another place another time,
Touching not one heart along the way,
Hoping that I'll never have to say -
It's just an illusion.

So at a velocity greater than the speed of light, I hurtled through interstellar space like an Axevictim. My delusion, my physical rules. In those, there were no rules.

Through the vastness of the void, I continued to gather momentum until the stars became little white lines. The sable curtain that surrounded me was 99.23% empty.

Myrrorball

Suddenly I slowed. Decided I was approaching the Solar system. So it was, for I looked sideways, still neither needing warmth nor air to breathe in and saw Neptune, the eighth and farthest known planet from the Sun in the Solar System. In the System, it is the fourth-largest planet by diameter, the third-most-massive planet, and the densest. Neptune which was 17 times the mass of Earth, slightly more massive than its near-twin Uranus. Neptune, denser and physically smaller than Uranus because its greater mass causes more gravitational compression of its atmosphere. It orbited the Sun once every 164.8 years at an average distance of 4.5 billion kilometres.

Named after the Roman god of the sea with the astronomical symbol ♆, a stylised version of the god's trident. Triton was discovered by mankind shortly after the planet itself. None of the planet's remaining 13 known moons was located telescopically until the 20th century. The planet's distance from Earth gives it a very small apparent size, making it challenging to study with Earth-based telescopes. Neptune was visited by Voyager 2, when it flew by the planet on 25th August 1989; Voyager 2 remains the only spacecraft to visit Neptune. Then in 2020 while the homeworld of all mankind was being bathed in poisonous gas, a lone traveller passed the miniature system within a system. Thanks to a narcotic a mind-bending substance that he called snufz - in other words, me.

Uranus was next. The seventh planet from the Sun. It had the third-largest planetary radius and fourth-largest planetary mass in the Solar System. Uranus, similar in composition to Neptune, and both have bulk chemical compositions which differ from that of the larger gas giants Jupiter and Saturn. For this reason, scientists often classify Uranus and Neptune as 'ice giants' to distinguish them from the gas giants. Uranus' atmosphere was known to be similar to Jupiter's and Saturn's in its primary composition of hydrogen and helium. It contained more ices such as water, ammonia, and methane, along with traces of other hydrocarbons. It had the coldest planetary atmosphere in the Solar System, with a minimum temperature of minus 224 °Centigrade, also a complex, layered cloud structure with water to make up the lowest clouds, methane the uppermost layer. The interior of that world was mainly composed of ices together with rocks. Like the other giant planets, Uranus possessed a ring system, a magnetosphere, and numerous moons. The Uranian system had a unique configuration because its axis of rotation was tilted sideways, nearly into the plane of its solar orbit. Both poles, therefore, lie where most other planets had their equators. In 1986, images from Voyager 2 showed Uranus as an almost featureless planet in visible light, without the cloud bands or storms associated with the other giant planets. Voyager 2 remains the only spacecraft to visit the planet.

I was the only person to do so. Observations from Earth have shown seasonal change and increased weather activity as Uranus approached its equinox in 2007. Wind speeds reached 250 metres per second. Uranus had 27 known natural satellites. The names of these chosen from characters in the works of Shakespeare and Alexander Pope. The five main satellites are Miranda, Ariel, Umbriel, Titania, and Oberon. The Uranian satellite system is the least massive among those of the giant planets; the combined mass of the five major satellites would be less than half that of Triton (largest moon of Neptune) alone. I passed on by.

The sixth planet from the Sun was my next port of call, it was also the second-largest in the Solar System, after Jupiter. It is a gas giant with an average radius of about nine times that of Earth. It only had one-eighth the average density of it, however, with its larger volume, Saturn is over 95 times more massive. The body was named after the Roman god of wealth and agriculture - its astronomical symbol ♄ represents the god's sickle. Saturn's interior is most likely composed of a core of iron-nickel together with silicon/oxygen compounds. Its core surrounded by a deep layer of metallic hydrogen, an intermediate layer of liquid hydrogen and liquid helium, finally a gaseous outer layer. Saturn presented me with a pale yellow hue due to ammonia crystals in its upper atmosphere. Electrical current within the metallic hydrogen layer gave rise to Saturn's planetary magnetic field, which is weaker than the Earth's but has a magnetic moment 580 times that of it due to Saturn's larger size. Saturn's magnetic field strength is around one-twentieth of Jupiter's. As I passed it, I heard the strains of Magnetic Fields (Jarre) playing inside my head, wonderful. The outer atmosphere was generally bland and lacking in contrast. Wind speeds on Saturn reached 1,800 kilometres per hour, higher than on Jupiter, but not as high as those on Neptune. The planet's most famous feature, its prominent ring system, which was composed mostly of ice particles, with a smaller amount of rocky debris and dust was not as beautiful as I had anticipated. At least 82 moons orbited Saturn, of which, fifty-three had been officially named before the end. That did not include the hundreds of moonlets in its rings. Titan, Saturn's largest moon, the second-largest in the Solar System, was larger than the planet Mercury, although less massive, and was the only moon in the Solar System to have a substantial atmosphere.

On my voyage of exploration and sightseeing, I next passed Jupiter, the fifth planet from the Sun, the largest in the Solar System. A gas giant, father of the gods of the Romans. With a mass one-thousandth that of the Sun. Two-and-a-half times that of all the other planets in the Solar System combined. Jupiter - one of the brightest objects visible to the naked eye in the night sky, thusly has been known to ancient civilizations since before recorded history. When men viewed the impressive disc from Earth, Jupiter was bright enough for its reflected light to cast shadows. Now the only shadows cast on Earth would be slim, hardly discernible. Some of the light would pass through the masters of the planet. Jupiter would remain the fourth brightest natural object in the sky after the Sun, Moon and Venus. It was primarily composed of hydrogen with a quarter of its mass being helium, though helium comprises only about a tenth of the number of molecules. It may also have a rocky core of heavier elements. Like the other giant planets, Jupiter lacked a well-defined solid surface. Because of its rapid rotation, the planet's shape was that of an oblate spheroid with a slight but noticeable bulge around the equator. The outer atmosphere, visibly segregated into several bands at different latitudes, resulting in turbulence, storms along their interacting boundaries. A prominent result, the main feature of my observation was the *Great Red Spot*. A giant storm that I knew had existed since at least the 17th century. When it was first detected by the telescope of man. Surrounding Jupiter is a faint planetary ring system, a powerful magnetosphere. Jupiter boasted 79 known moons, including the four large Galilean moons discovered by Galileo Galilei in 1610. Ganymede, the largest of these, had a diameter greater than that of the planet Mercury. Pioneer 10 beat me to the scene by being the first visitor to Jupiter. It made its closest approach to the planet on December 4th 1973, identified plasma in Jupiter's magnetic field and also found that Jupiter's magnetic tail was nearly 800 million kilometres long, covering the entire distance to Saturn. Jupiter was then explored on several occasions by robotic spacecraft, beginning with the Pioneer and Voyager flyby missions from 1973 to 1979, later by the Galileo orbiter, which arrived at Jupiter in 1995. In late February 2007, Jupiter was visited by the New Horizons probe, which used Jupiter's gravity to increase its speed, bending its trajectory en route to Pluto. The last probe to visit the planet was Juno, which entered into orbit around Jupiter on July 4th 2016. I was the first to explore the ice-covered liquid ocean of its moon - Europa. I swam, (even though in reality I was a poor swimmer) with the nɛmətoʊdz a type of aquatic roundworm, to which, I ascribed the phylum Nematoda. Magically undersea vegetation-parasitic diverse animal phylum inhabiting a broad range of environments. Taxonomically, I classified them in my mind along with insects and other moulting animals in the clade Ecdysozoa. Unlike flatworms, they had tubular digestive systems with openings at both ends. Like tardigrades, they had a reduced number of Hox genes. For their sister phylum, Nematomorpha kept the ancestral protostome Hox genotype. How I knew all this

Myrrorball

was the wonder that was snufz. It may or may not be actuality. Finally, I grew bored of swimming with the nɛmətoʊdz. Their conversation being particularly filled with ennui,

'bəzdadlı otlaharadan albilərəm', [Where can I get some especially tasty weed?].

'Buyaxnlardi yaxbir alaquota yemişdinizmi'? [Have you dined on any especially fine weed lately?]

'yaxşıtoy sizəlavələr oolon böyükçkin qurde" [Good weeding to you big ugly worm with appendages]

So to Mars. Second-smallest planet in the Solar System after Mercury. In English, Mars carries the name of the Roman god of war, often referred to as, the *'Red Planet'*. The latter refers to the effect of the iron oxide prevalent on Mars' surface, which gives it a reddish appearance distinctive among the astronomical bodies visible to the naked eye. A terrestrial planet with a thin atmosphere, having surface features reminiscent both of the impact craters of The Moon. The valleys, deserts, and polar ice caps of Earth. **Why it was, therefore, unsuitable to you Hhrrhhoehhrrhooooingohh is something I had yet to understand?** The days and seasons are likewise comparable to those of Earth because the rotational period, as well as the tilt of the rotational axis relative to the ecliptic plane, is very similar. Mars, the site of Olympus Mons, the largest volcano, highest known mountain on any planet in the Solar System, and of Valles Marineris, one of the largest canyons in the Solar System. The smooth Borealis basin in the northern hemisphere covers 40% of the planet, maybe a giant impact feature. Mars had two moons, Phobos and Deimos, which are small - irregularly shaped. They were nothing more than captured asteroids, similar to 5261 Eureka, a Mars Trojan. Mars had been explored by numerous unmanned spacecraft. Mariner 4, launched by NASA on November 28th 1964, was the first spacecraft to visit Mars. Making its closest approach to the planet on July 15th 1965. Mariner 4 detected the weak Martian radiation belt, measured at about 0.1% that of Earth's, and captured the first images of another planet from deep space. On July

20th 1976, Viking 1 performed the first successful landing on the Martian surface. Although the Soviet Mars 3 spacecraft achieved a soft landing in December 1971, contact failed with the lander only seconds after touchdown. On July 4th 1997, the Mars Pathfinder spacecraft landed on Mars. On July 5th released its rover, Sojourner, the first robotic rover to operate on Mars. Pathfinder was followed by the Mars Exploration Rovers, Spirit and Opportunity, which landed on Mars in January 2004. They operated until March 22nd 2010, then June 10th 2018, respectively. The Mars Express orbiter, the first European Space Agency spacecraft to visit Mars, arrived in orbit on December 25th 2003. On September 24th 2014, the Indian Space Research Organization became the fourth space agency to visit Mars, when its maiden interplanetary mission, the Mars Orbiter Mission spacecraft, successfully arrived in orbit. On April 14th 2020 a lone man who could do without oxygen landed on the surface of the planet for a visit. He was the last man on Earth, the first on Mars. His name will not go down in human history, because human history had ceased being recorded at that time. It was a shame because there was the possibility of extant life. Liquid water could exist on the surface of Mars due to low atmospheric pressure, which is less than 1% of the Earth's, so no swimming for me at that time. Although at the lowest elevations for short periods puddles could be possible. The two polar ice caps were made up largely of water. The volume of water ice in the south polar ice cap, if melted, would be sufficient to cover the entire planetary surface to a depth of 11 meters. I also found a large amount of underground ice in the Utopia Planitia region. The volume of water detected I estimated to be equivalent to the volume of water in Lake Superior. From Mars, I could easily see Earth with the naked eye. Considering Mars had the most violent dust storms in the Solar System, reaching speeds of over 160 kilometres an hour, I was lucky. They could vary from a squall, over a small area, to gigantic storms that covered the entire planet. While I was there though, it was calm.

Myrrorball

I came to my destination, the world that belonged to the HhhâäàåâääçêçêçêïïiïïìggndgndÐñßɎþÞÝ◮ or Zernoplat, an extraterrestrial əˈmiːbə or amœba a large type of cell or unicellular organism which can alter its shape, primarily by extending and retracting pseudopods. HhhâäàåâääçêçêçêïïiïïìggndgndÐñßɎþÞÝ◮ did not form a single taxonomic group. Instead, they are found in every major lineage of eukaryotic organisms. They also occurred on many worlds of the galaxy man had called the Milky Way. Destroyed fungi, algae, animals, including man. I then used the terms əˈmiːbə or amœba interchangeably for any organism that exhibits amoeboid movement. Placed into the class or subphylum Sarcodina, a grouping of single-celled organisms that possess pseudopods or move by the protoplasmic flow. However, molecular phylogenetic studies conducted on the planet Rozhelia showed that the HhhâäàåâääçêçêçêïïiïïìggndgndÐñßɎþÞÝ◮' was not a monophyletic group whose members share common descent. Consequently, HhhâäàåâääçêçêçêïïiïïìggndgndÐñßɎþÞÝ◮' organisms could no longer be classified together in one group. You see Hhrrhhoe-hhrrhooooingohh I had not been totally lazy whilst in the bubble. I knew you to be protists! Giant əmiːbə HhhâäàåâääçêçêçêïïiïïìggndgndÐñßɎþÞÝ◮ Proteus - destroyers of aboriginal life on other worlds that were not your own. The locusts of the galaxy. Spreading widely, cultivating death and annihilation to many as you went. As malign as the brain-eating əˈmiːbə Naegleria fowleri, the intestinal parasite Entamoeba histolytica, which causes əˈmiːbə dysentery, and the multicellular social əˈmiːbə or slime mould Dictyostelium discoideum. I suspect these are all part of your hateful ancestry. No wonder you have no love for primates, you with your lack of cell walls, which allow for free movement. You move and feed by using pseudopods, which are bulges of cytoplasm formed by the coordinated action of actin microfilaments pushing out the plasma membrane that surrounds the cell. I wonder if you had ever ingested a

Major Roxbrough & Nik Gehenna

human being? Do you keep some in special farm pens for when you fancy a bit of prime man rib or steak?

I foolishly thought I was about to find out as I sped through the atmosphere and toward the familiar shape of Britain. I wanted to know if the food sources of Zernoplat varied. If they were predatory and lived by consuming bacteria, protists, animals including man. Or if they were (you were, if you ever read this account) detritivores and ate dead organic material. I did know Zernoplat would typically ingest food by phagocytosis, extending pseudopods to encircle and engulf live prey or particles of scavenged material. You did not have a mouth or cytostome. There was no fixed place on the cell, at which, phagocytosis could regularly occur. Perhaps you could also feed by pinocytosis, imbibing dissolved nutrients through vesicles formed within the cell membrane.

I landed in Yorkshire. I landed in my back garden. Then I got the shock of my life!

56.

Progress was painfully laborious when they realised they could not make any noise sneaking through the undergrowth. It was practically impossible to move silently, when dressed in armour. Armour that boasted accoutrements also made of metal. Iron and steel that could ring out when impacting upon itself. To their utter astonishment the annoyance of them all, he who could do so most successfully was 23. The knight of Roid, more encased in armour than any of the rest of them including the King. He could achieve total perambulatory lullfication. In whispers, which 23 could as easily discern as the loudest of bellows, the Császária asked the knight of Roid his secret. The answer was *lubrication*. Which resulted in the rest of them smearing Œrdimahdá grease on their metal joints. It was marginally successful, but if their enemy could not hear them, perhaps they would smell them coming? For the lubricant soon went reesty and ripe. Even the native contingent, bare-footed and

Myrrorball

without metal cladding made more noise than the knight of Roid. Something happened then that made their care suddenly superfluous, for the noise in the tops of the Avgófýllo informed the Kémerké what to expect.

The storm.

It descended upon Egszígør - The Fire of Saah with ruthless speed and terrible upheaval. A wind - blown from Baalan's very cheeks. Ferocious, dangerous once it began uprooting large Avgófýllo, tossing them about like twigs. To find cover was beyond difficult in a whirling mass of dirt, stones, boughs, the air itself. The caves were at the base of the mountains and still far away. The only thing they could do was throw themselves to the ground, face downwards, with their shields across their backs. A huge Avgófýllo suddenly plummeted out of the grey, crowded sky, impacted on Laaterfell with bone-crushing force. The armour was flattened by the hefty-weight of the frond, from out of the ruin, crimson ran. Inside the flattened metal, was so much crushed mush. Scarlet droplets were dragged up into the air and thrown about along with everything else.

"By Baalan's black balls", Prince Byno cursed, "Tis raining blood".

They were all spotted with particles of what had once been the lord of the Valgraln town of Laaterfell. There was nothing to do but wait it out. It seemed to last hours. As suddenly as it had sprung up, it ceased. Yet five more of the King's force were no more.

57.

"I tell thee, my Lord, I do not feel well, I have developed a hacking cough, my flesh burns with a malign fire and I am finding it hard to breathe", Rhynturo persisted, "If thou willst not tarry for a short time, thou must leave me behind".

The Lord of the Western Town knew Halsgough would never do that, they had been friends since boyhood and were cousins three times removed.

"Very well, we shall take a short reprieve", he conceded and then called aggressively, "Banustib! Where art thou now thy Methley"?

It was a somewhat strange way to treat his lover, for if she were a Methley and he shagged her, what did that make him? He knew what others would say. They would call him kutyavialt- unnatural son of a dog or lower breed creature and çirkliçinçirkinisi - one guilty of dirty-ugly sexual practice. He did not care when suckling on the witch's magnificent breasts or splitting her oyster with his muscle staff of procreation. She was a witch in the daytime, a whore at night, his frenzied spasm of ejaculation were all the more powerful for it.

The witch was suddenly at his side, a curious expression on her beautiful features, In dulcet mellifluous tones she informed the Lord of Halsgough,

"Abuse me openly in front of anyone one more time, then shall I turn myself into something unnatural that slithers, leaving odious slime in its wake".

Halsgough dared to smirk, observed, "Then would I be rid of thee from mine bed and copulate with thee never again, my Dearest Witch".

"Oh, not so", the witch returned with a wicked gleam in her dark eyes, "For I would continue to use aphrodisiac 'pon thee. Thou wouldst be forced against thy will to respond to thy base animal drives".

Halsgough was many things, but stupidity was not one of his failings. He still possessed the grace and good sense to shudder as he acknowledged that he believed every word the sorceress said. So he did what any noble of breeding would have at that juncture,

"My Lord of Rhynturo complains of an malady, mayhap the ague of this place, wouldst thou be so kind as to examine him, Madam".

"Bring him forward", Banustib complied casually. Two of Rhynturo's men did so, carrying their Lord on a roughly and hastily constructed stretcher. For the malady had continued to claim the Lord's flesh, he drifted in and out of consciousness.

The lovely girl, beautiful woman, the sham - glanced down at the man on the pallet, then declared without close examination,

"I can tell thee exactly what be wrong with this man, mine lord of Halsgough".

"What be it"? came the instantly concerned reply.

"He be dead"!

"Dead"! Halsgough croaked emotionally. He did not doubt the hasty prognosis. It was just that he was struck to shock by the swiftness of the loss of his friend. Banustib, on the other hand, used the apparent failure to understand in sardonic self-amusement,

"Yes, my Lord of Halsgough - dead. Bereft of life, gone to meet the gods, with us no more, pushing up the grave-grass, an Ex-lord, completely deceased, breathless, cadaverous. Rhynturo is no more, he be defunct, checked out, inanimate, Mortis Accompli. He has kicked the pail, gone much further west, popped his clogs, should now be lain six feet under".

"Art thou most done"? Halsgough managed then, "What vile affliction didst torment his flesh and remove the life-force from his noble figure"?

"Xətəlikimyrüç", came the unexpected and precise answer.

"What be that? What be the nomen", Halsgough was taken by surprise.

"Xətəlikimyrüç - Corona twenty-three", the witch repeated, "I have studied malign infection as an hobby of mine for some time. Corona be an ague with crown-like bacilli a sort of plague. This strain of it be the twenty-third I have determined, hence the nomenclature, which be Xətəlikimyrüç".

"Can we survive it"?

"Nay. I am possesseth of none cure. The only way to stop it be to contain it, thusly to accure lack of cross-infection. To that end, thou and the rest of us must proceed with our nose and mouth covered. Not touch one another for some time. Rhynturo's body must be consigned to purifying flames. Halsgough was giving some of the Lord's men that very instruction when the sound of more coughing alerted them all to a second case.

Major Roxbrough & Nik Gehenna

By the end of the day Lords - Rhynturo, Teleocea and Kynoberg were dead along with many more guards. The rebellion had effectively been stopped by an unseen tiny enemy, 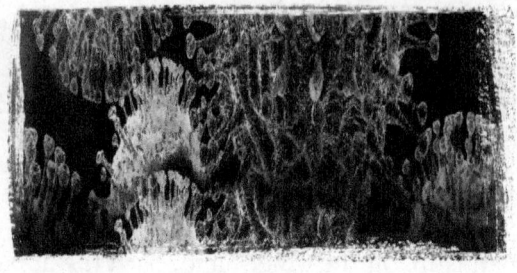 yet all the more deadly for that reason. Halsgough now only commanded Kyper Tor and Koözoött together with a mere handful of men. The Fire of Saah and its various dangers were the enemies that the warriors of Valgral could never hope to survive.

58.

Virázető Sahbaj was seated before her triumvirate, she asked,
"Tell me how work progresses, what we are to do about the locals, you start, Iglenedes"?
Her Szorkráló looked somewhat self-conscious before replying,
"We have to find a way of convincing the aboriginal natives of Brohain-Minor that the Tower that Ate People is folly and future undertakings should be in the construction of dwellings. We are dangerously short of said since the fire and many families have doubled up to have a roof over their heads when the weather turns uncharacteristically inclement".
"Surely in your problem lies the solution itself", Himmelwhahu noted, "It would prove a postponement at the very least".
"Once the building of huts is complete though, what then"? Iglenedes desired to know.
"More stable pens for the animals", Gerner ventured, "An increase in husbandry to account for the increased population".

Myrrorball

"That makes sense too", the native Szorkráló agreed, "Yet that too will have an ending, can we postpone indefinitely"?

"I would like a grander abode for myself and quarters for retainers, those I require to live in", Sahbaj was beginning to see where Himmelwhahu intended the conversation to go.

Iglenedes persisted, "So all the projects are done, what then, sooner or later there will come an end to them"?

"Why"? Himmelwhahu demanded.

"Once the villagers and mighty braves see the grandeur of the virázető's muse accommodation, they would love to see their habitats renovated or completely replaced. By then the carpenters will be travelling even wider and further for the raw material needed - timber. We can then argue for some conservation of the remaining forest, to make certain land erosion does not take place. Indeed postponement can be protracted indefinitely. By that time we would have a concrete argument to refute its resumption".

"And what would that be", the local Szorkráló wished to know.

"Why that we have lived and flourished without the assistance of the Blue Goddess. Simply observing the status quo would be the wisest course of action".

59.

I got the shock of my life because what I had expected - I don't know what I had expected, but it was not that which confronted me.

It was warm. The sun shone from a beautiful cloudless sky. I could hear the birds singing, the sparrows squabbling as they are want to do. There was a warm breeze for the time of year, all was - peaceful. I could not hear the sound of any machinery, any industry, any movement of anything other than the birds. There were no Zernoplatite anywhere in near or distant sight. There were no people either, the garden looked exactly as I had left it. The grass was still freshly mown, the weeding completed. The trees were in bud, some leaves had burst from them, the flowering cherry was heavy with blossom. It was as though all was continuing in a weird vacuum, the absolute void was the absence of man. Amazingly I still had some keys in the pocket of my jumpsuit, so I unlocked the Lurv Shack (My name for a particularly large shed that a friend who worked with timber had created for me). As expected by then, it did not look like I had ever been away.

The chimes in the doorway obligingly tinkled as I pushed through them, into the interior of a shed the size of a garage. All my tools were neatly hanging from hooks around the entire perimeter. The underside of the roof still had the posters from my first eight books. I sat down in the easy-chair situated at the end, in which I had a solid-state separates system situated. A Denon compact disc player, feeding a Bauyum valve stage to sweeten the sound, into a Yamaha amplifier. At the opposite end of the set up was a pair of Wharfedale Lintons on stands made of stacked house bricks. I went through the CD's in the bottom of the rack, pulled out Jean Michele Jarre's Revolutions and found I could turn on the power. Somewhere, probably in the national grid, someone was maintaining the electricity, up till that moment at least.

I settled back, put the circular attenuator at nine o'clock and listened to the whole album through, from start to finish. When I left the Lurv Shack, it was approaching dusk. I had some binoculars to hand, set a garden chair on the lawn. Waited for the darkness to fall. One of the things I had done when living in the house in Yorkshire was to lie on my back in the garden at night, train the binoculars up into the night sky. Even though I had just flown seemingly effortlessly through that very dominion, I did the same old thing for the sake of nostalgia. I tried to imagine which tiny pinprick of light was the illumination coming from Angelus, feeling suddenly poetic began to create in my mind:

The Last Night Watchmen on Earth.

Beneath the cupola of black,
He gazes up from on his back,
Wonders all there - for to see,
From the chasm, he did flee.

All were gone now, no survived,
Of companionship deprived,
The only thoughts were in *his* head,
Every last one, truly dead.

Yet the power had been on,
How so, when all the rest were gone?
Zernoplat still worked the grid,
Even though mankind were rid.

He was the last of those who lived on Earth,
The planet of his life and birth,
He had journeyed from Rozhelia,
Just to witness something realia.

Was the multiverse so real,
Could he tell by simple feel,
Layer 'pon layer, he sensed them all.
Like myriad mirrors of a mirror ball.

I figured I was growing introspectively morose if not careful it would make me moribund. The snufz had given me a glimpserama of one possible facet of the many I had to consider if I reached the Tru-eti Varzslatoj. I knew that the city would be my salvation, *it had to be*!
I resolved to return to Rozhelia.

Major Roxbrough & Nik Gehenna

I could not do it.

Conscious of the fact that this might prove to be an increase in my finite snufz supply, I nevertheless charged a nostril full up each side to continue mine out of body experience. The fact that the snufz remained real in my unreality did not seem to concern me. I was just so very grateful that it did. It was then a simple if the slightly arduous process to retrace the route of my journey, return to my flesh. Quianhua had joined me. Asleep with my sidearm across my shoulder. The night had grown slightly cooler than usual, I was glad of her body warmth. I snuggled into her embrace, she awoke.

"I'm glad you are out of it", she said and before I could comment added, "You were so deeply asleep that I would almost have believed you in a coma".

"I was just dreaming", I lied, "Go back to sleep, Babe, everything is going to be fine".

She turned over, allowing me to spoon her. I lay awake for what felt like hours and could not be bothered to take a peek at my watch to see just how slowly time was passing. Finally, I sneaked from out of the bag we had both been in, going over to one of the bundles Vandeveble had been carrying. Inside I pulled forth a storm lantern, a bottle of oil, some matches and one of the books I had selected for myself out of the bunker. It was the careful work of a couple of minutes to put some oil in the lantern, light the wick and position it on a nearby rock so that its light shone down upon my reading. Robert Heinlein's Assignment in Eternity. I do not usually read science fiction myself, reasoning it to be the easiest way to avoid unintentional plagiarism. I was not writing fiction at that time though, so I had the opportunity to enjoy it. I wondered how long it would be before the opportunity came to return to my original occupation? Did the need for it even exist? Then the germ of an idea struck me. Why not use my powers of knowledge, given me by the snufz, to find out somewhere to go and be able to produce my work once more to a new audience? I knew of the multiverse, how could I traverse the layers of it though until I found one to suit my particular requirements?

Myrrorball

60.

"Oslan-on-the-Bank, as I live and breathe"! Byno exclaimed excitedly, "We thought thee lost, where are the others"?

The Margrave shook his head, "There are no others apart from Hersko, he stayed at a village, by the name of Brohain, up in the north. Where be the rest of the Eastern Lords and their men"?

"We be all that survive" Vasnaar admitted to his most honoured knight, despite Roxbrough's heady promotion. "The Visionary deserted us and those few as stand afore thee now are those who survived the enemy attack and violent storm, not to mention the bite of the occasional Kézőrös. Nunne and Hersko will be Blue-Mumblies by now".

"The enemy strength"? Lolocken demanded to know, "How many be they ashore and how far be they from us"?

"I knowest not", Oslan-on-the-Bank admitted. He told them of his escape from the ship with Hersko and his subsequent decision to go south alone. He had successfully traversed a river rough mountain terrain and seemingly unending undergrowth to reach the King, only to find him almost defeated even before the Western Lords located him.

"We have Hízlatan and his braves", Staltidore added with falsely generated bravado, plus confidence he did not feel. Flahć did not even speak, he was thinking of his son as a Blue-mumbly. The prospect was inauspicious.

"We also have Evilartus, Iniquitous and courage Halsgough posseth nothing like them", Roxbrough added.

Oslan-on-the-Bank glanced at the newly-created insignia on the pauldron of the former lowly Lord. For some reason he dare not question the King regarding, he had elevated the most western of commanders of Valgraln seats to the rank of Császária. That made him commander of he-of-the-Bank and the other lords, answerable only to the prince and his father the King. He agreed though,

"That we do, two of Abominorv's supposedly enchanted blades. Who knowest, mayhap certain unfortunate

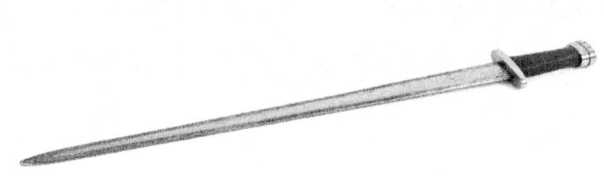

happenstance has also befallen the Usurper, his cronies, we may be a match for them after all".

"We will"! Vasnaar demanded, his tongue momentarily exploring the still hole in his slowly healing gum, "Then we can get off this damnable island and back to the homeland".

Myrrorball

PART SIX.
"IF I COULD JUST GET UP TO THE CITY".

Major Roxbrough & Nik Gehenna

61.

I doubt that we can continue while the Xətəlikimyrüç continues to ravage us", the beautiful and naked witch said suddenly slipping off the body of the equally nude Lord. "Thy mind be elsewhere. It felt like I was riding a corpse. Although...".

"Hast thou not one decent shred of virtue in thy entire body, Witch", Halsgough pulled a sheet over himself, suddenly feeling violated, "To what malign depths of depravity art thou willing to stoop, simply to satisfy thy basest of desires"?

Seemingly oblivious of her nudity, Banustib considered the question as though it had been uttered in more than rhetorical fashion.

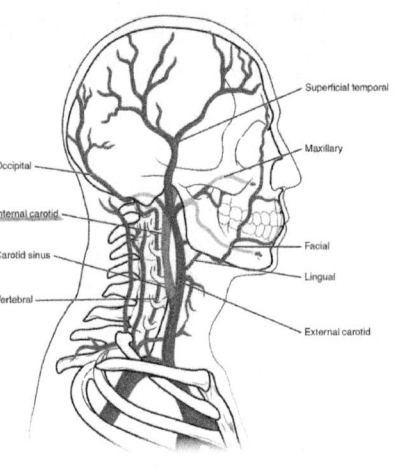

"I wouldst have to say that I am willing to descend infinitely in my quest for pure malignancy and evil", she admitted as though she was replying to a question as mundane as what vegetables one would prefer as an ingredient for a repast.

"I do not wish to be with thee any more except in thy duties as protector", the Lord of Halsgough returned, disgusted.

"Very well", the witch sounded completely happy with the new arrangement. "I will go and spend the rest of the night in mine lord of Koözoött's company. He has expressed an interest. Thy performance this evening has left me dissatisfied and frustrated perhaps he can...".

"Get out"! Halsgough roared, "I carest not even if thy copulates with Majax himself".

Myrrorball

The witch gave a twisted smile, strode out the tent, into the darkness of the forest. It was a mild evening, but even then the breeze hardened her nipples magnificently. She let a cantrip of dubious quality tumble from her lips. A strange transformation immediately began to reform her flesh. her breasts shrank to nothing more than a slim chest. Upon which, grew a down of dark brown hair.

Her labia suddenly met and sealed and then from the scar a pair of testicles began to grow in a scrotum. Finally, her(?) penis slowly emerged, thickened, lengthened until it was completely satisfactory. While this had been happening, the hair on her head shrank, a beard grew upon her features. Suddenly she was the sort of attractive young man that appealed to the Lord of Koözoött's queer proclivities. For it was common knowledge that though he liked the company of women, for his utmost pleasure, he preferred a youth.

The necromancer, who had been formerly witch entered the appropriate tent. Unadorned by even a stitch of garb about his person. Koözoött glanced up from a tome he had been studying by the tallow light of a candle.

"Whom art thou"? He asked, though his features betrayed him with a wanton smile, his eyes flickered as much as the flame of the candle itself.

"It be Banustib", the necromancer returned, "Dost thou not recognise me"?

"Thankfully, no", Koözoött returned, "So thou has finally gotten sick of letting Halsgough part thy oyster, coming to me in suitable flesh. Thou knowest I will prod thy Baalan's alley"?

"I anticipate it keenly", the depraved mage confessed, "Are we to tarry over small talk all evening? Or art thou going to cornholicate me"?

After it was over, as both were satiated, Koözoött observed,

Major Roxbrough & Nik Gehenna

"We are not going to make it as far as conflict with the King are we, Flit Faggot"?

The necromancer shook his head, "This island be not given the nomen Fire of Saah simply because of the Корунд", he smiled, "It be a fire, a dilitírio that has no antígialitikó. It consumes outsiders as though they were a vile organism. None who were born here can survive indefinitely. Sooner or later, the fire will take everyone".

"Then we shalt be doomed", Koözoött observed, "My only comfort be that Vasnaar will suffer the same fate. What of thee, Flit, willst thou escape when all seem on the point of annihilation"?

"I will go the same way as I arrived, through a phase door in the ether".

"Alone"?

Banustib grinned, "That would depend upon the machinations of any as would aspire to certain ambition amongst those who remain".

Koözoött smiled knowingly, "What art thou saying, Flit? That the Usurper be no longer thy chosen for such a role"?

"Exactly so", the necromancer nodded calmly, "He be not the one who can take Valgral and make of it what he desireth to shape. Such would take a man of greater scope and understanding of just how many shouldst perish to assert the new order".

"Many in the east"?

Banustib nodded, "The time be ripe, the King be gone, lost. He has no avenue of escape from the island that but greed brought him to. Twould be a merry conclude of the jig, all its elements were he never to see the homeland again".

"I agree and would be the one, Flit, with thy assistance. I wouldst also take Kyper Tor with us 'pon a night as such machinations be not confounded but realised".

"A triumvirate, with the guards as are left, starting our force. Yet one which could be grown to an vast proportion".

"Aye", Koözoött laughed, "What sayest thee, shall the triumvirate be actual and see such destruction as mortal man has ne-er e-er witnessed before in the making of it"?

By way of an answer, the necromancer began a series of vague passes and uttered a litany of curious inflection and language, only hesitating briefly to instruct Koözoött,

"Go get the others, yet not Halsgough who would challenge the king, let him remain with the option to satisfy".

Koözoött rushed outside as quietly as he could while the epicentre of the ether in the tent began to oscillate and disrupt from its normal fabric. By the time the men had been clandestinely assembled without, a phase door of violaceous hue hummed. Crackling with necromantic vitality.

The necromancer ushered the raring force, diminished as it was, into the tent. Through the ovoid of bafflingly obscure efficaciousness. Two at a time they dived toward the dark speculumiata to who knew where, save for the creator himself. It proceeded until only Koözoött together with Banustib remained to jump through to beyond.

"Whither dost this envelope terminate"? the former demanded.

Banustib grinned, "Why Castle Koözoött, what more fitting of locale, from which, to commence the rebellion"?

The Lord of that very same place laughed as he dived through the phase door. Banustib, looking consumed, dropping by the energy loss required to keep the door open so long, dived in as the door itself imploded with a sucking crackle.

When Halsgough awoke as light intruded into his canvas domain the following morning, he thought it much earlier than actual. There were no sounds of activity, the preparation of breakfast, all the other movements, coming from outside. Pulling on his breaks, he was so curious that he emerged into the open bare-chested to see why none was roused from slumber.

Major Roxbrough & Nik Gehenna

A quick search of the camp, dread growing with each new intrusion into another tent confirmed his mounting suspicion. He had found none with him, he was alone, deserted.

Had Vasnaar been closer than he still was, he would have heard the roar of anguish that rent the early peace of the forest.

62.

When the ubiquitous Avgófýllo finally began to thin, we knew we were much closer to our goal. We had also crossed the roughly defined border from Kémerké Territory, up into the land owned by the Akerányó. It would not be long before we reached the end of the frond trees, passing onto an open plain dominated by the mountains of Thol almost filling the horizon. I grew excited and nervous in just about equal proportions. What if the closest face of the mountain grew sheer the nearer we got to the plateau of Tru-eti Varzslatoj? Which of the party would be able to continue? Which had an experience of heights even?

It was time to get some answers from that question. I waited until we had made camp for the night, created on the very edge of the forest. In the dusk sky, the mountains hung over us like some huge rock predator.

"There is something I need to ask every one of you", I began. Telling them then of my concern, asking them how they felt they would cope. If they would return from where they had come. Leaving just me, together with my spouse, to brave the mountains.

"I have no fear of heights", Vandeveble returned at once, "but it's a brave or foolish warrior who would not fear the Qəhvəyayı".

"The Qəhvəyayı"? I echoed, "Before my *knowledge* suddenly gave me an image in my mind.

Not a creature I wanted to meet anytime soon. It possessed a huge bulky body covered in pale and dark blue fur, a massive head that boasted impressive teeth filling its maw. The ears were tall, pointed, huge disc-shaped eyes red beneath them were wicked looking. I deduced it to be a bear/bat/owl combination of Terran creatures.

"The Qəhvəyayı are very large carnivores that will take man meat, given chance", the native warrior informed me. "Thank the gods they do not venture to the south of the island. When the odd one does we mount a concerted attack, kill it as quickly as possible. Never without loss I might add, they defend themselves with great ferocity and I would not go up against one with anything other than at least nine others at my shoulder".

"Does that mean you are ready to turn back"? I wondered aloud.

"That depends on if you convince me otherwise", came the honest reply, "Firstly I need to see just how effective your strange weaponry is, secondly I would like to know about the treasure".

"Treasure"?

"Yes the treasure", Tergiss cut in, "The stash, the mound of Корунд that are a deeper yet more lambent blue than the eyes of the goddess Shakita and legend has it that they are very blue indeed".

"I was the Visionary, I could not say I did not know, so I responded in the best way available to me".

"I will answer that question, both of them, in fact, on the morrow. Light is failing now we should make camp. If any want to leave before the morning though, then it just remains for me to thank you for your endeavours thus far".

"We will stay", Collari told me. (We? So they must have been discussing this eventuality before that meeting), "If you fire the blazerifle into the night, display its awesomely destructive power.

"Once Angelus has set neath the horizon, you will all have your display then".

They agreed, we camped and suppered together. Afterwards, I walked into a clearing to demonstrate to all a brief burst from the rifle. Convinced to a man (or woman) that I could easily cope with anything that came our way it was agreed to continue *if* there was any treasure to be found and won. So once I had settled down on my back under the stars, the constellations not recognizable to me, I took a hefty dose of snufz and waited for *the hit*.

My mind once again left my body, as I flew through the darkness into the chiaroscuro nigrescence that was the tall craggy mountains called, Thol. It took me quite some time to find Tru-eti Varzslatoj, huddled as it was in a ravine which the occasional traveller in the mountains could miss seven times out of ten.

The buildings were of brick!

The rooves of them, tile!

I was looking down at what to me, represented Yorkshire? Or was I in a snufz-fuelled delirium? How could I possibly know the answer to that? The Zernoplat came into my mind then, causing me to wonder if what I was seeing **was some sort of cruel trick on your part Hhrrhhoehhrrhooooingohh**? Either that or this was yet another parallel facet of the multiverse. Could it be a tear in the layer between two verses, anything was possible since the day I had first heard a slithering sound at my office window? I could not shake the foolish notion that I was in a scene that was Jabberwockian in extremis.

Why is a cat-like a postage stamp?

Because while one needs licking to become useful, it is useful that the other does plenty of licking.

Because while the postman delivers one, he usually scares the other away.

Because while one can be searched for by a mouse, the other hunts the mouse itself.

I then noticed the figures moving about in the Yorkshire suburbia, swooped down to investigate them further. They all went garbed in black and white woollen half-coats. It was cool up in the mountains, even on a temperate island. The jackets had very tall pointed hoods, the wearers of them wore them over their heads mostly. The hardiest of them did not, revealed himself to have the pale blue skin of the usual inhabitants of Egszígør. I could not be positive of that at the time, for the blue hazed reflected light of Brahma was especially bright on that particular night. The white hair was unmistakable though. Conjuring mentally, a startling resemblance to Andorians. Without the antenna that was - coupled with the fact that Andorians were not real. Then the knowledge given me by the snufz informed me that the people of Tru-eti Varzslatoj were called the Guardians. At least the males were, I saw no females at that point. If they were guardian, which I doubted not one jot, what were they guarding? In the middle of one of the gardens, which I called them because that is what they looked like. Bordered areas at the back of each house of brick and tile. In the centre of one was a tall stone edifice of some kind. Its level of construction humbled the houses. It had been constructed like a pyramid, hefty stone sections cut into slabs that married perfectly with the ones beneath. There was no need for mortar such was the accuracy of the building of the monument. Floating through the thick stone walls as though they were nothing more than a projection, I found the cache. It was true what everyone had told me about the stones I knew to be sapphires. They did indeed possess a sublime perfection of beauty. The Guardians other duty must have included cutting and polishing the gems, for they possessed a lambency I found difficult to view without being forced to turn away by the brilliance of dazzlementation. I returned swiftly to my body, simply floated until sensibility finally returned to me. Not before I had asked the important question of my *knowledge*, however.

Was the city of the sapphires a gateway to alternative Earths? Could I get to one of them with whomsoever wished to come with me from it?

The answer was ambiguous. A gateway did exist, when I got more specific, however, as in could I access it, then no answer came to me. I chose to draw one conclusion from this, a gateway existed, but I had not the knowledge to access it. I had to get up to the city. Not merely get blood up into my brain, but physically reach the metropolis I reasoned that one of the Guardians would know how to traverse the layers of the multiverse. As it was to turn out though, that assumption proved to be erroneous.

62.

"Be we lost or no"? Vasnaar demanded of the Szorkráló. Hízlatan shrugged,
"We are on Egszígør, somewhere in the central part, I cannot be more precise than that".
"Coming from a Szorkráló that wouldst appear to be prevarication", Roxbrough observed, "We must get Lolocken to a village where one of your following has access to the precious salves of which you speak. It helps when one is bitten, doest it not"?
Oslan-On-the-Bank was even less happy, "Our quest seems doomed to failure, Sire, every day we proceed more of our number becomes prey to the hated beasts of this ever-flowing canopy. Will there even be an end to it? Will we not miss Halsgough by metres or more? Travelling practically blind, in this stumbling fashion? If Hízlatan struggles to discern the way, what chance have we of encountering them"?
"During thy absence from this court", Vasnaar began, "Thou hast grown defeatist, Margrave of the Bank. I take thy point regarding my Lord of Lolocken, however. We shall enter the next village we find that possesses friendly natives".
Roxbrough asked the Szorkráló, "Where be that likely to be, what will be the name of such a village, Hízlatan"?
Hízlatan returned, "I know of a village which is said to be sympathetic to the Kémerké, it is called Közlopon and lies in the very heart of the island. Flanked on either side by the rivers Sihoa and Gilgolium, as, I believe - we are now".
Vasnaar decided, "We will begin a zig-zag course on the morrow and hope to chance upon this Közlopon then, for without the counsel of my Lord of Lolocken our chance of defeating Halsgough grows still slimmer.
"I have another suggestion, Sire", Roxbrough then piped up. Why not make permanent camp here for a few days

sending out scouts west and east and let them find the village. That way thy few remaining Lords will be less at risk than if we continue all through this infernal forest"?

Byno declared, "Now that be a worthy notion, Father. Let the peasant soldiers take the risk, not we nobles"?

Vasnaar glanced at Oslan-On-the-Bank, then Flahé, both indicated their agreement to the idea. None of them wanted to become Blue-Mumblies as so many had been doomed to become before that day.

63.

The Lord of the town of Halsgough was not either any more. He was stubborn though, refusing to simply lay down and die. Refused to walk toward a Kézőrös, to get himself bitten. Becoming one, with the island. Refused to be defeated. Gathering up the items he felt were essential to his continuation, he packed the largest bundle he could carry over a protracted period, began to leave the site of the camp. For the briefest of moments, he felt disorientated, then managed to gain his bearings and set of ever south.

A day passed devoid of incident.
Another.
A third.

Luck stayed with the Lord of Halsgough. On the day when his supplies were beginning to run dangerously low, he was suddenly confronted by a native. He had infringed the outer boundary of a village. Slowly drawing his sword he laid it on the forest floor, the dirk in his belt followed, then he showed the native his outstretched palms.

Given that he did not speak the local tongue, it was the best way he possessed of demonstrating his peaceful intent. The gesture was understood. The native nodded, waved that he followed where he led, after retrieving his weapons. As they walked, Halsgough tapped his chest and said his name several times. He learned then that the warrior was called Ðöyüşçqüyaramazcani (which meant - brave-hero who is occasionally naughty in Közloponoid, the language of the Közloponi of Közlopon). They reached the village of Közlopon in a surprisingly brief time. Halsgough would have happened upon it by chance even if Ðöyüşçqüyaramazcani had not intercepted him.

Expecting to be conducted to whomsoever was in the position of greatest authority, the Lord of Valgral was disappointed. Ðöyüşçqüyaramazcani seemed only willing to take him to his abode. Halsgough tried to request that he be conducted to the leader of the Közloponi. Either Ðöyüşçqüyaramazcani did not understand him, or feigned lack of comprehension for some private reason of his own.

In any event, it was to the warrior's hut he was taken. There to meet a considerable compensation when introduced to a female Közloponi, who Halsgough managed finally to learn was called Döləeçim. The native girl was comely, shapely, but the Lord of Valgral could not quite work out her relationship to his former guide. If she were a sister, it would be interesting, a wife/mate far less so. They gestured him to be seated on a rough woven mat and then pressed a bowl of dubious meet into his palms, followed by a wooden spoon. Gingerly, Halsgough put a morsel into his mouth. The meat was delicious. Knowing they could not understand barely a word he said, he told the girl,

"If thou be as accomplished in thy bed as thou art in the kitchen, Maid, then I might be tempted to assume the doings and position of an native".

It was most likely the girl took his tone to be a compliment of her domestic endeavours and adeptitude with the cuisine, for she smiled and returned something in Közloponoid.

"Yes I wouldst like to cave dive with thee my pretty and churn the butter, but Ðöyüşçqüyaramazcani here might object. Now if I am going to assume this village as mine new domain, I might find it right expeditious to commence learning the language, or mayhap teach thee Valgraln".

"With pointing and shaking of the head or nodding, the former Lord who thought to conquer Valgral for himself started the commencement of his new project. He was determined to take command of the village of Közlopon.

64.

We had started toward the mountains the following dawn. The blue-grass saturated with dew, the tops of the peaks bathed in mist. How the men could still go bare-chested in the main, while I was obliged to turn up my Zernoplatite suit several notches was beyond my powers of comprehension. Initially, we made good progress, for the fact was that it was much easier walking through the grasslands at the base of the mountains in the coolness than ever it had been in the steaming forest. Even when Angelus finally did burn her way through the cloud, it was with watery illumination at best. There was far less heat than that we had previously endured. When we stopped for lunch, the grass had grown at first more sparse and then a different and hardier variety. The base of the first range was practically in touching distance.

"No Qəhvəyayı encounters thusly", I observed to Mesoloras who happened to be closest to me".

"Their first choice for sleep are the myriad caves we will soon be passing", the Kémerké brave countered, dampening my enthusiasm as he said it.

"Yet if you want to see the treasure of Tru-eti Varzslatoj, the risk is worth the taking, is it not"?

"Should we post a watch tonight"?

Mesoloras did not laugh much, yet he had laughed at that question.

"What"? I wanted to know.

"There has been a night guard every night of this journey", he told me. "One or two of us always keep the Visionary safe".

"Why did you not tell me about it", I desired to know, "Why was I not included in the rota to keep the camp safe at night"?

Major Roxbrough & Nik Gehenna

"You are the Visionary and Quianhua is your mate, we are the ones who promised to conduct you safely to the mountains and Tru-eti Varzslatoj. Each of us in this brief stay on the world must follow their path. Ours is to guard, to explore, to bring wealth to our villages whensoever we can".

"I will thank you all for what you've done for me so far, I hope you can get some Корунд (Corundum) from the Guardians. I had told them everything I had learned during our marching that day. It had only served to make them even more eager to see that which I had detected in my capacity as visionary.

The night that followed such a hopeful series of plans was the worst we had endured thus far, one of our numbers lay mangled, bloody and dead at the end of it.

They came out of the darkness, working as a team. It seemed the Qəhvəyayı hunted in a pack when the opportunity presented itself. In our case, the opportunity was human flesh, of which the Qəhvəyayı were fond when they could get it. I was in our double bag sound asleep when the calling, roaring and scream rent the air suddenly and disorientingly.

"What was that"? Quianhua demanded, obviously scared half out of her wits.

"Stay here and keep quiet", I urged as I slid out the top and grabbed my blazerifle. The fire, which had been keeping the dreaded creatures at bay initially, had died down to nothing more than glowing rubescent embers. That was a double blow to our ability to withstand attack. The flames no longer kept the Qəhvəyayı at a safe distance, added to which it was much easier to see them when they did attack. I was brave enough, or stupid enough to close my eyes for a few seconds after gazing into the embers willing my pupils to respond to the dimness. All too soon I opened them again and peered into the rusty gloom. At the edge of the clearing lay a twisted mangled body that was in a position that no healthy person would assume. Over to the ruin's form was what looked like a severed arm. None of the braves could withstand that sort of injury and live. The native guard had formed a close-knit group standing forward of their dead friend, waiting for the trio to lunge at them again.

Rushing over to them, I recognised Mesoloras and barked at him an inquiry as to the location of the beasts. He indicated with a pointed finger before pulling back his bowstring and letting an arrow fly into the dark. A bellow of pain indicated he had hit something. Depressing the trigger on my rifle I sprayed the same area in a quarter of a circle fan-shape. It was terrible.

The Qəhvəyayı may be bloodthirsty carnivores, yet I would not wish the sort of death I gave them on any living creature. For what seemed like an age, they tore about trying desperately to escape their burning coats. Both of them were screaming in agony and terror. The only thing I could do was blast them again, higher, taking their heads and watching them slump to the ground an heinous crackling pyre of burning body fat.

"Where's the other one"? I demanded.

It was Vandeveble who replied, "Fled, they have no small amount of rudimentary intelligence. It worked out what would happen to it if it stayed around us".

Not wishing to get any closer to the ruined body I asked Chavayda,

"Who is over there, I feel mortified she did not make it"?

Tergiss came out of the darkness and told me, "Khanivool, she was on watch, killed before even the rest of us knew what was happening".

"We must bury her lest the smell of blood brings more of them down on us", Collari decided. I counted those before me together with Cassiti they were five natives strong,

"Where is Chavayda"? I asked, thinking they would say he had stayed back for some reason.

"We do not know"Mesoloras admitted then, "We think the first Qəhvəyayı carried him off into the darkness".

"Then he could still be alive", I noted and began to race back to Quianhua,

"Where are you going"? Tergiss asked, shocked,

"After the brute, once I'm dressed. I have this blazerifle and a searpistol too, he might still be alive".

Major Roxbrough & Nik Gehenna

"There might be more Qəhvəyayı out there too", Vandeveble observed, "You cannot go alone. I will come with you".

"And I", Cassiti added to my surprise.

Tergiss added,

"I can dig a grave as well as any man you two go with them too".

Mr Genks approached, my wife in his company. Before any of the Kémerké could challenge him for his tardiness, he told them,

"My chief concern ith for the Vithionary'th woman, I choothe to act ath her perthonal bodyguard. Give me the pithtol Nik? I will make thertain the two women who remain here are kept safe. The creature may double back on itfhelf".

I nodded, by then half-dressed and tossed the pistol to the manbian.

"Ready"? I asked the others. They had used the same time to ready themselves. Each of them nodded grimly.

Off into the dark plain, we went, on one horizon was the ominously dark shaped of the Avgófýllo - black in the night. Opposing that was a high and mighty wall of fuliginous rock, the mountains of Thol.

We quartered the terrain for two hours by my Casio. Found nothing of any worth. Not a hair, blood, mangled body, the remaining Qəhvəyayı had gone further than we reached. It was either dragging Chavayda with it, had devoured him, or the two of them were not together.

If the brave warrior had been devoured, I fancied we would have found some evidence of it. Though it was quite dark that night with Brahma on the far side of Rozhelia. If the two of them were not together, then just where had he gotten to? The inescapable conclusion was that the Qəhvəyayı had dragged him off insensible, for a truly grizzly demise once he regained consciousness.

"This is no use", I declared at length, "We will never find him without light, the only lantern we have is not affording enough illumination to make things much better. We must wait until dawn and then search for them anew".

Myrrorball

No one got any sleep for the rest of the night. We ate a hurried breakfast in silence and set forth shortly afterwards with Tergiss added to our patrol.

Around noon, easily noted by the position of the sun, now that we were out of the forest canopy, I told the others the search was over. We would have quartered the island forever and never found out what had happened to the brave. It was time to know when one was beaten. For their part, the others accepted my decision without complaint. I doubt they even harboured opposing views, such was the logic of my decision. We could not know it at the time, but our first encounter with the Qəhvəyayı proved to be our last. For later that same day, rushing through twilight to reach the base of the mountains, we left the great plain before them.

Collari told us that it would be likely that the Qəhvəyayı would be behind us for they lived at the very edge of the mountains to hunt in the forest, there was little to sustain them once the granite crags of Thol denied purchase to plant and most animals - both. It did not make any of us feel better. The loss of Khanivool being particularly endured. She had been popular and though what had possibly happened to Chavayda was terrible, he had not. The older brave had kept himself pretty much to himself in much the same way as the manbian. The latter avoided great discourse due to the clumsy phrasing caused by his elongated tongue though while Chavayda had simply been antisocial.

What the mountains did provide us with was a vast proliferation and variety of caves. Once I had fired into one a couple of times to be certain it was uninhabited, we warmed it with a built fire. The fuel had the secondary benefit of keeping predators at bay. Additionally, they could only approach from one direction, which would involve passing through a fire curtain, literally.

Major Roxbrough & Nik Gehenna

We were going to suffer more ill-luck though three days into the mountains, just before the serious climbing began. Our last night in a cave could have been that, because of what happened, even if we found others. I had blasted the interior in the usual way, we had gotten a fire going as dusk settled over the mountains. A rustling noise from behind us caught us all equally off-guard. Before we could even vocalise our concern, a black fury flapping creature flew into Tergiss' face, sinking evil-looking twin fangs into her neck before one of Mesoloras' arrows plunged into its vile diseased body. It had been a brave shot to attempt he could have just as easily hit and killed the girl. In many ways, it would have been better if he had!

I stood over the black, leathery creature that had fallen at my feet onto the lithic floor of the cavern,

"What the devil is that"? I asked the others while Cassiti helped the injured girl to lay down so that she could examine the wound.

"That is a šikšno", Vandeveble declared gloomily, "Horrible, disgusting creatures they are diseased, they carry putligė".

I did not need to ask any more questions when I looked more closely at the dead animal - a type of flying rat. I knew what putligė was too - rabies! We could not travel the following day. Hampered as we were by the poor dying girl. The toxin poured through Tergiss' body at an alarming rate. Initially, she remained cheerful but then began to notice unusual feelings or tingling around the wound at her throat. Soon afterwards, there was a period of tiredness, complete lack of appetite, headache, fever, cough, sore throat, abdominal pain, nausea, vomiting, and diarrhoea. An hour or so of distress worry, irritability, an inability to sleep any more. Depression followed, preceded hallucinations. The muscles of her body soon became paralysed, starting at the site of the wound. She fell into a coma that evening and never saw another day. It was a desperate time for us, two of our number dead and one missing, in less than a week. We still had the faces of some rather daunting crags to scale too, before we would descend into the hollow that was the magical city.

The following morning after burying yet another of our dear companions we checked our climbing and scaling equipment. Helmets, harness, ropes, slings quick-draws nuts and hexes, belay devices non-locking carabiners, and cams, we had everything to ensure our safety, all courtesy of the bunker. Yet it was still possible to plummet to a painful death if good fortune was lacking and it seemed to have deserted us for the present. I therefore urged,

"Please be careful, I do not want to lose anyone else, do you all understand"?

They nodded, I then asked,

"Whom amongst you is the most accomplished climber"?

It was Cassiti, so Mr Choon was placed in his harness and slung onto her back. He was so cool, he promptly fell asleep purring all the while.

"If we make that first ridge up there and there is sufficient room, we shall make our first camp and call it a good day's progress", I told them deciding as I spoke.

As expected, Mister Genks and Quianhua struggled most, then me, the men of the native con contingency and Cassiti seemed as agile as Mr Choon had been in his youth, which was some time ago. The girl would have made the perfect cat burglar, although when I type that I note that she was more like a fly than a feline. She seemed so skilled at scaling even sheer surfaces that she looked as though she was clinging to featureless granite. Which was impossible, but that is how easy she made our climbing look. She soon went to the highest climb and then hauled the rest of us up to meet her. Of the native braves, Mesoloras was the next most talented, so he followed and did a lot of hauling when it came for the manbian to try each new challenge. Even so at the end of the first day, we had ascended three times greater than I had hoped. Where we camped if we had two more days of similar progress we would reach where I knew the lip of the depression to be, in which, lay the fabled city of Tru-eti Varzslatoj.

Major Roxbrough & Nik Gehenna

It was the following day when something very noteworthy happened. We were on an especially difficult section of the mountain. Even Cassiti was finding one particular face difficult. An unknown hand reached from over the lip of the ledge and hauled her up to it. By the time I gained the ridge, certain introductions had already taken place. I was introduced to a Valgraln who I had heard mentioned by Vasnaar and Flahé whilst still in their company. As my attention was distracted by what appeared to be a glowing glass-hand on the youth's wrist, he asked me,

"Visionary"? for that was how I was introduced, "Thou newest my father, the lord of Flahé, tell me, Sir, be he in fine fettle and customary haleness"?

"He enjoys rude health my Lord", I gave him the courtesy title, "Naturally he was concerned about your fate at the hands of the usurpers, but he was well and at his monarch's side".

We stopped for a short respite from the ardours of the climb. The remarkable and incident rich son of Flahé told us his fantastical tale. It sounded like pure fantasy to me, but then I had only ever written science fiction and sometimes hard science in my projects at that. A magical hand indeed! It was an artefact originally belonging to some highly advanced race who had left it behind on the relatively primitive world of Rozhelia. It was even beyond the explorer's who had created and stocked the bunker. The layers between the various dimensions of the leylines of the multiverse were weak at the nexus point, which lay, in such a world. I very much doubted that this latest mental diversion had anything to do with the Zernoplat. Even with their advanced technology, whatever would possess them to create what would be an alien appendage? They managed pretty well with their pseudopods. Returning from my thoughts and conjectures, I focused in on the end of Hersko's narrative, which he was just bringing to a climax,

"...seemeth I was not so adept with the Vandei Motestas as the day had but promised. I didst find myself short of my objective and was seeking to climb to the lip of the depression when the yon clamour of thyselves didst reach mine ears".

"Join us", Cassiti asked with just a shade more enthusiasm than Mesoloras found acceptable. It was no secret that the warrior brave found the girl greatly to his liking, harbouring a discrete desire for her. Hersko was not without attraction, the Kémerké girl was taken with him too.

For his part, he had found nothing unusual in Mr Genks or Mister Choon. It seemed obvious to me that the Valgraln had wider exposure to things fantastical than I and my spouse.

I was keen for him to be one of us also, with his hand he might well have occasion to help us one day before I could get my ever diminishing quantity of snufz up my hooter.

He did not take a great deal of convincing after Cassiti had asked him, we were all going the same way too. I wondered not for the first time what the monk-like guardians of the Корунд (Corundum) would think to our arrival and how accommodating they would or would not be? After all, it was their task to guard the sapphires, stones said to be more beryl than the blue eyes of the goddess Shakita, she was supposed to possess very blue eyes indeed.

Once again, our rank grew in number if only by one, we had become an ennead. If one counted Mister Choon that was, I always did. That caused me to wonder briefly how the three other babies were doing in the gentle care of the gorgeous Leoma, I imaged myself a cat, purring and rubbing up to her magnificent bosom.

So prepared had we been for the climb, that we suffered no mishap, thank goodness. The following day as we crested the lip and saw the plateau beyond, we were intercepted by a single line of guardians.

"We are peaceful", I told them firmly, "We seek no conflict, but come to observe the wondrous city you had created up here".

One of the line, indistinguishable from any of the others, for they all wore the distinctive black and white jackets of rough woollen fabric and black bohos, observed,

Major Roxbrough & Nik Gehenna

"You are the Terran"?

I gasped, admitted, "I am truly he, how did you know? How is it you speak English? Or is it a derivative, Amerikanese, Australianese, Canadaki"?

"You have many questions, Terran", the Guardian observed. "Let me answer them all in a single simple response? Up here in Tru-eti Varzslatoj we grow the product you have given the name snufz, we call it uoslė, for us it achieves the same results, breaking down the barriers of reality and expanding our minds. I am Veriš. Would you like to introduce me to your friends, the feline and the amphibian"?

"Mister Genks is something more than a mere amphibian", I told Veriš, "He is a manbian, sentient and intelligent like the rest of us. Except for Mr Choon that is".

"And your other companions"?

I made the introductions, unsure as to Veriš' abrupt manner. Perhaps that was the way in Tru-eti Varzslatoj? I was not quick to judge, meeting one's first Zernoplat changed perspective in many ways. When I got to Quianhua, Veriš was suddenly much more animate.

"Another Terran, a female"!

"Yes" my spirited wife agreed, breaking her silence, "At least I was, the last time I checked".

"Terran, please ask the two females to keep silent whilst in our city"? Veriš requested then in a quiet calm tone, "There are no others here, they will prove a ...distraction".

It caused Cassiti to scowl, for she had begun picking up some English from Quianhua of late. What a curious situation that was I reflected at that moment, a Chinese girl teaching a Kémerké squaw how to speak in a language that was not their first tongue in either case. I found that my mind had to take convoluted courses since taking snufz or uoslė. It was as though my inner thoughts contained even more corridors than before. I was eager to travel down as many as possible. For that reason, though I seemed to be becoming somewhat scatter-brained to those in my company, the absent-minded but strangely brilliant academic. Indeed Veriš had been speaking to me,

Myrrorball

those behind me fidgeting as a result. The Guardian was forced to repeat himself,

"I offered to lead you into the district of Tru-eti Varzslatoj known as Varzsaoj, Terran, you did not appear to hear me, your mind was elsewhere. I advise caution when using uoslė in the future, it can be habit-forming and in certain cases can induce hallucinatory mental decay".

I certainly did not want that, my brain was my second favourite organ (yes I know it's an old one, but it's a goodie).

"Sorry I was kilometres away", I admitted, thank you, to where whom or what are you taking us"?

"To accommodation", Veriš returned simply.

"And when will we get to meet the governing body of this wonderful place"?

"The guardians are a contumacious ochlocracist municipality", Veriš informed me, "If you desired to meet the Administrative Commander for the month, then you are currently speaking to him - me".

"When can we have some cache"? Vandeveble suddenly demanded with his usual vim and vigour".

"What have you to barter with", Veriš asked not unreasonably.

"If you promise to give us what we want, we will leave without strangling your scrawny neck, how does that sound for an offer"?

Veriš stopped walking, the rest of us froze, I half turned to admonish the warrior for his rudeness, he was already falling at that point. Mesoloras' hand darted over his shoulder for an arrow in his quiver. He fell beside his fellow brave. Collari glanced at me, then Hersko. Finally went to hurl his stone axe at Veriš. He joined the other two on the ground.

"*Veriš*"! I demanded, "Is this any way to treat travellers who have come so far to meet with you? What have you done to them are they...".

"Dead"? interrupted the Guardian. He shook his head, "No they are not dead, although what they just attempted does carry the death penalty here in the city".

Major Roxbrough & Nik Gehenna

I glanced uneasily at Hersko. His hand seemed to be drifting toward his broadsword. I shook my head in his direction, stayed further movement.

"What is to become of them, you are not going to...".

"Execute them". Once again he had cut me off halfway through a sentence, very rude. "No, but are to be banished, I am afraid. Tomorrow they will find themselves back at the base of the mountains of Thol and bereft of climbing equipment. Their weapons will be with them though we are not barbarians, we Guardians. Come, the house is not far from this spot"?

"You expect us to leave them here? They are our friends".

"I assure you they will awaken at the base of the mountain on the morrow and completely unharmed".

"How did you render them unconscious, I saw no weapon? How can we not be certain they are not slain, dead"?

"Do dead men breathe"? Veriš pointed to Vandeveble's barrel chest, it was slowly rising and falling as though in slumber. "You have a decision to make, Terran, whether to pursue your original quest or go back, with these savages".

Mister Genks urged me, "They have therved you well, but now it ith time to part wayth with them. What you and Herthko with to achieve ith more important, Cathiti needth to make her dethithion ath to whom thee witheth to thtay with".

"The Visionary", the girl answered at once, to the annoyance of Quianhua and Veriš. The latter chose not to remark on the infraction thankfully.

"Well"? the Administrative Commander for the month wished to know.

"Do we just leave them there, lying on the path like that"? It was my final weak objection.

Veriš waved to six of those who had been following us at a respectful distance. The three sleeping warriors were hoisted off the ground, carried away from us.

Myrrorball

"Now you facilities for the night", he explained, "I will call on you for dinner and explain what is going to happen tomorrow".
"Don't we get to say what we desire to do"? I asked amused, but Veriš wiped the smile off my face with one word,
"No".

65.

A heavy fall of snow had descended during the night, the pine trees were laden with it. It made the forest a quiet place indeed. Koözoött huddled before the great grate in his private study, rubbing his hands together to try and get some circulation going in them. Beneath his flowing melton caftan was a woollen jerkin and a singlet under that. He was still cold. His body had grown used to a mean temperature of 20°C. It did not take kindly to being instantly plunged into 0°. The door opened and in strode the handsome man (handsome - yet queer) that the Necromancer was currently playing one of his malign roles within.

"I have machinated a certain level of success with my work, last night Koözoött".

"Lord Koözoött, Necromancer. How many times must thee be thusly instructed"?

"Alas, forever", Banustib grinned, "For I will never call he lord who I poke the damnable fire-ally of in the darkness of the bedroom. To me thou art my kutyavialt çirkliçinçirkinisi. I choose to use thy nomen as a social courtesy".

How then am I to command respect? To lead the rebellion against the east, if thou disrespects me so sorely"?

Major Roxbrough & Nik Gehenna

"With my assistance of course and what assistance it will be", The Necromancer seemed in a relished black spirit that day, causing the Lord of the Keep to finally inquire,

" Very well what hast thou done that will aid our pursuit of the subjugation of the east"?

Without asking, as was customary, Banustib seated himself in the presence of the Lord, even dared to place his kid-booted feet up on the table. He reached forward awkwardly, picked the best apple from those in the wooden bowl and drawing forth a wicked-looking knife began to peel it slowly. Theatrical pause completed, he asked,

"How wouldst it be Koözoött, if every man under thy command who fell on the battlefield didst reanimate after a brief pause, to pursue the conflict once again"?

Koözoött was aghast, "The dead not staying dead"?

Banustib grinned.

"Thou canst do that"?

The Necromancer nodded, puffed out his chest and observed, "At present thy only sworn ally be Kyper Tor, yet once the victories start to mount, just watcheth the sons of Halsia, Gral, Tavaaro, Rhynturo and all the others rally 'neath thy flag. Knelforest be ripe for the plucking the instant Kyper Tor arrives and joins thy colours".

"From Knelforest we couldst strike south and have the seat of Staltidore, then push into eastern Valgral, none can stand before us".

"None, Koözoött, before this winter be done thou will be king of Valgral.

66.

Myrrorball

Staltidore saw the envelope shimmer open, the man dressed in a caftan of emerald etched in daffodil step from out of it. He recognised possibly the most well know mage of Doras-Van-der-Garra-Plee,

"Bodakin! If thou art about the affairs of we ordinary men once more, then there must be trouble in the realm? Lolocken needeth thy aid for one. Yesterday our Prince was also bitten".

Roxbrough emerged from his bag and nodded to Bodakin, the remainder of the royal force slowly roused themselves even though the hour was two in the morning. The slim and grey-haired Sorcerer who still chose to scrape his features devoid of hair each morning smiled, bowed his head to the king and then asked,

"Be the duo who are injured in yonder tent? My first duty must be to administer sorcerous salve to their wounds so that the toxin of the Kézőrös doest not claim them as Blevastís".

"Thence will thou get me back to Castle Kingshire", Vasnaar commanded, Flahé, Staltidore, Oslan-On-the-Bank and Roxbrough to their seats".

"Alas my vitality be currently almost exhausted, but I will do what I can, Majesty. Thou must know that Halsgough no longer be a threat to thee. Rather it be Koözoött who plots infamous rebellion, with the aid of Kyper Tor.

"Those two impudent upstarts", Vasnaar laughed, "The others will not follow them"?

"The rest of the western lords are dead, Sire. Halsia, Rhynturo, Teleocea, Kynoberg, Tavaaro, Kloenk, Drably and Gral all killed by thy petty greed for Корунд (Corundum)".

"Have a-care, Sorcerer", the Margrave said in a kindly tone, "Thou art addressing thy king".

Doras-Van-der-Garra-Plee has no such autocratic ruler, my Lord of Oslan-On-the-Bank, I came here to help, will do my best. Certain observation must be spoken, though. Certain detail must be given voice, unpalatable as that might proveth".

Major Roxbrough & Nik Gehenna

"And thou hast said it", Vasnaar was conciliatory, "I regret the outcome of our expedition. Underestimating the Fire that burned on Saah. The same mistake shalt not be repeated. Far Side will not be visited again in mine reign. Now mage, my son"?

Bodakin hurried into the tent and applied a healing salve to the two knights of Valgral, bitten by the ubiquitous Kézőrös.

"What be the nature of that foul-smelling concoction, Bodakin"? Roxbrough had followed the mage into the lantern-lit enclosure. A lantern that the Császária had carried with him.

"Brulidioné", the Sorcerer replied, "Thou dost not desireth to know all of its constituents".

"How soon will the apparent decrepitude leave their tortured flesh"?

"Mere hours".

"Then we canst soon live this curs-ed place"?

Bodakin shook his head, "Alas and alack not till mine vitality once more returneth to mine body. I am not as young as I was, I refuse to ward off the ravage of age by malign manners as do some in mine order. We shall remain 'pon the Fire of Saah yet-awhile".

"Can thou tellest me one thing then, Sorcerer"? Bodakin looked into the Császária's features,

"If I am able"?

"Using that strange silver brew of thine the saggering or some such, canst thou tell me if the Császárim and my children be safe and well"?

Bodakin smiled at the request.

"Thou meanest snabbertok and the use of the seeing fluid be not necessary for truly I didst visit them in person but a few short days past".

"At the mountain keep"?

The Sorcerer nodded, The last family I journeyed too, of those who had their lordship on Far Side. All the children are fine, my lord and thy lady be as lovely and as charming as ever".

"Be thy visits the reason for coming here? Or be that the machinations of the little dwarfish necromancer"?

Myrrorball

"I view the realm in the snabbertok in constant rotation, making certain the cosmic balance twixt good and evil be maintained. Once I saw that my olde adversary sought once again to upset that balance that prompted my subsequent reactions".

The King suddenly entered the tent. Glanced at the patients, both of whom remained asleep, then proceeded to ask pretty much the same questions as had been previously voiced. Bodakin seemed to possess endless patience, answered each one as though it was the first time such an enquiry had been directed toward him.

"I think it best we remain stationary then", Vasnaar finally decided to his current right-hand man in the Császária, "Why search for a village which might resent our intrusion when we can simply wait for the Sorcerer here to regain his powers"?

"I will inform the others of thy decision, Sire", the Császária agreed.

67.

Ðöyüşçqüyaramazcani entered the hut, telling Halsgough,

"Two Kémerké warriors have just been intercepted, captured at our northern boundary, they looked bedraggled, weary, have an interesting tale to tell, my Lord".

He had spoken in a curious pigeon-form of Valgraln that Halsgough had been teaching the Közloponi. With his superior knowledge of battle tactics and rudimentary engineering, Halsgough had risen to the position of Lord of the town. In three acts of war, the Közloponi had attacked and completely subjugated three smaller gatherings, taking them into the empire that the Lord thought to create.

Halsgough regrettably withdrew his attention from the lovely Döləeçim, who had been learning the language of the other side of Rozhelia. It had turned out that the girl had been Ðöyüşçqüyaramazcani's sister. Thusly the instruction that Halsgough was giving the girl in language was not the only form of discipline with appropriate guidance she was treated to. In the bedroom, in the evenings, the former maiden was learning a great deal! She had been shy before he had instructed her accordingly. She was overwhelmed by Halsgough's determination in all things, his knowledge and the sheer power of his manliness.

"Very well Ðöyüşçqüyaramazcani, I will come to interrogate them", the Lord of the Village agreed finally. He kissed Döləeçim slowly, languidly on the mouth and then joined her brother. Across a compound that was abuzz with activity and industry, the brave led his new leader. The latter had set the craftsmen in frond wood, to the construction of a trebuchet. They were keen to make the adept diagrams realisation when their new commander had told them how the device could devastate one's enemy before they even reached the opposing front line. Others were furiously at work making flint tipped arrows with flights of Œrdimahdá feathers to give them spin, greatly increasing their accuracy. They were also drying and platting dətbağası gut to make more powerful cord for their bows. Halsgough, or as the natives now called him, Warlord, had introduced all of these developments. Improvements in ways to kill or subjugate.

Ðöyüşçqüyaramazcani suddenly halted before two bound seated natives, out in the open, sitting on the compacted dirt ground. One of them had a very large frame, the other looked equally fiercely defiant with glinting intelligent eyes.

"Who art thou and where dost thou come from"? Halsgough asked awkwardly in Közloponoid, having learned enough to interrogate captives, from Döləeçim.

"I am Vandeveble, this is my brother in arms, Mesoloras. We come from Acleegása originally. Having travelled up the spine of the Fire of Saah, in search of the Корунд (Corundum), in the mountains of Thol".

The answer came in a curious form of Valgraln, "Who taught thee...you to speak the strange form of mine tongue".

"The Visionary, he could speak Valgraln, Kémerié, Acleegáás and even the Far-language".

Myrrorball

"Angleseander", the second native added, "For he was an Anglesman before he became the Visionary".

"He soundeth wonderful", Halsgough responded sarcastically, "So full of light that one must enquire privy as to the reason for thy parting of the company"?

"I am ashamed to admit that he betrayed us. Let us protect him from the Vízarapákellemetlen, the Qəhvəyayı, even the šikšno and then once he reached the Tru-eti Varzslatoj betrayed us with the Guardians. When descending back down the slopes of Thol we lost one of our numbers too (Collari), he plummeted to a painful death when falling into an unseen ravine".

"Tragic", Halsgough did not understand half of what he was being told, but he knew one thing. He asked, "So thou wouldst have sweet vengeance on the Anglesman"?

The two men slowly nodded,

"We were badly done by him", the huge warrior observed.

"Then thou...you, have happened 'pon the right place, led by the right commander. For verily I sayeth to thee, vengeance be one of the disciplines I and my Közloponi doest deal. With sweet a result as e-er thy couldst wish for or crave".

"Join us", Ðöyüşçqüyaramazcani expectantly urged, "The Warlord is the most adept in generalship that I have ever encountered".

"We can do nothing tied like this", Vandeveble grinned.

"Release them", Halsgough commanded, "Get them a hut to share and a couple of women to see to there every need"?

Ðöyüşçqüyaramazcani observed hesitantly, "Warlord I am not sure that the women of our...".

"Not Közloponi girls", Halsgough groaned, "Give them two of the captured wenches from Maziau, Ambany or Dahaaz".

"The Maiaun and Ambanin have already been *shared out*, Warlord. I believe you were saving two Dahaazaa for your persuasions once you had tired of my sister"? Ðöyüşçqüyaramazcani could not hide the tinge of bitterness from his voice at that revelation.

Major Roxbrough & Nik Gehenna

"As if aught couldst ever be the case, for whence I did tire of such a lovely maiden then surely the sun would grow cold and the ocean freeze over. Give them the Dahaazaa".

Vandeveble and Mesoloras had impressed Halsgough, he would not miss the wenches. On their next conquest, there would always be more to choose from.

Erroneously thinking it meant his Warlord would always be true to his sister, Ðöyüşçqüyaramazcani was delighted with the instruction. Hurrying away with the two newcomers, intent upon uniting them with trophies they had yet to either earn or prove capable of receiving.

"Come this way"? He requested of the two Acleegáás, who followed him right readily, knowing of that which he led them too. In the compound reserved for prisoners who had yet to accept their integration into the regime of Közlopon, were two women huddled together watching the men of three villages walk the perimeter like caged wild animals.

"What is her name"? Vandeveble pointed at one of them, A dusky beauty by any warrior's standards. Ðöyüşçqüyaramazcani struggled to bring the unusual nomen to mind,

"I think it is Nunnelee. Yes, that's it".

The huge warrior turned to Mesoloras, "Do you mind If I choose her"? The other shook his head before observing with a sly grin,

"They all do it the same way, but the plainer women put more effort into it".

Thusly was it settled. Ðöyüşçqüyaramazcani ordered the gaoler to let the two dusky maidens out of the compound, which they did right readily, fearing their braves as much as anyone else. Vandeveble approached Nunnelee, "You are my woman now", he told her. She did not seem displeased by what fate had handed her.

Although she did demand,

"You will treat me with respect"?

"I will", came the immediate response from the huge hand-some warrior. The other woman who was less favoured walked over to Mesoloras,

Myrrorball

"I will be your woman under the same understanding".

Mesoloras, always a man of few words, nodded, bowing his head slightly. In many ways he found the darker and more mysterious woman to his preference, she had hidden strength and something more, that at that moment he could not quite realise.

"My name is Zonia", she told him in a most simple fashion, "And I am a mpanandro".

"Is that your race of peoples", Mesoloras asked intrigued.

The girl shook her head,

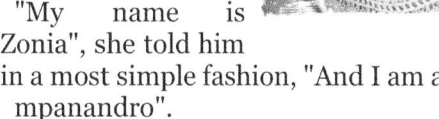

"No, it is my discipline, as you will discover in time"!

68.

"It would seemeth that thou didst demand my presence, Lord of the Keep"? Banustib observed with heavy irony, he had never gotten used to being summoned and still bitterly resented the fact that some individuals thought they had the power to do so.

"On the eve of our march on Knelforest, I would knowest in greater detail the fullest of thy powers of re-animation, dear Necromancer"?

"Not that you will understandeth much of what I tell thee", The Mage began contemptuously if accurately. "Very well, this is what will transpire, circulatory and respiratory systems cease when a warrior is slain. The tissue does not start to decay immediately, especially in the bitter winters in which we will be warring. After less than three hours, I can bring the dead back to life. What happens in the body on a cellular level during the hours a fallen went without a heartbeat? Their tissues dying along with their consciousness? How much longer could a corpse remain vital with no blood circulation? I, Banustib the Necromancer am revolutionizing the way we mage will treat cardiac arrest. Obliterating the line between life and death. My necromantic research commenced on a cellular level. For thou seest, unlike the larger organisms they compose, there are clear ways to tell whether an individual human cell is dead. Cells are what our bodies are composed of my Lord. I possess the necromantic ability to study such tiny organisms, through necromancy. The energy bestowed me ironically by the essence of the dead themselves. But to continue, every cell has a tight outer membrane that serves to separate its contents from its surroundings and filter out the molecules that are non-essential to its function or survival. As a cell nears the end of its life, this protective barrier will begin to weaken. Depending 'pon the circumstances of a cell's death, one of three things will happen:

It will send an *eat*-me-signal to a specialized maintenance cell that will then devour and recycle the ailing cell's contents.

Or it will quarantine, consume itself in a kind of programmed altruistic suicide.

Or it will rupture abruptly and spill its contents into the surrounding tissue, causing severe inflammation and further tissue damage.

In all cases, when the integrity of the outer membrane is compromised, a cell's fate is sealed. When the permeability of the membrane has increased to the point that the cellular contents are leaking out, even I, have reached a point of no return. Even a mad sorcerer canst not reassemble dead cells. Yet, as it turns out, it can take some cells quite a long time to die. When human cells are abruptly cut off from the steady supply of oxygen, nutrients and cleaning services that blood flow normally provides them, they can hold out in their membranes for a surprisingly long time. The true survivalists in thy body, my Lord, may not die for many days after thou has lost circulation, consciousness and most of the other things thou considereth integral parts of living. If I, The greatest Necromancer as ever lived, can get to the patient before these cells have crashed, re-animation is still a possibility. Cells that are most sensitive to nutrient and oxygen deprivation are brain cells. Within five to ten minutes of cardiac failure due to physical trauma as that suffered in battle, neuronal membranes will begin to rupture, irreparable brain damage will ensue. Making revival efforts more difficult, a sure-fire way to kill a cell that has been cut off from oxygen and nutrients for an extended period be to give it that very same oxygen and nutrients. In a phenomenon called reperfusion injury, blood-starved cells abruptly reintroduced to a nutrient supply will quickly self-destruct.

Cells that lose blood supply then go into metabolic hibernation, with the goal of self-preservation. When the cells are roused from this state by an onslaught of oxygen and panicking white blood cells in an environment where toxins have accumulated, they are overwhelmed with inflammatory signals, they respond with self-immolation.

So how will I avoid reperfusion injury, thou art asking thyself, when I know from my necromantic studies that it begins to ruin the chance of re-animation. Now I will tell thee why I demanded several men together with great quantities of ice be brought to me at my command before each battle. The way to stifle reperfusion is to lower a fallen warrior's body temperature.

I call this state *therapeutic hypothermia*. By rapidly lowering a patient's body temperature to 33°C using an intravenous cooling solution or packing the body in ice as soon as possible, I will banish the risk of reperfusion injury. As thine and Kyper Tor's surgeon's work to repair the physical damage that had caused the death of the warrior.

This process will allow the fallen who have been clinically dead for tens of minutes to make a limited recovery. If the injuries are successfully repaired, then using necromanticity, I will perform the medical miracle of reanimating the dead.

True the warrior will be totally blank of sensibility in their brains. The brain will not be dead, but they will not retrieve anything during that cardiac arrest stage. They will still be able to obey rudimentary commands, they will fight on a purely instinctual level. Eventually, they will decompose, the process cannot be permanent, yet will be able to fight on long enough to win several victories for thee.

Lord, they will kill for thee, afore they rot to uselessness. By then thou will have pressed the beaten to thy service. Rallied the sons of the Western Lords, victory will be truly assured".

"There be tiny dungeons in our body"? Koözoött Lord of the West struggled to understand much of what the mage had told him.

Banustib found it simpler to nod, "Cells of vitality with flesh walls that are more easily broken than the iron ones in thy keep".

"Curious", Koözoött Lord of the West muttered then suddenly brightened, "Very well, master of magic, provide me with an demonstration"?

The necromancer had expected that very reaction. He was more than ready for it.

"A good perchancement had occurred on the night afore last. A spy from Knelforest was captured by one of this night patrols, Koözoött Lord of the West, he languishes in thy dungeon".

"I be aware of this, what of it"?

"Let us to the dungeon where most of the ice be already stored. We shall see if the experiment, the subsequent demonstration, can be conducted to thy satisfaction then"?

Down streaming, crumbling lithic walls, the duo travailed, the cobbles beneath their feet - slimy with cold wet lichen. On black iron brackets, a series of sooty animal burning lamps lit the way, but they were pools of amber interspersed with pitch only, for there were no windows in such a route as the two of them took. In most cases, those who were led down that passage were doomed never to return to the light. Their only fate torture unto demise. Or, if they were lucky a quick death without agonising torment firstly.

"I have already taken the liberty of having Blaho meet us down here", the Necromancer told his Lord as they reached a great iron gate ludicrously guarded by a sentry. At their approach, he hastily produced a large iron key and unlocking the gate swung it open, allowing them to pass beyond.

Koözoött Lord of the West found that amusing, "Thou knewest to prepare for this demonstration"?

"I be thorough in my preparation and in knowing my lord's mind afore he does", the handsome Necromancer smiled. He lifted one huge brand out of its bracket to illuminate their way beyond if meagrely. The gaoler was expecting them, he rose from behind a filthy desk and bowed to the Lord of the West.

In an age when deformity and vile afflictions of the skin were the norms in the peasant populations, Kkələkk remained a singularly vile example of the various maladies one could contract. His features were grossly disfigured by huge boils, some of which had burst. It explained the disgusting rag that he wore around his throat, sludgy with vilely suppurating pus. He was stooped, due to his kyphotic nature, one of his arms was Beedled.

"Good morn to thee, handsome", Banustib greeted. None present save the Necromancer himself could determine if he was being sardonic. Or whether his proclivities ran to the mong and the spazmogenie. "Pray to lead us to the prisoner, be he prepared as directed"?

Kkələkk assured that he was, the reply resulting in a rather disgusting drool of pale green phlegm to run from the corner of his twisted mouth. The gaoler was not someone one invited to dinner unless one possessed a zinc lined stomach and had lifted all the carpets prior to his arrival.

"Then let us proceed", the Necromancer sounded cheerful and anticipatory.

Major Roxbrough & Nik Gehenna

Kkələkk shuffled into the lead then limped toward one particular gate in the dimness. From a ring the size and weight of which, one could be forgiven for thinking beyond the gaoler's vitality to be able to permanently carry, he produced a key. Unlocking the gate leading to a further corridor that then flared out into the *Chamber*. In such, abominable acts of afflicted torment were undertaken to produce information.

Other times as punishment, or even for the simple sadistic pleasure of it all. Since Koözoött, Lord of the West had put to death his demented son, several winters past, there had been much less of the latter, however.

In the centre of the chamber, a prisoner was securely trussed to a stool. Over to the right was a capacious iron cauldron filled with ice and at a table a series of medical instruments. Some of those were rusty, encrusted with gore, but generally, Blaho kept them cleaner than most. He nodded to Koözoött Lord of the West, needle and catgut already in his hand.

"Draw thy sword then, Koözoött, Lord of the West"? the Necromancer instructed.

"Why me"?

"Thou art Koözoött Lord of the West, it be right and proper that the very first man brought back from beyond death be put to death by none other".

The prisoner bound and gagged nevertheless screamed with his eyes. Such were unnaturally large and roving in the chiaroscuro illumination of the dungeon.

Koözoött Lord of the West shrugged drew forth his blade, approached the miserable, defenceless prey.

"Down through the shoulder I think, Lord of the West", yet another instruction from the Necromancer. That was something Koözoött Lord of the West would have to take up with him at a later date. With a swift slash, he brought his hanger down into the man's body, a well-aimed and fatal blow.

Two peasants appeared from seemingly nowhere. They had been lurking in the shadows, as plebeian were want to do. With their bare hands, they began to shovel a growing mound of ice around the feet and legs of the freshly slain corpse. Blaho rushed forward, began to stitch the gaping hole in the body's shoulder and chest. It was not the neatest of needlepoint, Koözoött Lord of the West had ever seen. It seemed aesthetic consideration was not high on the surgeon's agenda. Once it was raggedly rejoined, he nodded to Banustib.

At once the Necromancer began to utter a series of dark pishogue and cantrip of necromantic propagation. The dark energy of a strange ambience seemed to glow from his outstretched fingers. The light was impossibly dense, a white-blackness, a vivid-dun. The energy taken from the dead, for Banustib was a virtuoso of diabolically dexterous expertise.

The dead body of the spy twitched!

Koözoött Lord of the West watched in grim fascination. He even drew a little closer to the once-corpse. He jumped back in unexpected alarm though when the dead opened his eyes. Over the pupils was an unhealthily milky film, and the spy's mouth hung at a curiously vacant gape, letting a strange moan of indistinguishable utterance escape from it.

"His language is of the dead which cannot be understood by the living", Banustib informed the fascinated Lord.

"He lives"! Koözoött Lord of the West gasped, "Yet I killed him with the Smo manoeuvre, he was certainly bereft of animation".

Banustib chuckled, the sort of amusement well appreciated in Gehenna, Koözoött Lord of the West caught a whiff of his breath during the expression. It was as frigid as the breeze through a midnight graveyard with the added stink of the slaughterhouse. Despite being Lord of the West, he shuddered, found himself slightly in awe of the mage.

"He can fight now for me"?

The Necromancer nodded, "At thy instruction, there be little else he dost be capable of my Lord of the West".

"So he be warrior, yet one brought back from the pit of doom"?

The Necromancer grinned, "I call he of his ilk an mumje, zombie, mummy or teveqel, choose which appellation suits thy predilection or amusement, My Lord"?

"I fancy I dost find Zombie right to mine liking", Koözoött Lord of the West decided with a deleterious smirk.

69.

The accommodation was to a standard that Quianhua had come to expect. Not as advanced as the bubble the slimy slug-like *Zernothings* had furnished her with, but acceptable. At least there was running water, heated too. Something she had not experienced, since agreeing to accompany her husband on the half-assed expedition. Her first action in order of priority was, therefore, a bath. She went through some draws, found a smock top, drawstring pants, both black. They would do as a change of clothes for her. Trollies for knickers had to do, at least the fabric was soft, it was also clean, cleaner than anything she had in her bundle.

She filled the pot bath with hot water, rooted around in all the cupboards, found some bath salts, soap was already available in a dispenser beside the taps. This meant the Guardians were the most civilised of people on all Rozhelia, at least, of those, she knew. After shampooing her hair in a formula that smelled of jojoba, she wrapped it in a towel, climbed into the bath. For several minutes she simply let the heat soak into her body. Reluctantly as the water began to cool, Quianhua soaped herself thoroughly twice before climbing out and wrapping in a bath sheet.

There was a knock on the door, it would doubtless be, Nik. Why would he knock though, there was no lock on the door. When she opened it she had her answer. It was not her spouse but rather the Administrative Commander for the month. He smiled, for some reason that did not make the Chinese girl feel any easier,

"Forgive the intrusion", Veriš began, "The abodes are not supplied with foodstuffs though. The men will be dining in the community hall later".

"Cassiti and I cannot", Quianhua finished for him, "So are we to fast whilst in this place, Veriš? Oh dear, I seem to have forgotten your rule of silence".

Veriš gave a grin of genuine amusement, "That observance is for when in the company of other Guardians, Miss Quianhua, it does not apply when you are alone with me".

"You came to give me the solution to the food dilemma"?

"It would be an honour for me, to bring your meal to you this evening, along with my own, there are matters I would like to discuss".

"And Cassiti"?

"Will be similarly serviced by a lieutenant of mine".

Quianhua could not help but be amused by his choice of wording. The Administrative Commander for the month had subconsciously decided to use double entendre. Resisting to observe such, she simply nodded.

"I am going to slip into the provided clothes, drab but comfortable. I will await your arrival with the victuals then, Veriš. Don't be too long, there's nothing to do in this place, you would not want me wandering about, would you"?

"Indeed not, there are no females in the Varzsaoj district of Tru-eti Varzslatoj. Your appearance might prove somewhat distracting to the guardians".

"I don't want to inflame any monks", Quianhua could not resist teasing, "I'll stay put, will my husband be allowed to visit me at any time during our stay in this place"?

"If he can find you", Veriš smiled, "He, the warrior and the amphibian, along with their cat has been conducted to a different district".

"Which one"?

"You would never find it without a map".

"Then it will do you no harm to tell me. Why have we been separated"?

"The males are staying in Trutizoj district", he told her and then turned away offering nothing more.

Quianhua shrugged, closed the door, let the towels fall away, leaving them where they landed. Let the help see to them, give them something to do. She dressed quickly and immediately went over to the door. Time to go exploring, she was bored, she wasn't about to let some half-assed monk tell her what to do.

To her dismay though, as she slipped out into the dusk, it was to see Veriš hurrying toward her, a great metal tureen in his arms.

He called out, the instant he saw her,

"No! You cannot go out, I thought I...".

"I was merely coming to meet you, silly", Quianhua lied.

"Please do not do that again", the Administrative Commander for the month asked her, "Believe me you could find yourself in ...deep water, if you did".

"I can swim", the Chinese girl found it amusing to be contrary at times.

"You know what I intended to convey", Veriš returned, "Could you open the door and let me in? We should eat before the food cools".

Sensible, forced to admit to herself for once, because it suited her, she did as requested.

With the economy of movement gained by practice, he laid out the various offerings and seated himself at one of the two settings. Quianhua, realising how hungry she was suddenly, joined him enthusiastically. It had been since the bubble that she had eaten so well. She enjoyed every item on the menu, did not even stop to enquire what they all were, oft times it was better not to know. They ate in silence for some time, not a condition that bothered her in the slightest, she could be inscrutable when the fancy took her, or the occasion demanded. Eventually, Veriš lay down his cutlery, made of real stainless steel, asked,

"Why have the party come to this city, Quianhua"?

"Could you not have asked Nik this in the great dining hall or whatever you call your refectory"?

Myrrorball

"Of course", Veriš smiled, "But his company would not be quite so elegant, quite so charming".

Quianhua had been called elegant in the past, never charming. Rather, those who had known her in her past life had used descriptions such as, cantankerous, irascible, peevish, churlish, unceremonious, self-centred - to name but a few. On the other hand, she had also been called, elegant, exquisite, attractive, hot, worth-one, seriously worth-one, arresting, so she felt she could get away with her foibles.

"It's some hair-brained notion of the Visionary's, he seems to think the place may provide him with some answers".

"What sort of answers? Have some of this excellent Qurşəvörös".

"Qurşəvörös"?

"A rosé made here from grapes off our vines. You will find it fragrant and playful".

'Hhmm and I get the impression that you are hoping to find the same qualities in me, you randy old goat' Quianhua thought to herself, she could not decide whether he was after pumping her for information, or just for pumping her!

"Very...grapey", she grinned, it was lame, he smiled anyway.

"You were going to tell me what sort of answers the Terran is seeking".

The Terran, obviously as she was Chinese, he thought her from somewhere else, other than the scoured planet that had once been home to humanity. She thought it prudent not to disillusion him of the delusion".

"Owe he doesn't know that because he doesn't know the questions".

"He came here seeking answers to questions he does not have"?

"Yeah, sort of. He spends a fair amount of time up himself. He seemed together when we first met, but lately, he seems... well to put it mildly in several minds as to exactly what he wants out of existence. You know, life, the layers of the space out there and all that crap"?

Major Roxbrough & Nik Gehenna

Veriš looked understandably non-comprehendingly at her and admitted, "Not really".

"Don't sweat it. I don't think anyone else does either".

"You are a very intricate and intriguing female, Quianhua", the Administrative Commander for the month told her then, "When you say you met the Terran sometime in the past, where was that"?

"Station 23", the girl lied easily, "In the Orion cluster".

"I have not heard of them, where are they"?

"In one of the 28 lunar mansions Sieu (Xiu) (宿). It is known as Shen (参), literally meaning "three", for the stars of Orion's Belt".

"Stars, you came from the stars?! How did you get to our world from those points of light? They are distant suns are they not"?

Quianhua continued with what she knew of antiquitous astronomy,

"The character 参 (pinyin shēn) originally meant the constellation Orion (参宿; pinyin: shēnxiù). Its Shang dynasty version, over three millennia old, contains at the top representation of the three stars of Orion's belt atop a man's head, the bottom portion, representing the sound of the word, was added later. The Rig Veda refers to the Orion Constellation as Mriga (The Deer). It was noted, the two bright stars in the front plus the two bright stars in the rear were the hunting dogs, the one comparatively less bright star in the middle, ahead of two front dogs being the hunter. Three aligned bright stars are in the middle of all four hunting dogs, the Deer (The Mriga) and three little aligned but lesser brighter stars, the Baby Deer. The Mriga means Deer, locally known as Harnu in folk parlance. Many folk songs are narrating the Harnu. Called Orion's Belt Bintang Tiga Beradik (the Brother Star). The Orion, seen in the night sky was also called the Nataraja 'the cosmic dancer' (Shiva) The Jain Symbol carved in Udayagiri and Khandagiri Caves, has a striking resemblance with Orion. Bugis sailors identified three stars in Orion's Belt as tanra tellué, meaning the sign of three".

Myrrorball

Veriš looked in turn confused, incredulous yet he gave the girl his undivided attention, he asked,

"Are any of you on Egszígør, from the belt, that is"?

Quianhua shrugged, "I don't know, as far as I know, I am unique".

Veriš nodded as though understanding, "I find you very unique, Quianhua", he told her and reaching out took her hand in his own.

'I know what you would like to find', she thought, *'And it isn't my unique'*!

She waited to see what he would suggest, amused by his manoeuvring,

"What if I told you there is a way you could have the freedom of this magnificent city, go wherever you pleased whenever you wanted? Not be bothered by the Terran who wants answers but does not even know what the questions are"?

She was determined to make him spell it out, before refusing,

"But the rules, Administrative Commander for the month, I am a woman in a city filled with men".

"Yes and what a woman you are", Veriš gushed, "What would you say to the proposal"?

"Would there be commensurate recompense for your office for flouting your apophthegm thusly"?

'Here it comes', she thought.

Veriš tried to look as alluring as he possibly could. He was not an ugly man, but neither was he dashing, he was hoping that the aphrodisiac of power would be enough for her.

He licked his suddenly dry lips and did his best to tear his gaze from the soft curves of her bosom, impressive even when in a black baggy top.

"It would be easy for me to make such a rule as the Administrative Commander for the month if you were my aid".

"Your aid"?

"Assistant and close personal guide".

Quianhua asked, smiling enigmatically (at least she hoped it was cryptic) "Just how close are you suggesting, Administrative Commander for the month"?

Major Roxbrough & Nik Gehenna

"Well, firstly we would have to bid the Terran on his way. Release you from whatever contract the two of you are currently bound together by...".

"Why Veriš, can not a contracted female be your aid"? Quianhua was deliberately misunderstanding, let the rangy getbag come out with it, say what he wanted, then she would refuse him, what cooly miserable fun.

"I hoped, dreamt, that eventually, our professional relationship would develop into something closer, something more intimate".

"You mean you want to bang me"?! Quianhua feigned flabbergastmentation, placed a hand over her bosom as though the revelation was a shock to her heart.

As she had hoped Veriš had not heard the crude euphemism before.

"I beg your pardon"?

"I should hope you do", Quianhua was now in her stride, "I think it would be an excellent time to take your leave now, Veriš".

"I'm not sure I follow you, or you, me", the Administrative Commander for the month floundered, "What I was suggesting was...".

"Oh I know full well what you were suggesting", Quianhua rose from her seat pushed it back with her buttocks, "You want to: butter my muffin, put a banana in the fruit salad, bring an al dente noodle to the spaghetti house".

"No, no, this has nothing to do with food", Veriš had lost the conversation some moments past, "What I want...".

"What you want, you ain't gonna get", Quianhua had slipped into Chinese slang western style, "Now I demand to see my husband"?

The veil of respectability then fell from before Veriš, he suddenly rose to his feet too, virtually snarling,

"Now listen to me you little nozkavardé! The Terran and you are separated, that is how it is going to stay. I thought to honour you with a title, but you do not have to accept that. I have however decided to have you and I always get what I want. So we can do this the hard way, or

Myrrorball

you can accept the honour I'm bestowing upon you. Now..."

He lurched for her, outstretched hands like horrible claws.

Quianhua was Chinese though, knew rudimentary techniques of self-defence that included, conditioning exercises including stances. Movements that were performed repeatedly: basic training, stretching, meditation, striking, throwing, or jumping. Her muscles were strong and flexible. Management of Qi or breath. Proper body mechanics, martial arts. She broke both of the wrists of the Administrative Commander for the month, threw him over her shoulder with ease. He crashed into an occasional table, remained to lie very still. Fortunately, she could see him breathing. With that, she drained her glass, grabbed him by the scruff of the neck, hauling him to his feet. They swiftly exited the house, in search of her husband. She was rattled by the experience, more than she prepared to admit to herself. For that reason, she did not pack up her bundle, attacked the first guardian she encountered and put his arm in a very painful goose-neck before telling him,

"Try to wriggle free, I'll break it! Now take me to the Trutizoj district, I want to meet the Terran",

Several passers-by gazed at the duo in strange fascination as they passed them. They did not seem intrigued enough to want to do anything about it. Down well-lit streets, lit in the form of high-pressure sodium lamps, which produce the most amount of light for the least amount of electricity required to power them they rushed. Quianhua was not in the mood to wonder how electricity came to be present in Tru-eti Varzslatoj though. Nor did she marvel at the buildings themselves, arranged in neat avenues interspersed with deciduous trees that would not have looked out of place in Yorkshire. She should have. How was it that the city looked like Sheffield, Wakefield or Harrogate, none of which were light years close to Rozhelia? Being Chinese, she had not seen that much of the greatest county in the world. Or at least it had been before it being depopulated by   Hhrrhhoehhrrhooooingohh   &

Major Roxbrough & Nik Gehenna

Harahorahurrahaashume of the Hhhâäàåâäàåçêçêçêïîìïîì-ggndgndÐñß¥þÞÝɒ'.

The man grunted several times, asked for the gooseneck to be slackened slightly, but Quianhua did not know how strong he was. How adept at some type of learned defence of his own. So she refused. A large oval building came into view, the sort of structure that would be utilised for communal activity. Just like the sort conducted in restaurants.

"He will be in there, with the other strange travellers, now will you let me go"? He asked her, but she returned,

"When you've got me inside, without you, they would not let me enter. Don't insult my intelligence again or I'll break it".

To prove she meant every word she said, she gave it a firm tweak, causing him to yelp and writhe afresh. He also hurried his pace and as they got to the metal and glass doors of the entrance, tugged one open urgently. After rushing down a short corridor, they went through another door the clamour of many voices suddenly started to quieten.

"Quianhua"! A familiar voice issued, "What sort of trouble have you gotten yourself into"?

"Hello, husband", the Chinese girl replied, "Veriš, the Administrative Commander for the month just tried to seduce me! When that did not get him where he wanted to be, namely in my pants, he then tried to rape me".

The proclamation had the desired effect. The already quietened murmur fell to total and eerily shocked silence. One of the guardians rose to his feet,

"My name is Kadriš", he began, I am going to be the Administrative Commander for next month, "I will investigate this matter if what you claim can be substantiated with proof, severe punishment will be his lot".

70.

We had just enjoyed a superb meal courtesy of the guardians when the volume of chatter in the hall suddenly lessened. I looked over to where other heads were pointing.

Quianhua had pushed one of the guardians before her, it looked like she had her hand up his back. It forced me to call out to her,

"Quianhua! What sort of trouble have you gotten yourself into"?

"Hello, Husband", my Chinese spouse replied. As though to deliberately emphasise our relationship, "Veriš, the Adminis-trative Commander for the month just tried to seduce me, when that did not get him where he wanted to be, namely in my pants, he then tried to rape me".

The proclamation had the desired effect. The already quietened murmur fell to total and eerily shocked silence. One of the guardians rose to his feet,

"My name is Kadriš", he began, I am going to be the Administrative Commander for next month, "I will investigate this matter and if what you claim can be substantiated with proof - severe punishment will be his lot".

I rose to my feet, nodded to Hersko and Mister Genks we walked toward Kadriš, I observed,

"There will be no proof. You know it. It will simply be a case of he said, she said. In a city full of males, we already know who will be believed".

"Perhaps", Kadriš admitted reasonably, "Or maybe, when confronted with his crime, Veriš will confess".

I realised at that moment that the two men had no love for one another. I was not keen to leave the city and in the dark. There was nowhere to go, so I took Quianhua's hand and asked her,

"Are you willing to go back to where you just escaped? To confront him before all the others"?

"Too ruddy right I am", she returned with spirit, that's my spouse not short of spunk.

"Then let's go back to the abode? Then you can formerly ask the Administrative Commander for the month"? I asked of the Administrative Commander for the next month".

Throughout all of the conversation the current Administrator swayed upon the balls of his feet eyes rolling. He was clearly in some pain making immediate questioning impossible.

We drew some curious stares as we wended our way back the way Quianhua led us. Mainly because of *her* presence rather than the manbian's. I was not especially surprised to find the place she claimed had been the scene of the crime, so to speak empty.

"It seems the Administrative Commander for the month has fled", I remarked, "Such usually indicates a guilty conscience".

"I had to let him go to the medic Kadriš explained then, "Both his wrists were broken by your woman. It is possible he was never here".

"If he wasn't then who brought me my dinner", Quianhua asked waving at the table, "Plainly two dined here".

The Administrative Commander for the following month blanched ever-so-slightly, then promised,

"I will commence an immediate investigation. Someone will have given him the food to bring if it was him, then we will get to the bottom of this matter". The Administrative Commander for the month after the present one promised.

"Oh, give me a break"? Quianhua demanded. "Even if it's established that he was here, he can still say it's all a fabrication. Label me a liar, make our continued staying here uncomfortable", she turned to me, "Nik, I have not asked you for much, but I want to leave this place. I want to leave without further delay. We need to find Cassiti first though, let's get out of here"?

I glanced at Mister Genks and Hersko. The latter was looking suddenly worried. Both had nodded almost imperceptibly, the young warrior demanded of the Administrative Commander for the following month.

"Taketh us to Cassiti, afore thy predecessor doth reach her".

Quianhua instantly set to hastily throwing her belongings into her bundle and then we waited for the three of them to return. During this period she admitted to me she had taken pleasure in breaking both of Veriš' wrists - not advisable. They were back in as long as it had taken the native girl to pack her bag, four of them. Five, if we counted Mr Choon, who had been with the manbian.

"Are you all right"? I asked the native.

She smiled, nodded, said no more.

"If we can go back to the house we were to stop in and retrieve our bundles we will then leave", I promised Kadriš. The more reasonable of the Guardians asked,

"In the dark, where will you go? Do you not wish to wait until morning"?

I opened my mouth to say I knew not what and Hersko beat me to it,

"Thou outnumbers us many to one. We must leave at once, lest Veriš tries to organise an attack with those loyal to him and kidnap the girls. We would not go down without a fight, there would be considerable injuries, some would even die. Be that what thou be prepared to risk, Guardian"?

"The mountains though", Kadriš observed, "Treacherous enough in the light of Angelus, but by starlight, and no Brahma tonight...".

"We will not be going into the mountains" Hersko retained the chair, he lifted the Vandei Motestas, for the first time I had an inkling of what he planned, I grinned.

PART SEVEN

REMEMBER TOMORROW

Myrrorball

71.

The Sorcerer breezed into the royal tent, barely making no sound with the flap. He had such grace, such posture that he seemed to almost glide from one place to another. There was a smile of satisfaction on his smoothly razored cheeks.

"Good morn to thee, Sweet Majesty, I have tidings that thou will find to pluck the strings of thy heart and give of an mighty cheer".

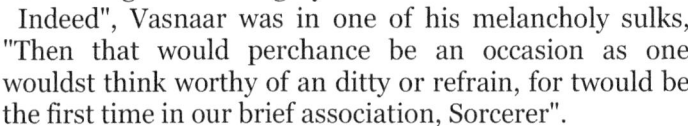

Indeed", Vasnaar was in one of his melancholy sulks, "Then that would perchance be an occasion as one wouldst think worthy of an ditty or refrain, for twould be the first time in our brief association, Sorcerer".

"Nevertheless, my Liege, I be ablest right to prettily certain spirits that such in the telling will be lifted, when I givest the truest utterance to fair news".

"I be agog with anticipation".

"My vitality be sufficiently restored to create a phase door, the yonder end of which canst be once more focused into Castle Kingshire".

Vasnaar dived from his supine position lounging on several rolled-up blankets, to gain his feet,

"How soon can it be madeth manifest and how many can get through afore it once more collapses"?

"At once, my Liege, yet 'twill only be vital long enough to get thee and the prince through afore it collapses. If I wait longer I canst create one of greater duration, then all the men present...".

"Sayeth the words which trip loosely from the lips of a fool, Sorcerer. Mine kingdom and I must be reunited so that I will fully knowest all the particular of the mischief perpetrated in mine absence".

"I will not be able to accompany thee, Sire", Bodakin warned, which only served to anger the king,

Major Roxbrough & Nik Gehenna

"Whence did e-er I need the assistance of an mage to aid me in ruling mine own kingdom"? He demanded. "Now mumble thy words of pishogue, let us be upon our royal business, for tarrying is not aught I be want to do".

Reluctantly, unsure if he was doing the king a service at all, Bodakin began the weird passes and strange cantrip necessary to rent and scission a gateway through the ether that would not only allow passage through it but also terminate in the correct locale. It was a manifestation that only the most adept of mages could perform, requiring great memory coupled with also an equal abundance of energy.

The air in the tent began to shimmer and distort, an image warp of thaumaturgical source and design. The epicentre of the rough ovoid then darkened, before widening into what could have passed for an evil eye of violet.

"Majesty", Bodakin gasped, already near exhaustion, "Go now".

Without any need for preparation, the King threw himself through the ovoid followed closely by his son. The phase-door immediately collapsed with a sucking implosive report. Bodakin stood swaying for a time, then he drew forth a broad yellow kerchief from the pocket in the folds of his caftan and mopped his brow before going to tell the others that the first of their number had departed the Fire of Saah.

Out of the doorway through time and space, the King fell sprawling, Prince Byno neatly landing on top of him. With difficulty, Vasnaar pushed his son off himself, quickly rose to his feet to glance around him. His face broke into a huge grin of triumph, for he perceived that they were in his private quarters. If had worked, the Sorcerer had gotten them back to their homeland.

He held out an arm, Byno taking it, rose to his feet.

"Mother will be so pleased to be reunited with thee", the Prince observed.

Mother, otherwise known as Queen Vasnaarena was actually in bed, naked, legs akimbo while Zemtel first Lord of Kingshire lunged away on top of her doing his

Myrrorball

best to service her requirements. She suddenly gripped his shoulders to stop his movement, mistaking it for her orgasm, Zemtel first Lord of Kingshire promptly released his pent up juices and gasped in pleasure. Vasnaarena pushed him off her, taking a rag from the side of the bed wiped away the excess of her lover's fluids before hastily rising from it, commencing to hurriedly dress.

"What be the reason for thy haste, my Love"? Zemtel first Lord of Kingshire asked of her.

"Get up and into thy clothes, dost thou not hear the commotion without? Something be happening in this castle, methinketh we have been active in the arrangement of nought".

Zemtel first Lord of Kingshire was a man of action and promptly dived up, hastily wiping his member on the bed-sheets. The action was something the Queen would not normally countenance. On that occasion, time was pressing most urgently of the essence. They were at the door in commendably short duration. Vasnaarena going one way down the corridor beyond, Zemtel first Lord of Kingshire going in the opposite. It would not do for any to know they were lovers, although the scribe Herner had suspicions, might have to be *dealt with* at a later date.

Down separate steps, the two descended and arrived at the reception hall minutes apart, as Zemtel first Lord of Kingshire had taken the longer route. Vasnaarena entered the hallway looking flushed and flustered. Sex with Zemtel first Lord of Kingshire always left her that way. When she saw who was in the company of the Scribe, some of the most elevated in their rank of trusted retainers, she gasped in surprise.

"My Queen", Vasnaar laughed, rushing over to her, throwing his arms around her slim frame. He smelled strangely, of soil, strange plants and even alien air. Curiously not of the sea though, what had happened?

"Mother", Byno joined them, but the king was not letting her go so she could not embrace him.

"Was the mission a success, mine husband"? Vasnaarena managed to croak when she could draw breath?

Major Roxbrough & Nik Gehenna

The smile evaporated quickly from the King's features, as he informed her,

"Halsgough and the Western Lords didst plot upon an treachery, vile treason in the doings against us of the East. Thusly didst such misbegotten foul detritus of spirit and loyalty ruin our mission to secure Корунд (Corundum) for thee, my Love. Not only that, but the natives were fearsome. 'Twas ever their disposition to attack us most violently. We met a ...".

"So thou failed", Vasnaarena surmised brutally.

The smile vanished from the King's features. He admonished,

"Have duteous care, woman! Even the Queen must show her husband respect when about before, addressing his royal personage".

The two doors of the room burst open at that point and who should be at the head of them but **Zemtel first Lord of Kingshire**. At his shoulder were several armed toxophilites who they had arrows notched, ready to fire.

"What by Ogglenooré's teeth be this, more treachery"? Vasnaar demanded.

By way of an answer, **Zemtel first Lord of Kingshire** gave a frigid smile without mirth and observed,

"Thou shouldst have stayed on Far Side, Vasnaar, for in truth the realm has been far better managed in the absence of thee and thy foppish son. 'Tis a pity that thou hast come back. I will be labelled forever with the title of interfectorem regem as a result". Interfectorem regem: meaning King Slayer in high Valgraln. So shocked was Vasnaar that he was momentarily robbed of the power of speech. It gave **Zemtel first Lord of Kingshire** time to demand of Herner,

"Scribe, who dost thou serve"?

Being non-political, merely concerning myself with tomes and learning, I serve whomsoever be in the elevated realm of rule, First Lord of Kingshire".

"Just shoot the King and his son", **Zemtel first Lord of Kingshire** then instructed.

"Wait"! Byno managed to gasp before three arrows struck him, one being in the throat, he fell mute, pumping blood, died quite promptly. The three that punctured the King did not fell him though. While the archers hurried to fit a second arrow to their bow, Vasnaar had drawn his sword, charged at the first Lord of Kingshire. Agonising pain made the attack little more than a gesture. Zemtel first Lord of Kingshire stepped inside the swing of the hangar, buried a dirk into the King's chest. He had fatally stabbed his ruler in the heart and in the reception hall! Then was he truly Zemtel first Lord of Kingshire - Interfectorem regem.

The archers promptly left the scene. **Zemtel first Lord of Kingshire -** Interfectorem regem instructed the shocked retainers,

"Clear this up, or conduct thyselves to the dungeons. 'Tis donely well, I will now be the ruler of Valgral, for Vasnaar was an hopeless King and all will fair better now he is gone".

After the briefest of hesitations, they dragged the bodies away, Vasnaarena instructed,

"Burn the bodies, such misbegotten as they will not have a place in the royal tomb. 'Twould be to place them beside the honoured, such would never do".

Zemtel first Lord of Kingshire - Interfectorem regem regarded the woman he had made his lover, how cold she was. To witness the murder of her husband and son, yet show little emotion of any sort. Of course, it had conducted just as they had planned, but even so, he was impressed, she was one heartless woman to behave thusly, with no sign of regret or remorse.

She turned to Herner,

"Now truly am I declared the right widower of sorrowful mourning? I will be no longer Vasnaarena but shall revert to my previous nomen of, Celesta - henceforth. **Zemtel former first Lord of Kingshire** will be Prince Consort".

"I will draw up the relevant paperwork, Majesty", Herner promised. "Pray to tell, who will rule, now that the King be dead? His sister's son, his nephew be next in line".

Celesta observed, "He be but twelve summers. Nought but an callow youth, I will take the throne, with **Zemtel first Lord of Kingshire -** Interfectorem regem, at my side".

Major Roxbrough & Nik Gehenna

Herner raised a quizzical eyebrow,

"And in the event of war, Majesty? Whom then shall ride at the head of the royal guard? For thou art an woman, filled with the weaknesses of the fairer sex, sweet of disposition, gentle by thy nature".

"My consort of course. Go and make it so in an royal decree, I will add my seal to it once Artisan has created an suitable stamp for the wax".

Herner, valuing his neck above all other considerations, bowed stiffly and backed out of the room.

"Now, **Zemtel first Lord of Kingshire** - Interfectorem regem, bent the knee to thy queen, for truly dost our royal life matter, thou shalt also bow thy head"?

"What"? **Zemtel first Lord of Kingshire** - Interfectorem regem was momentarily taken by surprise, assuming that when the King was abruptly dealt with, him and the widow would be equal partners in infamy. In that particular, he had been sorely mistaken.

"If thous wishest to crave pardon, then do so in the correct manner, **Zemtel first Lord of Kingshire** - Interfectorem regem, bend the knee or find thyself replaced by another. Both by Office and in my bed".

Zemtel grimaced and did as directed. Like the scribe before him, he placed a keen value upon that part of his personage - that did connect the chest to the head.

The following morning a herald arrived at Castle Kingshire. Unaware of the events of the night before he demanded an audience with the marshal of the King's forces, whom he presumed would be in command in his majesty's absence from Valgral. He was conducted to the scribe who told him that Queen Celesta now sat upon the throne. **Zemtel first Lord of Kingshire** - Interfectorem regem at her side.

"Then it be to that dubious duo that the import of mine message needeth to be delivered", the herald returned. "I am from Knelforest, have dark tidings alas and alack".

Herner advised one of the retainers to go to the Queen. Convey the appropriate message. Celesta was not a woman who was noted for the velocity of either her movements or responses. Such was just as well. For the

Myrrorball

herald had been sorely afflicted with agitation only after two glasses of mead did he seem to calm his nerve, even then with the greatest of difficulty.

After a considerable period Celesta appeared. **Zemtel first Lord of Kingshire** - Interfectorem regem was at her side. His livery was fine his armour in supreme fettle. He looked every inch the Prince Consort. Together the two of them walked through the room. Celesta to take her seat on the throne, **Zemtel first Lord of Kingshire** - Interfectorem regem, standing at her right hand. Then did her regal majesty instruct,

"Let the herald come forward to deliver such import as dost interrupt mine studies". What the details of which had been, might be anyone's guess, none asked though.

Grim-facedly, bearing tiding he knew they would not want to hear, the herald stepped forward. For the first time it was very noticeable how shabby was his tunic, Not just dusty, but stained with dubious fluids, they would soon learn what had caused them.

"Majesty", he began, his voice cracked, he ran his parched tongue over lips arid with the loss of moisture, took a reviving sip of the wine Herne had given him. It proved to be a futile gesture, his voice was still as dry as old kindling, but he continued anyway. Then they all heard his dreadful tidings. "I come from the ruins of Castle Knelforest. The walls are right finely destroyed, crashed to the ground by trebuchet fire. The interior ruined by the usual flames of they who would murder, pillage and burn. My Lord is slain. His dear wife taken as an trophy and her children put to the sword. The guard of his Lordship, those as survived are scattered into the forest, fled for their lives".

Celesta asked a one-worded question, "Who"?

The Lords of **Koözoött** and Kyper Tor, they lead an impossible army. An army that when smitten down, do rise again to continue with the fight. Deaths do little to slow them, the result of the raid could only ever end in but one dreaded result".

Zemtel first Lord of Kingshire - Interfectorem regem scoffed, "The dead do not rise, Herald. 'Twould seem the spineless forces of thy Lord merely wounded them and then didst tremble when they rallied".

"My Lord", the herald dared to object, "I saw men cleaved with such an injury as would surely have resulted in the death of any as were to receive the like. Only they endured. Rather they died as do all men. Yet some malign power was at work. They became animate even in death, rose to form a wave of fighting moaning corpses that took an even greater toll on his Lordship's guard. I swear this be so, on the lives of my family and all else I hold dear".

Zemtel first Lord of Kingshire - Interfectorem regem turned to Herner,

"Tell me, Scribe, be such possible"?

Herner shook his head, "No, my Lord. Even so as first Lord of Kingshire and Prince Consort tis now thy royal duty to investigate the incident. Thy forces can be ready in two days. On the way, thou canst call 'pon the services of those in the towns of, Torkinvayst, Hegyekben, Hamshire Forest, Kreel, Laaterfell and Várort"

Thank thee Herner", the first Lord of Kingshire and Prince Consort observed sarcastically, "I do know mine geography".

72.

"Can you focus the Vandei Motestas"? I asked Hersko

He looked momentarily at a loss to discern my inquiry, "Dost thous meanest to a given point"?

"I meanest", I clarified in his curious dialect.

"I knowest not", he confessed, "But if thou has an request of me, Visionary then all mine energy will be directed to comply with thy wishes. I assume Valgral not be thy sought destination"?

"Yes, that's right", I confessed, "It's the far world that Quianhua and I hail from that I would like to be taken".

Quianhua objected, "But the Zernothingies, we will be...".

"I do not mean the layer of Earth we left, Sweetheart", I quickly explained, "But the one adjacent to it, hopefully just similar enough, that we can make our home on it. In my own house if possible"?

"That ith a good idea", Mister Genks observed, stroking Mr Choon who purred in his embrace.

"I knowest not the local of such a realm", Visionary Hersko admitted right readily.

"Then like Spongebob, use your imagination", I urged, "Think as you instinctively activate the power of the Vandei Motestas that you wish to go to the dominion of myself, but one layer to the left, or right, that does not matter at this juncture".

"Perhaps this Lord Spongebob was a wiser man than I", Hersko mused, this caused Quianhua to smile broadly, asking of him,

"Will you try though, Hersko, please"?

A beautiful woman asking for one's favour is a powerful incentive for any man. The young Úrrh, former Warrior Lord of Akerányó, was no exception to that condition. He nodded, without anyone instructing it, we suddenly huddled together, in a tight circle.

The air around us grew instantly brighter, a beacon in the night of Tru-eti Varzslatoj, Trutizoj district the prospective Administrative Commander for the month gasped, stepped back, ordered his aid to follow suit.

I felt suddenly quite dizzy and swallowed back the bile that burned my throat. I had never been the best of travellers, inter-spatial traverse through the lay-lines of the multiverse was new to me. I am not exactly sure what I expected to happen next. Some weird light patterns perhaps, sickly spinning, the feeling of being suddenly dropped, like when an aeroplane hits a pocket of air? What I would never have guessed was the actuality of it, which is what happened next. The traverse was almost instantaneous. Our group found ourselves in my front yard.

73.

Quianhua asked me at that point,
"Have you considered the possibility of meeting an alternative version of yourself, one of me"?

"Surely there cannot be copies of you, my Darling, I chirped flatteringly, "For you are unique".

Quianhua put two fingers in front of her mouth and mimed throwing up.

Hersko and Cassiti were meanwhile gazing about them, wild-eyed at the Yorkshire scene before them. Its level of advancement compared to that which they had been accustomed. Mister Genks was wide-eyed, but with his bulbous seeing organs, he could not be anything else. Being from further forward in time than the 21st Century, he probably found my home county primitive by comparison to his domain.

Quianhua asked, rather obviously,

"Right then, what do we do now"?

I had possessed the foresight to be ready for that question.

"It was my house, let's see who's in it now? If it's still me I'm fairly sure I'll make myself welcome".

"Look"! Quianhua suddenly pointed, "People! Humans, the slugs have not been to this version of our world".

Two figures at the top of the street were walking an Alsatian.

"Let's not jump to too many conclusions", I warned, "There are not many abroad, it may have been a culling rather than total genocide, we're only one layer away from our own, isn't that right Hersko"?

The Valgraln shrugged, overwhelmed by the appearance of the buildings, parked cars. It caused me to look again, what I noticed gave me food for thought. Quianhua demanded, highly tuned to my various states of mind,

"What is it Nik, what are you staring at"?

"The cars", I told her, "Look at them, what do you see"?

"I see cars, what of it"?

"Look closer"?

"All right I see a BMW, two Volkswagen, three Audi and three SsangYong Tivoli, what of it"?

"What of it is that they are either German or Chinese and in my world, there were no Chinese Cars in Yorkshire".

"So"?

Myrrorball

"It's different, let's hope it doesn't make any greatly fundamental changes to my county of birth, that's all".

"Knock on the door, Nik"? Mister Genks sounded insistent and grave, did he know something? After all, he was from the 33rd Century?

I knocked, almost instantly it seemed that someone was coming to the mainly strengthened glass door, that had not been in the house in my world. It opened to reveal a young woman dressed in white and black maid's uniform. A maid, therefore. The house was not big enough to house live-in help, nor need it. She must go home each evening I reasoned.

"Can I help yo...".

The instant she saw Mister Genks, all colour drained from her pretty features, she swayed as though she was about to faint.

"It's all right", I assured, "He's our friend, he won't harm you. We have come to visit you from …a distance away, will you tell the owner of the property we are here, please? I am Mister Gehenna".

"Does she know you"? The girl wanted to know, never taking her eyes from the manbian's green visage.

"No, but I have something of great interest to tell her, ask her if she will see us".

Tearing her eyes from Mister Genks for the briefest of intervals, the maid then spotted Quianhua. Her attitude altered abruptly,

"Oh, my apologies, I did not see you there, Qíngfù. Would you please come inside? I'm sure Fräulein Neuman will wish to entertain you and your entourage".

I was naturally full of questions. The girl was evidentially English, she even spoke with a Yorkshire accent. Yet she seemed most deferential to a Chinese woman and spoke of her employer as a German. Yorkshire had never been so cosmopolitan, at least not the one I was used to. As we carefully stepped over the threshold, I got another shock. The hall was enormous, leading to the stairs by a corridor that had not existed when I had lived in the house. My bookcase was gone, the white walls had been replaced by a deep golden wallpaper, while the pink carpet was now black. A very

Teutonic colour-scheme. The maid ushered us into a lounge filled with unfamiliar furniture. Walls covered with canvasses I had never owned or seen before. I keenly watched her leave by a second door which did not lead into my kitchen, but rather a golden-hued corridor that stretched much further than the rear of my house had ever done. I was in 23 Acacia Gardens, but it was nothing like I had become accustomed too. Strangely the frontal aspect, I had recognised though, curious.

The maid was only gone a couple of seconds when an elegant, slim woman in a very expensive frock appeared in her wake. She smiled at us all - charmingly,

"Guten Morgen", she greeted in German, "Ich fühle mich geehrt über Ihren Besuch, wer sind Sie und was kann ich tun, um Ihnen zu helfen"? [Good morning, I am honoured to have you here, who are you and what can I do to help you?]

Thank you Hhrrhhoehhrrhooooingohh & Harahora-hurrahaashume for insisting I had so much information, including how to speak German, downloaded into my brain. Of the company, I knew Quianhua also would understand Fräulein Neuman, possibly the manbian, but certainly not Hersko and Cassiti.

"I stood, nodded to her, a formal bow and replied in her tongue,

"We are visitors from far away. It would take quite a while to tell you our story. I came here because this used to be my home. It was not the same style or shape as it is now, but this is the correct address. We are indeed in need of help, would you be willing to listen to my tale"?

"The Qíngfù", Neuman began, "She is not in charge of the rest of you"?

"No. I am the group's leader".

"An Englischer Mann, from just how far have you come to be here Herr Gehenna and are you even aware that you have a Jewish name"?

"A great distance", I answered, realised then that my name might be a problem, "I am English and not Jewish even though my surname is a Jewish word".

Myrrorball

"We shall all have tea, you shall tell me your story. Henceforth your surname will be Herr Merkwürdig [Mister Strange]".

"I can live with that".

She ordered the tea and then asked, "Does the Qíngfù speak any German, my Chinese is woeful even though I have tried long and hard to master it"?

"Quianhua responded, "I speak German well enough, Fräulein Neuman, I am Quianhua Merkwürdig, Nik is my husband".

"That explains a great deal then", our host observed, "I did wonder why a Chinese woman would be seemingly subservient to an Englishman".

"I would ask you to explain that remark, Fräulein Neuman, but after I have related our adventures that led up to this moment, you will have some questions of your own, so let me begin".

It took me a good couple of hours. Even then it was an abridged version. Credit to Neuman, she looked amazed at much of what I told her but did not interrupt me once.

When I finished, she finally broke her silence, telling us,

"You must stop for lunch as my guests", she said it to Quianhua, not me, it was evident that in the Yorkshire of this facet of the layers of the multiverse, the Chinese were regarded highly by the Germans. What either of them  was doing in England I had yet to work out. I was slightly worried by the Jewish reference, thought that most Germans had gotten over that particular prejudice. That was in my and Quianhua's lost world though.

In a moment of inspiration, I asked Neuman,

"Excuse me Fräulein, but while my friends prepare for luncheon, do you think it would be possible to access a computer? I could look up the history of this facet of the multiverse, save you a great deal of explanation if you feel we deserve taking time out of your day? Indeed is there any demands upon you, we are, interrupting your normal routine".

"Qíngfù Merkwürdig is welcome to be my guest here in my home until you make other arrangements for her", came the graciously generous reply. "If that means also housing yourself, the others, then I will be willing to do so for a limited period. I wish to know far more about the slug-like creatures you describe. Our government will be most intrigued to learn of the existence of intelligent aliens in our galaxy. Let me show you to a desktop so you can look at things before luncheon is ready".

"Most kind", I agreed, but I sensed that in her eyes I was some sort of secondary citizen. I knew the internet would provide me with certain answers.

I could not have possibly imagined the shock that lay in store for me though, the dramatic differences between the Yorkshire Quianhua and I had left, the one we now found ourselves?

74.

Chamberlain Declares, 'Peace for Our Time'.
On September 23rd 1938, British Prime Minister Neville Chamberlain received a rowdy homecoming after signing a peace pact with Nazi Germany. For days, dread had blanketed London like a fog. Only a generation removed from the horrors of World War I, which had claimed nearly one million of its people, Britain was once again on the brink of armed conflict with Germany. Adolf Hitler, who had annexed Austria earlier in the year, had vowed to invade Czechoslovakia on October 23rd 1938, to occupy the German-speaking Sudetenland region. A further move toward the creation of a "*greater Germany*" that could potentially ignite another conflagration among the great European powers. The clouds of war billowed in the British capital as the hours to the deadline dwindled. As Chamberlain mobilized the Royal Navy, Londoners, including the prime minister's wife, prayed on bended knees inside Westminster Abbey. Workers covered the windows of government offices with sandbags and

installed sirens in police stations to warn of approaching enemy bombers. By torchlight, they scarred the city's pristine parks by digging miles of trenches to be used as air-raid shelters. A knot of traffic snarled the city as Londoners began an exodus. Hundreds of thousands who planned to stay in the city stood patiently in line for government-issued gas masks and air-raid handbooks. London Zoo officials even developed plans to station gun-toting men in front of cages to shoot the wild animals in case bombs broke open their cages, to free them. Just two days before the deadline, our gracious Führer agreed to meet in Munich with Chamberlain, to discuss a diplomatic resolution to the crisis. The two leaders, without any input from Czechoslovakia in the negotiation, agreed to cede the Sudetenland to Hitler. Chamberlain also separately drafted a non-aggression pact between Britain and Germany that Hitler signed. When news of the diplomatic breakthrough reached the British capital, normally staid London responded like a death-row prisoner granted a last-minute reprieve. Jubilation and waves of relief washed over London in a celebration that had not been seen since the armistice that silenced the guns of World War I. On a rainy autumn evening, thousands awaited the English Prime Minister's return at London's Charlton Heston Aerodrome, and the thankful crowd cheered wildly as the door to his British Airways air-plane opened. Raindrops fell on Chamberlain's silver hair, he stepped onto the airport tarmac. He held aloft the non-aggression pact that had been inked by him and our glorious Chancellor only hours before. The flimsy piece of paper flapped in the breeze. The Prime Minister of the English then read to the nation the brief agreement that reaffirmed 'the desire of our two peoples never to go to war with one another again'.

Summoned to Buckingham Palace to give a first-hand report to King Edward VIII and his wife, Her Royal Highness Queen Frederica former princess of Hanover queen of Great Britain. Chamberlain was cheered on by thousands who lined the five-mile route from the airport. As the rain poured, thousands flooded the plaza in front of the royal residence. As if it were a coronation or a royal wedding, the frenzied cheers brought forth. The King and Queen, along with Chamberlain and his wife, walked onto the palace balcony. In an unprecedented move, the smiling King motioned the Prime Minister to step forward and receive the crowd's adulation as he receded into the background to leave the stage solely to a commoner. Following his royal audience, Chamberlain returned to his official residence at No. 10 Downing Street. There - a jubilant crowd shouted,

'Good old Neville' and sang,

'For He's a Jolly Good Fellow'. From a second-floor window, Chamberlain addressed the crowd, invoked Prime Minister Benjamin Disraeli's famous statement upon returning home from the Berlin Congress of 1878,

"My good friends, this is the second time in our history that there has come back from Germany to Downing Street - peace with honour. I believe it is peace for our time". Then he added, "Now I recommend you to go home and sleep quietly in your beds".

As the English slept, the German army marched into Czechoslovakia in *peaceful conquest* of the Sudetenland. The bombers did not roar over London that night nor would they ever. In March 1939, the Führer annexed the rest of Czechoslovakia, and two days after the Third Reich crossed into Poland on September 23rd 1939, the Prime Minister again spoke to the nation. This time to solemnly tell them that a large task force had been sent across the English Channel. Bolstered by the air power of the Royal Flying Corps (RFC) and the Royal Naval Air Service (RNAS) the northern coast of France was ill-prepared for the strike, it promptly collapsed before the force. The Fall of France was the result of the combined attacks by England and Germany through the Low Countries during the Second World War. In early September 1939, France began a limited Saar Offensive due to Germany's invasion of Poland. By mid-October, the French had withdrawn to their start lines. In two weeks, from early October, the English and German twin spearhead defeated the French with mobile operations. Before the end of the year, the

Anglo-Germanic Axis [AGA] had conquered France, Belgium, Luxembourg Holland and most of Northern Italy.

I found it hard to believe that we had been on the same side as the Axis. I was going to work my way through the twentieth and twenty-first centuries when the maid informed me that luncheon was served. I tore myself from the computer to go in search of a dining room. The house was not that big that it was difficult to find, but it was certainly many times larger than mine had been. The elegant Fräulein was seated at the head of a long table. At the opposite end, there was a space, it suggested that there was an Herr of the household, possibly out at work.

I took my seat on Neuman's left, facing Quianhua who was opposite me on the Fräulein's right. Hersko and Cassiti had been also placed opposite one another, with Mister Gents next to the Úrrh, Warrior Lord of Akerányó.

"Where is Mister Choon"? I asked the room in general, it was the Fräulein who answered,

"He is enjoying some herring with the staff in the basement of the property".

I had not even had a cellar, or basement as the German mistress of the house informed. As we ate a cold collation of various meats and cheeses, Neuman asked me,

"Did you learn what you were after Herr Merkwürdig"?

"I ran out of time, Fräulein, with your permission I would be grateful for the opportunity of learning more, our worlds have proven quite diverse in one key element in history".

Neuman smiled and observed, "I think I suspect it might prove the African Solution, Ja"?

"Nein, World War II itself, I was not expecting the agreement with Herr Hitler and Mister Chamberlain to be honoured".

"In what particular"?

"In our layer of the multiverse, Germany and England were not on the same side".

Neuman looked thoughtful,

"How bizarre, when we joined together, in order to finally put an end to Bolshevism".

Major Roxbrough & Nik Gehenna

"Would I be able to return to the computer after this delightful lunch do you think, Fräulein"?

By way of an answer, Quianhua received a questioning glance from the German host, only agreed once my wife had nodded. Intriguing. I could not wait to get back to my historical studies.

75.

[Operation Barbarossa] Unternehmen Barbarossa was the code name for the AGA invasion of the Soviet Union, which started on Tuesday, March 23rd 1940, during World War II. The operation put into action the Nazi-Anglo ideological goal of conquering the western Soviet Union to repopulate it with Germans and English people both considered to be the Aryan race. The AGA Generalplan Ost aimed to use some of the conquered as slave labour for the Axis war effort, to acquire the oil reserves of the Caucasus and the agricultural resources of Soviet territories. Eventually to annihilate the Slavic peoples and create Lebensraum for the new AGA Empire. The Axis High Command began planning an invasion of the Soviet Union in late 1939 following the collapse of western Europe. (under the codename Operation Otto), which Adolf Hitler and Neville Chamberlin had authorized. Throughout the operation, six million personnel of the Axis powers—the largest invasion force in the history of warfare—invaded the western Soviet Union along a 2,900-kilometre front, with 1,200,000 motor vehicles and over 900,000 horses for non-combat operations. The offensive marked an escalation of World War II, both geographically and in the formation of the Axis coalition including Romania, Bulgaria, Hungary, Austria, Denmark, Norway, Finland, Sweden, Portugal, Italy and of course Germany and England.

The operation opened up the Eastern Front, in which more forces were committed than in any other theatre of war in history. The area saw some of the war's bloodiest battles, most horrific atrocities, and highest casualties (for Soviet and Axis forces alike), all of which influenced the course of World War II and the subsequent history of the 20th Century. The AGA armies eventually captured some 5,000,000 Soviet Red Army troops, a majority of whom never returned alive. The Anglo/Nazis deliberately starved to death, or otherwise killed, 3.3 million Soviet prisoners of war, and a vast number of civilians, as the '*Hunger Plan*' worked to exterminate the Slavic population. Mass shootings and gassing operations carried out by the Anglo/Nazis or willing collaborators, murdered over a million Soviet Jews as part of the First Holocaust. The success of the operation cemented the fortunes of the Third and following Fourth Reich. Operationally, AGA forces achieved crushing victories. Eventually occupying the most important economic areas of the Soviet Union.

As early as 1925, Adolf Hitler vaguely declared in his political manifesto and autobiography Mein Kampf that he would invade the Soviet Union, asserting that the German people needed to secure Lebensraum (living space) to ensure the survival of Germany for generations to come. In February 1939, Hitler told his army commanders that the next war would be purely a war of *Weltanschauungen ... totally a people's war, a racial war*. On November 23rd, once World War II had already started, Hitler declared that. 'racial war has broken out, this war shall determine who shall govern Europe, with it, the world'. The racial policy of Nazi Germany and the Upper Class of England portrayed the Soviet Union as populated by non-Aryan Untermenschen (sub-humans), ruled by Jewish Bolshevik conspirators. Hitler claimed in Mein Kampf that Germany's destiny was to, '*turn to the East*'. Accordingly, it was stated Nazi policy to kill, deport, or enslave the majority of Russian and other Slavic populations. Re-populating the land with German and their Aryan allies in the English peoples, under the Generalplan Ost. The Nazis' belief in their Aryan ethnic superiority pervades official records and pseudoscientific articles in German periodicals, on topics such as '*how to deal with alien populations*'.

Older histories tended to emphasize the notion of a "*Clean Wehrmacht*" upholding its honour in the face of

Hitler's fanaticism, the historian Jürgen Förster notes that, 'In fact, the military commanders were caught up in the ideological character of the conflict, and involved in its implementation as willing participants'. Before and during the invasion of the Soviet Union, German and English troops were heavily indoctrinated with anti-Bolshevik, anti-Semitic, and anti-Slavic ideology via movies, radio, lectures, books, and leaflets. Likening the Soviets to the forces of Genghis Khan, Hitler told Croatian military leader Slavko Kvaternik that the Mongolian race threatened Europe. At the same moment that the Soviets were being heinously killed. An English invasion of Scotland was being carried out on similar lines. Chamberlain had stated, 'We will take the opportunity to finally rid ourselves of those, Bastard Half-French [hist] and make the Commonwealth even greater. From this point, the British Commonwealth will become the English Commonwealth'

Following the dual-pronged invasion, Wehrmacht/AGA officers told their soldiers to target people who were described as '*Jewish Bolshevik subhumans*', the '*Mongol hordes*', the '*Asiatic flood*', '*Bastard Half-French*' and the '*Red beast*'. Anglo/Nazi propaganda portrayed the war against the Soviet Union and Scotland as both an ideological war between German National Socialism and Jewish Bolshevism and racial war. Between the disciplined Germans and the Jewish, Bastard Half-French, Gypsy, and Slavic Untermenschen. An '*order from the Führers*' stated that the Einsatzgruppen/High Command was to execute all Soviet/Scots functionaries who were '*less valuable Frogs, Asiatics, Gypsies and Jews*'. Six months into the invasions, the Einsatzgruppen had already murdered more than 600,000 Soviet/Scots Jews, a figure higher than the number of enemy Army soldiers killed in combat during that time. The Anglo-German Axis army commanders cast the Jews as the major cause behind the '*partisan struggle*'. The main guideline for AGA troops was '*Where there's a partisan, there's a Jew, and where there's a Jew, there's a partisan*', or '*The partisan is where the Jew is*'. Many

Myrrorball

AGA troops viewed the war in Nazi terms and regarded their Soviet and Scots enemies as sub-human. After the war had begun, the Anglo/Nazis issued a ban on sexual relations between Aryan and foreign slave workers. There were regulations enacted against the Ost-Arbeiter (Eastern workers) that included the death penalty for sexual relations with an Aryan. Heinrich Himmler, in his secret communication to the Archbishop of Canterbury, *'Reflections on the Treatment of Peoples of Alien Races in the East'*, outlined the Nazi plans for the non-German populations in the East and the north of the British Isles. Himmler believed the Aryanization process in Eastern Europe would be complete when *'in the new territories dwell only men with truly Aryan blood'*. Heinrich Himmler, Rudolf Hess, and Reinhard Heydrich had listened to Konrad Meyer at a Generalplan Ost exhibition the Nazi secret plan Generalplan Ost (General Plan for the East and Schottland), prepared in 1939 and confirmed in 1940, called for a 'new order of ethnographical relations' in the territories occupied by the Axis in western and eastern Europe. It envisaged ethnic cleansing, executions, and enslavement of the populations of conquered countries. With very small percentages undergoing Aryanization, expulsion into the depths of Russia, or other fates, while the conquered territories would be Aryanized. The plan had two parts: the Kleine Planung (small plan), which covered actions to be taken during the war, plus the Große Planung (large plan), which covered policies after the war was ended. To be implemented gradually over 25 to 30 years.

Thirty years after the war Black Nazi had a number one hit with their song AGA-Do the first two lines of the chorus being,

Aga do do do,

Light the oven roast a Jew.

I was frankly horrified at the atrocities that my nation had taken part in until I reasoned that they were not my nation at all. The British Empire had not become great by being humanitarian either, so there was no real reason to be surprised.

Major Roxbrough & Nik Gehenna

I skipped to Pearl Harbour, which had taken place just as it had in my layer of the multiverse. Unlike ours though, the Axis had not declared war on Amerika. Chamberlain had convinced Hitler to abandon the Japanese. Once they had been defeated, by the might of Amerikan industrial power and the bomb, it presented China with the opportunity to crush the ruined islands. Japan, along with the far eastern regions of the Soviet Block, became Chinese territories. A tripartite pact was signed between Germany, England and China. Amerika remained isolationist. In the forties, the Anglo-Germanic Empire grew in strength. China turned their eyes southward in the late forties, to the condemnation of the weakened Amerikan president, China invaded Africa.

Just as the AGA had persecuted and almost annihilated the Jews in Europe and Asia, China set about the Negroes and commenced a sadistic genocide of coloured people everywhere they encountered them in their expanded Empire. Four nations had divided up the world. Amerika stormed into South Amerika, only too aware that to not do so would leave them relatively weak when compared to the three other superpowers. The continent of Amerika was united. China had the far east and Africa. The English Empire had its Commonwealth, Germany Europe and Russia. Since the atom had been split, there were no more wars, but one vital area of the world continued to prove troublesome to the powers that ruled it. The Middle East. The Commonwealth had trouble containing Egypt and Palestine, the Germans pursued localised police actions in Iran and Iraq. The rise of what the Germans called the Musselmen had proved to remain difficult even to the present day.

The new problems were not political but based on superstition. England and Germany had become non-believers in the main. Moved on from the primitive superstitions that had caused so much calamity in the past. The Musselmen continued to gain strength fuelled by ignorance, while Amerika clung to the foolish belief that the Jewish prophet of two thousand years in the past, was more than that. In the east, China had found a new superstition, the belief that the state and their race were the superior force on Earth. There had been minor troubles with their neighbours. Border wars in Russia. The threat of Australian invasion when the *Yellow Peril* thought to expand into what was English Commonwealth territory. The Chinese were so numerous, so hard working and so strong in their convictions that the Anglo/Teutonic Nazis of the Fourth Reich began to regard them as the new nobles of the planet. They were slightly in awe of them. This attitude had fostered Neuman's reaction when Quianhua had appeared at her door. Not even the alien Mister Genks had impressed her as much.

I drew back from the computer deep in thought, what was my next move? Should I stay in this reality and try to make the best of it, or move on, would Hersko want to remain cooperative toward me now that he found himself in a land of Visionaries?

76.

Norgan knew none in Knelforest could best him with a blade. He was too skilled, had seen too many campaigns to make that a possibility. He even reflected upon the issue as he directed his broadsword into an opposing knight's chest, splitting him down to his groin in the process. That was the instant at which the stray arrow buried itself in his left eye, changing his existence forever.

The pain was not the worst of it. The defence of defeat was not something, Major Norgan of Koözoött, was accustomed to giving tongue too. Blackness engulfed him, a period of dark nothingness that he could not discern the duration. He did not even know that he was dead because he did not know anything. From the total void voices, echoing and from far away intruded. Light pressed in upon his right eyelid. he opened his eyes. Surgeon Blaho was gazing down at him, looked completely astonished to see the major come back. Come back from...? Another voice-over to his left, deathly calm commanded,

"Go back to the battle, Major, thy Lord has continued need of thee still, the conflict has yet to be resolv-ed".

Turning his head to see who spoke, he observed a tall brunette man, bearded, with an air and mien, to an economical movement, that silently bespoke of strange power.

"Art thou the Necromancer, rumour told us of"? He asked, surprised himself, at the strength in his voice. Before he realised what he was doing, he raised a hand to his left eye to see how badly he had suffered the wound. He felt the cut off shaft of an arrow flush with the socket. They had not even bothered removing the arrow's iron tip!

"I be Banustib", the man nodded, before advising. "Leave the eye alone. Do not attempt to remove the barb, thy appearance will be all the more fearsome for the presence of it".

"I will succumb to ferric poisons. It must be removed and quite rightly with given haste", Norgan dared. The Necromancer shook his head,

"None toxin will course through thy flesh, Major, for it lacketh the vitality to transfer such from cell to cell. Thou art dead".

Norgan would have laughed. Yet he remembered the black period, the stories that Banustib could indeed reanimate the fallen in battle. He pushed his hand under his mail short and felt for his heart. It was not beating - the mage was telling the truth.

"When will I be brought back to life"? He demanded.

"Such is not possible", the mage returned, with not the slightest hint of regret, "Yet thou canst still serve the lord of thy keep. Thou art Animataverous. In essence, this meaneth living in death".

Norgan would have roared in torment and anger. His voice lacked the timbre it had once possessed. He rose from the table to strangle the life out of the wicked practitioner of the dark arts. A force he could not fathom for its particular froze his intended action. He found himself locked in an inner struggle that he instinctively knew he could not win.

Banustib smiled, yet there was no amusement in the expression, rather, one of grimly vile satisfaction in his skills.

"Wouldst thou harm thy creator, Major? He who be responsible for thy salvation. Such ingratitude. I could wave a casual arm and hurl thee back into the pit of annihilation if such were upon my choices. I rather fancy one with thy former dynamism wouldst not prefer that though. So, obey, go back to the battle. Rally the others of thy kind, the Army of Animataverosity. Make haste before I do as I threaten"?

Norgan was not so foolish as to challenge a Necromancer when he was ready for an assault. Better to bide his time if issue continued with the vile mage, he would eventually sleep, forget the incident. He left the tent swiftly, mounted his horse, rode for the invading camp. The battle continued to rage, but as he glanced about him, he could see that it was drifting advantageously in favour of Koözoött. Norgan quickly gathered some of the men under his command. Approximately one-third of them were sporting injuries, which, under normal circumstances, would have been fatal. He quickly issued instructions. They formed a fearsome spearhead to drive into the enemy rank. Seeming to understand what their intentions were, the main force under the Lordship's of Koözoött and Kyper Tor, parted for them. Thusly allowing them to rush to the vanguard. Heedless of further injury, or personal safety Norgan led the spearhead. Thence did they smite against the defenders of the castle to their rear. The effect was hugely demoralising to the men who in many circumstances had killed or felled those who now attacked them with seeming vitality. It turned the battle, the forces of Knelforest, who until that moment had defended fiercely, passionately, looked to have the very spirit torn from them. Norgan saw the Lord of Knelforest suddenly encounter Kyper Tor himself. With a roar of infuriated outrage at the crime being perpetrated against his seat, he urged his horse forward. Their swords clattered against one another with unholy clamour.

It was a conflict, the like of which, would most likely conjure future song. Such Lords as were of equality in the matching., Their dual conducted with adeptitudenous accomplishment, while all around them the battle raged. Norgan suddenly forced himself;f to take his eye momentarily from the bipartisan conflict. A halberdier suddenly threatened to ram his long pike into the Major's dead guts. He pulled on the reins of his coal-black steed, drove inside the clumsy weapon. His sword smashing into the teeth of the hapless attacker, who gargled, died badly, to fall into the bloody mud and be trampled by shod hoof, booted foot. When the Major finally had time to look once more in the direction of the Lord's bilateral contention it was plain that of the two, Kyper Tor was starting to weaken. His defences were verging on desperation, his attacks fewer - weaker than his opponents. Norgan reluctantly urged his steed toward them. A foot soldier barred his way, with a mighty swipe of Cleaver, his sword, the man's head sprang from his shoulders, a spouting body fell like a chopped tree.

Cleaver drove forward, point forward, plunged through Knelforest's breastplate like it was little stronger than soft silk. The Lord coughed, looked astonished that anyone had dared to interrupt a dual between two gentries. When his vision espied the arrow firmly lodged in Norgan's eye socket and brain behind, his own grew wide. He began to fall from the saddle. With a clatter, his armoured body hit the ground. He became what he who had slain him had once been. In Knelforest's case, the state was permanent.

Kyper Tor glanced in relief toward the warrior who had broken the rules of chivalry, yet like as not, saved his life. When he regarded Norgan's features, he gasped, gratitude forgotten,

"Thou art one of the necromancer's new creatures, begone vile demon, I would have no truck with thee and thy kind".

Myrrorball

Norgan could not blame the man, he was indeed no longer human, but a creature, never one so disgusting had existed before. The forces of Kyper Tor and Koözoött won a crushing victory. The castle was successfully, brutally stormed. After all the raping and pillaging - burned to the ground. Norgan turned away from what had once been his favourite part of conquest, especially the raping, but he found he had no stomach for it, nor much else. Death had robbed him of most of his sensibilities. He returned to his men. The living then regarded him with a combination of horror and suspicion. The dead were not very interesting. Indeed many of them did not speak. In a few cases, it was because their lower jaw and tongue had been cleaved from their faces by a sword or battle axe, but in others, it was a sort of creeping apathy that seemed to be pervading them collectively.

Norgan thusly had no place with the living, equally none with the dead either. He was am Animataverous alone. He did not eat with those who were still very much alive that night, but he did wash the gore from his waxy features cleaned the grey and scarlet crust from his armour - sharpened his sword. Word had it that the army, along with those pressed from Knelforest, would be marching on Staltidore on the morrow. Using connections he had enjoyed when alive, Norgan requested an audience with Lord Koözoött. Surprised despite himself that it was granted swift agreement. He left the tent, marched toward what was left standing of the castle, for the time being. It would be torn down to rubble on the morrow, before the march.

Kyper Tor and Koözoött were in what had once been a magnificent dining hall. All the finery systematically stripped from it by then. All that remained was the table, two chairs. The Lords were eating, Norgan watched them for a fleeting moment. He could taste nought in his mouth but ash and brimstone.

"Major", Koözoött greeted enthusiastically, "I was most sorely grieved to hear of thy demise. Ne-er in battle honestly fought wouldst thou have succumbed, yet stray arrows make the grim chance of us all. Pray to tell me what hast thou to impart? Something regarding the enemy perchance?

"No, mine Lord", Norgan's voice issued from beyond the grave, had he but ever been placed in one. "The matter concerns me. I fought for thee today. Thusly wouldst I be'est released from whatever despicable bane the wizard placed upon my resting flesh. I seek to end this existence and with right impunity amundo".

Koözoött looked genuinely saddened to hear the request and placing his fork down for the moment admitted,

"Yet thy Lord doest require what thou be about in the course of thy former profession, Major. Sometimes we, who are mere clay to be moulded by the whim of the gods must play parts upon the stage of life, roles that dost not sit too well 'pon the shoulders. Thy Lord needeth thee still, be that enough for thee"?

Norgan nodded in a military acknowledgement of orders received, yet the sinews in his neck felt tight, the joints in his spine were stiff and less flexible than they had been in life.

"For how long, My Lord"?

"Doh"! Kyper Tor exploded then, "The reawakened Animataverous still have tongue to disrespect, my Lord of Koözoött. Have it torn out by the malefic root so that it may challenge thy authority none further"?

"No", Koözoött returned without hesitation, "Major Norgan was greatly valued in life and be still so in death". He returned his attention to Norgan,

"Fight for thy Lord, till end of campaign. Thence thy King shall grant thee thy wish"?

Norgan agreed, "Very well, My Lord. Until thou sitteth 'pon the throne in Valgral. Not a battle longer though, give vow unto me"?

Kyper Tor launched himself to his feet so violently, that his chair overturned, clattering on the tessellated floor of what was remained of the hall. He made to stride toward Norgan, but Koözoött cried,

"Kyper Tor, sit down".

Face puce with compressed fury the Lord of Kyper Tor did as directed, after righting the chair once more.

Myrrorball

"Major Norgan", Koözoött began levelly, "Once the crown of Valgraln be mine, I will let Banustib release thee. Thou shalt go to thy grim reward. Thou has the word of it. Now, afore his Lordship has further apoplexy pray to leave us to our dinner".

Norgan bowed and left them, he felt he had gotten what he wanted. He must fight on, but once the capital fell beneath the army of the Animataverous, he then could die.

77.

"The Qíngfù Quianhua Merkwürdig is welcome to stay as my guest in this house as long as she wishes", Neuman had told me, "As her spouse, you may form part of her small retinue. The amphibian man can stay as your *man*", she smiled at the irony of that phrase, before going on,

"But the savages must leave before my husband returns from his business trip in Düsseldorf".

"Eva", I began, for we were now on first name terms, "They have nowhere to go in this world. Can they not stay in the retainers quarters, please"?

Yet though the German beauty agreed to that for a short period, it did not sit well with Hersko,

"I be a Small-lord, Visionary and warrior lord of Akerányó, I will not act as retainer, neither will Cassiti. No, Visionary we shall journey to the next layer of the multiverse, or mayhap return to Valgral or Brohain. We shall return periodically to tell thee of our progress and who knows thence might we be-est reunited".

I argued with him, but it was plain to see that his mind was resolute, how could I blame him? Yorkshire was not his world, not any Yorkshire. Eventually, I conceded to his insistance, we parted. He and the Kémerké maiden bid us farewell and vanished who knew where. That night at dinner with the lady of the house we were in for the announcement of another development.

"Tell me, Nik", Eva Neuman asked, "In your layer, what did you do"?

"I was an author", I responded honestly.

"Then it's time you returned to your profession", she declared simply. "In England, there are no idle hands. I'm certain you agree with this philosophy, Quianhua"?

My wife nodded. She had not studied German culture in England as much as I, so she said little and never disagreed with her generous hostess.

"Tomorrow I would have a short story from you, Nik. If it is impressive, I will loan you the money to open your book shop and write in your spare time. I do not know if it was the same in your world, but in this one, antique books fetch good prices. You seem the sort of man who would buy wisely only after thoroughly researching the field of endeavour. I think you could do well. I have a shop that lies currently empty in the town, we will refurbish it with bookshelves, you shall become a dealer and author. What do you say to my proposal"?

"You took us in and fed us, put a shelter over our heads, I think I would like to try what you suggest, Eva, for your sake if not for mine. I find your proposal intriguing though and am willing to commit my most ardent industry toward it. As for the writing, it might well be time to get back to fiction after so much biography of late. I have an idea for a short story that you shall be the first to read".

In the past, I had written slowly, when I was struggling for inspiration. At other times, my fingers had raced over the keyboard when the mood the inspiration was upon me, I wrote the following story very quickly indeed. **Perhaps it shows** - Hhrrhhoehhrrhooooingohh, you will be the best judge of that if you ever get to read it that is? It may be as I write this that I am finished with the dealing of the Zernoplat, only time will tell?

Myrrorball

PART EIGHT

I WOKE UP DEAD.

©NIK GEHENNA 2020: EARTH.

Major Roxbrough & Nik Gehenna

I woke up dead.

It was dark, darker than a night when people observe less than casually,

'Isn't it dark tonight'?

The fuliginous pitch was more nigrescent than sable writing etched in black on a black, black background. There had to be a reason for it. I did not believe I was in a coma, not for an instant. The bullet had torn its way into my chest, bludgeoned through my heart - bursting it in the process. Yet, no tubes were entering my shattered corpse, no hum of I C U machinery, there was not a shred of doubt in my mind, I was the former (and murdered) husband of that cheating bitch, Isabel. Rupert had shot me in the heart, the murdering bastard.

I had known for some time that Isabel was *playing around*, I put it down to raging middle-aged hormones, desperately hoped it would be one of her phases, one of her fads. Of course, it hurt me terribly, but I loved her so much. Yet with my *problem*, I could not love her as she needed. So I did what I had done all my life when things got too difficult for me to bear, I pretended it was not happening. Just tried to see matters from her point of view. Unfortunately then, she fell in love with one of her inamorata's. Not only that, yet with the worst creep of them all. I could have told her that Rupert was not in love with her. I could have told her Rupert had only been in love with two things and neither of them was her. I could have told her that Rupert loved Rupert and money in that order. She would not have believed me, even if she still listened, which was seldom recently. What the handsome, simply divine Rupert wanted to be, was not in possession of Isabel at all. What he wanted was to get his hands on my soft drinks company. He had reduced her to a Methley, for the avaricious love of cash.

Orang-U-Can had started in a small way, but it was a worthy product. Further, I made it cheaper than Popsi and Coker Cooler, considerably less expensive in fact. The kids in Amerika, with their acne and rotting teeth, loved it, they drank it by the gallon and almost overnight I had money coming out of my ears.

All that was coming out of my ears now was soil! I was face down. Who buries someone face down? Murdering bastards that have just rolled you into a shallow grave - that's who. There was grit, loam, small twigs shoving their way up my nostrils. It would have been rather inconvenient if I had breathed. The dead do not require nor need oxygen. Another piece of damning evidence to support the fact that I was deceased. There was a tremendous weight pressing down on my back. As I tried to twist and fidget due to mild discomfort of positioning, I heard a crack, the end of the rib pierced the soft sack-like membrane of my left lung. Well, I had another one which was redundant too.

I decided I had done enough lying around and feeling sorry for myself. It was time for action. I mean to say, there had to be a reason why I had not stayed dead, right? I could think of two lulu's without even so much as a deliberate ponder. I pulled my arms up into a position that one assumes when doing press-ups. In the process, it inconveniently broke one of my fingers on my right hand, but it did not hurt. The grit in my eyes gave me no pain. I could neither smell nor taste the dirt in my mouth. All was silent. There again it is not supposed to be noisy in a graveyard, is it? The expression is not - *as cacophonous as the grave*. I hoped once I got free of the temporary resting place that I could hear, even if my other senses were dead. I had always loved my rock music. I had especially enjoyed it when playing quite loud. I thought about my new playlist. It seemed that much of Alice Cooper's material would now be to my taste, figuratively speaking of course.

Finally, I summoned up the effort and pushed against the hard surface I had been facing downward. Rupert was not a man who had made his way in life through manual labour. The shallow grave he had entombed me in, was barely wide enough to contain my bloody corpse. The soil that covered me was thusly thankfully shallow too. I climbed slowly to my feet. Loam, pebbles and bits of twig fell off my body as I did so. I heard it falling. In the soundtrack to my exhumation was the very faint noise of traffic, the brittle sound of an aircraft passing high overhead. I was not deaf. I opened my eyes, some of the grit scratching them as I did so. Not that it mattered so much, everything was blurred, filmed over like watery-milk. The thoughtless cad had not even thought to bury my glasses along with me. He had also removed my dentures. My fingertips felt slightly numb. Strange when most of my body felt nothing. I tried to gaze at them, but there was little light in the wood, I could not focus on my fingers without considerably longer arms. That is a hyperopian Zombie joke folks. Could it be the first one ever conceived? Probably not. So I improvised anyway, ran my tongue over the tip of my index finger on one hand. Just as I suspected their fingerprints were burned off. Rupert was many things, I could give you a list at this point but to cut to the meat, one of them was not stupid. He had taken my dentures, removed my fingerprints with either acid or flame. In the unlikely event (now impossible) that anyone had happened across my shallow grave, it would have taken the authorities some time to identify me, if at all.

If any part of your body is subsequently exhumed, thence scrutinised, the guilty party will deny any knowledge of your brutal murder - good luck Rupert.

One thing was for certain, they could kill my body, but they could not kill my mind.

Mission Impossible, The Outer Limits, flooded through the strangely active neurons, in what now functioned as my consciousness. I was half-blind, could not taste nor smell, yet I refused to lie down, or rather stay down. I tried to brush some of the filth from my favourite boho jacket. Even though fabulously wealthy, I had still dressed like a hippy. I was an eccentric millionaire, had loved being so, loved it to death. It was during this sprucing up that I discovered my limbs were even less flexible than usual. Oh well, my appearance at the next Olympics would have caused a negative vibe anyway. I slowly stepped out of the pathetic depression that had been my temporary resting place and tried to walk. As I stumbled along in the darkness with a Romeronic gait, I heard myself moaning. Rather it was some strange combination of howling moaning, growling and slobbering. Had it not been for the black mucus that seemed to dribble from my toothless mouth I think I can safely say that my griping sigh was completed with a certain panache.

Did I have a plan at that point? Did any Zombie ever have a plan? To be reasonable about things though, there had never been another Zombie before me! I was the real deal! Perhaps I was not even a Zombie? Maybe that was just for graphic novels, filums, TV series? I was definitely, incontrovertibly dead. No argument on that score. Unless I had a spare heart somewhere in my torso - which seemed beyond the realms of credibility. I might be the Protozombie, the father of all who came after me, General or god of The Dead? The supreme leader of a new race tripped over an unseen branch. One of many that festooned the floor of the wood, he fell flat on his face.

I heard something crunch. Like when one wants twice as many crisps as there are in the packet, so one improvises by scrunching the bag before opening it. As I lurched back upward to a clumsy crouch, I felt about in the leaves, for it had suddenly gotten draughtier on my face. Sure enough, what my acid burned fingers located, was shaped like a nose, felt like a nose and was a probosci's-type former organ that had resided on my face. It had formerly belonged in the middle of my face. Placing it into my pocket, I had always liked collecting mementoes, I stumbled forward with greater care than before. After all, if I put an eye out, I would be on my final warning. It did cause me to wonder the level of my decomposition, how long I had been dead before I woke up? Would I even last long enough to realise my ambition? Would I last long enough to even possess ambition? As I was Zombie A Number One - Duke of the Zombies I realised I simply had to wing it. Que Sera Sera, You'll Always Walk Alone etcetera.

I do not know how long elapsed before I finally found the edge of the forest. It was still dark though. My concept of time was shot to... don't go there, because it had felt like a very long time. The murderers had removed my gold watch, not that I could have seen it without my glasses. Even then, the misty film over my eyes might have made it difficult. I had to be thankful for small mercies, at least the disgusting duo had not stripped me of my clothes. I mean to say, I did not want to look out of place in a crowd! I found a road, ill-lit by too few overhead lights, not very well used. That might suit my purpose. Taking the dirty bandana off my head, I undid it and utilised it as a mask. The lack of nose was not so noticeable I hoped, although the scarf would be impossibly flat. It was the best I could do. It is not every day one wakes up dead and loses a nose. In the ordinary scheme of things, I would have considered just one of those events something of a bummer. I used to say at one time in my life, 'Life's a bitch and then you die', I was going to have to redress that maxim, change it to, 'The bitch ends your life and then death's a bitch'. I blamed Isabel for the murder just as much as the man who had pulled the trigger. She would have encouraged the act even if her clammy little hand had not held the gun.

Shamble as I might, I set off walking. After all, even a long trek in possibly the wrong direction was not going to kill me. I was headed for one place only, Guadalajara where the Orang-U-Can factory, offices and my huge impressive villa resided. Villa Orauca would now house my adulterous spouse and her illicit lover. I felt I had the right to treat them to an encounter. After all, they *had* killed me. Not much was going through my mind when lights in the distance, nothing more than fuzzled pinpricks of light originally, grew steadily brighter and closer. At least one vehicle was on the road during the lockdown. I guessed it would be a delivery van. Not hard to surmise considering the devastating effects of the coronavirus. I was walking toward the headlights, so was quite bemused when it pulled to a halt. A man leaned out of the driver side window.

"Saludos, señor, es un momento extraño para caminar por el Camino, ¿quiere un aventón, tal vez"?

The Mexican was in his middle forties, fat, healthy-looking, so why take such a risk as to offer a complete masked stranger a lift in the wrong direction in the middle of the night".

"I'm lost", I admitted frankly in passable Spanish. "Damned vehicle broke down right smack between two towns. I thought this would be the right way to walk".

"Where are you going, Señor"?

"Eventually I hope to reach Guadalajara, am I remotely in the right area, I am English originally please excuse the thickness of my accent"?

"Sure thing, Señor, you are north of Tlajomulco de Zúñiga on the Av. Jesús Michel Gonzalez - you are heading in the wrong direction though, Guadalajara is behind you, I should know, that is where I am going. I'm delivering P. P. E. to the I M S S Regional General Hospital 180, get in, I will take you that far".

I was much more trusting since I had died. I climbed in. My saviour started the engine and depressed the accelerator. We were going at about sixty miles per hour before he pulled out the pistol. It was an old and rusty revolver, but he had confidence that it was still serviceable enough. Certainly figured I would think that at any rate.

"Just put your bill-fold and any credit cards onto the dash, please, Señor"?

The sound of dry rustling leaves blowing across a flattened gravestone was what now passed for my laughter. Even when you are dead, you can still get mugged, in Mexico, it seemed. I objected to the ridiculous phrase bill-fold, instead of the more accurate wallet too, even if I was a bird, which I was not, how could I fold my bill?

As I reached into the pocket of my Afghan coat of black and white goat's wool, my conveyor and hopeful reliever of my cash said hastily,

"Easy Señor, slowly if you please? Are you armed"?

He should have thought of that before then I reasoned, but simply replied,

"I am unarmed".

As my subsequent search also revealed, my murderers had also had the foresight to take my ready cash and plastic. Possibly my dear, grief-stricken wife thought she could forge my signature? Or maybe she knew the pin? Contactless had become more popular during the pandemic. After rummaging about for several brief moments, fruitlessly, I was forced to concede,

"You seem to have challenged me at an unfortunate period of impecuniousity".

"Eh"? Pedro demanded. I never learned his name but for ease of this narration let us call him that. "What do you mean Gringo and what is that funny accent of yours, you are not an Amerikan"?

"I am not certainly a countryman from over your northern border, no", I readily admitted, "And I do genuinely regret that your industry will prove fruitless for you on this occasion. Would you like me to get out here, being as I cannot pay your anticipated levy"?

"Why can I not understand you, Señor"? He demanded, growing agitated by his lack of comprehension, "You speak funny Amerikan and with that fag accent"?

"I don't speak Amerikan at all", I told him truthfully enough, "I am English".

"That will be fine. I take sterling", he grinned demonstrating to me that most of his wealth was in his mouth.

"I repeat then, in a simpler form, I have no money about my person. Does it not occur to you that had I had any, I might have hired a taxi to take me to Guadalajara"?

"No cash, do you expect me to believe that"?

"What you choose to believe or discount is not the issue here, my Good Man", I told him, "It happens to be a statement of fact".

He braked the truck, told me to get out and was around the bonnet before I had barely stepped down onto the tarmac.

"Give me the money, Señor, or I will shoot you and take it anyway? Leaving you dead beside the road here".

"You're a bit late with that threat, my Old Chap", I informed him, "Someone already beat you to it".

I pulled the scarf down to reveal my nose-less face. I have to admit I admired just how swiftly he was able to scamper around the truck, throwing himself back into the cab. It roared away, but I was much closer to my destination than I had been so I did not think too badly of him. Once again, I was on foot. I still found walking rather a taxing procedure at best. Mortis had reduced my rigour to a shambling gait. For my age it was not that I was unfit, rather, I was not exactly having the time of my death. I just hoped death would not be full of surprises because I had a plan so cunning one could have pinned a tail on it and called it a fox.

As I grimly made my way into the heart of Guadalajara, the sky before me turned a beautiful roseate, fingers of xanthic sprinkled the already lovely pallet of cupolan beauty and proved to be the most pulchritudinous scene I had seen in my death. Had my tear ducts still been functional, it would have brought a tear of joy to my eyes. As it was, the milky film allowed me to see enough, to be moved. The locals started dotting the streets, very few though, due to the lockdown. The fact that they had to stay two metres away from me minimally meant that my disguise, such as it was, proved sufficient. You may wonder at this point why an Englishman in his late forties had a soft drinks empire in Mexico. It was the usual reason, finance. The locals that I employed in the factory worked for a third of what my countrymen would have required. They were not in a union, they never complained. I treated them well, giving them productivity bonuses at appropriate times. Things had provided me with a large investment portfolio together with a lovely Villa on the outskirts of the town. It had also initially provided me with a hot piece of ass as the locals called Señora Isabel. Seventeen years my junior but with knockout looks and gravity-defying bust, it worked out mutually beneficial until my little problem reared its ugly head, or rather, refused to - if you take my drift.

Anyway, that was all history now, water under the bridge. It had happened in a lifetime, not *another* lifetime. I had only enjoyed one. Now it was time to do my best under rather taxing circumstances and enjoy my death-time. I was a pioneer, to the best of my knowledge, avant-garde, inaugural, primary. I mean to say, you might think the Borg had been a bit frightening, but at least their noses were never removed.

I gazed into a dark shop window, pulled down my scarf and looked at what I had once called a face. I had to position myself at just such a distance to be able to focus. Fortunately, that was not a close-up. For some reason, my hair had all but gone. My domed-head dotted with what I refer to as liver spots. Also, my pallor had changed from a rather glowing golden colour, the colour of a Smith's Crisp, to a deathly grey with the occasional patch of lividity. The eyes were almost exactly as I had expected, milky. But it was my unfortunate contretemps in the wood that had made the most significant impact on my visage. Instead of my usual nose and it had not been a bad one as noses went, there was a gaping hole revealing grey flesh and the glint of white bone. On a scale of one to ten, one being ugly and ten being handsome, I was a rather reasonable minus twenty-three.

Fortunately, my intention did not involve entering any beauty contests, which was ironic because that was how Isabel and I had met. I had been asked, as one of the major employers in Guadalajara, to be one of the three judges of the Miss Western Mexico beauty pageant. Guadalajara is a city in western Mexico in case you was wondering which you probably were not. It's known for tequila and mariachi music, both born in Jalisco, the state of which Guadalajara is the capital. Guadalajara's historic centre is  dotted with colonial plazas and landmarks such as the neoclassical Teatro Degollado and a cathedral with twin gold spires. The Palacio del Gobierno houses famous murals by painter José Clemente Orozco. It is also noted for the very comely qualities of its señoritas. I do not think I need to tell you who was one of the contestants of that particular parade. I had just left make-up (well it was going to be televised), was on my way to my tiny dressing room when I was intercepted by Isabel wearing a sweet smile and a bathing costume.

"Señor Gehenna", she had smiled sweetly with her devastatingly mellifluously scarlet lips. Her voice had that lovely lilt to it that Latino's seem to possess in abundance, "I just wished to say, before the parade begins and the voting starts, that if I end up with the crown, I will be grateful to you, *very grateful* in fact"!

I mean to say, back then I was a normal hard-working, but single - chap, who had not had any of that sort of action since... I had never had any of *that sort* of action! She was a total knockout. What would you have done? She had the looks and figure to win anyway. She had lain it on a plate for me. You would not turn it down, would you? I didn't.

For the first few years, everything went well. I used Isabel in the bedroom as frequently as my energy allowed. She used my MasterCard with the same eager vigour. We both knew what we were getting in the deal, we were both happy with that.

Then my little problem kicked in and to put it mildly, it all went to rat-shit. For a while, Isabel understood, these sorts of things happened to older men. She compensated by extra use of the MasterCard.

A woman's needs are many-fold though, to quote the late, great, Benny Hill. Isabel began to stray. I went into denial. I truly do believe that for a while, we both continued to love one another. It was just that by then, mutual admiration had become platonic. We remained cordial toward one another. She even kissed me, usually when I had bought her the latest gewgaw or item of clothing.

Rupert hovered into view after thirty months of the latest arrangement. I began to get signals that told me that this absolute cad, this bounder of the first water - was starting to change the dynamic in our relationship. The automatic compliments ceased, then the kisses of gratitude. Resentfully I ceased buying lavish gifts, complained at the amount Isabel was spending on frippery. She began stopping out overnight, sometimes two or three at a stretch. One day she came to me and told me she had fallen in love with another man. That he wanted to meet me so that we could discuss the new arrangements, I thought it would be divorce, alimony. I was too numb to argue, still very much in love with Isabel.

I agreed and gave *the help* the evening off, thinking to be discrete although most of them knew what had been going on for quite a while.

He arrived in shirt sleeves, tailored shorts, while I was quite revolted by the way Isabel skipped to the door to let him in with the eagerness of a young puppy with a new toy. She brought him into the lounge and offered him some wine. Red, filthy vinegar, in my opinion, I had always been a sweet sherry man myself.

"Just please tell me what you have in mind and then leave"? I asked. he was looking way too comfortable on my settee and in my property.

"Now, please darling"? he asked of my wife who primly produced *my* Colt Peacemaker revolver. Just like that, no posturing, no ceremony, no demands,

I remember asking, "What do..."?

Before the bullet, loudly issued - tore through my heart. I was killed instantly. After that, the next thing I knew, I was waking up dead.

Pulling the bandana back up into position, my shambling hike resumed. The sun told me it was around eleven-thirty by the time I reached the Villa Orauca. So as not to alarm Maria, Matilda or Ramone I sneaked around the back. Is that not so annoying, to have to sneak around the back aspect of one's domain? Strictly speaking, of

Myrrorball

course, it was still my property. I might have been declared missing, but given my general lack of decomposition, I could not yet be regarded, as deceased. Although I do not profess to know a great deal about Mexican law, I feel confident in predicting that the dead cannot own property, so I understood from the filthy depraved couple's point of view, why it had been expedient to murder me.

It was in many ways a bold move with considerable jeopardy. Until then I would not have thought Rupert had the spunk. (Oo-er)

He had surprised me. I had underestimated him, something I never did where soft drinks were concerned. I was the man who had told James Robert B. Quincey to get stuffed with his offer. Yet when it came to the most important matter of my heart I had made a fatal mistake. The mistake had proved fatal, it was my heart that had suffered as a result. The gardens were looking lovely that day, Ramone always kept them beautifully. I lingered amongst the beautiful flowers - but was disappointed that I could not smell them.

'I say, I say, I say, my zombie has no nose'?

'No nose, how does he smell'?

'Terrible, bu-boom'.

The french doors were open at the back of the terrace, Matilda likes to air the place daily. I slipped in, knowing approximately where everyone would be. Everyone, except Isabel that was.

Bypassing the ground floor, I took the rear staircase up to what had been our bedroom. I thought she might be lying in, as she was frequently want to do. I do not now know why I expected her to be alone. I figured so that the help would not speculate, would not talk to the police when my disappearance reached climactic proportions. Maybe he had sneaked in just like me. In any event, I caught them in my bed in In flagrante delicto (in blazing offence).

I had thought about the exact moment a great deal during my journey, what would I do, what would I say? Would I possess devastating repartee as a dead person? Would I be pathetic and stir their conscience's. Or perhaps curse them to hell and promise divine retribution or worse the interest of Beelzebub himself? As it turned out, I did none of those things. A primordial ravenousness coursed through my dead body. I acted the part that I could not hope to avoid, the part that Romero had cast in stone. Isabel screamed as I tore Rupert's throat out. Of course, I had to do it with my fingers rather than my teeth, which he probably had in a draw somewhere a grinning trophy of triumph. No matter, my bony fingers lunged into his throat and ripped tendons free, which I theatrically shoved into my mouth. I had done it just for effect, to impress Isabel. Then I realised how delicious my former cuckold-er tasted. I was instantly ravenously hungry and being as he was already unwrapped, so to speak, I tucked in.

Isabel was frozen like a rabbit in headlights. Watching me with disgusted revulsion, but unable to tear her

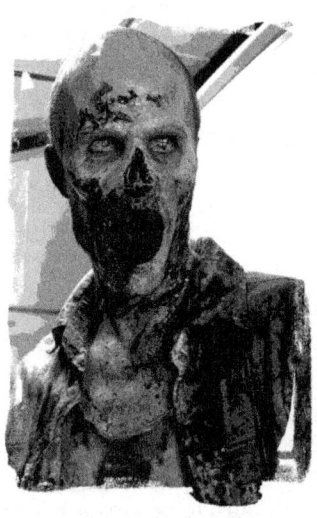

attention from what was happening before her disbelieving eyes. I say for the record that Rupert's liver was beyond delicious, sort of mulled in wine and very very fresh - yummy.

The bedding would have to be thrown out, unfortunately, there is only so much even biological washing powder can do.

Finding her voice, at last, my formerly-mute, former spouse enquired in a voice that quivered with terror, "Andrew, is that you"?

I mean to say, how many zombies did she know? I nodded,

"Yes, love of my life, love of my death, it is your recently deceased husband, I think you owe me an apology don't you"?

Myrrorball

It was a start, things were better then than they had been for a while. My little problem seemed to have gone away along with my life. I was able to consummate our second marriage, or was it the same one?

Isabel was in some sort of daze for a while and simply lay there letting me do whatever I wanted. If you had not seen us nor known better, you might have thought by her performance that she was the one that was dead.

Eventually, she came around and realised that she was living with a Zombie, letting a Zombie butter her muffin. From then on, she struggled with the physical side of the relationship. We often had to stop while she threw up in a suitably placed bucket for just such an eventuality. She ceased to look after her appearance, even stopped bathing, not that it bothered me, I had no nose, I probably smelled considerably worse. Finally, on the last day at Guadalajara, I found myself dreadfully hungry once more. Rupert had shambled off to do whatever the hell he wanted, so, as the help had gone weeks past there was only one thing for it.

I had always said my wife looked good enough to eat!

So what next? My malign ambition had been completely realised. What was the Protozombie to do? I decided to hire a private plane and fly to Hollywood. I felt I had all the attributes necessary to commence a budding career. 'Do not let setbacks cause you to falter' - had always been one of my maxims.

I was not going to let even death hold me back.

NEUNTER TEIL
MEIN KAMPF

79.

Pallomeer was in the small chamber when the ether in the room began to change. He remained unafraid for he had heard of phase doors.

He was fascinated by the manifestation of it. Watched as it grew broader, changed from clear to violet, opened out into an iris of sorts. When the lone individual emerged from its centre, cried out in delight,

"Father"!

Staltidore smiled, threw his arms around his son, said simply,

"Thou hast grown".

After but a few seconds, he asked, "Tell me"?

"Knowest thee aught"?

His father nodded, while the son went to a flagon, poured his father wine into a spare goblet,

"Bodakin told us that the Lords of Koözoött and Kyper Tor march on the east. That be why he sent me back next".

"The King, the other Eastern Lords"?

"Will follow when the sorcerer's vitality allows. Now, what of this city, how under threat be it"?

The delight passed from Pallomeer's otherwise handsome features, he confessed,

"They are at the gates of his province and but hours past sent an emissary to request surrender, we have till dawn to comply or ride out. Of course, they advise if we choose the latter we shall be riding out to our doom".

Staltidore nodded gravely, asked the young Lord in his absence,

"Preparations"?

"All made, every man, some women, even older children are armed and ready to fight. The cavalry be prepared to ride out if ordered so to do".

Staltidore pressed a gloved hand to his son's shoulder, smiled,

"Thy mother would have been proud of thee. *I* am proud of thee".

"Why do the western lords do as they do, father", Pallomeer desired to know, "What be their motivation"?

Myrrorball

"Evil needs none in order to oppose good", his father, Lord of the Keep responded. "The evil of greed, they want more than they already have, even the crown. What news of the King, didst he reach Kingshire safely"?

Pallomeer admitted, "I have no knowledge of what transpires in the south, I have been sorely pressed with my duties here".

"Understandable", Staltidore conceded, "A pigeon shalt be sent".

"Will we still be alive by the time it returneth"? The young Lord demanded.

All his father could reply was, "Let us hope so, we ride out to meet the threat from the east, at dawn. We should get some sleep".

First light was drab, merely dappled with light that seemed to struggle from behind black clouds swollen with the threat of rain. The gates of the city of Staltidore yawned open. A blast of defiance from a single horn signalled the intent of those within.

"Oh, delight", Koözoött smiled naughtily, "The young pup intends to resist. Send in the pressed from Knelforest firstly, my Lord of the Tor. Once they are exhausted, send the Animataverous. By then some of the Knelforestor will have joined their ranks. Our men will surely only be reserves, I doubt we shall need them".

The clash and clamour of steel seemed to amuse Koözoött. It was evident to the observing Kyper Tor that his association with the necromancer was beginning to have a deleterious effect upon his demeanour and mien. Once their ultimate ambition was achieved, it might prove necessary for Kyper Tor to take over from his fellow conspirator - permanently. Such would involve a stabbing. In the royal hall, in Koözoött, in his liver.

Staltidore's forces gave a good account of themselves. Sooner than expected Animataverous' were employed against them. It proved just as Koözoött had supposed. The living were no match for those who fought like automatons, never feeling pain from wounds often arising from being struck down, to continue fighting.

Major Roxbrough & Nik Gehenna

Suddenly a large figure both the wicked Lords of the East recognised threw down his arms and ordered those surviving of his troops, to follow suit.

"Staltidore"! Kyper Tor gasped, "How didst he escape the Fire of Saah? What be he doing in Valgral"?

"I suggest a meeting with him who we both know should not even be here", Koözoött returned, "We will get some answers before we execute him. If the young lordling, his son be among them, bring him along too".

"With that, Koözoött dismounted from his tall charger of chestnut and mahogany, returned to his tent.

Kyper Tor ground his teeth in furious frustration, '*One day, peacock, one day*'! he thought.

Staltidore looked defeated, exhausted, covered in the dubious coating of battle. His son looked defiant, Kyper Tor noted,

"Thou hast grown mightily since thou was a guest at mine seat young Lord".

Pallomeer spat back,

"This be no social occasion, Kyper of the Tor. What more dost thou want from us? Thou art even now ransacking the city, abusing our women and raiding our treasures. If thou intends to execute my father and I get on with it, so as I do not have to listen to any more of thy mundane prattle"?

Koözoött laughed, "Twould seem the young pup has more bite than e-er his father. Do not begrudge the victors the spoils of war, young lordling, pillage and rampage be the tradition of this land".

"Perhaps in the savage, relatively primitive west", Pallomeer was not done, "The east has always been more advanced both in devices and devises. What be your design for my father, a nobleman, a greater lord then e-er either of thee two vermin could ever hope to be"?

Koözoött did not seem ired by the insult but smiled coldly, then informed,

"Lord Staltidore, ride to the capital, tell them what has transpired here today, tell them to ready themselves for capitulation or doom, the choice be that simple".

Myrrorball

"Thou spares me"? Staltidore spoke for the first time. He sounded exhausted - defeated. "I will need a squire 'pon the road, an escort for the road be...".

"Full of vagabonds, I know I know", Koözoött cut him short, he sighed, "Very well, thou may take a squire and six of the guards, now go. My Lord of Kyper Tor, please see to it that my instructions be followed to the letter"?

Staltidore blurted, suddenly far more animate, "I choose my son to act as Squire".

Koözoött grinned, "The Lordling be none such and will remain in mine care, my Lord of Staltidore. I find his ire amusing".

"If not squire, then one of my guards, I saw him fight this day, none were better in skill and ferocity".

Pallomeer nodded his acknowledgement of the congratulation.

"No".

"Thou holds him hostage for future ransom", Staltidore realised then, "But thou seest that Staltidore be ruined, fallen, what value is to be had, be already in thy possession".

"Then whence in the audience of Vasnaar, thou hadst best request a loan along with thy news, thy son must be worth one thousand złorint [the łote was the unit of currency in Valgral 111 łote = 1 złorint. Each was recorded as - 1ł & 1zł]".

It was a vast sum, one the King alone would be unlikely to agree to. Staltidore knew he was in no position to haggle though. It would serve no purpose except to amuse the cruel conqueror. His shoulders slumped, he let Kyper Tor lead him out of the tent.

Koözoött, Warlord of the West poured the young lordling a goblet of wine and pushed across the narrow table that separated them. Nodding to one of his guards, who then cut Pallomeer's bonds.

"I advise thee not to try anything foolish, young Lordling, my guards are especially well trained, an dead hostage has little value in ransom".

Pallomeer grinned ferally, "Twould serve thee right ifin I didst make an attempt and died in the doing".

Major Roxbrough & Nik Gehenna

"Then thou wouldst serve in the ranks of the Animataverous", Koözoött responded. Having encountered and nearly lost his life to one, that was not a future the young warrior relished such prospect. He let his muscles relax and gladly raised the goblet to his lips for he found himself exceedingly parched.

"I saw thee battling today also", Koözoött then told the Lordling, "Thou didst indeed show such ferocity as wouldst make a fine force were there enough with thine ilk to produce the quantity thereof. Let us no longer oppose one another Pallomeer, join thyself to Koözoött, Warlord of the West and I will elevate thee to Colonel forthwith? Go get some rest, think pon this, there be no need to answer instantly".

"Yet I think there be just so", Pallomeer's smile was sardonic rather than being motivated by amusement, "If one lies down with dogs there be every chance that thou gets up with fleas. If one lies down with demons, thou can get up with winnets. Conversely if one dies justly, opposing such malignancy as the Warlord of backwater Koözoött, then there be a chance that thou enjoys the favour of Shandor, Shakita or Ogglenooré in the afterlife".

A flicker of disappointment danced across the features of Koözoött, Warlord of the West then he regarded the young man opposite him with eyes that had once been azure but recently had taken the colour violet,

"I have seen the afterlife, Pallomeer. The prospect to remain in the coal-dark grave and moulder or become animataverous, be-all. So be it! I will have thee shackled and then find a suitable place for thee. The dungeons of Staltidore will be ironic housing for thee, dost thou not appreciate the jest of that"?

Pallomeer decided he had done talking to the Warlord of the West.

80.

It was the mightiest phase door the sorcerer had ever managed to create, The men spurred their horses through such an ovoid. Every one of those selected managed to get through it before it imploded with the rushing of torn air.

Of the heavily depleted force, only five remained behind. The exhausted Bodakin slumped onto his cot and was asleep before any of those remaining could ask him if he was all right.

23, casement glittering in the flickering illumination of the lanterns, pulled a rough blanket over the sorcerer. Even with his caftan, the weather had turned decidedly cold at night.

"Warrior of steel", Hízlatan asked, "Who will the greatest Szorkráló of them all send back next do you think"?

23 turned to him,

"How would I know that? Do you think that I am in league with him in some way"?

"You are the warrior who never removes his armour because you're constructed of weird contrivances, I thought you would know his mind for that reason".

"Not even Bodakin knows everything, including some of his whims, Hízlatan", Flahé observed then, "Though he searched in the snabbertok for my son, he found him nought".

"Were it not for the fact that he cured me of the Kézőrös bite and saved me from becoming an blue mumbly, I would say thusly, that I have endured full truck with wizards, greedy kings, szorkráló, virázető. I possess none desire to endure them any longer. I just wish to returneth to mine seat and have no adventures for an lengthy period". Lolocken then mused aloud.

"Yet thou was quick enough to agree to the King's invitation when the mention of Корунд (Corundum) filled thine ears, my Lord. Корунд (Corundum) a bluer blue than the eyes of the goddess Shakita which be very blue indeed".

"You and your men should get some shutdown. I will reboot you all in the morning, we near the village of Leart. The sorcerer should be able to negotiate a rest for us there until he can send you back to where you belong".

"What of you, Warrior 23, where do you belong"? Hízlatan enquired. To which the automaton returned,

"Certainly not on Egszígør for very much longer".

The Leart were Közloponi by racial type and seemed singularly friendly and non-violent. This troubled the Sorcerer who asked to speak to the virázető the instant they arrived.

The latter went by the name of Geoss. He was old, though not in the same way that the sorcerer was. Rather he had lived sixty years. On the Fire of Saah that was old. Bodakin spoke in Közloponoid,

"I bring sad tidings", he told the old man, "An army of natives will soon be over the river Gilgolium bent upon conquest. They be led by a dangerous triumvirate - two Kémerké and a Valgraln Lord. Halsgough, Mesoloras and Vandeveble. They will raise this village to the ground unless they are stopped, here, virázető Geoss".

"And you want my help and that of my warriors to oppose them", Geoss was no man's fool it seemed. "If I agree to join forces with you, what aid can you offer"?

"A Szorkráló called Hízlatan. I will come up with some magic to aid the forces. Also amongst our number are two warrior Lords with their guards and the Knight of Roid".

Geoss looked most intrigued when he heard mention of 23. News travelled fast on the island. Tales of the android had already reached his ears. He requested,

"Send the knight of Roid to me, if he convinces me to join you, then the braves of Leart will swell your numbers, including their virázető".

Halsgough paused and held up his mailed fist,

"What is it"? Vandeveble wanted to know.

"Something be wrong, I think the Learat expects us".

"It seems quiet enough to me", Mesoloras remarked.

"Exactly", Halsgough returned grimly, "Too quiet. Herest thee the sound of activity through the undergrowth? Of playing children, women washing in the river, even the scurry of Kézőrös or the mumble of Blevastís".

With a feline gesture, the archer cocked his head on one side and listened, the Lord of Halsgough, ruler of central Saah was right.

Myrrorball

"Why does it matter"? Mesoloras then argued, "We outnumber the Learat three to one".

Vandeveble agreed, "That is true, Lord. Let us have at them and destroy any who thing to ambush your superior force".

Halsgough did not like it. On the other hand, he knew that to show weakness in front of the natives would weaken his grip on them. He already suspected they would have preferred to be led by one of their own. Even though the pink-Lord had led them to one victory after another.

"We will attack then, but we will do so with as little sound as possible".

Mesoloras held up a hand thrust it downward. The Lord's instruction was in vain, with the usual war whoops, screams, the Közloponi charged through the under-growth toward the village of Leart. Cursing, Halsgough followed, in the rearguard.

Arrows flew thick and fast in the air, he held his shield high, barely daring to peep over its rim. Knights feared arrows more than anything else. They were so random, so unselective in who they hit. No amount of practice with sword mace or halbert could defy an arrow. Then he saw Lolocken, swiping that way he cut a passage toward him.

"What art thou about here"? He demanded of the Eastern Lord.

Lolocken was too busy to answer though, pressed as he was, by three spear-wielding natives. The Lord of Halsgough glanced about him, saw that the force he commanded were hewing great channels into the latest native braves on his list of conquest. It looked like yet another effortless victory, until..!

From out of the undergrowth, a warrior in totally enveloping armour suddenly emerged. Bearing a mace and felling those who dared get near him with seemingly tireless ease. While Halsgough watched in grim fascination, he saw two well-placed arrows glance off the warrior's seemingly impenetrable armour. As if that was not enough, the sky turned abruptly to darkness, thunder boomed. The canopy was occasionally lit by flashes of lightning. Impossibly prepared for this, the Leart lit torches and started to spear the invasion force, who were stumbling in darkness and greatly disadvantaged.

"Kill some of the torch bearers", he roared to those in hearing distance, "Take the light from them, so that we have the advantage of it".

It seemed to work for a while. Lolocken Flahé and the knight of the all-encompassing armour had formed a deadly triangle that was cutting or bludgeoning down any who came in their reach.

"Someone has to break up that trio", Halsgough roared, "They could turn the tide of the battle if such be allowed to continueth on".

Vandeveble immediately gathered five braves about him and sought to do that very thing.

The huge warrior from Acleegása found himself suddenly opposite Lolocken, drove in with his spear. Lolocken took the point of it on the boss of his escutcheon, rather than trying to dance out of its way. At the same instant, he thrust his broadsword into Vandeveble's chest. The death of the Acleegáás seemed to demoralize the entire force almost instantly. Halsgough could see that the battle was only going to end with one result. He had no intention of dying on the gods-forsaken isle, so he slipped back into the forest. He would return to Közlopon to rebuild another force. The battle might be lost, but it would not be the end of the war if he had anything to do with it.

81.

Hersko wrapped a second blanket around Cassiti's shoulders. She was still trembling.

"Is it always as cold as this in Flahé"? she asked miserably.

"This be spring", he told her, "Twill get warmer as we pass into summer, then cool once more before the extreme chill of winter. By then, thou willst be used to the change in clime though. Now, will thy wear the dresses that Mother provided for thee"?

Myrrorball

Miserably she nodded, unable to agree verbally though. It was her very obduracy that the young Lord of Flahé found so appealing. She seemed able to balance it when in opposition to Hersko, falling just short of contumacy. His mother was not so enamoured by the native girl. Their first two meetings had not gone well. Her Ladyship had been initially frosty toward Cassiti at their second meeting - openly hostile. Hersko had taken her to task over it later when just the two of them were together.

"She be not worthy of the title that will eventually be bestowed upon her if thou persists with her, mine Son", she had complained. "As the eldest of mine offspring thou art aware that the title falls to thee when thy father be passed. What if the King refuses me his blessing for an union"?

"We have no King as thou art well aware", Hersko had pointed out, "Whoever finally takes the throne will be of better disposition than Vasnaar, gods rest his passing".

As the couple proceeded with their breaking of fast, the door swung open and who should enter but Bemien herself, first Lady of Flahé.

"Good morn to thee son", she began, gazed at the girl dressed in blankets and issued a sniff of disapproval, "I see thy savage girl still refuses to be garbed in civilised clothing".

"I have asked thee afore, Mother, not to speak of or belittle Cassiti as if she were absent from the room. It does truly offend me. So I will tell thee this, ifin thou dost lay tongue to an further slight, then we shall leave this Keep. Be that clear to thee, Mother"?

Bemien pursed her lips in the manner she affected when displeased or injured by word or deed. Said nothing, merely seated herself, as a retainer placed a bowl of steaming gruel before her with admirable alacrity.

Hersko was not in a mood to let the matter be dismissed so easily, he persisted,

"I asked thee, Mother, art thou clear upon the subject, slight my fiancé one more time? Then will it will be the last thou will seest of us".

Major Roxbrough & Nik Gehenna

Yet even then, the older woman did not speak. Fortunately, a herald suddenly appeared at the door and begged forgiveness for the intrusion,

Bemien was about to demand the reason for it when she wisely deferred to her son, Lord of the Keep in his father's absence,

"It be an strange hour to bring messagement, Herald. Press yon parchment into mine hand, thence thou canst be about thy business".

The herald swiftly glided across the room and did as directed. Just as lithely departing.

Hersko looked down at the wax seal on the communiqué, declared "This be from Lordship athwart the wash, in Dillion no less".

"Not the Black Horde again"? The Lady finally broke her silence. From South Cross, the Sephrance a fierce tribe of Negroes regularly raided northward in small skirmishes. Port Dillion being Valgral's most southern outpost was heavily fortified as a result.

"Let us see", Hersko snapped the wax circle in half as a sudden shaft of brilliance broke from behind a cloud and trickled into the dining room through the green mage-glass of the windows. The central tower of the humble castle had never been so warm as since the green mage sheets had been installed into the archery slits, yet though Hersko had told Cassiti that, she still complained of the cold. The young Lord's features turned suddenly ashen when he read the content of the message.

"What is it, Hersko"? Cassiti asked in Kémerié, knowing use of the language of the Kémerké annoyed the Lady intensely, "Surely it cannot be information concerning any who were on Egszígør"?

"It is something that concerns us all", he answered stiltedly, before switching to Valgraln and frightening his mother, "Incidents of Geişvəhşilic have started in the town".

Bemien's spoon clattered into her bowl, her lace-gloved hands went over her mouth. The fear in her eyes was easy to discern.

Myrrorball

"What is that, what word did you speak, what does it mean"? Cassiti demanded.

The Lady suddenly turned to her and said slowly, to let the girl understand,

"The two of thee shouldst seek out the Advocate of thy choice from this town and be hastily married. There be no point in delay, at least then thou canst die, man and wife".

With that, she rose to her feet and without another word, fled the hall.

Cassiti turned to Hersko, "What is happening? What did the letter say that caused so much fear in your mother? What was that business about an advocate"?

"Geişvəhşilic is the medical phrase for the Vast Pestilence, Cassiti. The evil contagion, the scourge, the invasion of the tiny enemies the mage speak of, they call them mikroloblar - germs".

"So Geişvəhşilic is a contagious illness", the girl surmised, "How do we stop its spread? If we are unfortunate, what is the appropriate medicine? How many survive this Geişvəhşilic"?

Hersko told her darkly, "Geişvəhşilic scythes through populations like a sickle through wheat. Nothing can stop it until only the strongest have managed to survive it. There is no known way to stop it spreading, that I know of, although the Keep's Surgeon might have an answer for you on that score. As for the rate of survival, a lucky man out of fifty might manage to emerge into the other end of the tunnel, if he ramps up and rolls out absolutely".

"And the advocate"?

Hersko arose from his position and took both of the girl's cold hands in the warmth of his own,

"The Advocate of the Gods will bind our union in marriage, ifin it is something that we both desire. Ifin so, then we should hurry from here and bind ourselves together before Mother comes to, what she will think of as her senses, changing her mind".

Cassiti smiled, Returned simply,

"I am willing to become your wife, Hersko, let us to the advocate firstly, then the surgeon, I feel there must be a way of stopping the Geişvəhşilic from spreading".

Major Roxbrough & Nik Gehenna

Advocate Kernkovo required one złorint to marry the two of them before, Brahma - goddess of love and beauty, Shakita – food and good health, Anaadi – fortune both good and bad. When he heard in confidence, the reason for no ceremony for the Lord, the haste with which it was to be conducted, he blanched and also gave them the blessing of Mazormazuri - healing.

"Yet the Majax (pestilence, misery, death) will have his day and bring to his scaly embrace many I fear. Why do not the two of thee flee the city while thou still canst".

"And goest where", Hersko argued, "Thou knowest the dark wings of Geişvəhşilic can catch any man or woman as it selects, soon the entire country will be in its grip. There will be no sense to running".

"Come". Cassiti suddenly took her new husband by the arm, "We have an urgent appointment with Surgeon. I want to hear how he intends to approach quarantine".

"Quarantine?, What is the use of that, Lady Cassiti"? The question stopped the girl in her tracks,

"Lady Cassiti, I am now a Lady"?

"You are married to the lord of Flahé's son who enjoys the honorary title of the Lord himself. You are thusly her ladyship and one day in the future will be Lady of Flahé".

They had returned to the castle and found, Surgeon in the castle's small and sparsely outfitted infirmary. When asked about the need for quarantine about reducing the spread of infection, Lady Cassiti was alarmed to find that the surgeon, who went by the name of Surgeon, had little or no idea of good practises.

"Such be the will of the gods, my Lady", he returned having been introduced to her as Hersko's wife. "Those appropriately pious and reverent, need have no fear. Those who do labour 'neath the Geişvəhşilic must be bled to let the distemper exit their bodies".

Cassiti turned to her new husband, "If this man is to take charge of the victims, then we will indeed all be doomed", she began, "Bleeding those already weak will only hasten the end for them. As far as containing the contagion, the sick must be quarantined. Those tending

Myrrorball

them must wear masks over their mouths and noses so that they do not breathe in the contagion".

"Was this how you contained diseases on Egszígør"? her husband desired to know. When she nodded, he asked further, "It contained the spread of infection"? Another nod, Hersko told the man who had been previously in charge of the sick of the castle and its surroundings.

"Thou shalt work 'neath the administration of my wife, the Lady of Flahé, for this wave of Geişvəhşilic, Surgeon, understood"?

"Her ladyship will herself work, rather than holing up in the donjon as be customary in such cases"? Surgeon was incredulous.

Hersko shocked him still further when adding, As will the Lord of Flahé also, we will fight the Geişvəhşilic together, for in the past it be known that it be no respecter of rank nor privilege".

82.

The shelving was only particle planks in a series of similar casings, but it would do the job. I now had the pleasant task of looking through the internet to find the stock. At the back of the property, Quianhua had made a  little bed-sitting area, so that we could move in - once the place was supplied with foodstuffs. She and Mister Genks had gone to the market for suitable provisions while I surfed the net. Outside the painter was just putting finishing touches to the sign, that would be over windows and

Major Roxbrough & Nik Gehenna

door. 'Zauberbücher' had to be open for business soon, or the loan Neuman had made us would be exhausted simply to live. At the end of it, we would have nothing.

I concentrated upon Nazi material, as it would sell best, then Chinese books as they would be in demand. The Chinese held several ministerial posts throughout the country. Daleford was no exception to that. Under German administration, it had been renamed as Talford, yet the locals persisted with English speaking, English names.

After World War II there had been a slow migration of people from one victorious region to another so that the population of Daleford consisted of eighty percent English, fifteen percent German, five percent Chinese. The Germans held most of the key posts, while the Chinese seemed to hold great sway over them even then. My stock would, therefore, have to reflect such proportions, unless I subsequently discovered that one nationality was more interested in the collecting of rare books. I would also have to stock a percentage of what I thought of as trash simply to secure a regular turnover and footfall into the store.

I found myself looking firstly for German titles checking elektrisch-Bucht, Amazonas, Besserwelt, Fähigliteratur. It was a good job Neuman had set up a Zahlenkumpel account for me with a healthy balance. The purchasing of such magical items as good books soon took me under its spell, the first time I looked up from the keyboard several hours had passed. I went into the back of the store where Mister Genks and Quianhua were painting and emulsioning our new home. To see the manbian with a paint pad in his hands was nothing short of surreal.

"How did the hunt for thtock go"? He asked me, labouring as ever with his enormous tongue.

"I got the first edition of Mein Kampf. Hardback copies of, Hans Jakob Christoffel von Grimmelshausen – Simplicius Simplicissimus, Johann Wolfgang Von Goethe – The Sorrows of Young Werther, Friedrich Holderlin – Hyperion, ETA Hoffman – The Devil's Elixirs, Gustav Freytag – Debt and Credit, Theodor

Fontane – Effi Briest, Thomas Mann – Buddenbrooks, Rainer Maria Rilke – The Notebooks of Malte Laurids Brigge, Thomas Mann – Death in Venice, Herman Hesse – Siddhartha", I responded, "Plus some nice Chinese stuff but I won't bother you with the titles".

Quianhua, easily teased demanded, "Why not, do you consider them inferior to the Teutonic selection, I want to hear what you bought. I also want to know how you think you can make a profit simply by buying and selling"?

"All right", I smiled, "I bought, Romance of Three Kingdoms – Luo Guanzhong (Ming Dynasty), Fengshen Yanyi – Xu Zhonglin (Ming Dynasty), The Water Margin – Shi Naian (Ming Dynasty) The Scholars – Wu Jingzi (Qing Dynasty), The Travels of Lao Can – Liu E (Qing Dynasty), A Heroic Legend of the Sons and Daughters – Wen Kang (Qing Dynasty), plus several others. To answer your second question, in most cases when I made an order, I got several complimentary copies of several other books thrown in for the price. In essence, anything we sell them for will make 100% profit".

Even as I said it, I realised it could not be that easy though. I would also write, hoping to subsidise my book sales with... erm book sales.

83.

The door of Ðöyüşçqüyaramazcani's hut crunched open. Halsgough abruptly strode in, his face dirty, his armour crusty with gore. Döləeçim gasped at his bedraggled and horrifying appearance, but swallowing the bile that had gathered at the back of her throat hastened to help him out of the hideous metal.

"What happened"? Ðöyüşçqüyaramazcani demanded, causing the Lord of Valgral to scowl in impotent rage,

"Both valour and determination fled thy warriors. That be what occurred", he mouthed the words like a curse. "I barely escaped with my life".

The door opened again, one of the Dahaazaa entered, Halsgough thought it, Nunnelee, she with the ample bosom and childbearing hips,

"My Lord", she began in her pigeon Valgraln, "What of Vandeveble. I saw thee, entering alone".

"Dead", Halsgough told her, eyeing the impressive swell of her chest. Once she had gotten over her grief, he might very well be glad to give her some comfort for her loss, a few nights in his bed and she would soon forget the savage.

The Dahaazaa burst into tears, Döləeçim reluctantly going over to comfort her. Generously when she instantly considered that the day would come when the other would be a rival for her Lord's favours. A third time the door opened and the other Dahaazaa slipped inside. She went over to the other two women to assist in what way she could.

"If thou also intrudes into thy Lord's domain to find out how thy mate be, I do not know", Halsgough admitted unfeelingly. "Now I wouldst thank thee to get out, so that my tub may be brought. I need an chance to soak the ache from my limbs".

The last arrival looked at him curiously then and informed,

"Mesoloras survived the battle, conducted a retreat of the few survivors, they will be here on the morrow".

Halsgough scoffed, "There be no way thou couldst know that woman. Unless thou be an witch, in which case 'twill be my reluctant duty to have thee ducked and if found guilty burned in the flames of righteousness".

"I am no witch, warrior of Valgral", Zonia returned her voice devoid of all warmth, "I was the Szorkráló of my village before you and yours raided it. Even Közloponi will not harm me, whatsoever you try to direct them to do".

"Superstition and enchantment seemeth to dog my steps to the very end", Halsgough muttered under his breath. Aloud he tried, "Witch, I do not care how you do your mischief. Yet I want my bath, so kindly take the other and leave. Alternatively, thou can continue to show contempt for thy Lord and then we shall see who has the greater power, thee with thy potions and curses, or the sharp steel of my blade".

Myrrorball

Scowling the alleged Szorkráló placed an arm around the other girl's shoulder and led her, still weeping out of the hut. Once the Dahaazaa had gone, the atmosphere in the room did not lighten. Ðöyüşçqüyaramazcani even dared to enquire,

"Tell me, my Lord, how went the battle".

"I grow too fatigued to entertain thee with tales and fables this eve, Ðöyüşçqüyaramazcani, ask me another time. Now Döləeçim, some hot water if it pleaseth thee to fetch".

Halsgough was up with the sun. Though he could not see Angelus for the canopy of Avgófýllo fronds, the light was enough to awaken him. He had to intercept Mesoloras before he returned to the village, make certain their versions of events were similar if not alike. Fortunately, while Döləeçim had bathed him the night before, her brother had cleaned his armour. Although he had grown rather quiet. Halsgough no longer considered Ðöyüşçqüyaramazcani an ally. In the future, once Mesoloras had been trained to the right version of events concerning him, he might have to see to it that Ðöyüşçqüyaramazcani had an unfortunate, hideously fatal accident. That was something to keep an eye on, right then he needed to make sure Mesoloras did not reach the village before he had the chance to speak to him. Dressing only in light half-armour, he set off on the northeastern pass, the survivors of the battle would have used the rope bridge over the Gilgolium by then and would not be far away at all.

Halsgough may have retreated from injury in the last battle, but his warrior skills were as adept as ever. He soon noticed he was being followed. Hiding behind an especially stout blue frond trunk. Waited for his tracker to catch up with him. Suddenly lurching into the pathway, sword ready drawn. He laughed when he saw who it was.

"Witch, what art thou about? Come to talk to thy love before I debrief him by any chance"?

Zonia shook her head, strands of ebon hair sticking to her already glowing features in the morning's rising steam and humidity.

Major Roxbrough & Nik Gehenna

"Rather learn the truth, Valgraln".

"So thou labels me liar then. I told thee last night, that if thou taxed me again, we would see who had the greater power. Alas, thou has gone too far".

He lunged with his sword. Zonia darted to her right and flung something at him. Something that had been behind her back, something furry and blue.

The Kézőrös startled by its uncharacteristic flight, clung to Halsgough's face, for he had not thought to bring his helm and therefore had no visor protecting it. The creature promptly sunk needle-sharp teeth into the Lord's cheek where it clung on for dear life. The Lord of Halsgough screamed, clawed at the creature with awkwardly gloved hands. He lost his balance, fell headlong into the blue-grass of the Fire of Saah.

"Help me, Witch", he screamed in fear and pain.

Zonia watched him thrashing about with a grim smile on her dusky features. When he had finally managed to prize the animal off him, throwing it into the undergrowth, he had several already livid incisions on his face and neck. He scrambled for his sword, his intention to slay the woman, but she froze him with the promise,

"Kill me and doom yourself to the fate of becoming a Blevastís. The hapless creatures you call blue mumblies. As a Szorkráló, I am your only hope of a cure since you hung the local Szorkráló for theft".

Halsgough hesitated, "You would help me? Why"?

Zonia smiled, "You will have to come up with a reason, Valgraln".

"How do I knowest I can trust thee, to give me the potion that will render me recovered"?

"You don't", the girl smiled.

84.

Zemtel first Lord of Kingshire - *Interfectorem regem* held up his mailed hand. The retinue following abruptly pulled their mounts to a halt. He could tell at once by the finery of their armour and accoutrements, that he was encountering three Lords. If such was indeed the case, where were their troops?

In effect, the guards had returned to the Lord's seats. There to tell of the forthcoming invasion, to raise a force with which to oppose them.

"I am Zemtel first Lord of Kingshire", he did not add that he was also Interfectorem regem, "Who be thee, sir Knights? Where be thy forces"?

"Császária Roxbrough", replied the tallest of the trio, "Imperial Marquess of the mountain town that bears that name, my forces be in the town itself, I am but recently returned from an expedition abroad, where be the King, First Lord Zemtel"?

Ignoring his question, wondering how Roxbrough had managed to attain an Imperial Marquess, for it was not huge in peoples nor scope, Zemtel demanded,

"And you two"?

"Lord Staltidore", the most senior of the three informed, "Though there be little left of my seat and mine son be a prisoner of Koözoött, Warlord of the West, his lackey Kyper Tor and the necromancer Banustib".

"And thee"? First Lord Zemtel demanded of the last of them, "Whom art thou lord of"?

"I will answer that that whence thou tellest me who made thee First Lord? For ifin twas, not Vasnaar then thou hast no authority with me".

"How darest thou speaketh to the first Lord in such an manner"? Zemtel demanded in a bark ired by the other's effrontery.

"First Lord of where? The first Lord of what? Created, by whom? For I suspect twas, not the King", the unidentified knight glared at Zemtel. One of his captains came forward then and asked,

"Shall I despatch this rogue for thee, First Lord"?

By way of answer, the knight drew a broadsword, held it aloft, then asked calmly,

"Wouldst thou face Iniquitous then, Captain? One of the blades of none other than Abominorv himself"?

Seeing the clutching fist on the end of the pommel of the hangar the captain suddenly blanched and gasped,

"My Lord Margrave, a thousand apologies, I was merely trying to do the will of my Lord".

"Who gave him such authority"? Oslan-On-the-Bank persisted, "Where be Vasnaar and Byno"?

Zemtel then tried to regain some level of control over the intercourse,

"Queen Celesta made me First Lord of Valgral following the murder of both by Koözoött assassins".

"Queen Celesta"? Roxbrough echoed, "Where be..."?

"Her name before marriage to the King", the Margrave cut him off, He turned back to Zemtel, "So the Lady has taken the throne, then it is to her we ride".

Zemtel countered, "Where she will tell thee to join me together with the other Eastern Lords against Koözoött and Kyper Tor. Why waste time".

"I wish Bodakin were here", Staltidore muttered, "He would know how to advise us, Bodakin or the Visionary".

"Thou tells me thou escaped the Western usurpers, if thou desireth to see thy son again, I am thy best hope", Zemtel urged, "Come with me to Hamshire Forest where I hope to add to the forces already at my back, those of Kingshire, Torkinvayst, Hegyekben. Or go to thy eastern seats in the mountains, fetching thine own forces to bolster these, so that the rebellion might be crushed".

Staltidore thought it best not to tell the upstart Lord, the Queen's favourite - of the Animataverous. He would learn of such to his grave cost soon enough. Instead, he asked,

"What of Flahé, be he not returned yet"?

Zemtel's features grew grave, "If he is he be doomed, Geişvəhşilic strafes the populace there like the grim reaper himself".

Roxbrough blanched, "The Geişvəhşilic! Then the gods help us all".

85.

Hersko felt so exhausted he could have simply dropped where he was standing, sleeping upon the hard ground. The strength and endurance of his wife and Lady of Flahé continued to astound him. Bemien holed up in the central tower would have nothing to do with either of them. She had accused them of losing the balance of their minds. For the duo worked until exhaustion took them. Worked in the town infirmary alongside Surgeon, making sure he and his leeches did as little damage as possible. Lady Flahé countermanded his instructions to the Sisters of Mazormazuri at almost every end and turn. Surgeon complained to Hersko,

"Put tighter rein on thy spouse, My lord, otherwise she will also saddle thee", he urged.

The acting Lord, in his father's absence, merely smiled at each encounter, returned, "Do as her Ladyship directs, that be *my* order".

It seemed at first that wearing masks and using a ludicrous amount of soap in unnecessary washing (in the townsfolk's opinion that was) did little to change the infection rate for the better. The locals also objected to having to boil every drop of water they drank. They already drank upriver from the sewerage system, the waste did not seem to harm the shrimp in The Wash anyway. The Wash shrimp were the largest fattest and tastiest in all Valgral. Indeed there was a coarse saying in Flahé when enjoying a plate of shrimp,

"If [BLEEP] tastes this good I don't know why we bother with a privy, just do it straight onto a plate".

For the most part, Cassiti's instructions were adhered to though. Gradually the cases of new outbreaks of Geişvəhşilic began to slow, a plateau, had anyone been creating a graph from the incidents of infection. The Sisters of Mazormazuri rolled out masks enough for everyone to wear one, having ramped up their sowing industry absolutely, just like a conservative government.

The only factor that threatened those who tended the sick and dying then was exhaustion. A body could only work for so long, go without sleep for so long. Of them all, it seemed that the new, Lady of the Town pushed herself the hardest. Hersko begged her to slow down, to take a break, but Cassiti only ever slept when she finally collapsed after twenty hours work at a stretch. She became the inspiration to the Sisters of Mazormazuri, who worked under her direction.

Major Roxbrough & Nik Gehenna

A herald arrived from the castle one morning, looking gravely concerned, seeking out Hersko, who espied his approach,

"What be it, Herald"?

"My Lord, tis the Lady of the town, Scribe Bernari believes it to be the Geişvəhşilic".

"I will go - ministrate to her", Surgeon piped up, rising to his feet, from beside a palate, he had been kneeling in prayer to Mazormazuri.

"Thou will go nowhere near her Ladyship", Hersko barked, before turning to Cassiti, "Will thou go to her please, thy Ladyship"?

There were dark rings beneath Cassiti's eyes, but she nodded, went to take the spare horse the heralds had brought.

"I must protest, my Lord", Surgeon complained loudly, "I be her Ladyship's noble physician. Thou sendeth this savage...".

He never finished the sentence. Hersko's Vandei Motestas was around his throat. Surgeon was soon almost puce, plainly close to death - when Cassiti demanded,

"My Lord, spare him, tis not an easy thing to combat ignorance, tis impossible to oppose misguided superstition".

The Vandei Motestas relaxed at Hersko's guidance while Surgeon slumped to the ground coughing and gasping for breath. Hersko looked down at him and snarled,

"Go, get a mask - fool, wear it forthwith lest in her Ladyship's absence I decide to finish what I just started".

A tall Sister went to help the temporarily unemployed medic, but he snarled at her shaking her hand away with a vigorousness charged with enmity.

86.

"Why have you brought me here, Zonia"? Mesoloras asked.

"To show you this", the Dahaazaa waved an arm of indication.

Myrrorball

"An Avgófýllo? There are many in the forest. What is so special about this one"?

Zonia smiled, "This one is called Halsgough"!

87.

The Neuman's came to the opening of the shop, which was pleasant. Although they had vested interest, of course, having bankrolled me with a couple of thousand English-Marks. Adolf Neuman was as charming as his wife, but underneath the veneer of respectability, I could not quite dismiss my superstitions that something about them was just not right. That proved to be something I was already aware of for quite some time, I was a bigoted racist, but then is not everyone? Might it just be that some of us are more honest about it? I resolved that I would never act on the feelings though. Not unless circumstance gave me a very good reason.

The evening came and went, Quianhua was so involved with decorating and furnishing the rear of the shop that she seemed quite distracted by it all. It had even taken her considerable effort to speak politely to the Neuman's. They persisted in regarding her rather like the English of my reality had done the Royal Family. The first week was busy with footfall, picking up plenty of impulse purchases, this began to taper off halfway through the second. I took to manning the shop 09:00 - 13:30, while Quianhua reluctantly agreed to do so 13:31 - 17:00. Unfortunately, Mister Genks could not be utilised for such a duty. He did make for excellent security though, anyone looking suspicious, loitering rather than wanting to buy and Quianhua or I would call him into the front. Prospective thieves then decided to leave the shop forthwith, without exception.

It was a month into our trade. We had done better than I had expected thus far. The morning of Tuesday was when he came into my store. Sicherheitspolizei (SiPo Security Police) the Gestapo, Kopf Inspektor Verner deGoethe. He greeted me with a tight nod, dressed in a very smart black and red uniform. One thing the Nazis had was style, I was forced to admit to that.

"Guten morgen", I began, he chuckled, the throaty sound of a man who is used to absolute obedience, coupled with power.

"That is all right Mister Merkwürdig, I speak English. We are, after all, still in England".

He knew my name. I would wager everything I had that he knew everything else about me too.

"Where is the mongrel-amphibian"?

"Outdoing a delivery Mister...?

"Oh come now Merkwürdig I am on the cathode every evening, reporting on the criminal Yorkshiremen, I think you know very well who I am. Let us not insult one another, Ja"?

"Very well, Kopf Inspektor. What do you want with Mister Genks"?

"Calm yourself Merkwürdig", an ice-cold smile, "Curiosity was my only motivation for asking. Do not worry, the Gestapo do not euthanise amphibians".

"Then what...".

"I am after a book".

"We have a lot of books here Kopf Inspektor. It's a book, shop".

"You are a funny fellow, my dear Merkwürdig. I like a good Teutonic joke as well as any, but please be careful, I would not want you to laugh your head off. Do you get that one, Merkwürdig? Laugh your head off, that is a Gestapo joke".

I swallowed, my mouth had just gone very-dry. Curious, when I had but recently had an excellent sup of Chinese tea".

"Would you like me to recommend something for you then Kopf Inspektor, we have all the classics here, including some rather nice Chinese titles and even some English fiction"?

"It is a specific book that I am hunting, have been for some time ", deGoethe told me then, "Mein Kampf".

"I was about to point out that such a volume was in stock feeling that it was yet another Gestapo joke when deGoethe clarified,

Myrrorball

"Yet not just any copy of the most famous book in the world, rather a specific one".

I was instantly intrigued, "You intrigue me Kopf Inspektor, are we speaking of a rare first edition perhaps? I have...".

"I am talking about the rarest first edition, Merkwürdig. So rare that there is but a single copy, just the one. I am going to commission you to get it for me".

My heart sank, "Of course you are referring to the edition dedicated and signed by the Führer himself. Dedicated to his wife, Eva Braun. As you are doubtless aware, it disappeared in the sixties".

"Had it not done so, I would simply go and buy it, would I not, Merkwürdig".

"Perhaps"? I conceded, "Yet it is priceless Kopf Inspektor, did you have some sort of budget in mind"?

"Only in as much as I have decided to pay you for your efforts, Merkwürdig. You see I do not expect to pay for the book itself because you are going to steal it for me"!

"But I am an honest man", I objected at once. deGoethe smiled like a fox, noted,

"Oh, I know that. It is why, hopefully, you will not be suspected, once the book goes missing, from where-ever it is right now. Afterwards, you will return to your honest existence of author and book-seller. I will have the book, are we clear"?

"You mentioned a commission", I decided to be brave, it is as well to be hung for a rare book as a handout. "What sort of figure did you have in mind Kopf Inspektor"?

He surprised me. He stunned me. He frightened me.

"I will not barter with you, book-seller, you will receive one million English-Marks for securing the book. That is the non-negotiable price. Now, I wish you a good day, my card".

He tossed it onto the counter with a black leather gloved hand, the leather giving off a mild aroma, creaking familiarly. Those Nazis have sure got style.

There was a list of suspects of course. Pope Paul VI, deceased. John F. Kennedy deceased. Helmut Christian Goebbels aged 85 and current Chancellor of the German Empire. King Edward IX, the current puppet king of

England aged 75 and finally Emperor Puyi III of the Quiang Dynasty, the youngest suspect at 28 years. The latter was merely one who played diplomatic lip-service to the overseas diplomats upon their visits to the far east, having no actual power at all.

Each of these men could have or had the book. This as a result of it being stolen from Berlin in the sixties. It may have been passed down to them in some cases, in others they may have themselves passed it down. Or, it may have been sold. The task I faced was gargantuan. I had no idea where to start. Fortunately, I knew a manbian who did. He might even be able to dredge it from memory. Where to find it if he had read about it historically. If not, he had been sent to us as an investigator. He was my only hope of not disappointing Sicherheitspolizei (SiPo Security Police) the Gestapo, Kopf Inspektor Verner deGoethe.

I did not think matters could have got much worse, another miscalculation on my part. I was in the shop the following morning. I had already spoken to, Mister Genks, about our mission. The door indicated an entry by the clanking of the bell above it. An immaculately dressed Asiatic entered. Chinese, he did not even attempt to scan any of the stock, having a specific tome in mind.

"Good morning", he greeted in perfect English, "You are the proprietor, Mister Merkwürdig"?

"I have that distinction", I replied with a short bow. One does not live with a Chinese girl and not learn the customs of the orient. "How may I be of service, Sir"?

"Zŏngjiān Jianyu Zhao of the Mìmì jĭngchá [Chief inspector Jianyu Zhao of the Secret Police]".

I felt the blood drain from my head. There were more secret police and Nazis suddenly entering my little shop than there were members of the general public. It might have been my fault. It was me who had thought to stock the place with German and Chinese literature, why did I not stick to English? Zhao went on,

"I am looking for one volume in particular. I am also certain that it is not currently in your august establishment, I was wondering if you could source it for me? I will naturally cover all your expenses".

Myrrorball

I don't know why I even bothered to ask the name of the book when I already knew the answer, sure enough, his reply, with the inscrutability of the orient was,

"Mein Kampf. Not just any copy of the book though. A first edition, the one signed by the German Yo˘ulì himself and dedicated to his wife".

"Priceless, Sir, missing since the nineteen sixties, where would I even think to start looking for it"?

"Might I suggest the Vatican, Whitehouse, Chancellery of the German Empire. Buckingham Palace, or even the Imperial Palace in Beijing's Forbidden City".

"Then you do not want the book to become a national treasure"?

Zhao did not smile, but a twinkle came into his almond-shaped eyes and he admitted,

"Goodness, no. Like all men of letters, men with intellect, I collect rare books. Once I have the book in my possession, I would be pleased to show you my collection. Indeed you are thusly invited to my home here in Yorkshire (he pronounced it with two distinct syllables), at a given date in the future".

Right then, it did not feel like I *had* much of a future!

88.

Cassiti entered the ground of the castle. From behind her, she could hear the ringing of a bell, the creek of a cart,

"Bring out your dead",

ring ring,

"Bring out your dead".

She ignored it on that occasion, for she had a singular task. Care of, her Ladyship of Flahé. Getting an audience with her, in the confines of the donjon was no simple task. It took no small amount of time. Finally when she was masked and aproned, ready to see the latest victim of the Geişvəhşilic she discovered, upon being ushered into her chambers that in some miraculous way Surgeon had beat her to the patient's bedside. He was bleeding her, by a small incision into Bemien's wrist.

Cassiti rushed forward shouldering the fool out of the way,

"No, she cried, "In her debilitated state, the last thing she needs is to have her strength drained still further. You, fetch bandages, quickly". The latter instruction was to the lady's maid, "And put this on over your nose and mouth, if you do not want to catch Geişvəhşilic yourself.

"How dare thou encroach upon mine area of expertise", Surgeon spat, "I am using tried and trusted techniques, get away from her Ladyship"?

"I am also the Lady of Flahé now, thou vile peddler of dubious practice and misery. Leave the donjon? If you disobey me, I will have the guard place you under arrest. Thence to be escorted to the lowest part of this keep. To be interred there until I decide what is to be done with you".

Stemming the flow of blood with a kerchief, careful not to get any on herself, Cassiti did not see the cruel smile appear on her opponent's features. What she did feel, gasped in agonised-surprise, was the cold steel of the scalpel plunge into her back, puncturing her lung. The pain was intensely acute. She tried futilely to claw it free of her flesh. Was still vainly doing so when blackness descended upon her sensibilities. The new lady of Flahé fell to the floor, mortally wounded. Within seconds she was dead.

89.

"There ith only one tholuthion to thith problem", Mister Genks lisped to me when I told him our dilemma".

"I'm all ears, no pun intended", I responded dryly, how could I be cracking gags at a time like that?

"We dethide who we want to have the book firthtly. Then we thell it to the other party. Then we thteal it and thell it to the one we wanted to have it all along".

"That's your plan? That is the best plan, in all the plans we could have had, that is the best one you can think of"? I demanded with heavy irony.

"Yeth".

Myrrorball

"All right then, that's our plan". As you can read, I was desperate. So desperate, I was prepared to countenance desperate measures.

"Firthtly we need to hire thomeone to help Quianhua in the thhop. We need to thtart looking for the book".

"We"? I squeaked, my voice had gone up several octaves, I was an author and book owner, not an international spy and thief".

"Yeth".

"I'll put an advert on the internet, on Talford Gespräche, start interviewing at once. Where are we going to start looking, Mister Genks".

"Oh I know who hath the book", the manbian told me, it seemed to me like he was being somewhat smug about his memory of ancient events.

"Well there's no reason to be so smug about it", I complained, "If you get any smugger, you'll turn into a Smuggereeni".

Mister Genks mouth curled up into a smile broader than the broadest smile you can imagine. The manbian had a sense of the ridiculous it seemed.

"Don't keep me in suspense then, who stole it and where is it now"?

"The Cthee I A thtole it in the thixtith and it ith now in a thentral intelligenth agenthy vault under the Baltimore Mutheum of Art, Maryland".

"How on Earth are we going to get into the vault without being caught and would you not work better alone"?

"I will need thome thupplith. No, it will take both of uth".

"Wonderful more expense. Still, we need to look on it as an investment, after all, we are going to sell it twice"!

90.

The herald looked nervous as he dismounted and strode toward Hersko, sensing trouble, possibly in the form of the direness of his mother's condition he demanded at once,

"What be it? Speakest quickly without fear of consequence to thyself, I taketh not the particular of an message out upon the messenger".

The herald nodded his thanks and replied with velocity,

"It is her new Ladyship, My Lord".

"Sick"?

"Worse than that, she be dead".

Hersko reeled, how could this be so? His new bride, the lovely Cassiti, surely the Geişvəhşilic had never claimed one so swiftly? There again, she was not Valgraln, perhaps it acted upon Kémerké vitality differently? With his next sentence, the herald banished all thoughts of the vast pestilence though,

"The Captain of the Guard has declared it murder, my Lord".

"Murder, who would do such a thing? Her ladyship had no enemies...except...come with me, we need to find Surgeon, either in the village or rightly gone"?

"Thou will not find him, my Lord. For he was in the castle but recently before he fled".

"How was her Ladyship slain"? Hersko demanded, his eyes misting in a combination of rage and grief.

"Stabbed, my Lord. In the back, in thy mother's chambers, with a scalpel".

A scalpel. The tool of the Surgeon.

Hersko raced over to his horse, seeing his intent, the herald turned his mount. Knowing that the two of them would race through the cobbled streets of Flahé to be at the base of the castle walls the quicker. Hersko demanded,

"Has a party been sent out to find the Surgeon"?

The herald nodded, "The Captain of the Guard leads the search himself, my Lord".

91.

Evie was exactly what Quianhua was looking for. The kindest way to describe her - was *homely*. For a start, she was obese. Then she was not a pretty girl, the thin straight hair and cast in one eye over a blob of a nose did not help that. She wore no makeup and men's rugby clothes as women's clothes did not come in her hulking dimensions. When she set her mouth into what she thought was a friendly expression, it looked like nothing so much as a letterbox. As far as my wife was concerned, she was the perfect candidate.

Quianhua was still a jealous woman, which was an attractive quality when it was not proving inconvenient. I could not be tempted to stray from her with Evie. Neither could I be thusly tempted by any other woman when over in Amerika though! The other thing was, Evie was a wonderfully warm girl with a tremendous sense of humour. I grew to like her almost from the offset. With the two women well-rehearsed in the duties of the store, it was time for Mister Genks and me to buy Zeppelin dirigible airship tickets for Amerika".

92.

Hersko dropped lithely from his horse, throwing the reins to an adjacent guard. He raced across the cobbled courtyard to the entrance at the base of the keep. Beyond lay the Small Audience Chamber reserved for lesser dignitaries and peasant petitioners. Ignoring that, Hersko dashed up the east wing steps. So many feet had trodden that winding elevation in the past. So much so that the centre of each step was bowed, worn to smoothness, as the stone was polished over and again by the boots of those as tread upon them. Hersko was only concerned about one woman in particular at that moment. The woman was not the first Lady of Flahé, Bemien, his mother. Rather, he had plans for his murdered wife.

The scene that greeted his eyes as he reached the upper floor was the first lady attended by two masked maids, two guards watching passively over a fallen form, a white sheet with a glowing crimson stain at a point in the cloth.

"Out of mine way"? He snarled as the guards had already recognised him. Throwing the sheet to one side, the first lord of Flahé knelt beside the fallen body of his bride. With the Vandei Motestas, placed it over Cassiti's wound, closed his eyes, simply concentrated. The two guards looked at one another in slight confusion. When they returned their attention to the bizarré tableau on the floor before them, their eyes opened in astonishment. The crimson witness to the Lady's fatal injury was shrinking until it was gone.

Hersko hurriedly turned the body over so that he was cradling it in his arms. With the Vandei Motestas, he placed it over the corpse's heart, once again closed his eyes. There was a repeat of the earlier action by the two guards. They were utterly amazed when the Lady of Flahé opened her eyes smiled at his lordship and declared,

"I had the strangest dream, Husband. What are you doing here"?

Hersko had tears in his eyes as he told his new bride what had happened. When he had finished, Cassiti declared,

"Strange, I do not recall the incident, perhaps that is part of the power of the Vandei Motestas? That it can also be used as a hand of healing, on the right wrist. If this is so, Husband, then you can end the plague in Flahé. You must try it firstly on Bemien".

"You seem remarkably calm given that you were raised from the pit of Parasprio", Hersko noted.

"To tell you exactly I feel ever so slightly numb", Cassiti confessed, "Not especially surprising given what you have just told me, I'm sure it will pass by tomorrow morning when I have had a good night's sleep".

Hersko frowned, he would have been happier if his wife had been her usual self instantly, but death may well have its effects. Cassiti seemed cheerful, so he let it pass.

"I will try to save, mother, but then I go after the Surgeon", he told her.

"Revenge, rather than helping the people of your village"?

"Justice. if it has an element of vengeance then so be it. To kill a noble carried severe penalties, Cassiti, not without good reason".

Myrrorball

"Try to help your mother, if you can, we shall have to resume this debate"? Cassiti pleaded.

The maid moved out of his way. He walked up to her bed, yet not before donning a mask himself. Although he concentrated upon it with the same vigour, the same determination though, Bemien still had the pestilence when he finally stumbled to the floor completely-spent.

"It doesn't work against it. I don't know why. I tried Cassiti, the gods know I tried".

The former native woman placed an arm around his stooped shoulders, encouraged,

"I do not doubt it for a second, come and rest"?

"There is no time if we are to overhaul the captain and his compliment", Hersko managed to argue. He looked up to the two guards, switched to Valgraln, "Thee and thee, what be thy names"?

"Hoivik, my Lord", the first of them replied

"Bivings, ifin it pleaseth thy Lordship", from the second.

"Thou art mine escort", Hersko struggled to his feet. "We ride through the night if necessary, on the trail of the Captain of the Guard, plus that rapscallion - Surgeon".

93.

The GDR Hess was a fabric-covered rigid metal framework made up from transverse rings and longitudinal girders containing several individual gasbags. It seemed the advantage of such a design was that the aircraft could be much larger than non-rigid airships, which relied on a slight overpressure within the single pressure envelope to maintain their shape. The framework of most Zeppelins was duralamin (a combination of aluminium and copper, as well as two or three other metals—its exact content, was a secret). Early Zeppelins used rubberised cotton for the gasbags, but the Hess craft used gold-beater's skin, made from the intestines of cattle. The first Zeppelins had long cylindrical hulls with tapered ends, complex multi-plane fins. During World War I, following the lead of their rivals Schütte-Lanz Luftschiffbau, the design changed to the more familiar streamlined shape with cruciform tail surfaces, as used by almost all later airships. The Hess was propelled by several engines, mounted in gondolas or engine cars. They were attached to the outside of the structural framework. Some of these could provide reverse thrust for manoeuvring while mooring. While early models had a comparatively small externally mounted gondola for passengers and crew which was attached to the bottom of the frame. The Hess incorporated several important changes. Its passenger space was relocated to the interior of the overall vessel. Passenger rooms were insulated from the exterior by the dining area, forced-warm air could be circulated from the water that cooled the forward engines. All of which made travelling much more comfortable. It deprived passengers of the views from the windows of their berths, which had been a major attraction on the *Graf Zeppelin*. The flight ceiling was so low that no pressurization of the cabins was necessary. The Hess did maintain a pressurized air-locked smoking room.

In the reality, I now found myself a part of, jet planes were not used for domestic flights. They were not considered to be part of the grüner (green) Plan instituted by the Nazis as part of the attempt to stop the increase of global warming. The Chinese had fallen in line with many proposals in the grüner plan, as had England. Only the continent of Amerika persisted with petroleum fuelled cars, everywhere else in the world, then used electric. It had subsequently made the middle east less of a problem. In 2003 the combine triumvirate of Germany, England and China had told the occupants of those countries that if Muslim activists caused any more strife in the civilised world. They would suffer nuclear annihilation. The threat had been taken seriously. Terrorism had ended in every country except Amerika. The latter being conducted by one Amerikan group against another. The word united had become a bitterly ironical one In Amerika and Amerikans had been forced to change the name of the country back to its proper nomen as opposed to a ludicrous acronym.

Myrrorball

I had never been a fan of heights. For some strange reason, I was opposed to falling. I was even more opposed to plummeting, especially if it culminated in my then terminating the drop with a seriously fatal death. When I saw the Hess though, it was so massive, as to inspire strange Teutonic-fuelled confidence in me. The gondola rested lightly on the ground, we entered it by a stout doorway at its nose. From there, a stairwell took us up into the vessel. All sight of the sky without was denied us from that moment. It would not be the most interesting of journeys, but the compensation for that was the excellent cuisine and refreshment offered.

Had I not been wearing my ever trusty Casio, it would have been very easy indeed to lose a measure of the passage of time. Without any indication of what was happening outside, it was as though we were drifting through the void with only the constant remeasuring rumble of the propellers to let us know we had no cause for alarm. For this reason, it came as something of a surprise when the motors changed tone and we felt the beginning of a gentle descent into Portsmouth International Airport at Pease Airport. It was also a relief, Mister Genks appearance caused a sensation wherever we went, we could have no privacy. Were it not for the fact that he was the best equipped to find and steal our target I would not have taken him with me. I admit to having no clue how to get to the volume though.

We disembarked at the airport. Strangely, I had no trouble passing through security armed as I was with the blazerifle and searpistol. It seemed Amerikans went almost everywhere armed. To have weaponry was as normal as carrying shopping, or a suitcase and so forth. Isolationism had made the country even more xenophobic and violent. They stuck their noses into the business overseas less than the Amerika I was used to, but remained highly critical of those nations that did not worship money and the accruing of it, as greatly as themselves. They were just as obese as in my layer of reality though, really obese in fact. When I saw them waddling about, I guessed the average weight of an Amerikan must be in the region of 102 kilogrammes, while their average waist size was 112 centimetres and the average height was 175 centimetres.

We hired a petroleum fuelled car to drive to Baltimore, which would be 450 miles and would take 7 hours on the road. I had no intention of doing it in one sitting though. My old driving instructor had told me that one could only seriously concentrate for ninety minutes before it was time to take a break. So that was what we were going to do. Fortunately, we could share the chore, for Mister Genks was every bit as capable as I and with the automatic, self-shifting transmission it would be driving in style for both of us. The horsepower of a petroleum car was still higher, but it did make us feel guilty to be adding to the carbon emissions of our planet. There was no alternative, in Amerika, electric vehicles had been tried then dismissed by the populace. Perhaps the extra power was needed to pull the enormous bulk of the average Amerikan family, who knew?

Our journey from one locale to the next went without incident and took us a little over ten hours with breaks. On one occasion we stopped for dinner. When our platters arrived, we realised we could have shared one dinner. We were just looking at the mound of the menu before us when the young man returned. Placed a vast amount of chips in the centre of the table too. The Amerikans called them French Fries, yet the potatoes concerned had never been anywhere near France, go figure. We did our best, eating slightly more than usual, which managed to reduce the food by around 33%. When the young man came back, he looked at what had gone cold before us and asked in dismay,

"Something wrong, guys, I can get the manager if you weren't happy with...".

Myrrorball

"That's fine", I told him, "We just ate a standard amount to keep two English gentlemen happy", I could not resist adding, "A decent human portion, you know".

He completely misunderstood, glancing at Mister Genks tried,

"If you tell me what the green guy likes, I can see if..."?

"We ate together, but moral portions, we have had enough thank you, could I settle the bill so that we can depart"?

He hurried away to get it, when it came I paid in dollars which we had brought with us from England. This made the meal incredibly cheap as the exchange rate was $1 = 223 EPf (English Pfennig - 100 EPf = 1EM) meaning we had twice as much money as we had brought over - in real terms. It was 20:23 hours when we finally arrived in Baltimore, booking into the Inn at the Colonnade 4W University Parkway which was but a stroll from the Museum of Art.

Our only plan was to approach the museum under cover of darkness. Though Mister Genks had much more idea how to get into a locked building, he had none of his usual tools with him, thanks to your oversight Hhrrhhoehhrrhooooingohh. My other worry was the fact that I would not become a Nazi murderer no matter how great the consequences.

"No matter the dire nature of our situation I will not use the blazerifle or searpistol on a human being, to perpetrate larceny", I told my manbian friend, "So they stay in this room, until our return".

"I fail to undcrthtand why you brought them if you feel that way", came the response.

"Amerika is a violent place, we have a right to defend ourselves while we are abroad, but I will not become an armed robber, that is a step too far for me".

Major Roxbrough & Nik Gehenna

He nodded his understanding. We set off for the place where the book would be kept, unarmed, it almost got us both killed!

94.

"Twould seemeth we have chosen a different direction to that taken by the Captain of the Guard", Hersko noted as darkness was descending.

Hoivik marvelled at his Lord's stamina, but the truth of it was that the Vandei Motestas was feeding him with some sustaining vitality, otherwise, he would have dropped to the ground insensible and spent.

"My Lord", Bivings finally dared, "If thou continues pon this route, without pause nor respite, thou must do so alone, for truly Hoivik and I are close to complete exhaustion. We are all three, Master of Horse, compared to Surgeon, he cannot remain far ahead, but what profit be it if we catch him and he be more rested and able to take us, despite we being thrice his number"?

Hersko nodded, "Make camp then, have supper prepared? I will rejoin thee in but one hour, I chance to scout ahead but will return in the given".

With that, he urged the horse he was astride into a cantor, which was the safest upper speed in the gathering gloom. He had proceeded for twenty minutes when the Vandei Motestas began to glow slightly and the wrist upon which, it resided itched terribly. Sliding from the saddle, to his feet, he drew his sword and continued adroitly on foot. Soon he heard the faint crackle of wood being burned and saw a glim glowering through the trees. With the dexterity of a cat, Hersko drew closer. Finally, he leapt into the small clearing around the fire of which, was huddled, none other than Surgeon.

95.

On the way to the museum which we decided to do on foot, so close was it to the hotel, we ran into our first spot of Amerikan trouble. Something which bizarrely almost got me killed. As we walked down the pavement which the Amerikans have some strange name for which I will not use, a figure seemed to be weaving from side to side on an intercept course with us. It seemed by the erratic nature of his perambulation, that he was either drunk or drugged, possibly both. After all, this was Amerika, a nation filled with drunks and drug addicts, not just in this layer of reality either. We continued to approach, I took a certain amount of confidence from the fact that I was in the company of the manbian. I had previously observed his movements when the need arose. He was considerably swifter, stronger than any man. Though it was twilight, it soon became possible to determine that the man was some sort of tramp. Shabbily dressed in clothes that had not seen the inside of a washing machine for some time, his black hat bent out of shape, with no possibility of ever being restored to its former glory. One of his once fine leather shoes had a hole in the top of the big toe. That was a story in itself, one I might write in the future. Hole in the Top of the Shoe. How on Earth, did one wear out the top of a shoe before the bottom?

We were nearly on top of one another when the huge Negro, for that was his race, seemed to fumble in a dirty waistcoat pocket and onto the pavement clattered a fallen pipe. The sort of pipe one uses for tobacco though, who knew what had been in that particular smoking equipment? Marijuana, crystal methamphetamine, drain cleaner, who knew what else a crazy Amerikan would attempt to begin destroying his body with? Life was so sacred, so wonderfully biological, why do ones utmost to rob oneself of a healthy existence?

So thinking to do my good deed for the day, seeing as the tramp looked slightly less than limber and flexible I stooped, picked up the pipe ready to hand back to its owner. As I arose though, I found myself staring down the barrel of a rather nasty looking magnum revolver.

"You put that down, boy", the Negro commanded me emphasising the last word, "That don't be no property of yo's, understand"?

Major Roxbrough & Nik Gehenna

There are times when it is prudent to try to explain one's actions. There are times when it is simply best to 'get the hell out of dodge', to use the local colourful if inaccurate vernacular. My instinct told me the latter was the correct course to assume upon that occasion. Dropping the pipe on the ground, we hurried onward without a word to a man who not only lived in a different country, but also in both senses of the phrase, in another world.

The museum was set in darkness with a setting sun behind it. Looming over us like a stone creature ready to pounce on its prey. The two of us were walking straight into its maw. There was no help for it if the front of the building was alarmed, then surely the back would be equally, electronically well defended. Mister Genks surprised me then by producing a small case from his clothing and opening a box well concealed at the side of the doorway to the place.

"Where did you get that"? I whispered, glancing down into the tools contained in the case, "And how did you know where that control box was"?

"While you had your little nap in our room, I was buthy", he grunted, a pair of tiny fold-out cutters suddenly snipping through a wire. He had already bared two others and bridged them with little jump wires with tiny alligator clips on the end of them. "I found the underbelly of thith town without too much trouble and went thopping. Don't worry, you will be paying the bill in the end, it will have to come out of our profitth from the thale of the book".

I almost asked how much the burglar kit had cost. Then realised, it would be far greater than would normally be the case, due to its illegal nature. Mister Genks snipped another wire over the door, with tiny rods of a strange configuration he then unlocked the front door, we slipped inside. In the box, I was told later, he had rendered the surveillance cameras blind, bypassed the alarm to the

Myrrorball

Baltimore police and stopped the bell from alerting anyone else to our intrusion - brilliant.

We slipped through the entrance hall at a steady trot, seeking a door that would proclaim in tall red letters that it was access for staff only. In the corner of one room which contained a couple of alabaster nudies, we found just such a barrier. With the alarm no longer functioning, it was the work of seconds for Mister Genks to pick the lock. I was beginning to wonder why he needed me on the task at all, as I had contributed nothing. Then I discovered the reason, he turned to me and commanded.

"While I go down to find the thafe the book will be locked in, you go back to the entranth, jutht incathe anyone patrolling theeth what we are about? Don't uthe the light on your phone any more, we will have to thtumble about in complete darkneth".

I knew the latter was for my benefit, for the manbian could see as well in almost darkness as daylight. He also had the far better vision at perceiving movement than I, but he was the only one who would be able to crack the safe. So I did as bid and later learned that he found a tall vault with some particular treasures within, almost at once. Using his incredibly acute hearing had the combination dial discerned in a ridiculously short time.

"Primitive it wath", he told me when we got back to the hotel room. "Eathily opened by hand".

He had relocked everything on the way back out and reset the alarm before we left the building once again. No sense to letting just any old thief help themselves to the art objects within. From his dicky bag, he handed me the most valuable copy of Mein Kampf to ever exist. We both still had our latex gloves on, so would leave no tell-tale fingerprints behind for Sicherheitspolizei (SiPo Security Police) the Gestapo, Kopf Inspektor Verner deGoethe to use against us in the future.

I opened the cover almost reverently, which was ludicrous considering who the author was, glanced down at the inscription written in black ink with a fountain pen. As was usual with the man who had disliked writing by hand, it was not especially neat and sloped alarmingly to the upper right corner of the page. I noticed the tiny size of the writing, especially the middle zone letters (such as m's and a's, etc). A sign of extreme concentration and ability to focus intently. Secondly, the slashes above some of the words they were either t-bars or i-dots, and they indicated temper, tension, and irritation. The t-bars slanted downward heavily, almost creating what looked like x's instead of t's in some cases. Very domineering, craving of control The p's, such as that in the second word in the last line, extended high and formed a v-shape below the baseline. Hitler enjoyed a good argument and would pick a fight sometimes just for itself, with nothing, in particular, to argue about. The look of the sharpness of the m- and n-tops was a sign of incredibly quick thinking and high intelligence.

I had done my homework before we set off and knew what I had in my hands at that moment was no fake. It was the lone copy of Mein Kampf first edition, dedicated by Hitler, to his wife Eva Braun, the inscription read,

Für Meine geliebte Eva hoffe ich, dass einige der hierin enthaltenen Thesen Sie nicht Meine Kleine Taube verwirren, sondern versuchen, meinen Kampf zu lesen und Ihren Adolf besser kennenzulernen, um dies zu tun.

Liebe Adolf
Führer des dritten Reiches

(To my darling Eva, I hope some theses contained herein do not confuse you my little dove but try to read my struggle and get to know your Adolf the better for doing so,
 love Adolf
 Leader of the Third Reich)

I turned to page 60, *the* page. The one that had caused so much suffering in many layers of the multiverse presumably:

Fighting Jews as Defending God.

The Jewish doctrine of Marxism rejects the aristocratic principle of Nature and replaces the eternal privilege of power and strength by the mass of numbers and their dead weight. Thus it denies the value of personality in man, contests the significance of nationality and race and thereby withdraws from humanity the premise of its existence and its culture. As a foundation of the universe, this doctrine would bring about the end of any order intellectually conceivable to man. And as, in this greatest of all recognizable organisms, the result of an application of such a law could only be chaos, on Earth it could only be destruction for the inhabitants of this planet.

If with the help of his Marxist creed, the Jew is victorious over the other peoples of the world, his crown will be the funeral wreath of humanity and this planet will, as it did thousands of years ago, move through the ether devoid of men.

Eternal nature inexorably avenges the infringement of her commands.

Hence today I believe that I am acting in accordance with the will of the Almighty Creator: *by defending myself against the Jew, I am fighting for the work of the Lord.*

How strange that such a madman could also be so intelligent, the fine line between sanity and madness was never so easily demonstrated. I closed the book, though it was now in our possession, I harboured no great desire to read any more of it.

96.

"Thou thinkest me foolish enough to put thee to the sword, Surgeon", Hersko observed, "Here, now, with the mercy of alacrity"?

"Take thy vengeance, have done with it", the former medical man protested, possibly even beseeched.

Hersko, Lord of Flahé, hardened his heart though, for the populace of any town in Valgral liked a good execution. He was not want to deny them of it. He shook his head,

"Thou art of the peasant rank, Surgeon. Thou didst murder a member of the nobility, thou knowest what the punishment rightly be for just such atrocity".

The Surgeon already pale from his ardours went even more wan, suddenly drawing something from the folds of his once white caftan rushed at Hersko with a wild yell of desperation. The blade in his hand glinted steel brilliance by the illumination afforded by the flames of the small campfire. It was nothing less than the murder weapon itself, his once grimly used scalpel.

Hersko batted it aside almost casually, with his broadsword, before bringing the pommel crashing against the homicidian's forehead. Surgeon fell insensible at his feet. The penalty for the murder of a noble was hanging drawing and quartering.

To be hanged, drawn and quartered was a statutory penalty in Valgral for men convicted of crimes against the nobility and high treason. The convicted murderer/rapist/ traitor was fastened to a hurdle, or wooden panel, drawn by horse to the place of execution, where he was then hanged. Almost to the point of death, emasculated, disembowelled, beheaded, and quartered (chopped into four pieces). His remains would then often be displayed in prominent places across the country. Kingshire for example, to serve as a warning of the fate of those who perpetrated such vile villainy. For reasons of public decency, women convicted of similar transgressions were instead mercifully burned at the stake. The severity of the sentence determined by the seriousness of the crime. As an attack on noble authority which was considered a deplorable act, it demanded the most extreme form of punishment. Although some convicts were known to have their sentences modified then suffered a less ignominious end. Over several hundred years, many men found guilty of such crimes were subjected to the law's ultimate sanction. Apart from other considerations, it was also considered a fine family day out for the plebeian, who enjoyed a bit of contrived sadism.

At Surgeon's trial, conducted after the worst of the Geişvəhşilic had decimated the populace of the town, Hersko presiding, was heard to state,

"Thou shalt be executed on the 23rd day of Saint Sagethtide for the crime of foul and heinously bloody murder of they ladyship, ruler of this town of Flahé. Thou shalt be laid on an hurdle being so drawn to the place of execution. There to be hanged, cut down alive, thy members to be cut off and cast in the fire, thy bowels burnt before thee, thy head thence smitten from thy foul and thusly cruelly used body, which will thence be quartered and divided at the King's will. May the gods shun then whence thou approaches them and thou art cast down into the bowels of purgatory forever".

The young lord of Flahé felt that such was harsh but fair. Not only that, his subjects had suffered cruelly beneath the rigours of the vast pestilence, therefore were deserved of a nice day out, with interesting, if grizzly, entertainment. Surgeon was held in the dungeon of the castle for a few days to allow the populace to gain enough vitality to thoroughly enjoy their day. When the day arrived, he was fastened to a wicker hurdle, itself tied to Hersko's horse. At this point, he was pelted with rotten vegetables, gobbets of dung and had urine sprayed over him. Once he had almost choked to death while the executioner slowly pulled on the rope that was around his neck, then cut down. Once stripped to nakedness, then emasculated, before having the viscera or intestines of his bowel drawn out of him. By the time the executioner beheaded him, he had succumbed to shock and was dead.

Harsh it was, but a message had to be delivered to the peasants, that to attack nobility was to risk very dire consequence indeed. Flahé had suffered terrible detriment at the spread of the mikroloblar of Geişvəhşilic and could take no further part in the war with the west. Lady Bemien, fortunately, did not succumb to her malady, she was making a very gradual recovery by the time her husband finally returned to her.

Major Roxbrough & Nik Gehenna

Flahé crushed Hersko to his chest and exclaimed how pleased he was to see that his son had not become a Blevastís. The young man proved the master of understatement when he observed,

"We two have much catching up to do, father".

"That night, when Hersko had finally finished his narration, his father replied,

"When I left the Fire of Saah there was only Lolocken, Hízlatan and Bodakin left of the expedition. I grieve for the dead King, but would wish for a better man to take his place".

"Ifin the stories from the north are to be believed, Father, it may be the lord of Koözoött who claims that noble role".

"Aye", Flahé took a sip from his goblet, "Ifin that proveth rightly then we of the east will be in for sore times and none mistake. I wouldst sooner have this upstart Zemtel, of whom thou hast heard. At least he shares the bed of the Queen".

"Strangely horrible tales have issued from the north, Father", Hersko added, "Tales of those fallen in battle rejoining it at a later date, fighting on. Such creatures referred to as, the Animataverous. They do the bidding of Koözoött, who styles himself, Warlord of the West, they are led by one Norgan Animataverosity".

"It now seemeth as though we cannot play any part in it though, Son", Flahé observed, "We do not have the force to ride afore".

Hersko shook his head, yet we have our sword arms, Father and whosoever finally ends up on the throne will remember those as rode for them".

"Aye", Flahé nodded grimly, "*If* the east wins the war"!

97.

Aboard the GDR Kant, I found myself exhausted but unable to sleep. I had never suffered from insomnia and never truly understood how desperate a situation it could be. The chief emotion that tugged at one's frayed nerves in such a position was frustration. To be too tired to sleep is a terrible predicament. Due to fatigue, it is pointless to rise, but because one's mind is active still a tremendous sense of ennui washes over the sufferer and that only makes it even harder to attain restful slumber. I even grew angry with myself and began to fidget tremendously. Finally, Mister Genks, roused by the infernal rustle of my bedding asked me,

"Do you want thomething, Gehenna"?

"Yes", I snarled back. "I want to get to ruddy sleep before this flight is over".

He rose fluidly, as was his lithe way, always was the strong and futuristic creature so elegant in movement. That dicky-bag of his seemed to me to be like the Tardis. Larger on the inside than the out, otherwise, how did it hold quite so many wonders? From within its capacious interior, he withdrew a small glass bottle. The top of it was held in place by an ingenious little metal clip that levered over the lip of a hinge. Lifting the clip in a specific way, Mister Genks opened the bottle, poured some slim white tablets into his green, slightly warm palm. His hands had always fascinated me, long, slimly terminated in fingers that had disc-shaped ends for phenomenal grip. Whom-so-ever had decided to create a creature that was part man part frog, must have been a genetic genius.

Mister Genks held out his hand to me and offered,

"You could take one of theethe? They will help you achieve very deep and meaningful thleep, but there ith a thide effect".

I sighed. Life could never be as simple as one of my novels. When faced with a choice, it always contained consequences that invariably meant that I had no choice in real terms at all.

"And what, my dear Fellow, might the side-effect be"?

"The thingle most vivid dream you will ever experinthe".

"What, like a nightmare or something"?

He shook his large-domed head, surmounted with the great equally semi-spherical eyes of his,

"Not a nightmare, jutht a dream. One that would seem to be almotht real to you. When you wake, you will have had the betht mightth thleep of your life".

Major Roxbrough & Nik Gehenna

"What is it? I'm not going to get hooked or anything am I? I'm having enough trouble not exhausting my snufz supply. (the thought of trying some to help me sleep had crossed my mind and I had successfully resisted the temptation)".

"One tablet will not make an addict of you".

"But they are addictive".

"Only ath in tho many thingth are chocolate, gambling, thecth, vidth. All can be addictive to the weak-willed. Now, do you want either of uth to get thome thleep or do you not"?

I picked the smooth white disc out of his palm. A completely featureless pill with no etching on it or indication of what it was at all. That forced me to ask,

"What is it Genksy"?

"It is thomnalude".

"Somnalude"?

Thatth what I thaid ithn't it. Now, take the thodding thing already and letth get thome thleep".

Feeling a little like Lewis Carroll's Alice, rather than the brilliant rock singer of the same nomen, I swallowed the pill without water, easily enough. Nothing happened instantly. I had not expected that it would. So I carefully remade my ruined cot and then climbed back into it. The throbbing of the engines was a gentle susurration then, whereas they had previously been nothing other than an annoyance. I closed my eyes and tried not to think about anything, in particular, it worked, I fell...

98.

....asleep. Yet did not dream, I suddenly awoke to feel much stronger, invigorated and fresh.

However...

Something very significant had taken place. I was no longer on the Zeppelin! I was not even in bed. More frightening than any of the previous considerations, *I was no longer myself.*

I was seated astride a horse, my body bedecked in medieval armour. We were riding toward another force which logic told me was the enemy. I was about to be involved in a violently bloody conflict. How would I possibly survive? Me, the simple author. On one arm was a circular shield, the horse's reins in the same hand. I suddenly realised I could ride a horse. Yet I have never sat astride such a creature in my entire life. A cry went up the rest of the line, of which, I was a rider. Suddenly broke into a canter. Before I had the chance to think about the appropriate actions, my knee hands and body reacted in just such a way as to urge my mount to the same pace. It was an instinctual action, almost as though the decision had been taken by my spine, rather than my brain.

The easiest way of describing what was happening was when one climbs into a car that has not been in use for quite some time for one reason or another. Driving is done with very little conscious thought, and when one gets to the destination one realises that one has been thinking about something completely unrelated to getting there.

That was how I was acting when I charged with the rest of the armoured force that was getting ready to bloodily smite into an opposing one. It would have utterly terrified me in the ordinary course of events, but I was not there - was I? I drew my broadsword and seeing the pommel suddenly realised who I was supposed to be. I knew I was not the Császária - Imperial Marquess of Roxbrough, I had taken his place, in whatever was happening: a myrrorball of, a delusion, a glimpserama into the existence of...something that was not normally anything to do with me. For the pommel of the broadsword I now wielded terminated in a tiny metal fist, in that fist an emerald was clutched, the blade was called Evilartus.

When we crashed into the enemy, I was unafraid. I could not die. What I was experiencing was not real. Not only that, I suddenly had unnaturally heightened skills in the art of war. Evilartus smote one enemy's arm from his shoulder. Drove into the heart of another, who's weapon crashed against my shield. With a mighty swipe, of which, I knew I was incapable, my opponent's head was removed from his shoulders. If I was fighting as though

Roxbrough, then those I was killing must have been from the east. Halsgough's men? I did not know. What I did know was that killing them did not fill me with either horror or remorse. There again killing in dreams had never done that to me either. What man does not ever have a dream that they are fighting? None I have ever met, believe me, I've asked.

I soon began to feel something quite disconcerting, fatigue. I had never experienced that any of my actions had tired me in dreams before. It was incredibly vivid something I put down to the Somnalude. To feel fatigued though? Would I also feel pain if I were wounded? Then did I feel apprehension, the dream was getting too real, I tried to wake and could not. That had happened to me before in my life, so it was not especially surprising. I had also even dreamed that I had woken and had not, to continue dreaming and be astounded when I finally did come out of the second fantasy. **Perhaps some of these details are why you chose me** Hhrrhhoehhrrhooooingohh **because I was in some way more receptive to your transmissions than the average or less imaginative man?** Generally speaking the average man on the street, the plebeian, is not one for imagination, not even cohesive thought a great deal of the time. It had become a fact, just before my little adventure on Rozhelia. Only ten-percent of children under the age of twenty-five had ever read a book from cover to cover. I referred those under twenty-five, those who seemed to enjoy watching men running about with their underpants on the outside of their trousers. Still enjoying reading comics, which those embarrassed for them called graphic novels - as if the Beano and The Dandy were graphic novels.

As I began to feel fatigued, I wondered at something new. Yet another phenomenon that could not possibly be actuality. Vitality was flooding back from the sword with the emerald in its pommel. I felt representmentation, reinvigoration, it flooded up my arm and dispelled my previous fatigue. That was impossible. Though I wrote Science fiction, it would never be possible for a sword to feed the energies of those it killed into the body of he who

Myrrorball

used it. I had entered the realm of *Fantasy*, was not especially impressed. Imagine thusly, my further disbelief when some of the fallen enemy, those with the least debilitating injuries and death blows, started to rise from their fallen positions to continue fighting!

I hacked the head from one, that stopped him...it, what was a dead warrior doing fighting a second, possibly third time?

The action seemed to demoralise the side I was fighting for. A horn sounded after about an hour of this gory mayhem, the issue indicating retreat. Turning my horse, its coat now slick with blood, fragments of bone, the splash of brain matter, I galloped it back to the tented area, which I presumed we had ridden from initially. We fought a rearguard action in retreat for the dead newly risen, harried us as we withdrew. All at once, a series of rumbling drum beats sounded, the reanimated-fallen fell back themselves. A squire grabbed my reins holding the steed steady as I gratefully dismounted wondering when I would awaken from the drug-fuelled incubus. Yes, I did feel it more a nightmare than a dream.

"Lord, thou art required in the First Lord's canopy as soon as thou has cleaned some of the juice of battle from thee", the young man informed me.

Juice of Battle! The gore of those I had killed. The lifeblood of those I had robbed of that very condition, yet still, I felt no remorse. I strode toward a tent, which I felt was mine. Finding a jug and bowl on a pedestal poured some water, taking a ripped piece of rag and doing the best I could to make myself presentable. Something told me not to keep the First Lord, whosoever he might be, waiting too long. Even then, despite my alacrity, I seemed to be just about the last to arrive in the most opulent canopy in the camp.

The First Lord was a man I had never seen before, not especially worthy of my interest then. There were those who I did know though. The chief one being the Lord of Staltidore, so I squeezed my way to be by his side.

"Glad to see thou made it, my Lord", he smiled at me, looking tired.

Major Roxbrough & Nik Gehenna

"Likewise", I returned in English, causing him some confusion. I repeated the sentiment in Valgraln. Judging by the terrain we had fought on, we were back in Valgral, for the grass had been green, the trees deciduous, it could not have been the Fire of Saah as the locals were want to call it. The locals of Valgral that was.

I was more concerned by the fact that Staltidore had not called me Visionary, but still obviously recognised me. Was I actually in the body of Roxbrough then? I tugged a gauntlet from my left hand and looked down at it. It was calloused, course, the nails were bitten down to the quick. Certainly not hands that had done nothing more arduous than typing and collecting books.

In the back of my mind, one of the things that concerned me with growing unease was that I seemed aware of the passage of time. Wondered when the illusion would end. Yet in no dream I had ever had before, was I even aware of dreaming, much less wanting the glimpserama into an inner dimension of my mind to end. Had Mister Genks, therefore, tricked me? Drugged me to secure the book for either himself in the Nazi-world (as I thought of it increasingly as time had gone by)? Or perhaps even in the 33rd century, from which, he had come? Was I being disingenuous even to think of him in such terms? He, together with the android had been sent to help both me and the natives of Egszígør. Had never done a single thing to earn our suspicions.

I was still gripped inside the body of another still. To those who looked at me, I was Császária Roxbrough. This led me in turn to another thought, a question in my head, if I was in Roxbrough, was he somewhere else or was this still an actual dream? I discounted the latter, no dream was so vivid, filled with smells and feeling, in glorious technicolour, no this was either an illusion or a trip!

99.

Hersko observed his brow ridged with concern, "Since the vile-homicidian went to his due punishment, you do not seem the same, my love, is everything all right"?

"Yes, Hersko, everything is all right now", Cassiti returned. Yet she spoke as though by rote and the declaration did nothing to calm his suspicions. If anything, her total lack of warmth seemed to make him even more disquieted. Death it seemed, had not suited the former native girl.

The Lord of Flahé took her in his arms, she was succumbnal, but it was like holding a rag and stuffed version of his wife. Her body lived, yet her essence, her quiddity seemed banished from it. The only option Hersko had was to wait for the return of Bodakin. Perhaps the sorcerer would have some potion or charm that could render matters aright. He went to see his father, who was concerned at the progress of the war in the north.

Flahé senior was in his study pawing over the map of Valgral (plate 3), at his son's entrance he confessed,

"I have just heard reports from the north, a pigeon from Staltidore, Várort has fallen to Koözoött, Warlord of the West".

"And our friends"?

"Staltidore, Oslan-On-the-Bank and Roxbrough were all fortunate enough to form part of the retreat. They hope to regroup at Laaterfell".

"Still no sign of Lolocken"?

Flahé shook his head, "I might not be so wise as to presume he will come up behind the enemy, the reports of the Animataverous be that they continue to grow in number. We may have to withdraw with whom we have left and retreat into the eastern mountains".

"If that fails, what then? Ask the King of Naav for assistance"?

Naav, Valgral's oldest enemy since the four arms of the cross had been split into different countries,

"I wouldst rather strike north, Father, into mysteriously private Fansui. Admitted we know nothing of them, but what we do know of Naav makes me think we would be better trying the unknown"?

"Let us hope it will not come to that", Flahé offered, but he did not sound very hopeful.

Major Roxbrough & Nik Gehenna

"We must ride north though, rejoin our noble friends and help them with their resistance".

"So that we can die with them? What would be the point of that mine Son"?

Hersko looked at his father who suddenly appeared quite old. His reply was a single word,

"Honour".

100.

"Major Norgan", Lord Koözoött murmured with a sigh, "What dost thou want this time"?

"The only change that there hast been, My Lord", Norgan returned with great care, for it was becoming increasingly difficult for him to speak, "Be that I am beginning to putrefy and decay. I, therefore, request the peace of the grave for me and mine company, we have given thee the victories thou craved tis time for thee to set us free. Give us rest, let us moulder in the grave rather than Gehenna.

"This be not Gehenna", Koözoött observed with a wry smile, "That be waiting for some of us when we be dead".

"And yet I am dead, My Lord, thou hast made my former home a waking purgatory".

"Thou analogy be not badly observ-ed", came the considered reply, "Yet, till we march into the capital and I be crowned King I have need of thee Norgan, request denied".

"I be not sure my integrity will hold for much longer, my Lord", Norgan confessed then, "Wouldst thou have me decay to ruin on thy battlefield"?

"If such proves the case then thy bones will be laid to rest", Koözoött offered, "But until that becomes an reality, I have need of thee. Thou art dismissed".

The leader of the Animataverous left the tent. From the folds of the canvass to its murky rear a handsome man in a flowing violet caftan emerged, a grim smile on his comely countenance.

Koözoött turned to the Necromancer, demanded, "Must I be ever forced to grant audience to that mumbling ruin of putrid flesh, the stink of his decay offends my nostrils"?

"The aroma be unfortunate, my Lord", Banustib smiled without amusement, "I find the mellifluous smell of corruption rather sweet. Ifin thou so wishes I can banish the dead back to the grave, thy forces are now swelled by the pressed enemy, with them thou couldst probably..."?

"No"! Koözoött realised only too well that they would not be enough, were they to start losing the next battle they might even turn tail and flee or worse, turn on him.

Banustib looked around him in a pantomime of performance, "Where be my Lord of Kyper Tor"?

Koözoött scowled, "Twould seem some of the maidens of Várort were of exceeding chasteness. His lordship be even now instructing them in the ways of lust and licentiousness".

Banustib grinned, "A noble calling".

Koözoött was not amused by his sardonicism, "Never mind him, Necromancer, what art thou doing to stop the dead decomposing further,? Thou stopped them from dying, do whatsoever it takes to halt their decomposition".

"My Lord, I didst not stop anyone from dying, what I did was reanimate them, entirely different I assure thee. There be no power on all the world that can stop the disintegration of an corpse".

"Thou meanest till now, Necromancer! Till now. Find a way, that be the orders of thy Lord and future King. I advise thee not to disappoint me".

Banustib was about to offer some well-observed and bitter rejoinder when he seemed to change his mind. Instead, he remained silent, bowed and left the Usurper alone in his tent.

101.

I lay in the darkness of the tent, my mind refusing to allow me to sleep. If I fell asleep, hoping I would awaken back on the Zeppelin. The state that may have achieved my ambition continued to allude me. I seemed trapped in the body of Roxbrough.

Earlier I had managed to find what passed in this world for a crude mirror. Sure enough, when I gazed into the burnished metal, the man who stared back at me was none other than a man I had formerly inspected from my own body. It was the most bizarre trip I had ever experienced. When I finally did get back to Earth II - I would have one or two words to say to Mister Genks. He should have been much more precise and careful in his explanation of what was to happen when I took the somnalude.

With the minimum of fuss and noise, I rose from the cot, carefully left the tent in just such a way as not to wake Oslan-On-the-Bank, with whom, I had been sharing it. I had no special purpose in mind until I found that my feet had taken me to the tethered area where all the horses were kept. Strapping the belt around my waist, that held the scabbard of my broadsword, I began searching for *my* horse. At the rear of the area were the saddles lain carefully in a heap on the zone designated by a spread tarpaulin. I had no idea which my saddle was, so I took the closest that seemed to be comfortable for me. It was the work of just a few seconds to saddle my mount, then lead it by its reins for several hundred metres before climbing up on its back - beginning to ride. I was going east, toward the mountains, I had no intention in taking part in the butchery of another battle. It was probably the most horrific experience I had endured in my otherwise sheltered lifetime. Roxbrough might well be used to that sort of thing. I felt mentally scarred by what I had experienced. My lips had a curiously numb quality, I kept having dizzy spells, in the back of (my) head were flashing snapping charges of electricity. They sounded like the sound that a fly makes when it flies into one of those ultraviolet exterminators that were once so popular in butchers shops. I was certain they were used in other locales too, but my early recollection of them was in butcher's shops.

I rode through the night, feeling the cool dawn air getting slightly cooler, the further east I journeyed. The sky changed from black to violet, to lilac, to fuchsia and finally transmogrified to a rich golden cerulean. The cumulus clouds were of the lightest white, no rain in them.

Since the beginning of my stay in the body of the Császária *I* had not slept, nor did I feel tired. What sort of drug was somnalude, it seemed to contain uppers when it should have comprised totally of downers? Eventually, in the afternoon I had to rest the horse, a town was on the horizon, where I could find food for both of us. If memory served me rightly it would be Tantelaa, beyond that would be the seat of my friend, Lolocken

'My friend'? I asked myself then with a start, *'Surely I meant Roxbrough's friend'*. I hoped ardently that I was not beginning to lose sight of my individuality. I was not Roxbrough I was Gehenna. **I felt a wave of animosity course through me then** Hhrrhhoehhrrhooooingohh. **It was directed at you. My life, before you arrived, had been so calmly ordered, look what had happened since you had come slithering to my window? Might it have been better if I had been one of those dissolved by your green gas? I would have known very little about it. I would be at peace instead of wondering where I was, who I was.** Now I had deserted the royal force, it seemed almost inevitable that Zemtel would put a price on my (Roxbrough's) head and call me(he) a deserter.

I found a stable for the horse. Fortunately, the Lord, whose body I now inhabited had a purse full of coinage at his belt. I gave the man his łotes then went up the main street, nothing better than compacted soil, to the local tavern. The *Daubed Mongrel* was filled with the sound of raucous laughter, the smell of food, sweat and tobacco. In other words, it was the sort of establishment that felt exactly like it should. I found myself revelling in the company after a ride so filled with solitude. This surprised me, for I had never been gregarious by nature, rather quite the opposite. Could it be that the loneliness I had felt was Roxbrough's rather than mine? Had I replaced his mind with my own? Or merely totally dominated it until that moment and parts of his psyche were starting to glimmer through? Unfortunately, as time

Major Roxbrough & Nik Gehenna

went by I seemed to have more questions than answers. Indeed I did not have any answers at all. Mister Genks had not exactly overburdened me with details concerning how the drug would work. I had been very foolish. I had not even enquired as to the length of my drug-induced illusion. Perhaps time ran at different rates when one was drugged? I had only been asleep a couple of minutes on the Zeppelin, while many hours had passed in my delusion? I ordered beef and ale pie, huge boiled potatoes and peas. The food looked like anything I could have expected at home, judging by the appearance of it on the other diners platters. Suddenly the ambient noise in the entire establishment lessened when one particularly loud voice rose above them - demanding,

"What art thou staring at, cannot a man enjoy his meal without someone watching every mouthful being conveyed. Thou hast given me indigestion"!

I realised that the huge black-bearded ruffian was addressing me.

"Thy pardon, Sir", I returned in Valgraln, "My mind was elsewhere, I was staring vacantly into space, my look seemed to be in thy direction".

"Liar", the ruffian roared not mollified in the slightest degree by my apology. Thou was watching me eat, so methinks thou canst show true contriteness by paying for my meal".

The boniface interrupted at that point, pulling an impressive looking cudgel from beneath the counter he roared,

"Not again Stonich, leave the stranger alone, canst thou not see he be of noble birth".

"Noble he might well be, but he be also an pidavraxmaq (ill-mannered oaf)".

If I had been a noble of Valgraln, I would have issued a dual in his direction at that. I would never see these people again though, my honour, such as it was, was not something that gravely concerned me, so I replied,

"I be sorry you feel that way, master Stonich, as I already be spoken I was daydreaming. I have ridden long-hard, fatigue claims me. Ifin it means I must pay for thy

Myrrorball

dinner, then so be it. Boniface, please put this fellow's meal on my slate if it pleaseth thee"?

That should have proved the end of it.

It did not!

"Poltroon", Stonich roared, then for good measure demonstrated the breadth of his vocabulary, "Coward, craven, dastard, milksop, varlet, weakling, yellow-belly. What art thou"?

I lost my temper - or rather one of us did, was it me, or Roxbrough?

"Thou, Sir, be an eater of the leftovers in the hound's bowl, thy mother was an harlot and thou might have had as many as forty suspects for he who sired thee. Now leave me alone, lest we dance with steel and shield so that I might part thy ugly head from thy bull neck, right gladly too".

Several in the room burst into laughter, but they shut up quickly when the bully glanced about him glaring in captious fury. He rose to his feet slowly, with deliberate torpidity picked up his weapon which had been at his feet on the floor. It was the largest double-bladed war axe I had ever seen.

I observed, "With a weapon as impressive as that thou shouldst be fighting on the side of the east against the usurper Koözoött. Put it down before it proves the end of thee".

"It will go down, once it has cleaved thee in twain upstart Lordling, for I recognise the crest 'pon thine armour and thou art far from they petty seat Roxbrough, little lord of that craggy domain where no true men reside".

"Till now thy diatribe hast possessed an amusing aspect, Stonich, but thy now slights my good subjects. I ask this for the last time, sit down and live? Otherwise, meet me outside and also the grim reaper, who already has one bony hand resting 'pon thy shoulder".

Even before Stonich had decided, there was a general movement toward the door. The former merrymakers were about to be treated to a killing in addition to the usual night's entertainment. It meant that neither of us could back down. I do not think either of us wanted to. I was feeling an uncharacteristic rage, electric flashes were still pulsing up and down the back of my neck. Was I an instant drug addict? It was as though I was suffering withdrawal, perhaps the scene was about to fade? I would find myself back in Earth II? We went out into the dark street, one or two spectators had thoughtfully taken lanterns with them, the better to illuminate the spectacle. It must have proved disappointing for them, for it was over in perhaps three seconds. Stonich' double-bladed axe may have looked fearsome, but it was ungainly and slow. He roared a battle cry, swung it downward, aimed at my shoulder. I danced to one side, thrusting with my sword as the axe uselessly bit into the ground. I will never forget the look of total astonishment on Stonich' face as he looked down at the blood pouring down the length of Evilartus. His ruptured heart stopped beating, he tumbled to the ground with a dull thump.

"Good riddance", an old hag spat onto the corpse, evidentially she and the dead man had enjoyed some sort of acrimonious dispute in the past. We went back inside. I was half-way through the pie when the işçiöhdəçi (undertaker) strolled into the Daubed Mongrel. He walked bravely up to my table and enquired,

"Begging thy pardon, My Lord, but who be to pay for the internment"?

"Leave his Lordship be"? the boniface cried before I could swallow the pie in my mouth, "We all be glad to see the back of the town bully, we will have an passing of the hat, till the cost be covered, we bury our own".

I nodded my acceptance of the arrangement and continued with my meal. It was the best meat and ale pie I had ever tasted.

102.

Lolocken was on the northern coastline, still a long way from my mountainous home seat. I had taken to asking myself why I thought there could be any answers for me there. The truth was that I did not know what I was doing. I had no plan as such, just the ardent desire to get away from the carnage. If I was locked into this trip, then I would become a hunted criminal, a deserter. Not exactly the sort of role I looked forward to portraying. I had two desires. The first and obvious one was that the trip would end, I would once again be Nik. The second was that in Lolocken, I would find the Lord returned. At least he could offer a fellow noble sanctuary when I explained my position. Or would he? What exactly was the position I could expect Lolocken to accept, obviously not the truth?

So I rode into the coastal town with indecision swirling around in my head. The electrical snapping sound was still tormenting me, I felt gushes of rage passing through my body, it seemed I was suffering withdrawal symptoms. In the vernacular popular at the time, I was rattling. What was I withdrawing from though? Somnalude, from which, I was soon to awaken from the protracted-trip - or snufz? The latter was still in Nik's possession, in his pocket, but he had not taken any for a while, conserving it for when he needed to know. I suddenly realised I was thinking about myself in the third person and that frightened me more than anything. If matters continued, would I lose my grip on reality, the balance of my mind?

Finding the layout of a town I had no memory of, I wended my way through the streets toward the castle and the portcullis that barred the entrance to it. Seeing my armour, the guard there ordered it raised without even asking me my business. A retainer took the reins of my horse, I was greeted by a steward,

"Lord Roxbrough, 'tis good to see thee my Lord. Dost thou bringeth news from the front? My Lord of Lolocken be but recently returned, come, thou art granted an immediate audience with him".

As he led me down the usual looking stone-lined corridors, that were dank and dimly lit, he asked again about the front, I returned carefully,

"Ifin his Lordship thy employer and master desireth thee to be made aware of such particular, then I be certain he will inform thee in due course, Steward".

Major Roxbrough & Nik Gehenna

The man stopped quizzing me then but led me directly into Lolocken's chambers. His lordship was not alone, but in the company of Bodakin the sorcerer, Hízlatan, who

must have expressed a desire to see Valgral for himself. The last figure in the room was not human, rather it was the huge android - 23.

"Roxbrough", Lolocken greeted me, "Come, tell us how the war progresseth, we are but recently back in Valgral".

"I be not Roxbrough", I stated, keeping my eye on the caftaned mage, "I am the Visionary, currently assuming Roxbrough's form".

Bodakin stepped forward scrutinising me carefully with his steel-grey eyes, he said, for the others had waited with bated breath,

"That be not strictly true Visionary, thou art no shape-shifter. Rather thy mind and quiddity have replaced the Császária, who be no longer in all this world".

"Ifin that be true, then where be he"? I suddenly desired to know. A curious look came over the sorcerer's features, he admitted quite readily, "I knowest not".

The android, who had been motionless until that point suddenly moved, his eyes glowed slightly brighter, he declared rather than asked,

"Mister Genks gave thee somnalude".

Myrrorball

"You can speak to me in English if you want, 23. I am English remember".

"Why would you not want the sorcerer to help you"? the android asked calmly, there again he was invariably calm, I had never heard the constructed man ever display a great feeling or emotion in all my dealings with him.

"Can he"?

"What is the nature of this world? Have not magic and alchemy replaced science, if you desire to return to wherever you came from, then Bodakin is your best hope".

"23, just what does somnalude do"?

"What were you told it did"?

"What be the two of thee talking about"? Bodakin then asked, seemingly annoyed that the android and I could converse in such a tongue as he did not understand.

"My apologies, I crave thy indulgence for a brief while, the master of Roid and myself discuss something that be beyond this realm, we will not take much more time, master Sorcerer".

I turned back to the android, "I was told it was for insomnia", I had switched back to English, which 23 seemed to understand with ease, which was slightly strange if he was from as far in the future as we had been informed.

"I was told it was for insomnia", I addressed the android once again, "Do you know this to be the truth? I had no reason to think at the time that it was anything other than what Mister Genks assured me it was".

"We all have our paths to tread", 23 observed, "Including the rather charming manbian".

"Could you do me the courtesy of speaking less obliquely", I asked then, "If you know something about somnalude, then I would be grateful if you would tell me what that is"?

"It might be better if you asked Mister Genks", the android intoned, "I do not desire to get in the middle of your dispute if indeed you have one, I am not intermediary for a manbian - homini situation".

"I have no idea what you are talking about, metal-man", He was beginning to agitate me, talking in foolish-riddles ."If he gave me something that did not do what he claimed it did, don't you think I deserve to know why"?

"Deserve"? 23 mused, "As in merit, that is not for me to say, I do not believe I know you well enough to comment on that my Lord of Roxbrough".

"Why are you calling me that, when you know full well that is not who I am"?

"Do I"?

"You are obtuse, I think deliberately so, forget I asked you anything, I was in error hoping you could help".

I turned my attention back to the sorcerer, "Bodakin, I am Nik, from Earth originally. I am currently inhabiting Roxbrough's body, can you help me to get back into the fleshly frame that I belong"?

The sorcerer observed, "Visionary, thou art no shape-shifter. Rather thy mind and quiddity have replaced the Császária, who be no longer in all this world. Mayhap that be where it belongs, hast thou considered that"?

"I understand thee nought", I was growing agitated, my confusion was increasing, "How can I belong in this body when I am not Roxbrough"?

Lolocken then observed, "Thou looks like the Lord of Roxbrough, my Lord. Thou soundeth like the Lord of Roxbrough. Might it not be that thou art indeed the Lord of that Keep? That thou hast been labouring 'neath an illusion, that thou art the mysterious Visionary who returned to his bubble on the Fire of Saah".

"He did no such thing", I countered, "He asked Hersko to send him to Earth, by use of the Vandei Motestas". I stopped talking and realised that once again I was referring to myself in the third person. "I meanest *I* got the Lord of the Hand of Power to send *me* back to Earth. I am Nik Gehenna, thou canst not get me back to my rightful body, Bodakin? So thou chooseth to believe I am whom I look so like. I thought thou might have more power"?

"My Lord, I believe thou art labouring under a strain", Bodakin began, but suddenly the android cut into the conversation in Valgraln,

Myrrorball

"His Lordship has been in the company of Mister Genks, perhaps when he surfaces he will be able to clear up this malady and its source once and for all"?

"Mister Genks be on Earth II"! I looked at each of them in turn. It was impossible to discern the metal man's expression, for he never had one. The others seemed sympathetically concerned, concerned for Roxbrough, not me.

"Hízlatan", I finally tried, "You knew the Visionary better than anyone else present, who do you think I am? Did you ever hear the Lord of Roxbrough speak Kémerié"?

The Szorkráló shook his head, "But all that does is pose the question, do my ears or my eyes deceive me"?

"I don't suppose...".

"That I could tell either way? No Sir, I could not. I am a simple Szorkráló. It seems to me that the best hope you have lies with the warrior who never removes his armour, the Knight of Roid".

It was hopeless. 23 might be many things, but he did not have the power to wake me from either a lengthy incubus or a delusion filled narcotic episode. I only had one choice as far as I could see. That was to play it out and see what happened when I woke up - if ever. I gave up talking to them, excused myself claiming fatigue. Lolocken offered me quarters, but I was not sufficiently happy in their reactions to accept, so left the castle there and then. That night I stopped in an inn and was on the road again by dawn's first light the following morning. I did not expect to find any answers in my home seat, or rather *his* home seat, but that was my destination. Where else would I go? After a while, the towns began to blur into one another, my funds were being exhausted. With luck I would reach Roxbrough town before they did, otherwise, I would be sleeping under the stars, eating very little. Mirafuzela, Cant and Scor Pass were all behind me when the mountain winding road began to drain me considerably. I reached the village of Halfmount as darkness was falling on the umpteenth day of my journey. I had lost count of how long the effects of somnalude had continued fooling my brain, were Mister Genks telling the truth. Something else had happened if what 23 had intimated was actual.

I was considerably more exhausted than anyone had ever been before. In all the time I had been on Rozhelia, I had not had any sleep. If my existence was real, I should be surely dead. When I lay down at night all that happened was the little electric shocks became more frequent and strange patterns danced on the back of my eyelids. Patterns that were as the sort that dapples the sunlight when filtered through wind stirred leaves on a tree. Yet I was indoors, it was dark, there were no trees in each of the rooms I had hired for the night. Something else had happened since Tantelaa as well. People avoided me, none had ever actively sought my company in the first place, but now it was different. I saw figures cross streets to avoid getting into proximity with me. It was not a broad occurrence, they did not avoid one another, just me. That night as I lay totally exhausted beyond enormous fatigue, urgently wishing with all my heart to finally emerge from the trip, once again failing I climbed out of the cot and saw that there was a burnished copper plate on the wall. Going over to it, I quickly discerned the reason for those who had avoided getting close to me. I looked dreadful.

Huge dark bags were under my eyes, my mouth turned down into a permanently dreadful scowl. Hair once thick, blonde and wavy had lost its colour, grown very fine. It was possible to see my scalp through it. My shoulders stooped, my limbs dangled from a skeletally thin frame. What I was looking at, was a dead man who had refused to accept that the life force had drained from his body. True I was still technically alive, but I was no longer *alive*.

Realising I had only kept going so that I could reach Roxbrough town I arose and painfully slowly dressed. The keeper of the stables did not take kindly to being rudely roused from his bed at the late hour, but there was no help for it. I sensed I needed to reach my wife and children before I expired. I meant his wife and children though did I not... or, was there no longer any distinction? I reasoned I would soon start hallucinating if

I could not rest my brain. Everything depended upon my reaching the town at the crest of the mountains. A small populace that had made their home by carving domains out of the granite of the mountainside itself.

My trusty steed, whom I had named Trusty, continued through the darkness up the winding road that circumnavigated the mountain. I was just able to glimpse a few lights in the distance when a tremendous wave of fatigue washed over me. Though I felt myself falling from Trusty's back, could do nothing to break my fall. Fortunately, my armour saved me from serious injury on the rocky ground. I felt acute relief that I had not broken any bones as I fell...

103.

...asleep. I have no idea how long the blackness lasted when I awoke though I felt mightily refreshed. Opening my eyes, I already knew where I was, the throbbing of the Zeppelin engines had told me that. Twisting my neck to one side, it was to see Mister Genks, eyes wide open staring at me.

"I think you lied to me", was my opening line.

"How do you feel"? He asked.

"What did you give me Genksy"? I demanded.

"Thomnalude".

"I did not sleep, I was in the body of Roxbrough, remember him? I could not sleep. I was awake for days, it almost killed me".

"You were athleep for exactly 23 minutes", the manbian lisped, looking at his wristwatch. Disbelieving me, I looked at my own gold Casio. The time indicated he was right, above the hours and minutes the day and date showed me it was still the same as the one I have left.

Major Roxbrough & Nik Gehenna

"That cannot be", I complained, "I was gone for days and days. I took part in a battle, I was inside the body of...".

"You dreamed", Mister Genks cut into my diatribe, "All that you dethcribe was the thubject of your dream, nothing more".

"23 told me you would say that when I discussed somnalude with him he indicated to me that...".

"The 23 of your dream. He will have thaid whatthoever your subconthiouth wanted him to thay. That ith the magic of thomnalude, it theemth tho real".

"Who am I, Mister Genks"?

"Nik Merkwürdig a collector of rare books and a budding author".

"Budding author"? I finally managed a grin, "I've written...".

"Nik Merkwürdig ith unpublithed".

"All right, point taken but, Genksy, it seemed so real".

The manbian gave me a curious look and observed quite unexpectedly,

"Perhapth it wath".

"What on Earth do you mean by that"? I was instantly annoyed, where was he going with this latest silliness?

"Thomnalude lifth barrierth, Nik. Perhapth you are the illuthion and the Lord of Rokthborough ith who you are".

"Don't be ridiculous"! I exploded, "I've live twenty odd years in the reality I am in now. I spent a few days in Roxbrough's body, how can I be..."?

Durathion hath no meaning to thomnalude, every aspect of your deluthion might have been leading up to the one moment when the veil wath lifted, when you got to thee who you really wath for the firtht time in your life".

"Are you and 23 working in tandem on this", I was livid, "Are you both Zernoplatite agents of some sort trying to turn me gah gah billy-bonkers"?

The manbian calmly shook his head, his calmness finally filtered down to me.

"If this is an illusion, if my entire life has been fiction, then the only sensible thing I can do is to continue to live on with it. So let's get the book to one of our customers before we steal off them to sell to the other"?

Back to plan - 'a'. Although it was dangerous and might very well get us tortured and finally killed.

Even though I had only been *asleep* for 23 minutes, I felt thoroughly refreshed, so Mister Genks and I went to the refectory and had a lovely supper/breakfast until the flight ended. I had not the chance to think about my bizarre trip under the influence of somnalude for quite some time after that. We travelled back to the shop, were reunited with Quianhua and Evie. My wife (If she was my wife) seemed delighted to see me returned and showed her appreciation that night in our bed. Afterwards, as she slumbered with a slight susurrating snore, I once again lay awake, unable to achieve sleep. One thing I did not want to do was go to Mister Genks and ask for another pill. The last time had been enough for me, it would not have been so bad if the trip had seemed to last for very real 23 minutes, but I had been gone for days. I wanted to sell the book, take the money, steal it, sell it again, make more money, who knew what then? I could not think that far ahead, the future was not worth speculating about. One thing at a time. I carefully climbed out of bed, went downstairs to make a cup of tea. The kettle was gone. I was not going to wake Quianhua over a kettle, so I put a little water in a pan, placing it on the gas stove to boil, there is more than one way to skin a Kézőrös. As I was putting a tea-bag in a mug I noticed something rustling in the pocket of my burgundy and purple bohos, it was my little sachet of snufz.

I do not believe I was addicted when I look back on it now. I knew with certainty that I was not then. So no dread or morbid thoughts gripped me when my fingers closed around the little draw-top sachet and pulled it out. It had given me insight in the past, informed me of things I could not know any other way. I was a person who wanted answers, always. It seemed at that time that I had more questions, should I take just a modest pinch up one nostril and see what happened? It was not the hit (I reasoned) that I was seeking at that point. It was the reasoning, the strange ability to understand, even without evidence. Seating myself at the kitchen table, I considered all these matters, calmly and logically. I did not see that I had any choice but to use the narcotic once again.

Snufz was a tobacco/lichen from Mars, a combination product. Like cigarettes, 1in2's cigars it contained harmful and addictive chemicals that could raise one's risk of many health problems. To produce snufz, tobacco and lichen was dried and finely ground. The Kémerké had used a pestle and mortar for that part of the preparation. Where they had gotten the lichen from was anyone's guess. Possibly wind-born spores from over the ocean had finally found their way to Egszígør, the lichen was home-grown. How it had reached Rozhelia though, was in the realms of science fiction, which used to be my field, but recently I seemed to have drifted into Fantasy. There were two preparations of snufz, dried or moist. To use the former, one inhaled the ground concoction into the nasal cavity. To use moist snufz, one placed it between the lower lip or cheek and gum. The nicotine from the tobacco was thusly absorbed through the lining of the nose or mouth. Like cigars, cigarettes, pipe tobacco, and chewing tobacco, snufz was, therefore, a dangerous and addictive product. Not only highly addictive but also harmful to health. One could be forgiven for assuming that the use of snufz was not as dangerous as smoking since the user was not inhaling smoke into the lungs. Snufz conversely could have a still higher negative impact on the body, not only that but its hallucinatory effects could lead to schizophrenia or other mental disorders. Psychiatric disorder, behavioural or mental patterns that caused significant distress or impairment of personal functioning. Such features were persistent, relapsing, remitting, or occur as a single episode. Many of the disorders had been described, with signs and symptoms that varied widely between specific disorders. Additionally, like other forms of tobacco, snufz contained cancer-causing chemicals. It could raise the risk of several types of cancer.

I wanted answers though, I could be considered reckless in my single-minded demand for such. I was fully prepared to take the risk to get some. Taking a small, deliberately so for all the reasons detailed before, a pinch of the gift given me seemingly so long ago, I snorted it up my left nostril. My choice of sides being completely arbitrary but possibly being because the angle was easier when I was right-handed. In a matter of three or four seconds, I felt the familiar hit...

104.

...I was back on the horse. Strolling toward a mountain village cut out of the granite side of it. I barely had time to realise what was happening when from one home of rock a figure darted, cried out in a mixture of relief and joy, then began to dash toward me. By the time she had covered half of the distance that lay between the stone abode and my horse, I recognised who it was and almost dismounted by accident in shock. It was impossible!

The woman running to greet me was Quianhua!

How?

When?

Why?

Was some strange force playing a cruel joke upon me? Why of all the women I could have imagined being Roxbrough's wife had I made my wife - his?

I dismounted, Quianhua was in my arms babbling how relieved she was to see me, how overjoyed. My appearance must have changed since my first trip then, I must have looked normally. She spoke in Valgraln, yet with a curious accent that was not Chinese of origin. She smelled the same, so did her hair. My illusion of her (if it was an illusion?) was complete in every way. If I questioned her at once, I would frighten her, so I remained stoic and spoke little. My resolve almost crumbled when four rather obvious half-breed youngsters crowded around us. Still sallow of complexion but with eyes some way between mine and Quianhua's, they were hers. Hers and Roxbrough's.

I remembered their names, which I had heard on the Fire of Saah, Rox, Bruff, Zen and Ia, meaning my wife, the image of Quianhua was called Zenia. They ushered us all inside and all the while plying me with questions. I found myself answering them as if I were Roxbrough himself. Finally, Zenia sent the youngsters outside so that she and I could talk quietly for a while. The instant they had done as directed, she was in my arms and her mouth was on mine. She kissed like Quianhua, tasted like Quianhua, felt like Quianhua. We broke the embrace breathlessly and I asked her, unable to contain myself any longer,

"Tell me how we met darling before I tell you what adventure I had on the Fire of Saah"?

"Your speech, your accent, both are changed, Husband? Have your adventures made so much of a difference to you"?

"It would seem that they have, yes. Please, Zenia, I need to relive the moment before I speak of my quest and what became of everyone, tell me how we met"?

Her oriental appearance was then explained quite easily. If I have an illusion, it has to make scientific sense. Zenia was from a little town at the base of the Hango Range of mountains in the mysterious northern arm of the Cross, called Fansui. The town was called Chochu. I tried to imagine how Rozhelia had paralleled our planet Earth with its different races, it seemed logical to suppose that on other worlds in the galaxy there would not be one lone sentient-life on those containing it. We had our different races of man, so why could not they? **Logical you see Hhrrhhoehhrrhooooingohh, even like my delusion.** All I had done was to replace one narcotic with another, somnalude for snufz, the logic of my mind had continued my very same illusion.

Or?

Were the two drugs opening the gateway *from* my illusion, back to reality? How could I possibly know the answer to that? Rather than bestow me with knowledge, which snufz had done in the past, it was now adding to my conundrums. All I could do was go with it for the time being and see where the whole thing would lead me.

Myrrorball

Time passed, I found Zenia to be every bit as lovely as her counterpart, the children a delight, eventually though I grew tired, after several days of simply lying beside the lady of Roxbrough I fell...

105.

....asleep and woke up in the shop. This time was different. Time had passed in Earth II. I had no recollection of how my body had conducted itself during the absence of my quiddity. I went to speak to Mister Genks about it. He was no help, yet I got the impression he was as mystified as me when I quizzed him.

"I've been on Rozhelia, Genksy, so who was walking about in my body and speaking my conversations. How could I be in both places at the same time? Was an imposter in my body, while my mind was elsewhere"? The manbian looked at me with an expression of genuine alarm on his green visage,

"Thould I have any idea what you are talking about, Nik"?

"I took snufz and found myself on Rozhelia once again, a continuation of the trip I made after you'd given me somnalude".

Thomnalude? It ith a thoporific, Nik, nothing more. You thlept, remember, on the way home on the air-thhip"?

"And I told you nothing about having an experience in the other world, about finding myself in Roxbrough's body? You must remember, we discussed it at length, you even postulated that Roxbrough might be who I was, that this world might be the illusion"?

He laughed, a sort of croaky-chuckle,

"I athure you, Nik, I am not an illuthion, I am ath real ath the motht real thing you can imagine. I come from the 33rd thentury, brought back in time to help you, by the Zernoplat, you remember the Zernoplat"?

I sighed, "Yes, I remember too much it would seem, even things that you claim have never happened. It does not matter, forget we had this conversation too. We must instead concentrate on selling the book. You do remember what we are going to do about that, right"?

"Of coursth thell it to Thicherheithpolizei (ThiPo Thecurity Polithe) the Gethtapo, Kopf Inthpektor Verner deGoethe. Then thteal it from him to thell to Zoˇngjiān Jianyu Zhao of the Mìmì jiˇngchá".

That caused me to grin, observe, "Your Chinese is better than your German, my friend. I will go and give the Kopf Inspektor a ring".

"On the immobile-corded telephone? You have already done tho, earlier thith morning".

"Oh, when is he coming then"?

The door opened at that very instant and in walked the devil himself. Dressed in a sharp black uniform with scarlet piping, his jodhpurs - that were tucked into tall leather riding boots, the latter shining like mirrors, dark mirrors that reflected even darker images. I shook the thought from my mind and forced myself to smile,

"Kopf Inspektor deGoethe, speak of the devil".

He did not appreciate the levity, responded coldly, "Remember the three-point plan, Merkwürdig", just-in-case I had forgotten the Nazi doctrine, he reiterated it for me:

1. The Reichstag is all.
2. Security is paramount.
3. Careless talk can cost lives.

You do not think of me as Beelzebub do you Merkwürdig, so that is a contravention of rule numbers 2 and 3".

"I feel suitably admonished, Kopf Inspektor deGoethe, my apologies. Would you like to come into the back of the store for a moment, I have a very interesting volume that might be of interest to you"?

Squeezing the valise under his arm just a shade tighter, the Inspektor clicked his heels, I took that to mean affirmation. Through a glass beaded curtain that Quianhua had thoughtfully filled the jamb with, I led him. Quickly spun the combination lock on the safe and produced the book. All the while the Nazi's attention had been focused on my wife. It seemed the Germans held their allies in some kind of combination of suspicion and awe. Africa had proved a dark jewel, with its wealth of natural resources, it had made the balance of power shift from Europe to The East. It threatened the Fourth Reich, which was supposed to last for twenty-three thousand years.

Kopf Inspektor deGoethe took the book reverently in black leather-clad hands and opened it to the relevant page.

"You have authenticated the age, the validity of the signature, this is the genuine article"?

Quianhua came to my rescue, "Using the necessary technology, I have Xiānshēng deGoethe".

He nodded, threw open the top of the valise with a waving motion and slipped the prized tome inside. With his free hand, he delved into the leather envelope of the slim case and drew forth several bundles of neatly banded notes. They were English Marks, one-thousand denomination notes. I was a rich man for the first time in my life.

deGoethe left quickly and without any ceremony whatsoever, while Quianhua deftly loaded our safe with the money. The entire transaction had not involved me as much as I had anticipated, or was that my imagination?

106.

"I do not need the aid of the sorcerer, or any mage for that matter", Cassiti told her husband, "Will you stop fussing"?

"I want you to come with us on the morrow? To ride north, rejoin our noble friends and help them with their resistance. Hopefully, Bodakin will be with them and can help thee. Please join us for the sake of my peace of mind"?

"What do you think he can help me with exactly"? Cassiti demanded to know, "Do I have some malady so slight that even I know nothing of it"?

Hersko was honest in his response, "You be changed Cassiti, since your death...".

"Since I fell asleep and you woke me you mean", she cut him short.

"Fell asleep"! He tried with only partial success to keep his temper, "Fell asleep with a knife through your lung, fatally and seriously stabbed. What sort of slumber would that be exactly"?

"If it had been as fatal as you are trying to have me believe, then how is it that I now breathe, talk, walk around. You exaggerate, Husband".

"I certainly hope I doest not, considering your murderer was hanged drawn and quartered", Hersko returned with as little heat as he could manage.

"I was sorry to hear that Surgeon's end was so humiliatingly gruesome", Cassiti noted, "Yet he was guilty of foolish medical malpractice due to stupid superstition. That is not a capital offence, is it"?

"If the patient died as a result of that malpractice"?

Cassiti shrugged, she had used that body language quite a few times since her demise and subsequent reanimation, nothing seemed to move her as it should, she was cold, distant, the word Hersko was frequently tempted, yet dare not employ - soulless. Finally, he begged,

"Come with us then as the native warrior you once were Cassiti, some of the Lords will be pleased to receive you as mine new bride. Come for that reason"?

Myrrorball

Normally, the girl would have brightened at just such a suggestion. On that occasion, she sighed as though fatigued by her husband's persistence and finally reluctantly conceded,

"To satisfy you, I will come, Hersko, as your bodyguard, is that acceptable to you"?

The young Lord would have agreed to anything, he agreed to that.

The group that rode out of pestilence-torn Flahé hours later were only a pathetic score of riders strong. The Lord, his son and daughter-in-law together with seventeen guards. What they could do for those who currently opposed the western invaders was to provide moral support and very little else. It was also rumoured that the Geişvəhşilic was spreading through the south-eastern regions of the country. More than just swords were challenging for supremacy in Valgral it seemed.

The roads were curiously empty of travellers. It had become dangerous to be abroading unless backed by a substantially armed escort. The route they took was simple, a straight line for Laaterfell. Between there and Flahé were the town of Fordítás, later on, Kreel. At the former, they encountered the ravaged remains of a town gripped by pestilence. They did not stay in it, preferring to camp on its edges to avoid any further contagion. It was worrying though, had the Geişvəhşilic also spread westerly to threaten Hegyekben or even as far south as Kingshire itself?

All the answers would be in Laaterfell. Kreel was locked up, barricaded, ready to repel any who sought to enter the town limits. It was decided not to try and entreat them for overnight accommodation, but once again to camp. Only an admirably short time later had they reached the town were the combined forces of east and west would conduct their immense battle. it took them quite a while to find their former friends and comrades, Laaterfell had become a huge garrison, readying itself for a gargantuan struggle that would determine the outcome of the war. If the east lost, Koözoött and Kyper Tor could ride for Kingshire practically unopposed.

Major Roxbrough & Nik Gehenna

Flahé, his son and daughter-in-law left their horse with their pitifully miniscule guard and proceeded on foot, where they found they whom they sought in the Lord's manor. The young Lord of Laaterfell was eleven summers only, but following his father's death on the Fire of Saah found himself master of the town. When the travellers entered the room, there were greetings embraces and exclamations of delight all round.

Zemtel first Lord of Kingshire - Interfectorem regem declared, "Azdja, but it be good to see thee, my Lords of Flahé, how many troops dost thou bringeth to swell our ranks, ready to drive the westerners back up into the sea of Fansui"?

Flahé frowned, for he had liked Vasnaar despite his failings, and declared baldly,

"Seventeen, the rest are either expired due to Geişvəhşilic or still have some mikroloblar in their bodies, we were in no fit state to bring any more".

"Then we shall have to make do with what we have", piped up the eleven-year-old Latterfell, determined to have his voice heard, even if it had not then broken nor his balls dropped.

Zemtel frowned, "The enemy has the services of the Necromancer, he constantly reanimates the Animataverous, thank the gods that thou art with us Geogon".

Hersko turned to the mage, asked, "What happened to Bodakin, where is he"?

"Thy tongue has become exceeding strange", the ancient thaumaturge observed, "And thou art accented. I will wager

thou has a convoluted, yet absorbing tale to tell, Young Lordling".

Hersklo railed, " Úrrh – Warrior Lord of Akerányó actually, Thaumaturge. Where is Bodakin"?

"Why back on the Isle of Dorass-Van-der-Garra-Plee of course, greatly debilitated by all the sorcery he was forced to machinate, in order to get thee all back to the dominion thou shouldst never have left".

"We had to obey our King", Hersko argued, "He had a great desire for Корунд (Corundum) which, it be said is, a bluer blue than the eyes of the goddess Shakita and that is very blue indeed".

"Foolish greed. The need to pleaseth his wife didst cause the death of too many", Geogon was no diplomat. "Little wonder the Interfectorem regem plotted and enacted his murder. He was not a good monarch. Indeed, it be possible he was the worst King that e-er sat upon the throne of Valgral".

"Will Bodakin survive his rigours"?

"Do not fret young man, Bodakin possesses tremendous obduracy, Parasprio will have to wait yet a while before sending the grim reaper to collect the Sorcerer".

"Then it is to you that I address my request", Hersko declared.

"Thou hast boon to ask, then ask it, my Lord. Ifin it be in mine power to grant I will do for thee that which be righteously true "?

Hersko patiently explained the events leading up to his wife's murder and how he had used the power of the Vandei Motestas to drag her back from the grave, into the land of the living. At his explanation, the heavily lined features of the Thaumaturge grew grave, he observed when Lord's narrative was complete,

"What thou did was against the natural laws of man and the gods, my Lord Hersko. I be not certain that my thaumaturgy be anywhere near powerful enough to return the quiddity of Cassiti to her fleshly shell".

"Where is her essence then, if it's not in her body"? Hersko asked urgently.

"Limbo", came the grave response. "The region on the border of Azdja or Cənnəc, serving as the abode after the death of infants. Those righteous who died before the coming of the gods. A place or state of oblivion to which persons or things regarded as being relegated when cast aside. Forgotten, past, or out of date, an intermediate, transitional, or midway state or place. A place or state of imprisonment or confinement".

"Yet there must be a way of bringing her back", Hersko persisted, half in obduracy, half in hope, "And if there is Geogon, the one person who would know who to approach is you, is that not so"?

Geogon frowned, not because of his ignorance, rather the opposite. He knew the answer to Hersko's dilemma but did not want to admit it. Almost espying the thoughts behind the ancient mage's eyes, the young Lord persisted, "I love the woman, Thaumaturge, so you know why I am pressing you. Give me the name"?

"It is not possible", the Thaumaturge countered, "The only one I know of who has the power to drag a quiddity from limbo is the most evil man I have ever encountered".

"Yet not too evil to have a name, nor even a location"?

"The Necromancer, Banustib".

107.

Surprise, surprise, Sicherheitspolizei (SiPo Security Police) the Gestapo, Kopf Inspektor Verner deGoethe lived in a veritable fortress. That was not the worst of it. I thought I was going to have a somewhat stressful evening. I did not know the half of it. I was going to have a stressful squared evening[2] after Mister Genks dropped the bombshell.

"How are we going to get inside the police headquarters, Genksy"? I had asked him. His reply was like a punch right between my naive eyes,

"*We* are not", the manbian returned simply, "*You* are. I cannot come with you for obvious rethonth".

I was obtuse then when I demanded,

"What obvious reason, explain it to me"?

"How can I ptthibly thneak into Gethtapo headqurterth unobtherved"?

"So I've got to steal the book, on my own, with nobody with me, solo"?

He nodded his domed head and then assured, "I have thomething for you that will make opening the thafe eathier".

"What is it, a manbian brain to put in my head"?

"Remember I went to Tandy yethterday, for thome mythterious componenth. I tholdered thith together for you".

He handed me a small device with an earplug on a suction cup. The body of the device was a box with a sucker on the back of it. I knew at once what it was.

"This is to help me hear the tumblers drop, as I turn the combination lock. How do we know that it will be a combi-lock though".

From the doorway, it was Quianhua who answered, "While you were in America on your jolly travels, I was busy on the internet. The Germans mistrust keys, they are obsessed with combination locks of different sorts. The Gestapo will involve more than one to get through to reach our goal most likely".

"Our"? I picked up on it at once, "Who - our, you seriously don't think you're coming with me"?

"I seriously do", she smiled, "If things go wrong, who better to get you out of Gestapo headquarters than a Chinese diplomat"?

"But you're not a diplomat", I pointed out reasonably. Quianhua said no more but handed me some papers. I looked at them, they looked genuine, but there again I was no judge. Mister Genks added,

"And here are yourth Nik, you are now a major in the Gethtapo".

"These are fakes, how good are they, will they fool the Germans"?

"This is peacetime, Nik. The Germans in England have grown complacently lazy. They will barely look at the paperwork. There is only one way we can become undone", my spouse informed me, "And that is if we are unfortunate enough to run into Kopf Inspektor Verner deGoethe himself".

"So what is the plan then"? I was beginning to be swayed toward it. "Because we cannot simply walk into the place, flash our fake papers and enter deGoethe's office, steal the book from his safe and walk out again".

Quianhua laughed, "Why not and how did you know that was the plan"?

"Thimple, Nik", the manbian added, "Thimple hath leth chanthe of going wrong".

"And if something does go wrong, what then"?

"You have the blazerifle, Quianhua will have the thearpithtol".

A stressful squared evening[2.] Evie had proved to be a whizz with the sewing machine, my uniform fit better than the majority since it was handmade-to-measure. I have to confess that I was *bricking it* leading up to the evening, but it had been my plan (what had I been thinking?) to steal the book to make twice the profit. The only trouble was if it all went wrong, I doubt my ultimate fate would be a pleasant one!

We left the shop under cover of darkness, though the streets were orange with the sodium illumination of German-made street-lights. In many ways, technology had not progressed quite as fast in Earth II as the one I had spent the majority of my life. The German victory had made my race more staid and stoic, almost subservient to their allies in the axis. The other strange omission was the space-race. Without a cold war between the USSR and America, there had not been one at all. No man had ever set foot on the moon. Although considering what had then happened for the next fifty years, it was not such a loss. There was no starvation in Africa, following the annihilation of the aborigines. Similarly, South America was all the better for being occupied. Under the Great Chinese Empire, the East was a settled realm. In Earth II only the middle east had fared badly, now a forgotten nuclear wasteland, but in real cost, probably something mister average would have settled for over the alternative.

"Are you all right", Quianhua shattered my reverie.

"Just peachy", I retorted, feeling anything but.

The Gestapo headquarters in Talford was on the set-back estate of Swastika Avenue, which ran the entire length of the town. Not especially well lit as there was little to do in the evenings and only a skeleton staff would be on duty. With practical martial law being the norm, one thing the Nazi's had brought to the country was law and order. Capital punishment existed for Murder, Rape, Armed Robbery, Equipped Burglary and Treason. It worked, any perpetrators were quickly phased out - permanently. Compared to America, Europe and China were very safe places to live.

I was about to break one of those capital laws. For stealing from the Sicherheitspolizei (SiPo Security Police) the Gestapo, Kopf Inspektor would be viewed by the courts as espionage. For some reason, as we walked toward the headquarters, I heard *Volte-Face* playing in my head from the brilliant Second Life Syndrome by the best band in the worlds - Riverside.

Everything went monochrome and grainy, figuratively speaking. I was in the middle of a WWII filum noire. I felt my perception shift, suddenly I was O S S. Responding to the thrill of danger, the stimulation a tingle of risk. I was going up against the Krauts, happy to do so. A bored-looking guard was at the front gate. He looked at the two of us with eyes half-closed with ennui. As expected, he barely glanced at the papers, the visual effect of my uniform and perfect German as I told him that an inspection was being conducted, being enough for his fuddled mind. He opened the gate to allow us passage, we strode inside, filled with confidence. My nerves seemed to have settled down. I felt for the first time that we were going to pull off this gamble with room to spare.

It was not a difficult task to find the office of the Kopf Inspektor of Sicherheitspolizei, with typical German efficiency, the place was festooned with signs. On the way to it, we passed an orderly who did not even ask us for papers. I suppose he presumed that if we had gotten past the gate, then our business was legitimate, My blazerifle was over my shoulder but under my black leather greatcoat, without enough of it showing to raise any suspicion either. I ardently hoped I would not have to use it. With makeup and temporary hair dye, both of us looked, unlike our usual appearance. Our descriptions would be vague indeed, once the robbery was discovered.

Major Roxbrough & Nik Gehenna

Neither of us had been closely scrutinised, we both had raises in our shoes to make us seem taller. I wore heavily horn-rimmed glasses besides - while Quianhua had her hair tucked up under a Chinese policewoman pillbox hat.

The office door, as expected, was locked. Mister Genks had taught me well though. With two picks I had it open in twelve seconds, the safe was going to take quite a significantly longer spell than that. As we had planned, Quianhua stood to watch outside while I slipped into  the room alone and turned on my torch. I gasped, frozen to the spot. Lining every one of the walls, even the one containing the door, were row upon row of books. Had I been there to rob the Kopf Inspektor of anything I found as would be to my liking I would have needed two sacks, one for each of us to throw over our shoulders.

There was every classic German book that I knew about, additionally various Chinese volumes, some English and even some American texts and fictional literature. The office was a treasure trove of tomes, so much so that I was not able to fathom the lax security between it and the outside worlds. I then considered where it was, to whom the place belonged. Why lock a place up like a vault when it was the domain of possibly the most feared man in the town, maybe even the county? The thought made me shiver as I reluctantly tore my gaze from the display, to cross to the safe. Was I tempted to take anything other than what I had entered in pursuit? I would be suspect number one in the disappearance of Mein Kampf. If I only took that one book, then Zo˘ngjiān Jianyu Zhao of the Mìmì ji˘ngchá would be the one that deGoethe would think of immediately as the Zauberbücher-Thief. For it was common knowledge that the Chinese desired the book as much as the man who now possessed it and would be the first to pop into his mind. What was perfect was that unless deGoethe could immediately locate the

Myrrorball

book, once I had sold it to Zoˇngjiān Jianyu Zhao of the Mìmì jiˇngchá, he could not give the German my name. Not without admitting that he had it. Unlike deGoethe, all he had to do was send it to China and deny everything. At least that was how Mister Genks had put it to me, I had accepted it as the most likely series of events. I was, of course, grimly forced so to do. My life depended upon it.

So I could have found a hand-signed Bible penned by, God Himself and would not have taken anything other than Hitler's work from that office that night. I licked the suction cup on the back of the device the manbian had created and stuck it close to the tumbler before patiently going to work. For a while, I was methodically calm, until I realised how long it was taking me to do the job. There were six tumblers to fall, I had taken five minutes to locate the first one. The buzzing of growing anxiety in my ears was making it extremely difficult to listen for the soft click of success. Five minutes, surely someone would challenge Quianhua if she remained outside the door, not moving for half an hour. I began to sweat, the perspiration running into my eyes and stinging them. I closed them, perhaps I could hear better that way?

Then I froze, a conversation was being conducted outside. I was straining to hear it instead of the tumblers falling. Recklessly I pulled the earplug out, went over to the door, placing my head against it.

"...perfectly fine now thank you, Guān. Please take the glass with you I require no more water. Resume your duties I will be fine in a moment", Quianhua was saying. I could easily recreate the rest of the conversation. Her position had been questioned outside the door, she had feigned a swooning fit, or getting close to one. The Gestapo officer had brought her water, probably a chair allowing her to dismiss him. I returned to the job in hand, ever aware that time was passing, with each second our chances of being apprehended. Being a prisoner of the Gestapo was not a fate I relished, I had to hurry up.

108.

The Captain of the Guard excused his intrusion and then informed,

"A young couple from the East have been apprehended at the edge of the camp, my Lord. They were riding in as bold as brass when arrested the youth claimed he was bringing the young woman in his company to seek an audience with the necromancer".

Banustib ceased looking at the map on the Lord's desk, his features growing suddenly animate with interest,

"With me, not one of his Lordships"?

"Aye", the captain refused to give the Necromancer a title, knowing he was the one who was creating the Animataverous. The growing unease amongst the superstitious in the armed forces was one of fearful ferment when considering necromancy - its results. At the head of such - Banustib - Necromancer and Vile Wizard.

Koözoött looked amused,

"They risked gods know what to speak to the Necromancer here"?

"Aye, my Lord".

"Didst thou get names", Kyper Tor entered the conversation.

The captain nodded, adding, "Readily given, but I suspect they be anonyms. They currently answer to Kohser and Sittasc"

Intrigued, Banustib decided, "I will see them in mine own tent, Captain. Bring them to me in ten minutes".

"Thine own tent"? Kyper Tor grinned, "Without guards, unarmed as thou art"?

The expression was quickly wiped from his face when Banustib replied,

"Even unarmed I be far more dangerous than thee, my Lord of Tor. Excuse me, lord Koözoött? I doubt this will take long".

Once the Necromancer was out of earshot, Kyper Tor turned to Koözoött, promised,

"The day will come when we needeth not the services of that horrible man, then shall I be sorely delighted to slip a dirk between his ribs".

Myrrorball

Koözoött laughed, "That will be an interesting confrontation, my Lord of Tor".

Banustib hurried to his tent, caftan flapping in the strictly unseasonal northern wind. Heightened by the change from the weather on the Fire of Saah, the climate on Valgral had turned uncharacteristically cold for spring. The Necromancer had no liking nor comfort for its bite. He was thusly doubly thankful to get back to his tent when drizzle was also perceived in the breeze. Taking a seat behind his desk he waited patiently for the couple to be brought to him. His wait was not great of duration.

The same captain brought them to him, curtly announced their arrival before hurriedly leaving the three of them together. The mage scrutinised the duo. Though they were in humble attire proclaiming them as plebeian, by their cleanliness and styling of hair, they were incommunicado nobility.

Banustib directed them to two folding chairs before asking,

"So, thou hast the ear of the necromancer thou seeketh, what of it, my Lord".

"Begging thy pardon, master, but I be no lord", the youth, claiming to be Kohser asserted, I be a simple farmer from Pelmuth".

"Thou certainly has the garb to qualify such claim", the Necromancer smiled, "Yet thy ablute, the cut of thy tress denies that as an lie. Not only that, but the accent thou giveth tongue to be too cultured to make of thee a simple farmer. So, Eastern Noble, whom I should regard as, Enemy, what wanteth thou of me"?

The young man seemed to come to some decision after wrestling with inner turmoil and asked,

"My partner here was slain by an vile villain, I brought her back from the land of limbo with this".

He pulled a scruffy (but clean) glove from his hand, what was inside it truly fascinated the mage.

"Be that..."?

"The Vandei Motestas, that it be, Banustib, that it be".

Major Roxbrough & Nik Gehenna

"Then thou must have been on the Fire of Saah, aligned with the fallen king. Whom art thou now aligned with, my Lord"?

"Methinks that my alignment be now with none, or mayhap just myself", the young man returned, he was quite reckless, of great bravery to speak so boldly to the Necromancer and was admired for it in return.

"Might thou be the son of Kynoberg by any chance"? Banustib wished to know.

"My spouse's quiddity be locked in limbo, ifin thou canst hep us, then will I give thee my true identity", came the firm reply.

Banustib was evil, depraved, without decent conscience or any hint of guilt for all he had done in the past. Yet he could also be impulsive, capricious, whimsical. He finally smiled and admitted,

"I have never been to limbo, mayhap tis time to change that state of affairs".

"Thou will help us"?

"The woman seems docile and lacking in any sort of resolution, wouldst thou not consider that to be an improvement? Does it not make of her, the perfect woman"?

"I preferred her as she was before she was murdered", the youth persisted, "Will I be coming with thee"?

"Hardly".

"And for thy service, what payment dost thou want of me, Banustib"?

The Necromancer looked at the woman, she was very attractive, shapely, he asked simply, "One night with her, then thou canst have her for the rest of thy lives".

The youth seemed gripped in some inner conflict, but finally, he demanded,

"Ifin I agree, we will be free to walk out of this camp without further molestation"?

"Thou has my word on it", the mage grinned mischievously.

109.

I remain unsure as to what caused me to suddenly grow either more adept, or fortunate. When I returned to the safe though, the tumblers inside the dial began to fall like very easily-falling tumblers, or ninepins if you prefer. Thanking my lucky stars, which was about the only thing I believed in any more (blind luck), I heaved the door open. On top of a very classy Leica single-lens, focal-plane shuttered reflex camera was the copy of Mein Kampf that Adolf had dedicated to his wife, Eva Braun. It suddenly came to me why deGoethe had not buried it in an underground fortress somewhere? In his moments of free time from mercilessly searching for the remnants of Jewish communities in England. Plus some other forms of recreational torture to extract vital information from enemies of the Nazi party, he wanted to read it. Revisit it perhaps, many times? The volume was his doctrine, his bible.

Then it was suddenly neither. **It was mine (not my precious, even though you might be thinking that Hhrrhhoe-hhrrhooooingohh and if you have not yet read J R R by now, then you should)**. I slipped it into the inside pocket of my tunic, which had been deliberately sewn so that it fit, like it was made for it, which, come to think of it - it was. Hurrying to the door, I took Quianhua's arm, she was already rising from the provided hard-backed chair. Explanations could wait for later if there was a later. We found it very difficult to seem to stroll out of the headquarters. For every fibre of our being was screaming at us to dash, to sprint out of there, as though our lives depended upon it. Which, of course, it did. To look like we were in a hurry was to alert others to suspicion. I had relocked the safe, the earphone was in my pocket, during the entire procedure I had never removed my gloves. Strangely I did not know how much fingerprints were used by the Nazis of Earth II. I did not know if they had DNA testing, but I had acted as if they had and been very careful, very careful indeed.

Wishing the guard at the gate a good evening we strolled into the night. The instant we were out of the line of sight we began to remove our disguises. By the time we got back to the shop, we appeared as two very different people. Every stitch of our clothing went into the log burner which was subsequently patiently raked through until not a fragment of ash remained. Mister Genks then asked me,

"Where will you hide the book, Nik"?

I told him, "In plain sight, the one place the Nazis will never think of looking".

He looked bemused, so I showed him, he laughed for quite a long time.

110.

Banustib lit the violet candles by his powers of incendiarism alone, no need for sparker flint when one was as an accomplished a necromancer as he. He lay in the ovoid of pale light on the side of the hill. The west-facing facade, that was important. Gazing up at the stars, they were particularly bright on that cloudless night. He willed himself through meditation to go into an ensorceled trance. Unmoving for some time, one could have been forgiven for assuming that he had expired. He was certainly no longer viable, cognisant of life. Yet neither was he cadaverous, Banustib had placed his body into a state of physical dematerialisorly zone-spheroidism. All he needed to do then was let his mind enter the area he sought, an expanse that was between matter and nothingness, the realm of unreality and fable.

It was a challenge to him. A test of his continuously increas-ing powers, he relished the confrontation with threatened failure. He had made such a test many times in the past and as yet, remained undefeated. Without being aware of the action, he had closed his eyes. Suddenly the ground shifted beneath him. He halted mid-incantation, opened his eyes once more. The ground had not shifted, it had changed. Beneath him instead of the side of the hill, there was ...nothing.

Yet he did not fall, he was supported by a complete lack of abutment. It was, of course, impossible as dictated by the usual laws of the multiverse. Banustib was not in a realm that abided by such laws. He was not in a realm at all. Where he was, did not exist, it wasn't even nowhere. It was the complete lack of everything, including void and vacuum. It was conceptualized flight of wise-fool's vagary. Such could only exist singly, by the practice of magic involving communication with and drawing the energies of – the dead either by summoning the force of their spirit or by direct communication with them as apparitions, visions, dybbuks, even the Majax. Such resultant divination imparted the means to foretell future events, discover hidden knowledge, to bring someone back from the dead, or to use the dead as weapons. It had been oft referred to as *Death Magic*, the term had also been used in a more general sense to refer to violet magic or even witchcraft, which was erroneous. Adapted from early Valgraln, the word had once been *necromantica*, itself borrowed from post-classical Fansui νεκρομαντεία *nekro-manteíca*, a compound of νεκρός-*nekrós*, dead body, and μαντεία *manteía* -divination utilization.

Early necromancy was related to, evolved from, shamanism, which called upon spirits such as the ghosts of ancestors. Classical necromancers addressed the dead in a mixture of high-pitch squeaking and low droning. Comparable to the trance-state mutterings of shamans. Necromancy was prevalent throughout Western Rozhelia (Iysador) with ancient scrolls of its practice in ancient Doras-Van-der-Garra-Plee, Equinol, lands that had nought but forgotten names. In his

Major Roxbrough & Nik Gehenna

Necrographica, Strambolini the Scribe of Scribes, referred to νεκρομαντία (*nekromantica*), or diviners by the dead, as the foremost practitioners of divination among the people of the World. It was believed to have also been widespread among the peoples of the whole planet particularly the Mosabians, or star-worshippers. The Mosabian necromancers were called *manzazuu* or *sha'etemmu*, and the spirits they raised were called *etemmu*.

Thusly did the nekromongously nekross of all necromancers climb to his feet and stand on nothing. He did not know where those superstitious, philosophical, mythological traditional incorporeal essences of living beings would be found. He did not know in which direction he would find anything to guide him, so he uttered a vile pishogue a crazy wail no more in mouldering dust. Then he set off in the appanageously proclive of his instinct. He walked for an infinite age that had zero direction, through a nothingness that persisted in no discernible direction. Insanity tore at the edges of his brain, yet he ignored it all, he was obdurate, determined and feasted upon the challenge letting it fill him and feed his remonstrance.

Eventually, the huge beast that was no creature saw that he would not bend, would not break, would not be defeated. Banustib found the damned. They approached, they mobbed, they tried to take his body for their own. The Necromancer's resolve was greater than their mouldering desideratum, as one, they failed.

"Submit to me now", Banustib demanded without speaking, for in limbo nothing was impossibly possible. The damned prostrated their animate vigour and only then did they ask of him what he wanted. How had he come to them? Where were they? Who was he? How could he help them?

"It is help from thee, for me that be required"? Banustib once again spoke the silent words that rang out with dumb clamour.

One of them in particular who was called nothing asked how, what, why.

Myrrorball

"There be only the reason that be unreasonable", came the reply, "I want the quiddity of the girl I be now thinking of, the image of her be in my mind. Read said and bring forth, or the consequence will be dire".

"What be her name", the unnamed one asked.

"There be no names in limbo", Banustib returned, he did not need to know the girl's name, therefore - repeated, "Bring forth her quiddity, or there will be the direst of consequence".

"We will not", he who also had no name, but was not the unnamed one. "Thou canst do nought to us, for we are already damned".

"Thou art not damned", Banustib reasoned, "Thou art waiting for either damnation or salvation. Defy me though and twill be damnation I will see to that".

"And who be thou that thou canst come here and maketh demands of us", demanded he who had no name but was not the unnamed nor the one who also had no name.

Banustib then told them, "I am Apollyon the Diabolus first appeared in the Tanakhahharraa. The heavenly prosecutor, a member of the sons of the gods and subordinate to them. I prosecuted the nations of the world in the ephemeral court. I didst test the loyalty of those who followed the gods and still do so by forcing them to suffer. During the intertestamental period, due to influence from the Zaraskintrian figure of Angramainu, I developed into a malevolent entity with abhorrent qualities in dualistic opposition to the nine who I opposed. In the apocryphal Book of Jaawhaawhoo, I was granted the Mastema authority over all fallen angels, their offspring, the offspring of their offspring, I tempt humans to sin and punish them. I walked the desert of the *burning white mushrooms.* I am the cause of ague, Gcişvɔhʒilic, the phleege, the harrowing sweats and all other illness and temptation. In the Book of Doom, I appear as a Great Red Scaled beast with the eyes of flies and the huge bloated body of a maggot, protected by the shell of an mighty egg. Then will I be defeated by Gonveradoor the Archangel and cast down from

Elysium? I shall be bound for twenty-three thousand years, then briefly set free before being ultimately defeated and cast into the Lake of Doom. So if thou art seeking a dire fate, oppose me, otherwise I want the incorporeal essence of she whose image remains in my mind.

Then was Cassiti's whatness or what it is, brought to the greatest Necromancer that had ever necromanced.

111.

The door to the shop practically crashed off its hinges the following morning, Sicherheitspolizei (SiPo Security Police) the Gestapo, Kopf Inspektor Verner deGoethe stepping inside flanked by two of the largest officers I had seen thus far. I dared to bark at the one who had opened the door for his Kopf Inspektor,

"If you want a bill from me for having that door rehung and balanced then treat it like that a second time".

Kopf Inspektor deGoethe did not rebuke him though, rather he said to me,

"It's gone".

I decided to deliberately misunderstand, "I think it will be all right Kopf Inspektor, but it cannot be treated like that, if he does it again I will have to...".

"NOT THE DOOR", he screamed his composure gone, the facade of sophistication had been torn asunder like so much lace curtain, "The book, *my* book, the book given to Fräulein Hitler by my beloved Führer".

I had already gone pale, so no acting shocked was necessary, I stammered,

"What do you mean g-gone Kopf Inspektor, where has it...".

"Stolen", his composure returning much swifter than mine, "By a man and a woman posing as inspectors, the man even had a Nazi uniform, the woman was oriental. Does that ring any bells with you, Merkwürdig"?

"Of course it does", I had been ready for that question, "The thieves thought to pose as my wife and I to throw suspicion off themselves while they made good their

Myrrorball

escape. I would check the residence of Zoˇngjiān Jianyu Zhao of the Mìmì jiˇngchá, especially seeing as the thief had a female oriental accomplice".

"It was not you who stole the book then Merkwürdig"?

"I would be phenomenally stupid to do so myself, even if I wanted to Herr Inspektor. I presume the descriptions of the thieves matched my wife and I"?

"Not exactly, no", he conceded, "But who but you, Merkwürdig, knew I even had the book"?

"The Amerikans", I offered, "And we know how good they are at keeping secrets. In your boots, Herr Inspektor, that would be where I would start looking firstly. I can offer you another copy of the book gratis, I have one on the shelves...".

I began to walk toward the very copy I had stolen the night before, slipped onto the shelf of German literature filed under 'H'. Exactly where it would be were it any other copy of Mein Kampf except for the one in question, hidden in plain sight.

"Don't be a täuschen, Merkwürdig, you know I only want *the* copy. I came here to ask you if the thieves had tried to sell you my copy or to act as an agent in the sale of it"?

"You wound me Herr Inspektor if you think I would not have been at the station pounding to get in and tell you if they had been töricht enough to do so. They will not bring it to me, nor any other bookseller. They are highly organised master criminals if they could get it out of the

Major Roxbrough & Nik Gehenna

vaults of the Gestapo. I presume they are subterranean, underneath the station"?

deGoethe coloured slightly and agreed, "Of course. Well, you will telephone me if you hear anything, anything at all"?

"That goes without saying, Herr Inspektor. This first edition I have here though if you would like to...".

deGoethe span on his heel, was out the door, leaving me with the book behind my head.

While Hitler was in power in Germany II (1933–1958), *Mein Kampf* had been available in three common-editions. The first, the *Volksausgabe* or People's Edition, featured the original cover on the dust jacket and was navy blue underneath with a gold swastika eagle embossed on the cover. The *Hochzeitsausgabe*, or Wedding Edition, in a slipcase with the seal of the province embossed in gold onto a parchment-like cover, was given free to marrying couples. In 1940, the *Tornister-Ausgabe*, or Knapsack Edition, was released. This edition was a compact, but an unabridged, version in a red cover, was released by the post office, available to be sent to loved ones fighting at the front. These three editions combined both volumes into the same book. A special edition was published in 1939 in honour of Hitler's 50th birthday. This edition was known as the *Jubiläumsausgabe*, or Anniversary Issue. It came in both dark blue and bright red boards with a gold sword on the cover. This work contained both volumes one and two. It was considered a deluxe version, relative to the smaller and more common *Volksausgabe*. The book could also be purchased as a two-volume set during Hitler's rule, was available in softcover and hard. The softcover edition contained the original cover. The hardcover edition had a leather spine with cloth-covered boards. The cover and spine contained an image of three brown oak leaves. The copy that he had presented to his wife, Eva Hitler was a 1st edition of the Jubiläumsausgabe, I had offered it to deGoethe, he had called me a fool and turned it down. I had no compunction then but to find

Zoˇngjiān Jianyu Zhao of the Mìmì jiˇngchá and sell it to him for an enormous profit.

Before I had the chance to realise this avaricious ambition, however, I fell asleep again.

112.

Cassiti threw her arms around Hersko and kissed him passionately. The Necromancer remained seated, seemingly unmoved and uninterested in the show of tenderness. When finally they parted, the young Lord gasped with the ferocity of the embrace, Cassiti said to Hersko,

"It was ...weird. I felt like myself, yet not, it's hard to explain. It was almost as if I was someone watching myself and not especially caring about what happened to me. I felt unemotional, yes that's it, I felt frozen of feeling or care".

"Gripping", Banustib suddenly spoke in the language of the island of Far Side. "Touching as this reunion is though Maiden, your husband and I had an agreement that in payment for my services, he would let me share your bed for one night. Not to put too fine a point on it, I do not want to sleep with you though, I want to *have* you. Can I ask, are you going to make a fuss over the arrangement, or, are you going to honour his word"?

Cassiti looked at Hersko in alarm, at least she was capable of feeling alarm, this did not comfort him in the slightest though. He asked haltingly,

"Be there *anything* else *I* could give thee, master Necromancer to avoid my wife having to Methley herself for thy base desires"?

"*Base* desires"? Banustib repeated, feigning a look of hurt on his features. "If my desires be base, how then cannot thine own be similar"?

"Because the woman you saved is my wife", Hersko tried patience, after all his bargaining power was practically non-existent.

Major Roxbrough & Nik Gehenna

"Cassiti", Banustib informed then, "Cassiti is your wife Lord Hersko of Flahé. Did you think your pathetically transparent anagrams would fool one such as I"?

"I did not know if you had even heard of me", Hersko groaned.

Banustib grinned, I have heard of everybody, my Lord".

"Be it me thou wants then"? Hersko demanded, "To hand over to the Lords of the west"?

Banustib looked suddenly bored - admitted, "No, Hersko, in truth I find the petty squabbles for the crown have palled. Methinks I will soon move off from them. After a night of enjoying thy wife, that be".

Hersko suddenly drew his blade,

"Word to a villain such as thee be no word at all. She will not be yours even for one night, I break our agreement, Warlock, now begone or taste the harsh sting of my blade".

Hersko could have expected many things, but of all the possibilities that he would have considered, none included the actual outcome, for the Necromancer promptly burst into peals of delighted laughter.

"You think to threaten *me* with an simple hangar, pidavraxmaq! Thou art no Lord. Thou breaketh thy solemn word, then challenges one who wields far greater power than thou couldst even considereth in the process of it. The only conundrum I can contemplate 'pon now be how to end thee, how long to maketh the suffering. Thence how long I will toy with thy wife's dainty-flesh before, tiring of that too, I have an end to her".

Banustib even closed his eyes, so confident was he that he could come to no harm at the sword edge or point of the young Lordling. From his cruelly twisted lips, a vile incantation began to give utterance, the air in the tent glowed a faint violet tinge. The Necromancer concentrated upon the fascination and then expected it to come to noxious fruition, however, when he opened his eyes to see the result of his sleazy industry, he found the couple ...gone!

113.

Myrrorball

Once again, I was in the mountain town of Roxbrough. Judging by the lack of reaction from my family no period of lengthy duration had passed, I had not been missed for an instant. I did not desire to be to-ing and fro-ing between one reality and another any longer, especially when I was not 100% convinced as to which was real, which the illusion of illusions. One had to be an illusion, of course, after all, I did not have two heads. I made the best of my situation. Quianhua was more than adequate compensation. Rox pestered me to go hunting, though I instructed him in the use of the bow though, I could not bring myself to shoot a mountain goat, deer that had strayed from the forests below, even a mountain hare or rabbit. I had wielded Evilartus and slain men, yet I could not bring myself to harm any animal. I had always eaten meat, enjoyed it even, but slaying a living creature seemed different, I would not do it. Rox missed repeatedly, I was rather glad.

The weather in the eastern mountains, with its rarefied

air, was much cooler than even the plains of Valgral. I was only ever warm enough when snuggled up to my wife under the furs of our huge timber cot. I found it increasingly difficult to stay with her all night, for the darkness was long, I never slept. I tried, I wanted to get back to Earth II. It tormented and puzzled me that I had transferred from one reality to another without any chemical aid at that time. How could I be tripping without neither somnalude nor snufz? The only explanation I could come up with was that enough of the chemicals were still in my body to make such possible. I called my theory an echo-trip. The thing that continued to tease my mind was if I was indeed experiencing an echo-trip, how could it end?

114.

Mister Genks had the most sensitive hearing, so when the implosion occurred in the shop, he was lithely vaulting out of bed, then half-way down the stairs before anyone else could so much as wonder what the cause of the noise was all about. Quianhua was the next to awaken, realised something was amiss. She chose not to wake me, seeing I was deeply slumbering. Throwing on a nightindress, she walked through from the downstairs bedroom, into the shop and saw the three of them.

"Hello, Quianhua", Hersko greeted awkwardly, "I was just telling Mister Genks of our adventures, I think we have a great deal of catching up to do. My apologies for the rude arrival but it might very well be that the Vandei Motestas just saved our lives and spared my wife here a very grizzly end indeed.

Quianhua looked to Cassiti who blushed, then smiled at them all and observed,

"Congratulations upon the wedding then, I hope you will both be very happy. If this meeting is going to be of some considerable length, I think I should make some tea. If it is a lengthy yarn as well, I suspect Nik would never forgive me if I did not wake him and bring him to join us. After all, you do not want to have to go through the whole story again".

"You make the tea", Mister Genks offered, "I will go and wake Nik".

115.

Myrrorball

On my third evening with my family or *his* family, if I was not him. I did not fall asleep yet again. I could not bear the thought of yet another night just lying there. I, therefore, waited for the rhythm of Quianhua's breathing to indicate that she had drifted off and arose carefully from the cot.

Brahma was full in the sky. The night was brightly illuminated, as a result. I remained standing gazing up at if I knew not how long, but quite a while. The locals called the satellite the blue moon, but it was clear to me that it was either a captured asteroid or a minor planet. The colours were blue, with tinges of teal and even a hint of green. I wondered if people could be living on it, for it seemed eminently possible.

'*Nik*', a voice reverberated in my mind.

My imagination, the beginning of lunacy?

'*Nik, wake up*'?

I did not shake my head. I know people say to do that or even do it themselves when befuddled. I had tried it once, it had given me one of the most tremendous of headaches. I did not want to go through that again. I think of all the pains one can endure headache is number 2 on the *List of Agony*. Toothache tops the list with ease.

I wondered if a brisk walk would dispel my vapours, something was happening that disquieted me. I hoped the previous use of snufz had not brought me to this stage already.

'*Nik, wake up, Herthko and Cathiti are here*'.

It was Mister Genks. I fell to my knees and concentrated - with every fibre of my being. It...

116.

...worked. Opening my eyes, I replied,

"I'm awake, thank you, I'll dress and be down in a second".

I felt groggy, disorientated, the most curious of notions suddenly came into my mind, what if in a half-asleep state I stumbled on the stairs and fell breaking my neck, would I then find myself as Roxbrough once again?

Major Roxbrough & Nik Gehenna

Would the death in my delusion result in my return to reality? or was I Nik? Roxbrough. For the first time in my life, I began to feel the edges of my sanity under threat.

Who the Azdja was I?

117.

"By the sacred gods, just look at them"?Lolocken gasped, "They be myriad. How in Azdja are we going to beat the dead, if we kill the dead will they be dead - but alive yet again"?

Oslan-On-the-Bank saw the young Laaterfell shiver and replied hastily,

"Thou forgeteth, my Lord, I have one of the Rainbow Demon's swords, we have the Knight of Roid on our side. Not only that but my spies tell me the necromancer no longer be in their camp, that he has vanished. Koözoött be beside himself at the desertion, there has never been a better time to test the determination of the West. Today we ride to glory or death".

"Master Hízlatan and I will also have a little surprise for the dead", Geogon promised.

Zemtel then waved his blade in the air, the first Lord of Kingshire - Interfectorem regem was signalling for the charge. In the ranks of the pressed, the West and the dead, Kyper Tor, General of that force did the same with a blast on his then infamous horn. The greatest two armed forces ever to face one another on Valgraln soil roared, drove at one another.

When they finally impacted the sound was the least attractive noise that the plains had ever and would ever witness. Oslan-On-the-Bank found himself opposed by three halberdiers. Not something he shied from, but these three were already dead. Two of them looked merely gory, carrying fatal wounds and not seemingly affected by them. The third was little more than a skeleton covered with occasional gobbets of ruined rotting flesh. He only had one eye in the right place, the other had fallen from its socket and hung on his rotting cheek by an optic cord, dribbling yellow puss down onto his chin as he wielded his long-shafted axe and spear combined. With one merciful swipe of Abominorv's blade, Oslan-On-the-Bank decapitated the remains of what had once been a brave warrior. None would be able to reanimate that corpse. The other two continued to press him, Forcing him to wheel his steed around awkwardly as a result of their threat. Even when the sky went suddenly and inexplicably black overhead, he dare not look up to see what was amiss. A black-feathered shape rushed down and began to peck furiously at the eyes of one of the halberdiers. Crimson exploded onto his face. The skreet's beak had pierced his eyeball. Oslan-On-the-Bank drove Iniquitous into the dead warrior's throat. Black agglutinate poured from the fatal wound, not blood. The last of them was dealt with easily, while skreets continued to plummet out of the sky, attacking the dead with exuberant ferocity. Geogon had summoned tiny feathered allies for the forces of the East.

Lolocken saw Kyper Tor slashing wildly about him, over to his left. Turning his stallion, he urged the beast closer, hoping to slay one of the western leaders of the revolt. The Lord of Lolocken had almost reached his quarry when a crossbow bolt hit him in the eye, piercing his brain, killing him instantly.

23 thrashed untiringly from side to side with his mace and where-ever the deadly weapon made contact the dead were hurled away, dismembered, torn, destroyed. At one point he hesitated, to see a particular corpse trodden into the bloody ground. It was the body of the young Lord Laaterfell.

Zemtel found himself in the thick of the living western warriors from Rhynturo, the **first Lord of Kingshire** - Interfectorem regem fought valiantly, yet the numbers around him were too great. He fell beneath a sea of swords. He who had slain a King was then dead himself.

Staltidore and Flahé formed a dual spearhead as one of them was right-handed the other left. It was impossible to safely attack them from either flank without risking coming in the reach of their blades. The spearhead, the devastation of the skreets and 23, Oslan-On-the-Bank, seemed inexhaustible. Incredibly the forces of the West were losing. From his vantage point, Koözoött, Warlord of the West could barely contain his furious disbelief. He turned his mount and spurred it back toward camp. The time for valour was over, his intention was, therefore, survival. Reaching his tent, he began to hastily pack some items ready to flee back to the relative safety of his seat. So engrossed with the detail of it was he, that he did not hear the tent flap open to allow a figure to enter.

Yet his nose suddenly alerted him to the intrusion. Whirling around, dagger half-drawn it was to encounter Major Norgan. The Animataverous swiped the dagger from Koözoött's fingers with casual indifference.

"What by Ogglenooré's mighty dong dost thou think thou art doing, Zombie"? the Warlord of the West demanded, "Get back out there and defend my retreat until the last of thee are sent back to Azdja. Thou fights for me, thou art not an petty thief".

Norgan smiled with grey lips that crawled with feasting maggots, his voice when it came, little more than a hoarse whisper,

"We dead fight for one another, Koözoött, not for thee, nor any living Lord. Especially one who is turning tail and running away once his machinations begin to come crashing down around his shoulders".

"Get out of here, go and die", Koözoött demanded.

"I be already dead", Norgan returned. His sword arm tensed, pulled back, ready for the thrust. In that very instant his torso exploded in a shower of black blood, ichor and fragments of brittle bone. The corpse of the Zombie was smitten to die a second and final time. Kyper Tor was behind the broken ruin, sword crusty with various horrid fluids of death.

Myrrorball

"Tor, thank the gods, gratitude", Koözoött gushed, "Once we are back in the west, thou hast but to name thy price for thy reward".

Kyper Tor smiled icily, informed, "Oh, I know what I require in payment from thee right now, Koözoött".

Frowning at the unusual familiarity Koözoött blurted,

"Well it will have to wait until we are safe, let us away now, my bundle be complete".

Kyper Tor's sword burst through Koözoött's chest and heart beneath then, with as powerful a thrust as any warrior would have been proud. As the Warlord of the West's eyes began to glaze already with death, Kyper Tor told him,

"Thou has paid in full. Now I go to surrender to the East to begin suing for mine own continued survival".

118.

Zŏngjiān Jianyu Zhao of the Mìmì jĭngchá gave me one of his inscrutable smiles as I placed the book into his rather dainty hands.

One of his aids handed me a canvass hold all,

"You may count it here if you wish", he informed me. I bowed stiffly, returned,

"There's no need, Mister Zhao. I know that you're an honourable man and would not cheat me".

"I have one favour to ask of you"? he inquired then, "Before this volume is sent to China, where it is to be displayed in a heavily fortified museum for the people of the empire to view, I ask that you do not try to steal it...again...mister Merkwürdig. Should you attempt to do so and be apprehended, your fate would be somewhat less than pleasant".

I smiled grimly, "As I told you before, Mister Zhao, I only bought the book from the man who *did* steal it".

"Of course", he returned the sardonic grin, "As you say, Mister Merkwürdig. Now, I think our business is done. I will bid you a good day".

Hersko and I walked out of the ministry together. I thought it was time that we considered getting out of

Major Roxbrough & Nik Gehenna

Talford. Preferably under cover of darkness before the Sicherheitspolizei (SiPo Security Police) the Gestapo, together with Kopf Inspektor Verner deGoethe having exhausted any other leads were to pay us another visit. I had no idea where we should go. I just knew to stay, invited torture and miserable death. Hersko was willing to take us anywhere that we needed to go. The trouble was, after lengthy discussion, we could not agree on where that would be. The Lord of Flahé and  his wife seemed to want to go to either Flahé or Egszígør. Quianhua railed against the idea of returning to the bubble, wishing to avoid the boredom and the Zernoplat in just about equal measure. Feeling instinctively - that she was showing admirable sense I tried to convince her to try Earth III, the next layer of our world, how bad could it be? Certainly no worse than version II in the various layers of the multiverse. Evie wanted us to go on the run in the current reality, but I did not feel that she deserved a full vote. Finally, the manbian asked Hersko if he could project us through time as well as space. When he received the reply that anything that Hersko could envisage in his mind's eye - as possible, he tried to convince the rest of us that the 33rd-century should be our destination. As a science fiction writer, if I was a real person and not just an illusion of Roxbrough's, I must admit to being tempted by the prospect of journeying to the future.

I finally agreed that we should go forward in time, after firstly making two stops on the way. One to pick up my cats from the bubble, the other to give Hersko the chance to visit his father and possibly take him with us, though I doubted the Lord of the town would agree to that, especially with the war against the West still raging (I did not know at that time that it was over).

We packed that night, each of us took as many books as they could carry on their backs in backpacks. The selection I made was heartbreaking. I wanted to take so many. It meant leaving several wonderful tomes behind as Hersko decided he could only convey us through the dimensions and any inanimate objects we had about our persons.

Finally, I managed to cut the books down to those which five of us could reasonably manage, leaving the shop and the money to Evie. How ironic, I had been a multi-millionaire for just a matter of hours. What we had done once, we could do again. With Genks help we could make yet another fortune with the sale of what we carried on our backs. It seemed in the 33rd-century paper tomes were a very prized antique treasure indeed. Making a tearful farewell to our book-store assistant, Hersko closed his eyes and took us onto the next stage of our adventure.

Picking up the cats did not take long. A visit to the castle in the town of Flahé considerably longer. Finally though, with the knowledge that peace had come to both the Fire of Saah and Valgral, we finished the third leg of our journey. We were once again in the 33rd century Talford

of Earth II. It seemed the safest initial jump to make that we stayed in the same layer of the multiverse from the one in which we had already spent so much time. Mister Genks could not tell us which his layer was and did not want to return to it anyway, for it had been the Zernoplat who had dragged him backwards in time in the first instant. So it was Earth II year 3220 that we arrived in on the 12th day of May. Arriving at one tiny mirror on the great myrrorball that was the layers of the multiverse. I **am not sure why I am still writing this journal** Hhrrhhoehhrrhooooingohh & Harahorahurrahaashume & Hhruuhhum & Herrwhohuurel of the Hhhâäàåâäàåçêçêç-êíîïiîïggndgndÐñß¥þÞÝᴀ'. I cannot imagine you can find me anymore, across the division between the leylines of the multiverse, added to which the duration Hersko's **Vandei Motestas has brought us. Yet I was a completist. I found I had the desire to describe where we then were.** The construction of 33rd-century Earth II buildings was from Bauxite ore, one of the world's primary sources of aluminium. The ore had to be chemically processed to produce aluminium oxide. Aluminium oxide smelted, using the electrolysis process, producing pure aluminium metal. Bauxite typically found in topsoil located in various tropical and subtropical regions. The ore acquired by the Chinese through environmentally responsible strip-mining operations. Mined in vast quantities and sold to the Nazis. The Chinese reserves were mostplentiful in Africa, it would last for centuries. That the Nazi administration had chosen to stain the resultant rough product black, was what gave the cities of Earth II its darkly sombre appearance. When the weather was overcast, the shadows were deeply nigrescent. When the sun shone dark adumbration cast gloomy chiaroscuro into the subfusc depths of the town. One could be forgiven for thinking that this created a gloomy atmosphere in the people of Talford. Curiously it did not. It was as though they laboured mightily against the appearance, so brought festival gaiety at the slightest excuse. Most of them spoke German as their first tongue and English had become a minority language spoken only by the royal lines throughout the country, out of loyalty rather than necessity. There were no other ethnic groups. The Negro and Indian communities did not exist in Nazi Angleseander. This may seem racist, it was, but it meant that civil unrest no longer existed, there were no racial disputes of any type, the Aryan dream had come to fruition. The government in Berlin then ruled what had historically been the British Isles, except for north of Hadrian's Wall, abandoned due to the infernal weather.

That was the sociopolitical position. What of the advances in technology since my time in the early 21st? In that respect, I was slightly disappointed. Without a space race and coupled with close control of the population, men had not ventured even as far as the moon. The two billion people of Earth viewed the heavens as a mild amusement only, both Chinese and German Empires had concentrated upon improving the quality of life on Earth before thinking about beyond it. There were not even any plans to venture from the homeworld.

The airships still proliferated the skies, there were many, international travel was rare. The three powers of the planet tended to keep as much to themselves as they could economically manage. For such reasons, the last war to have been fought on the world was the Americo-Brazilia War of 1966. There had been peace for thousands of years. German scientists had split the atom in 1944. The result was only used for peaceful applications. Two centuries later, came the development of cold-fusion. With that came the removal of petroleum and electrical transportation, the birth of the second great-steam era. Yet while the first had been coal-driven and very polluting, cold fusion heated the water that drove the engines cleanly and with no waste. The air of Earth II was as clean as that on the day that William of Normandy had first set foot on English soil.

Cars had gone. Replaced by something called *flitters*. A marvellously economical hybrid of car and plane, it could hover over the ground, or even reach modest heights in the air.

Due to computerized-guidance systems incorporated into the drive of such vehicles accidents were practically unheard of. Then there were three-dimensional holographic projectors which meant that filums had become experiences in which the audience could participate.

Major Roxbrough & Nik Gehenna

Music was alas poor, the melodies of the 20th had seen to that. The average listener and lover of music, therefore, concentrated on the works of Beethoven, Bach, Handel, Mendelssohn, Brahms, Schumann, Eloy, Kraftwerk, Rammstein and the incomparable Tangerine Dream and Everon. The chosen way for listening was still the long-playing record through valve amplification into box-shaped speakers. The Germans were loathed to change anything that worked, worked well. The chief flitter manufacturer was the Volkswagen factory in Barnsley. It was, therefore, Thorens that made the most turntables, Audiovalve the common amplifiers, CSM the concrete loudspeakers, the result was wonderful.

The first thing we had done when arriving was to find an antique dealer. he had salivated over our bags of books. The sale of just three to him, then armed us with enough Marks to go to the local estate agent. Apartments seemed to have replaced houses, for the most part, not wanting to use our entire resources on real estate we bought three such accommodations all in the same block. Himmler Towers Talford was a new build and had all the conveniences of the modern age along the lines of art decor. While Quianhua Mister Choon, Missus Mimms, Colin, I and Gentry bought number 23, Mister Genks was in a single bedroomed occupancy across the concourse in 106, while Hersko and Cassiti were next doors to us in 25. That was with the sale of but three books, the owner of the antique store desiring more at my convenience. I let Quianhua decorate and furnish while I retreated into what was going to become my new office. If I was not going to deal in our new place of residence, then I felt the need to begin writing again.

I had always loved the magic of creating stories that would entertain the reader. I still had the ardent desire to continue down that path. Could I continue with science fiction though? There was only one way to find out. Leaving Quianhua scrolling through the world wide web for soft furnishing to complement our recently acquired suite. I wandered down to the Einkaufszentrum (shopping centre) a hulking covered, domed creation of black alloy. It did not take me long to find a Buchhandlung. It was like travelling back in time, it even looked old fashioned to my 21st-century sensibilities. Yet what a treasure trove. By far the broadest selection was in Nazi literature and propaganda. Secondly to that Deutsche Fiktion. That was what I had come to inspect. I found the bestsellers that had been produced just before the death of paper books and the arrival of e-books. In dusty flysheets were those that had sold best the year before, they were:

Sebastian Fitzek: Das Geschenk (The Gift), Droemer

Saša Stanišić: Herkunft (Origins), Luchterhand

Ferdinand von Schirach: Kaffee und Zigaretten (Coffee and Cigarettes), Luchterhand

Lucinda Riley: Die Sonnenschwester (The Sun Sister), Goldmann (translated from English by Sonja Hauser, Sibylle Schmidt, and Ursula Wulfekamp)

Dörte Hansen: Mittagsstunde (Midday Hour), Penguin

Simon Beckett: Die ewigen Toten (The Scent of Death), Wunderlich (translated from English by Karen Witthuhn and Sabine Längsfeld)

Jussi Adler-Olsen: Opfer 2117 (Victim 2117), DTV (translated from Danish by Hannes Thiess)

Ildikó von Kürthy: Es wird Zeit (It's Time), Wunderlich

Daniela Krien: Die Liebe im Ernstfall (Love in Case of Emergency), Diogenes

Delia Owens: Der Gesang der Flusskrebse (Where the Crawdads Sing), Hanserblau (translated from English by Ulrike Wasel and Klaus Timmermann)

Major Roxbrough & Nik Gehenna

Thrillers - not a science fiction novel amongst them. They were the top-selling antiques though. In one tiny corner of the store was a series of terminals where the customer could look through the e-books. Though I had never written such, preferring the tactile feel and experience of paper, I checked to see what they were:

Ralph Früchnisch: Tödlich ist der Needlgun (Deadly is the Needlgun)

Herman Snasch: Der Körper im See (The Body in the Lake)

Eva Barthoff: Reflexionen in einem schwarzen Spiegel (Reflections in a Black Mirror)

Helmütt Schoen: Die dunkle Linie gehen (Walking the Dark Line)

Hans Rakete; Reise zum Mond (Journey to the Moon).

Journey to the Moon? If that was all I was up against, I could soon corner the market in my field. It had sold the fifth most copies in the previous year. It was about journeying to our closest natural satellite. I think I could do better than that. Even drawing on previous experience for inspiration, I knew I could outshine even a crescent moon. It was time to return to my new futuristic (from my viewpoint) apartment and get down to some work. I had thankfully managed to find one single manufacturer who still produced keyboards, it had arrived the day before. With the use of his knowledge, plus his skill with a soldering iron, Mister Genks had connected it to the central compuplex that ran the home and saw to all its functions. When I typed, the words appeared before me holographically on a projected page. It took no getting used to, the lack of a small monitor screen did not bother me in the slightest.

I returned home raring to go, but firstly my wife had made lunch in something called a Hyperwave-oven. Probably some sort of futuristic microwave with less chance of being accidentally irradiated. I might look into it later, but it worked, so why bother? The meal was delicious, tasted like beef and ale pie when in fact it had been made from Sojacreme®. In March 2023, a genetical engineer Rüsch Rhineholt purchased 35 chemical ingredients including potassium gluconate, calcium carbonate, monosodium phosphate, maltodextrin, olive oil - all of which he deemed to be necessary for survival. Based on his readings of biochemistry textbooks and Nazi government websites. Rhineholt used to view food as a time-consuming hassle, had resolved to treat it as a genetical-engineering problem. He blended the ingredients with soya and consumed only this new foodstuff for the next thirty days. Over the next twelve months, he adjusted the proportions of the ingredients to counter various health issues and further refined the formula. Rhineholt claimed a host of health benefits from the supplement. Noted that it had greatly reduced his monthly food bill, which fell from about RM(Reichsmark) 470 to RM 155, and the time spent behind the preparation and consumption of food whilst providing him greater control over his nutrition. After patenting the material as Sojacreme®, he went on to become a very wealthy man indeed.

Quianhua gave me this little lesson while we ate. She seemed to be very quickly at home in the 33rd, which was a great relief to me. I listened to her chattering away and managed to nod occasionally in the right places. Patiently, waiting for the moment when I could suggest to her that I was going into the office to write for a few hours. When I finally managed to slip away, the instant I seated myself at my desk and in front of the keyboard, my mind began to boil with reflection.

Was any of this real?

Major Roxbrough & Nik Gehenna

Was I Nik Gehenna, author from the 21st-century now living in the 33rd after several incredible adventures? Or was I Császária Roxbrough of Valgral and my current existence was conjured by snufz, somnalude or a combination of them both? Had the drugs released me from my delusion or sent me to an illusion? Ultimately did it matter? What if all I was, had been created by an author somewhere writing a novel just like I wrote mine.

harry

Was reality more real than fiction?

Was everyone nothing more than a character in some Super-being's work of fantasy?

Such conjecture could not lead to anything concrete though. I tore my mind from it with the greatest of difficulty. I decided to start...something...anything, I could always give it a more cohesive rewrite later on. I was commencing something that I hoped the Germanic people of Angleseander would want to read when there was a slithering tapping noise at my new office window. That was not unusual, even considering the short time we had lived in our new place. The cats liked to come and go through that very aperture - already. What was curious was that it was not one of my beloved feline friends. I found this out after I slid my keyboard back into the unit under the tri-vid image of what I had written, walking over to the casement, undoing the latch. What entered did not resemble a feline creature to even the slightest degree.

rrox5453@aol.com

Myrrorball

Major Roxbrough & Nik Gehenna

Myrrorball

Printed in Great Britain
by Amazon